BRIDGE

Over the

VALLEY

A Story of Heroism, Tragedy, Triumph & Healing

Gary A. Freedly

BRIDGE

Over the

VALLEY

Langdon Street Press
212 3rd Avenue North, Suite 290
Minneapolis, MN 55401
612.455.2293
www.langdonstreetpress.com

ISBN - 978-1-934938-82-9
ISBN - 1-934938-82-3
LCCN - 2010924839

Cover Design by Alan Pranke
Cover Art by Michael Rasmussen
Typeset by James Arneson

Printed in the United States of America

Dedicated to all the heroes in Valley City, North Dakota, who saved their town from the flood of 2009

CONTENTS

PROLOGUE

Randy Spencer

I don't have a thorough explanation as to why the valley ended up where it did, but here it is in the middle of the flat, sloping prairie. One day, back in the distant past, something happened and the prairie bottom collapsed leaving a one-hundred-seventy-five-foot deep picturesque valley. The valley is enclosed by a series of small hills stacked one on top of the other. Erosion has sculpted the mounds into bluffs, some with steep drop-offs. This is a river valley teeming with wildlife. Moose live in the bottomlands and shelterbelts. Deer, fox, pheasants, waterfowl and the occasional cougar inhabit the valley. The rare and endangered whooping crane finds solace in the fields overlooking the valley during its semiannual migration. In the past, the river flooded the bottomland. Today, the river's contrary moods are mostly constrained upstream behind a dam and large reservoir.

It is safe to live in the valley and seven thousand people, mostly Lutherans and Catholics, have chosen to do so. The neighborhoods are close knit and interconnected by a series of advantageously placed bridges that cross the lazy, slow-moving Cheneau River. A canopy of trees conceals the town that is named Cheneau Valley. Passersby on the busy interstate, which weaves around the top edge of the valley, only see the three exit signs and little of the town below.

The railroad originally built the track through town, but descending down into, and climbing up out of the valley, proved unprofitable. In 1908, the railroad ignored the valley by going over it on a single-track high bridge, thousands of feet long, standing one hundred sixty two feet above the Cheneau River and the town. An incredible engineering feat, the railroad bridge spanning the valley is an architectural landmark that is hard to miss. Throughout the valley it is referred to as the Dakota High Bridge, and the high school adopts it as their mascot. High school athletes are known as "High-Bridgers" or just "Bridgers" for short. The townsfolk support the Bridgers whether they are boys or girls playing basketball, football, softball, baseball, hockey, wrestling, tennis or golf. The Dakota High Bridge is the backdrop to the city appearing on postcards, the local paper, official documents, and letterheads.

Above the city, on the prairie, the landscape resumes its flatness and is covered with fields of grain, soybeans and corn. Tractors work the rich prairie soil along the high bluffs that border the valley. Half-million-dollar combines take the harvest from the far-reaching edges along the bluffs, seemingly ignoring the steep drop-offs they expertly avoid.

Considering the land was settled mainly by those of Germanic and Scandinavian descent, many ponder the origin of the name Cheneau (pronounced shey noh.) Tradition imposes the theory that a Frenchman, working on a railroad survey crew in the 1870s, admired the quiet, lazy river that snaked through the valley and named it using the French word for canal. Later, the name evolved to a word meaning cornice, describing the decorative hilly features that beautify the valley ridges. Without dispute, Cheneau Valley is a charming little town hidden deep in the vast North Dakota prairie.

We have everything we need here. There is St Catherine's, an eighty-bed acute care hospital with its good doctors, Cheneau Valley State University, Cheneau Valley High School, and two grocers. We are the county seat with the courthouse, judge, jury, and jail. Most here are Lutheran but we have churches for many faiths. There is a country club, an Eagle's club, two city parks, and a football field. The university has its own field house and stadium. Every season has its sports and theatrical productions. Life is busy in the valley.

The town couldn't exist without the multipurpose Swenson's Parlor, which provides us with an Internet café, Espresso coffee bar, photography, and bookstore. Swenson's is the social gathering place for the locals to enjoy some Scandinavian treats while discussing the latest happenings about the town.

It is unnecessary to drive to Fargo when everything you need is in the valley. People are not content nowadays. Folks, at least the younger generation, seek out the big box stores and entertainment venues of Fargo. Fargo, an hour east in the Red River Valley, is the low place of the Dakotas. Everything tips towards Fargo. The streams and rivers in Eastern Dakota flow toward the Red River in Fargo. The whole state from Bismarck east, inch by inch, slides down into Fargo. Fargo is sucking the town of Cheneau Valley dry. Merchants are having difficulty staying in business.

Here, newcomers are viewed with some suspicion. If you moved here from Fargo, that was understandable. Folks who wanted out of the city, away from noise, crime and pollution were welcome in the valley. Usually these folks shared the same values as the valley residents. But the folks who move in from far away are viewed with some suspicion. Why would you move here? What were you running away from? Newcomers with no ties to the agricultural industry, the university or to family living in the valley are suspect. These might be the same people arrested later for operating the meth labs set up in abandoned shacks in the countryside. It will take time and patience before this veil of suspicion can be lifted, allowing the new arrivals to penetrate the tight social structure of Cheneau Valley.

Life isn't always easy here. We learn to survive the brutally cold winters, the floods, the droughts, and tragedies that life brings. We are proud of our town, of our university, our schools.

We can trust the sheriff and the justice system. It seldom fails us. We're a proactive community. We feel the pressures of a changing world. We cope, we adjust, and we strive to do our best. We succeed.

I contemplate where I should be buried. Folks are not buried in the valley. There is no space for the dead down there. Two cemeteries decorate the sloping bluffs to the east. The Catholics have their burial place at St. Xavier's, which looks out on the busy interstate. The Lutherans and others prefer Hillcrest, sitting on the opposite knoll. The gravesites are mostly unkempt and messy from the tree droppings. Inaccessible in winter because of snow cover, bereaved families of the deceased endure months or weeks of waiting for the snow to melt so they can have the final graveside committal ceremony, which is so necessary in the practice of their religions. During the winter when the graveyards are closed, corpses in their coffins, stacked one on top of another in an unheated metal shed, harden in the bitter cold. During a wet spring, burials may not happen until late April after the water table drops.

As I stand here atop a bluff, looking down from a corner of my wheat field, I have a commanding view of Cheneau Valley that is fit for the artistry of Norman Rockwell, whose art we loved as it appeared on the cover of the *Saturday Evening Post*. In the foreground, the Dakota High Bridge stretches across the valley. I love to stand here and watch the long grain trains slowly move across the bridge heading west to the port of Seattle. I've never been to Seattle and I don't care to go. There is too much country between here and Seattle. I don't know one single person in Seattle. All of my grain goes there and is shipped overseas. Those trains have kept us financially afloat all these years that I've struggled to make ends meet on the farm.

Now that I am seventy years old, I worry about the future of this land that I have cultivated and protected for so many years. Everything is good. The bridge, now one hundred years old, still

4

stands and trains still take my grain west to Seattle.

I would prefer to be buried right here. I could donate maybe an acre of this wheat field, cut on two sides by steep bluffs, for a burying place for friends and family. It could serve as an everlasting memorial to my life here in the valley. During the winter, this field is usually clear of snow as the trees on the west act as a snow fence and wind carries what isn't trapped further east. Clear of snow, the grave-digging equipment easily penetrates the first few feet of the frozen ground, and underneath it the rich, black prairie soil can be moved. I like the idea of an all-season cemetery.

Families would need to decide on how to place their dead in the field. Lying prostrate with the head pointed south, there would be a view of the valley. Feet to the north, if you preferred, there would be that eternal view of the prairies and the multicolored sunrises. I, for one, would be buried feet to the south, in view of the bridge, autumn colors, and sunsets. I have approached my ninety-five-year-old mother about this subject.

"Would you be open to being buried at the west edge of my wheat field up on the bluff overlooking Cheneau Valley?" I asked when I thought her mind was crystal clear and she could process the question. I let that set in before I finished.

"I'll move dad over from Hillcrest and put him next to you."

"Randolph Jerome Spencer!" she exclaimed. "You know me better than that! Why in God's green earth would anybody want to be buried up there?"

I can't discuss this with my wife of forty-nine years, as she can't come to grips with her mortality. For the present, I have to keep these thoughts to myself.

Prairie Farm Life

David Olsen

It was barely daylight this clear, crisp March morning when I looked out across the driveway from the kitchen toward the barn. I realized that the steer was left tied in the stall all night since it wasn't out in the corral as it should have been. It wasn't like that kid to forget.

Immediately, I walked across the yard to the barn and led the halter-broke steer outside so he could drink. He was a really nice animal, but he didn't place well in February's Winter Show. Travis couldn't stay focused on it. You can't play hard basketball and raise cattle at the same time. The steer was a big disappointment for Travis, who now has been disengaged from his show cattle responsibilities. In a few days, the animal will be butchered.

I stood there for a moment watching the animal drink. Suddenly, my attention was directed at the brilliantly colored sunrise, and then to the west at the multicolored clouds. The sprawling two-story ranch home I owned, and helped build, was fully illuminated in the morning sun. I have to admit, in spite of all the difficulties, I have the perfect setup for farming, and most importantly, I have the perfect family. I don't mind helping Travis with his steer. We will have some good steaks from that animal. I can already hear them sizzling on the barbeque. Travis has had a lot on his plate. It is okay that he forgot.

As I walked back across the yard to the house, Laser, our five-year-old Border collie mix, greeted me. I spoke firmly to him.

"Sit, Laser. Sit."

Laser yawned, his throat sending forth a white vapor trail in the morning chill. He obeyed, but stretched out his paw for approval. When I brought him home as a puppy, Travis was twelve years old. He called him Three Spot. Laser had a white tip on his tail, a large white spot on the nap of the neck, and a white ring around the nose. Part of him was white like snow and the rest of him was black as night. When he chased the deer, Travis said he looked like a huge skunk running across the prairie.

As I stood there for a moment with Laser, I tried to blow smoke rings just like I did on the coldest of winter mornings when I was a kid, pretending to inhale from a cigarette. I love the mystic that accompanies a cold, windless prairie morning in the spring of the year after the snow is gone and the ground tries to wake up. The grass under foot was hard and crunchy from the night's frost. It will be awhile yet before the spring planting begins. Travis will be pushing me to plant as early as possible. Travis will be anxious and it will be harder for him to stay focused in school when so much farming blood flows through his veins during the planting season.

I walked back to the house and sat down at the kitchen table. My wife Lynn is a good wife and mother to our three children. I'm thinking that it is past time for the kids to be dressed and eating breakfast already, according to what they said last night. I thought they would be leaving early. That instant, my fourteen-year-old daughter Terri appeared in her robe, wanting to borrow some of her mother's accessories. I shouldn't have to, but I went to check on the boys. Tanner was dressed and almost ready for school, but a knock on the bedroom door where Travis slept produced nothing but silence. Travis, the typical teenager, stayed up too late studying and talking to his friends on the computer. When I pulled on his foot, Travis flung his lean, six-foot-six frame up off the bed like he was on a springboard and darted for his bathroom, stopping a second to turn on the shower before pausing to relieve himself. I walked back downstairs to finish my coffee and listen to the morning news.

Suddenly, Tanner, our youngest boy, let go with a series of shrieks. He was laughing, screaming and crying all at once. Figuring he did something to earn the wrath of Travis, I went upstairs to investigate. We didn't usually have this much commotion in the morning and I tried to disavow myself from the sibling spats, but I didn't want them to be late. Lately the boys just can't seem to get along and my wife has been ragging on me to monitor the situation. Trouble is, we never see exactly how it all comes down. Travis never tells us his side of the story. Tanner always blames his big brother for everything but usually starts the trouble.

Seizing his opportunity to irritate, Tanner filled a small pail with ice-cold water from the bathroom that he and Terri shared, entered Travis' bedroom, opened the shower door and threw the cold water on Travis, who was barely awake but just starting to enjoy his hot shower. Travis hates cold water. He won't step in the shower until he is assured the water temperature is perfectly copasetic with his internal chemistry. Evidently, Travis must have perceived what Tanner was plotting to do as he pivoted around, pulling Tanner in under the shower. Tanner, who was already dressed for school, received a thorough drenching.

Soon, Travis emerged with his backpack, ready to leave. More intense emotion was displayed before Tanner, who had to change his clothes, came stumbling into the kitchen not wanting to be left behind.

Travis gulped down a protein shake he had quickly blended up with milk and a banana. Lynn stuffed an energy bar and apple in Tanner's pack. Travis, Tanner and Terri piled in the 1966 vintage Ford Mustang fastback. They drove onto the county road that took them to the interstate and Cheneau Valley six miles away. Terri and Tanner got dropped off at their cousin's house, where they studied or goofed off until it was time for them to go to school. Terri is best of friends with her stepcousin Josie, who is also in her eighth-grade classes. Travis had arranged to meet with his English and debate teacher, who would help him rehearse a speech for the class that he was taking on the campus of Cheneau Valley State. Travis, a high school junior, was enrolled in the Fast-Track program for college-bound high school students. Students with a B average or better were allowed to receive dual credit for high school and college courses. These courses, any of several from the approved list, could be taken at the campus located a few blocks from the high school.

Travis had excellent writing skills but he was a mellow kid who spoke in a low, monotone voice. His speeches received high scores for content, but not for delivery. Like his dad, he was a man of few words. Today's speech assignment would require that he demonstrate some feeling and passion.

The most important event in the life of Travis so far was being voted as most valuable player in the Eastern Dakota Division after his basketball team took second place in the divisional tournament held the first week in March. This honor was bestowed on him by members of the coaching staffs from the ten Class A schools within the Eastern Division. It was rare that a junior would be considered for that award. The coaches usually nominated, and voted for, outstanding seniors.

He did cherish being recognized as the most valuable player. He didn't know if he could express it in the speech he had prepared for today's class. This whole speech class had really freaked him out. As a kid he grew up concealing his emotions and now, barely a man at age seventeen, he had to suddenly become an actor convincing the audience, comprised mostly of strangers, how he really felt. Travis met with the speech and English teacher, who made him practice, recite, practice, and recite some more. She and her debate team brought home numerous championships.

The speech went very well; he knew because of the applause after he finished. The class always applauded their classmates' work, but for Travis the applause was sometimes halfhearted. He knew the intensity of the clapping had a direct correlation to the grade he would likely receive. He only hoped the applause was a result of his delivery and not to acknowledge him being voted most valuable player. After lunch at the campus, Travis returned for his afternoon chemistry class.

After school, Travis hooked up with his best school and basketball buddy, Brad O'Connor. Brad and Travis had a lot in common being farm-raised, first-string varsity basketball athletes. Brad's parents, John and Sara O'Connor, are about ten years older than Lynn and me, and for various reasons we don't circulate socially. Brad's only full sister, Dana, is in her third year at University of Minnesota in Morris, a few hours to the south. Brad and Dana have been very close during their growing up years. Dana adores her younger brother. She had been his babysitter and protector during their years growing up on the farm. Travis thought the world of Dana, but was often annoyed with the controlling hold she had on her brother. She was the kind of girl, Travis said, if she was only five years younger, he would try to reel her in for himself. She was a well-put-together young lady. Brad indeed was Dana's hero and she was very proud of him.

I'd like to be a strict parent. I don't like to vary far from principle. Travis calls me every afternoon to get my approval for the evening's plans. I insist on it. I have to be informed about who was doing what, where and when. Tonight, Terri and Tanner are to be on the school bus. Travis always has a plan he wants to follow. If it makes sense, I go for it and make Tanner and Terri conform to what Travis and I decide. When Terri called to say she was staying in town with Josie, the answer was no. It was always no if Travis said something different. If Travis said they were to be on the bus, then they were to be on the bus. Terri and Tanner thought when it came to certain issues of their lives, Travis had a chokehold on them. I don't see it that way. He's the older brother and it's good for him to take some responsibility in looking after them. He is a bit overprotective of them, though mainly of Terri. He tells me how attractive she has become to other boys. I know he's going to be hard on the boys when they come around. Overall, Travis usually makes sound decisions. I trust him.

When I asked Travis what he was doing, he said he was having dinner with Brad and they were going to study chemistry. Travis was to have the Mustang home no later than 10 p.m. My instructions to Travis during the spring thaws are always to come home via the interstate. I don't want him driving on the county and township roads that are shorter and more direct. I don't want the Mustang on roads that are full of chuckholes, ruts, and mud. The roads are okay once it dries out, but this early in the spring, it's too wet. Driving the back roads carries a greater risk of running into deer. Travis drives too fast.

Other than the costly investments in farm equipment, the Mustang is my one and only expensive vice. The Mustang belonged to my dad, who died when I was twelve. I have spent a small fortune restoring it and have spared no expense to keep it running. The Mustang has become the family heirloom. The car means a lot to me, and I hope it will to Travis. I want him to have it eventually. For that reason and that reason only, the car is stored in the implement shed during the winter months. Now that the snow is gone I'll allow it to be driven, but only on the paved roads.

Travis came home at 10:20 p.m. I was in the den doing some work on the computer. Travis came in and excitedly told me all he learned about the O'Connors' plans for next season's crops. I listened with amazement. I had to agree they had some good ideas, but that wasn't going to have much influence with what we were planning. Travis knows that the bulk of the farming activities had to be discussed with my stepdad and two stepbrothers, who were heavily involved in our operation. I don't have total control over every aspect of our farm operations like John O'Connor does.

My mom is part owner in a certified seed business that my stepdad Paul and his two sons operate. My mom goes by the nickname of Granny. Dad got sick when I was ten. They said it was an aggressive form of lymphoma. The cancer specialists at Fargo said they had seen that form of cancer before in farmers. They thought there might be a connection between the disease and the use of insecticides. I knew something was wrong one day when I saw my mother crying. She never did that. She and dad were always happy. I never heard them speak a cross word to each other. She told me dad was sick, and that he wasn't going to get well. That's all I knew. She never said he would die, so I didn't expect him to. It was her way of coping. Mom pretended that nothing was wrong. She had to have her head on to do the crop contracting and other farm business so we could get the crops sold. She didn't want to lose the land. Dad was sick for two years. I saw him getting worse. His illness took a toll on mom. The first year dad was sick, we were cheated on some poorly written crop contracts. It almost ruined us financially. The medical bills were piling up and bill collectors were starting to hound her. After two years, mom was burnt out with caring for dad. It was one thing after another.

Something had to give. So she sent dad down to her friend's place in Fargo. Her friend and her sister, my aunt, took care of him until he died. The hospital wouldn't take him because they said he was terminal. Mom didn't have the money anyway, and they balked at doing any more for him since it wasn't going to make him well.

When mom finished with the farm business, she dropped me off at my friend's house in Cheneau Valley and left for Fargo to help take care of dad. I never saw her or heard anything from her for about two weeks. She called where I was staying, but never when I was there. She didn't want to talk to me. She just checked up on me to see that I was okay. I don't think she could face talking to me. She knew I would ask about dad, and she couldn't act as if nothing serious was happening to him.

The day my dad died, Granny's priest came over and told me that my dad wouldn't be coming back, and that I'd be going on vacation with these folks for a few days. They took me north to a lake, where we fished and camped out for a week. The priest didn't say that he died, but I knew. That was obvious. I knew dad wasn't coming back. Mom didn't call me or anything. She didn't want me with her in Fargo, so I went on this fishing trip with my friends and never gave it another thought. Then, when it was over, she never mentioned him again. It was like dad never existed.

When it comes to farming, what I do usually works, and if it doesn't so be it. I'm pretty comfortable farming the way I do. I had to learn it on my own, because I was too young when my dad died to learn anything much from him. Farming is always a gamble, even though this is good farming country. The land here is good to the farmer but Mother Nature has her ways. I get hailed out, rained out, frozen out, dried out and snowed under. The only solution for that is crop insurance. It is easy to get in a rut, and Travis thinks I'm in one. It's a good rut. I stick to what I know: soybeans and wheat. I'm pretty conservative, but Travis is more progressive in his thinking.

When I was old enough, I went to work in the fields. I operated machinery and learned the business. Granny had a good business head. She could add, subtract, multiply and divide and come up with the right answer. She could manage. I could do the work. I learned my managerial skills from her. We began to make it after we had a couple really good years. She paid off dad's medical bills. I was able to lease machinery and do some contracting as well as farm our four thousand acres. Suddenly, it all came together. I had to grow up fast. Travis would be the same way if he had to. He's growing up fast. I'm very proud of his self-reliance.

Travis reads, he studies the latest research, he questions and challenges everything I do. He keeps me honest. He was trustworthy with the machinery by the age of twelve, and during harvest you couldn't get him out of the field. He absolutely loves farming, and the money that can be made from it when managed properly.

Travis knows the pros and cons of every piece of machinery; its cost, what it can and can't do. When he is along, we can't pass an implement dealer without stopping to see what is on the lot -- new or used. The dealers know Travis and they call him when new equipment comes into their lot. If they can sell Travis on it, that is the first hurdle they jump over to push it off on me. I have banked on the fact that Travis will always be on the farm. He is my son but he also is a best friend, business associate and confidante. Truth be known, I rely heavily on Travis. When he graduates from college he will get involved with Paul's seed business. They had better get ready for an upheaval. He'll know everything there is to know about growing certified seed, and probably a lot they don't want to know about the seed business.

Paul and my mom, Granny Norlund, live just across the driveway from us in their ranch-house rambler. It was Paul's original home, where he raised his five kids before he married mom. The seed business is about two hundred yards behind us. There is a small elevator and numerous granaries. There is ample room for the supply and grain trucks to pull in by the elevator and out again. It is a good business and keeps the family going. Travis has a keen interest in its operation. When he gets bored with the routine here at home, he's over sticking his nose into their business.

Mom's marriage to Paul seemed to be a marriage of convenience. Money married money, they said. It was a very short courtship. One day it just happened. It was a good marriage, but there were a lot of problems when mom and I were forced to assimilate into the Norlund family.

Granny was previously known in the valley as Cecelia Olsen. Shortly into the marriage, Paul's grandkids started calling her Granny. They readily took her to be their grandmother. Granny loved the outdoors, and prolonged exposure to the elements had contributed to her face wrinkles. Her face is full of wrinkles. She might pass for being older than she is. She doesn't mind being a Granny.

Today, Granny is mom to the five Norlund kids and grandma both to her twelve grandchildren on the Norlund side and to my three children. They all adore her. She worked hard to earn their love and they have reciprocated. She spoiled her stepchildren rotten and they loved every minute of it. At times, I was somewhat jealous during the time we were growing up together under the same roof. They could get by with a lot more than I could. Through it all, we have all remained good friends and we were fiercely loyal to each other. I loved having brothers and it somewhat filled the void of not having a dad. Paul was always good to me, and he certainly was to mom, but he never stepped up to the plate as far as parenting me like he did for his own kids.

Granny's pride and joy is Travis. She feeds his pride and he feeds hers with his basketball talent, his academic achievements, and his farming abilities. Travis doesn't take to her affection so Granny keeps her distance. Granny tends to lavish affection on Tanner, who doesn't like it either but stands reverently still as she hugs him. Granny gives Terri attention too, but not like she does with the boys. Terri is pretty much her mamma's girl. Folks will tell you that without debate, Travis is also Lynn's favorite. Everybody caters to Travis. He's everybody's favorite.

Tanner has been the odd kid on the block who isn't particularly close to his mom or me. Ignored by his older brother, Tanner fights for attention by badgering Travis. If you push Travis over the edge, it isn't worth it. Tanner is beaten up by Travis almost daily but never seems to learn his lesson. I mostly just gloss over it, thinking someday Tanner will grow up and be good friends with Travis. I know it will happen. Lynn sees more of it than I do and it disturbs her. I can't referee every fight they get into. Travis is a peaceable guy, but he'll only take so much and he'll not back down from any opponent. Travis teases Tanner, telling him he was the result of an accident. In a sense, it is true about Tanner being conceived accidentally. Lynn had a hard time carrying and giving birth to Travis three years before Terri was born. Terri was a problem to carry and birth as well, so we decided to be satisfied with the two we had, rather than trying for another. We didn't have a set number of kids we wanted to bring into the world. I was fine with a boy and girl three years apart. Granny wanted more, and she was crafty in the hints she dropped, indicating her preference for more kids. She wouldn't relax until she knew the direction we were leaning.

But as fate would have it, less than a year after Terri was born Lynn was pregnant again with Tanner. Lynn refused to use birth control so what do you expect? This time, for some reason, the pregnancy went smoothly. I was thrilled when I learned it was a boy coming.

Lynn always has Granny's approval and they get along well. Granny loved her the minute she laid eyes on her. She was "cute as a button" as far as Granny was concerned and just the right one for me. Granny brags about Lynn, saying she is the most capable person there is, but then Granny might say that about the next person. She's not beyond flattery. Granny's love at first sight for Lynn is somewhat based on Lynn's Italian-Catholic roots. It was rare in the Northern Plains to find an unmixed Italian girl when most are of Scandinavian heritage. Granny is pleased that her grandchildren are so Italian-looking, having the dark features, long eyelashes and olive skin. They stand out so perfectly among the white-skinned, blue-eyed blondes who comprise so many in the community.

My mom is deeply religious. Granny has a deep faith in God. She believes He is omnipresent. Everything is for a reason and part of the bigger picture that we don't see. Granny's philosophy is to make something good happen from something bad that happens. Everything is sort of pre-planned, she believes.

She hangs tightly to her Catholic faith. The scandals and improprieties that continue to shake the church tear her apart. She refuses to disfranchise herself. She continues faithfully. I feel badly for mom that none of us attend Mass with her. Every Sunday, if the roads are clear, she drives herself into Cheneau Valley for Mass. When Lynn is in the mood, she will also go. Paul is not religious, but she knew that when she married him. His kids went every way that the wind blew when it came to religion. Most turned out to be Lutheran. As a kid, I was sent to Catholic school for the first six grades. I received my Catholic education and that was all I wanted. I went to public middle and high school. That said, I respect my Catholic upbringing and I want my kids to embrace good morals. They need to believe there is a higher power who governs and rules in the world. They need to understand that they don't own their lives. They don't have total control of their lives as far as fate and destiny. There has to be a higher power involved. They need to understand that life is precious, and if they lose it, they can't get it back.

Lynn and I chose not to send the kids to Catholic school. This did not set well with Granny. Lynn feels guilty about this. We did allow them to be baptized in the Catholic Church, according to our family tradition.

Travis thinks Granny's spirituality is a bit too creepy for him. Travis doesn't want anything to do with religion. That would have all changed, Granny reasons, if Travis had gone to parochial school and had some religious education along with the three R's. If my kids get any religious blood flowing through their veins, it won't be from me.

Lynn Olsen

Travis couldn't let go of a basketball for any length of time. Before the spring farm work was into full swing, Travis was itching to get his half court put back together in order to shoot baskets and practice his game. Basketball brought Travis and Tanner together and put their love-hate relationship on hiatus. Without being asked, Tanner followed his big brother outside to help clean up the concrete court and portable goal that was stored in the implement shed during the winter.

I stood at the kitchen window and watched Travis and Tanner as they unloaded the pallets of tiles for the synthetic basketball court that would be laid down on the concrete slab.

They looked too heavy for Tanner. I clutched the edge of the sink and gasped as they lifted the four-foot sections of synthetic tiles off the truck trailer onto the concrete court. Travis had no idea how much Tanner could lift. He would push Tanner to the limit, just like he always pushed himself.

David left with a load of wheat for Cordsville, fifteen miles down the interstate. Before he left, I overheard him tell Travis to wait until he came home, but when Travis wanted something he became impatient. I knew David didn't intend for Travis and Tanner to lift and assemble those tiles without his help. It was a half-day job to put the floor together, even with David's help. The manufacturer's guarantee covered outdoor exposure, but to Travis, the floor was sacrosanct and he refused to leave it outdoors at the mercy of the subzero winter weather. Without question, the investment for the new goal and outdoor floor was well worth it. It was the perfect contrivance for the boys to hone their basketball skills. Now that Travis was playing at such a high performance level, it was a thrill to stand at the window and watch him sink three-pointers, free throws, and layups. Tanner would make use of it, too. When he was older, he wanted to follow in his brother's footsteps. When David came home in the early afternoon, he just shook his head.

Once it was laid, the court, with its green field and red key was an attractive addition to the back yard. Travis owned it, and he protected it with great veracity. Unfortunately, the court was in a direct line between the back door and the farm buildings, including the open lot where the equipment, trucks, and guests sometimes parked. Nobody dared walk on it, not even Laser. By the end of summer even Granny's cat, the last on the block to learn any new trick, stepped around it rather than face the wrath of Travis.

The boys hauled out the bin full of basketballs, cleaned them up, and begin practicing. Trying to achieve ten for ten, Travis moved the full one hundred eighty degrees along the three-point arc trying to sink as many consecutive shots as possible. After the first shot was in the air, Tanner threw another ball to Travis, who moved to a different position on the arc.

"Don't you make most of your points inside the key?" Tanner asked.

"Be ready to play from anywhere. Always adjust your game as the circumstances dictate." Travis always gave the same answer.

"But Brad makes more three-pointers than you do!"

"Not for long, buddy. Not for long." Travis seemed to ignore the insult only because it was true. Brad was deadly from the arc. Now, if Tanner had said that about Aaron, Travis would have beaten him up for it. As yet, Travis had not accomplished a full ten for ten, but more than once he made eight out of ten from the three-point line.

"How come you don't float your three-pointers like Brad does?" Tanner asked, knowing that Travis' shots were always off the glass.

"That's Brad's method. He concentrates harder than I do," Travis explained. "The opponents always have two guys on me under the key. That leaves Brad open to take the better shots. I have to make my attempts with lightening speed. I'm at a disadvantage. I go hard off the glass," he concluded. "Tanner, do you know how many assists I had last season?"

Tanner knew Travis wasn't a selfish player. He pulled down the rebounds and if someone was open to score, he threw the ball to them. Travis never threw the ball away by taking bad shots. Travis shot seventy-six percent from the charity line and he intended to move that up above eighty percent by the next season. Tanner dropped on his haunches while he watched Travis sink one after the other. Tanner was impressed with the consistency of baskets Travis could make from the free throw line.

"Free throws are my bread and butter. They often win or lose your game. They are free points." Travis reminisced about the final minutes of a close game where his opponent was repeatedly hit with reach-in fouls trying to stop Travis from scoring inside the key. "That's the difference between me and Aaron. Aaron is less than forty-five percent at the line. He needs to up his game!"

Aaron Richards, the team's first-string guard, was the substitute center when Travis fouled out or when Travis had to rest. Travis was capable of playing the whole game, but the coach liked to give him a rest during the second half, if possible. Travis never liked to be benched. Everyone in town knows about the rivalry between Aaron and Travis. It didn't interfere with their game, but it was a big concern for coach Epperson, who stressed a cooperative team effort. I always took my son's side in the disputes he had with Aaron. Aaron had a cocky attitude about him. He spoke impudently to everybody, including the coach. He was often benched for that, too. He grew up with older stepbrothers who weren't the best influence. In spite of his attitude, Aaron was a good kid. He worked hard on the farm for his dad. He was tough. He knew more about worldly ways than Travis did. We didn't let Travis involve himself in some of the things Aaron had done. Aaron bragged about his exploits. He and his dad considered themselves to be better farmers than most. He gets a lot of his arrogance from his old man. They grew a bigger variety of crops than we did. Travis outperformed Aaron in basketball. Scholastically, Travis was way out in front of Aaron because Aaron didn't study that much. Aaron planned to stay on the farm. He didn't think he needed to go to college. Travis never particularly liked him, but David told Travis that when you live in a small town you had to get along with people and overlook their faults. Travis pretty much listened to David because David was a good role model.

Tanner stood at the baseline and threw the ball to Travis as he jumped for a layup. Travis did twelve layups and made every single one. Fatigued, Travis grabbed his brother and wrapped his right arm around his neck and the other arm around his middle. He locked him in a tight hold.

"Little bro!" Travis yelled. "How many of them did I miss?"

I wanted Tanner to answer him. Tanner was trying to wiggle free of the vise-like grip Travis had him in. He couldn't. His face reddened. He couldn't breathe. I could feel the pressure and gripping strength of Travis' long arms as he held Tanner tight like a python with its prey. Tanner is stubborn. He's not going to give in. In a second, Tanner was going to start crying and that would end their togetherness.

"One?" Tanner cajoled

"How many?" Travis didn't let up on the pressure. Tanner was in pain, so he answered wisely.

"Zip, zero, nada!"

"And, bro, how many layups are you allowed to miss?" Travis kept up the abuse.

"Zip, zero, nada!" Tanner answered correctly, so they came in the house for a drink.

Travis averaged twenty-five points per game on a good night, and most of his nights were good. As high school juniors, Travis and Brad O'Connor were two of North Dakota's leading scorers in high school basketball. When Travis grabbed the rebounds, he'd try and set Brad up to shoot if he couldn't get it up himself. They worked together that way but it often upset the other players.

David Olsen

The spring planting was right on schedule. When the weather cooperated, it took four to six weeks to seed eight thousand acres. Granny owned four thousand, I owned two thousand, and I leased two thousand. Depending on prices, I liked to also do some contracting. When Travis was available to help me, we made some extra cash by contracting. It was good money when the prices were favorable.

On the weekends, Travis followed me behind the seeder, pulling the field roller with an almost new John Deere tractor. He was a strange kid. He liked driving tractors better than cars. If John Deere made a tractor for the road and one for fieldwork, Travis would be quite happy. When he was a little kid, Granny made him a pullover. It had a picture of a fawn on it. Underneath it said, "Travis is a Deere." Travis claimed that John Deere tractors were arguably the best machines ever made. He's still stuck on that brand name. The fact they are manufactured here in our little town doesn't detract from his enthusiasm.

Travis was being heavily recruited by Iowa State University. Iowa State had scouts at the tournament exclusively to watch Travis play. The head basketball coaches wanted to meet Travis. They had the curriculum and a massive basketball program with membership in the Big Twelve Conference. I urged Travis to travel there on an official visit that would be at their expense. I was sure they would make him an offer, but he wouldn't go because he knew he wouldn't play center for them. He wasn't tall enough for that. His pride couldn't digest the fact that he was destined to play on the perimeter for whatever school he attended. He saw it as an insult to his ability. He wanted to limit his visits to schools where he thought he could play center. It was genes, not ability.

It was the last Bison Visit Day at the North Dakota State University campus in Fargo. We put the fieldwork on hold. It was such good weather to seed that I hated to stop, but Travis wanted to make a decision.

We had appointments with the coaches and some faculty members in the College of Agriculture. This was Travis's second unofficial visit to the Athletic Department. They wanted him. They tried to get him last fall. I told him to wait and see what else was offered. They didn't push him, but had they done so, he would have committed and the possibility to attend Iowa State would have been moot. The college here was good that way. They didn't want you to sign until you were sure that they were a good fit for the athlete. But, when they offer you a scholarship, they see you as a good fit for them.

"And, if you know what's good for you," I said, "you won't tell Granny about the recruitment letter from Notre Dame."

"Aw! It's just a letter," Travis said.

I told Travis that the letter from Notre Dame would mean a lot to Granny, and she would be gnawing on his butt to go there and interview. A grandson playing basketball at Notre Dame would be the top echelon of achievement in Granny's world.

"Why wouldn't you go to Indiana and visit Notre Dame? It could be an official visit on their money."

"Because I don't intend to go there, so why waste their money on a trip?"

I could see his point of view. Travis got his bullheadedness from Granny. I knew he would never go to Notre Dame and be that far from home or the farm. No matter how much you tugged and pulled, he wasn't changing his mind. I insisted that he consider all offers, including South Dakota State. I wanted my son to use this opportunity to travel the country to larger campuses to see their programs. Then, in my view, after he laid everything out on the table, he could make his decision. Travis was not your usual seventeen-year-old. He was focused and a lot more mature than I was at his age.

I told Travis to talk to the coaches on his own, but I wanted to sit in on the discussions with the College of Agriculture. Travis could filter out things he didn't want to hear. He tended to downplay the academic part. In my book, that was the bigger item. Travis wanted more information from the faculty about how easy it would be for him to do a double major in crop and animal science. Both majors were big, with little overlap. He wanted to make sure he could get all of his classes and get out of there in five years. I tried to tell Travis these professors had to teach in the morning and spend some time with their graduate students in the afternoon and do their field research. The Fargo campus had a huge graduate program. I didn't know how easy it would be for him to get his classes, because it seemed they were all bunched together in the morning. He had to get the most recent curriculum from both departments, dig into their class schedules and see how they were arranged. He didn't want to do that. He took whatever they said and ran with it. Granny was intent on setting Travis up in the cattle business and Travis was not about to be swayed from doing the second major in animal science.

We went right to the offices in the Athletic Department. Travis hit it off well with one of the assistant coaches. The guy had been very helpful and had not pressured Travis to come there, but why should they when Travis gave the impression he had already decided to play for them? The coach, still very young, told about his experience being recruited. Travis told me to stay with him when he met with the coaches, so I did.

The coaches gave us a rundown of the program again. They were excited about some of the new recruits. There would be more roster changes. They were still saving his spot. They asked when would he be ready to commit. Their conference schedule was going to change and there would be a couple more preseason tournaments to play in. I could just see it. Travis's adrenalin was flowing. All the blood went to his brain. He had that excited look he gets when he is about ready to land a trophy fish. Finally, they announced they had attained NCAA Division I status. They previously had been on probationary status. It wasn't for sure last fall, when they made Travis his offer of a full five-year scholarship. To me that was big. I really wanted Travis to attend an NCAA Division I school, where he could have a chance at the big dance. Everybody wanted in on "March Madness."

That did it. Goodbye Iowa State. They asked Travis if he had made up his mind and Travis looked at me and looked at them and said he wanted to sign.

"Where do I put my signature?"

They made it look ceremonial, took a picture, wrote up a press release, and brought out a letter of intent for him to sign. We had to make a run for the student grill and grab a bite to eat, as it was nearly time to meet with the School of Agriculture. The coaches wanted a little more pomp and ceremony but there wasn't time.

"Travis, I'm a little bit peeved at you. I should have made you pay for my sandwich. Today's trip should have been done as an official visit where the coaches buy the lunch."

"Oh sure, dad. Let them run us around town too, huh? Maybe we could tour the Fargodome, splash around in the Red River, and I could get your picture in an old Viking ship. Dad, we live here! We don't need to make official visits here!"

That wasn't the point, I explained. If he came with the intention of signing, why not make it an official visit? Everyone wanted him, and he had not gone on a single official visit anywhere.

I told him what we were embarking upon this afternoon was more important than basketball, anyway.

"Look Travis," I said, "As they say, 'you are one injury away from never playing the game again,' but I say you will be a farmer for the next forty years. What you get out of the School of Agriculture will outlast any basketball program that they offer."

We met with one faculty member who taught in the soil and crop sciences department. He gave an unofficial "yes" to the double major, saying it would require at least five years. The professor went over the curriculum for Crop Production, the program Travis wanted, and he explained the options available in the Animal and Range Sciences Department. The longer the guy talked, the more excited Travis became.

Back in the car headed for home, I asked Travis if the coaches knew about him being recruited by other colleges.

"Oh yes," Travis answered, "They sure did."

"And?"

"Well, I told them about Iowa State. That made them really nervous," Travis said as he laughed. "Dad!" Travis sat up in the seat and stretched his arms across the dash. "I'm in. Could you see how badly they wanted me to come there and play?"

"That's a lot of money, Travis. Five years of tuition, room and board, and books, and they won't pull it unless you don't perform right?"

"Dad. I'll perform for them. They know it. Why would I suddenly not perform for them? They know in a couple years, I'll be performing at a much higher level than I am now."

"I wanted you to visit Iowa."

"How far is it to Ames?"

"Over five hundred miles. It's an eight-hour drive."

"It would have been a waste of time. I'm just not interested in going that far away from home. Besides it is more than twice the size of North Dakota State. I would have been lost there."

"If you are happy, mom and I are happy. You can live your whole life in North Dakota. Five years might seem like a long time to be away from home. If you factor in the whole of your life, five years is nothing."

Travis continued to argue that he needed to be home for the farm work. I responded that the farm would go on without him. I pointed out the fact that Travis would miss the spring seeding, as he would be in school until the middle of May. He would be at home for some of the wheat harvest in August but miss all of the soybean harvest in September. In other words, it would be the same as when he was in high school. The Cheneau Valley School District did not allow absences from school in order for the farm kids to work the harvest on their family farms. It would be the same in college. He couldn't miss classes to work on the farm.

"Dad," Travis asked, "Don't you think I landed a pretty sweet deal today?"

"You bet! A really sweet deal from a cow college!"

"I wish there were some way I could get out of being a freshman redshirt. You know how much I hate the bench. I don't see how you can get all ramped up in practice and then not play in any games your first year."

On our way home, Travis called his mom.

"Hey mom. Guess what?"

"What, Travis?" Lynn asked.

"I signed!"

"Go Bisons!" she said.

Raising Trevor

[Seattle, Washington (ten years back in time)]

Susan Jensen

I was extremely frustrated sitting there in traffic trying to find the Kensington School of Martial Arts. I was unfamiliar with the streets in the Fremont District on this side of Lake Union. I wanted Trevor admitted to this school, and I didn't want to be late for his audition. I'd had a taxing day keeping up with the kids' hectic schedule. I felt a migraine headache coming on as I sat under the Aurora Bridge, stuck in traffic. Whatever was blocking the intersection ahead, I hoped it wouldn't delay us too much longer. Trevor was looking out the back seat window, mesmerized by the concrete Troll that sat under the bridge. This giant work of public art was intriguing, and the kids had not seen it before. In fact, I didn't even realize it was here when I turned on North Thirty-Sixth trying to find the Kensington studio. I had read about it when it was created by a local group of artists a few months back. Trevor wanted to get out of the car and go over so he could see it up close. The windows and doors were locked so he couldn't open them. Trevor began his usual pattern of defiance, arguing why he should have his own way. As I sat there, still idling, I looked over at six-year-old Paula and five-year-old

Amber, who had been wonderfully behaved, and I wondered what we fed Trevor that produced his tenacious personality. Now eight years old, Trevor was a challenging piece of work and it was a constant battle to keep him reined in.

I kept a log of the children's activities. Thanks to Trevor, I kept a good and a bad list. The good list included such things as reading books, hanging up clothes, being polite to one another, and helping me with simple tasks. It also included scholastic achievement. It wasn't too hard for the kids to have their good lists full of accomplishments. Items on the bad list canceled out what was on the good list, and Trevor usually ran a deficit. I tried to put as much as I could on Trevor's good side to counterbalance what went on the bad. This time when Karl returned from Europe, Trevor's bad list would be long. He talked back numerous times, threw tantrums, and said some vulgar words. For a kid his age, he racked up quite a record. He didn't understand why we put so much emphasis on bad behavior. In his mind the good behavior should cancel out the bad.

Just as Trevor commenced to throw a tantrum, I had to remind him that if he said one more word about getting out of the car, I would add that to the bad list I had prepared for Karl. After that threat, Trevor was quiet. As the traffic began to move forward I looked through the rear-view mirror and saw that Trevor had that "curled upper lip" look he gets just before an emotional outburst. His cheeks were bright red. Tears were streaming down his face and I knew what would happen next. I figured we were close to the studio and I wanted him in a good mood for the audition. Trevor was an emotional kid who cried when he was minimally upset. A long episode of crying induced bronchial spasms as a result of his asthma. Definitely to be avoided just before an audition.

The audition went well and Trevor was given a high score. However, he wasn't accepted into the program because of his age and the fact that he already was, in their opinion, engaged in too many disciplines. I knew that might happen. It was hard to get into this school. It was suggested that he continue with his dance and gymnastics, but come back in two to three years for another audition. This studio, acclaimed to be the best in Seattle, was on the way home from the gymnastics class, and that was why I wanted to fit it in, for the convenience. Trevor was a "can do" kid, wanting to participate in every sport and activity he possibly could. The busier he was, the happier. It fit his personality.

I was happy to be a stay-at-home mom, but on days like this I often wondered what my life would have been like if I had pursued a career in civil engineering after graduating from college. I met Karl Jensen, the man of my dreams, my junior year in college. I married young and was soon pregnant with Trevor. I gave up the possibility of a career to raise my kids.

The kids are home-schooled by private tutors in order to provide flexibility for the variety of extracurricular activities. Due to their dad's passion for the performing arts, they have been enrolled in ballet, guitar, tumbling, and gymnastics. Trevor had his first guitar at age six. Paula takes piano lessons and Amber will also begin music lessons next year when she turns six. Most days of the week, I have little time for myself. I continually transport the kids from one class to another. I prefer staying on the east side of Lake Washington where I can utilize the educational services in the Kirkland-Bellevue area as much as possible.

Just as we left the studio, I made a right turn and passed a homeless person who stood by the curb. Trevor wanted me to turn around and go back so he could give the man some money. Trevor started whining and wasn't going to stop without another confrontation. It was raining and the poor man appeared to be cold. Giving to the less fortunate was something Trevor insisted on doing. His dad started him doing it. Trevor was convinced it was his obligation to be charitable. He was passionate about it. Reluctantly, I made a left turn and went back. The man was still there. I pulled up to the curb and handed Trevor some money from my change purse. Trevor handed the money to the man, who was completely taken aback by this act of generosity from a little kid in the back of a Mercedes. I pulled away from the curb and Trevor waved enthusiastically to the man. I then headed for the 580 Freeway to our home in Kirkland.

The rain was heavy now, and soon we were in stop-and-go traffic. Trevor started trying to convince me to remove some other bad things he did from the list I'd prepared for Karl. Trevor was a good negotiator and he made some pleas and promises in an attempt to convince me to see his side. He was deathly afraid of his father and worried what Karl might do if everything on the list was mentioned. He was so sensitive and sincere in his pleas that I sometimes caved in to him. Karl said that I immediately lost all control when I did that. I tried to remember what all was on the bad list. It was so bad this time that I couldn't remember everything that was listed, but I stood firm that some of the things on his bad list were going to be held against him.

There was one deed, though, that wasn't getting cut from the bad list. I made it very clear to Trevor that he would have to receive his dad's justice for that. The behavior in question was reprehensible. He had talked back to me in Spanish, using an expletive. It was not the first time he had done that. When Trevor was learning Spanish from little Jose, he also learned some obscene words. They were words Jose Sr. used when he was cleaning out the horse corrals we have on the property. Little Jose's mom, Lilly, helped me in the house and Lilly overheard Trevor and little Jose talking. Lilly knew the standard of the Jensen home. No vulgar language. Jose Sr. didn't use foul language around Karl, either. Karl would display such a professional air that no one would talk dirty around him. Lilly was afraid that if I knew what little Jose was teaching Trevor, I would not let her bring little Jose to work. That would mean that Lilly and Jose Sr. would be forced to pay a babysitter.

Trevor loved to be with kids. He and little Jose played well together. They never fought. Trevor was always happy to share whatever he had. He gave his stuff to little Jose because he knew Karl would replace it. Karl admired the generous traits Trevor seemed to have. Due to his class schedule, Trevor wasn't around kids. His classes were usually one-on-one with the instructor. His ballet classes were mainly with girls. Karl had pushed me to get him into the Kensington studio to learn karate. Karl wouldn't be happy they didn't take him.

One day, Lilly privately told Trevor that if she ever heard him say that word again, she would tell his mother. She and Trevor had a serious discussion, and Trevor understood her perfectly. However, boys will be boys and Trevor didn't mind her. Trevor sassed me again in Spanish and called me a bad name. I don't know any Spanish. I knew he was talking back to me but I didn't have a clue as to what he said. Lilly overheard him and made good on her word. She came right in and told me. Karl had made it very clear to Trevor that it was not to be repeated. Well, he did it again. This was the most serious incident on the current bad list, and I couldn't remove it.

Thanks to the global economy, my Dutch-American husband Karl was gone for twelve days on a business trip to Northern Europe. As a lawyer, Karl's specialty was Business Law with an international focus. He worked with a group of lawyers who had contracted themselves out to various enterprises. The last several months, Karl had been away more than he had been home. It had been rough on me, and this time being alone with the kids had not been easy. On the other hand, I realized Karl's good-paying job had enabled me to stay at home and live a comfortable life. In fact, in a few hours Karl would be boarding a plane in Amsterdam for his flight home.

It won't exactly be happy landings tomorrow, after I show him everything on the list I have chalked up against Trevor. All these problems stemmed from the fact that Karl wasn't home to help me reinforce the discipline. Karl and I agreed to work together as a team when disciplining the kids. When in the presence of the kids, we agreed even if we didn't, and I didn't always agree with Karl. Karl thought I was too easy on Trevor so I couldn't go against Karl by removing the very items from the bad list Karl had worked so consistently to correct. But then again, Karl expected too much. He and Trevor would make an agreement to do something and if Trevor didn't do it just the way Karl expected, then Karl didn't count it as worthy for tthe good list. It was more like a business contract than parenting. Everything Karl did was focused on business. I wished, sometimes, that Karl could somehow stop being a businessman and just be a parent. When Karl was gone that long, Trevor's bad list was always long. I couldn't lie to Karl. Once I did that, Trevor would take full advantage of me. I had to stick to my guns but I didn't like it.

Finally, we were off the bridge and able to resume freeway speed.

"It has been a long day hasn't it, kids? Why don't we stop off at the next exit and have a Burgermaster?"

"*Yes!*"

The kids gave a resounding answer. It was the kids' favorite place to eat. At this location it was a drive-in and the kids enjoyed giving their order directly to the carhop.

"Husky Pup," Trevor loudly announced his preference.

"Weinermaster," Paula announced.

"That's a "Husky Pup," Trevor corrected her.

"Muffinmaster," Amber barged in on the discussion.

"That's for breakfast only. You can't have that now," Trevor argued.

"Chickenmaster." I chimed in.

The noise level worsened as we discussed what we could and could not have and what to call it if we could have it. The Husky

Pup was what Trevor and Karl ordered at the Burgermaster over by the Husky Stadium, where they also had a sit-down restaurant. I was pretty sure they didn't serve it here, but whatever. Trevor would find out soon enough. I pitied the carhop who had to wait on us.

The scene was bedlam when the kids screamed their orders simultaneously at the poor, unsuspecting girl. Thinking that there must be some advantage to be first, Trevor shouted out his request ahead of the girls who were usually a step or two behind him. The poor girl, who spoke with an Asian accent, couldn't get the order right with everyone shouting at her in unison. I knew I should take control of the situation and speak to her myself, but the kids were having too much fun yelling at her, my headache was in full swing, and I was too tired to even care. It was also amusing. The Asian clerk couldn't understand them and they couldn't understand her broken accent. She was confused about Trevor's request for a Husky Pup. So Trevor yelled it back in Spanish, and when that didn't work he tried a little Dutch his father had taught him. Finally, after gaining control of my laughter, I shut them all up and tried to regain my composure so I could politely recite the orders, but she gave up on us. The supervisor came outside and started speaking to us in Spanish. I got it. She thought the problem stemmed from the fact we didn't speak English. I played along with that, allowing Trevor to restate our orders in Spanish. He was always ready to practice his Spanish. He didn't know all of the Spanish words for the menu items so it became a hodge-podge of both languages. Trevor was very funny. Trevor demanded they serve him a Husky Pup. At this location it was listed on the menu as a Weinermaster. It was almost the same but Trevor insisted they make it as close to a Husky Pup as possible. He knew exactly how it should be done and told them so. Amber couldn't have her Muffinmaster and settled to split the big Burgermaster with her mom.

The next afternoon, Karl's direct flight from Amsterdam arrived early. He caught a private shuttle home. It was still raining when the shuttle pulled up into the circular driveway, unsheltered from the damp weather. Karl, dressed in a business suit and trench coat, got out of the car while the driver unloaded the bags. The kids wanted to run outside and greet their dad but I wouldn't let them. Trevor had been using his inhaler. They had all taken a chill yesterday and I was afraid we all were coming down with colds. Karl looked weary. I knew it would take a couple of days for the jetlag to wear off. I didn't want to unload on him right now. There was never a perfect time. He would want to know immediately how they all behaved.

The kids stood at the window with wild anticipation. He came home with more bags than he took. He brought gifts. It was what they all expected. The longer he was gone, the more things he brought. He always brought back nice gifts. I kept the kids inside while I went outside to greet him and help with the bags.

When he came in and unloaded his things, there was an aurora of excitement parallel only to the night before Christmas. Karl sorted out the boxes and set them on the dining-room table. In one of the larger boxes were three additional place settings of my favorite dishware. He reached inside his carry-on and pulled out three long sleeved T-shirts. Next, Karl walked over to Trevor and put a baseball cap on his head. On the front of the cap was the inscription "Cheese Head." Trevor removed the hat and examined it.

"I'm not a cheese head," he exclaimed.

"You're Dutch, and that makes you a cheese head!" Karl stated and they all laughed.

There were three boxes left on the table. Karl gave each of the girls the two small ones. Inside each was a porcelain doll.

Now Karl said, "Before we go any further," he looked at me before he continued, "Were there any lists that had to be made?"

37

Trevor sat down on the floor and began to fidget.

"I made some good lists," I said.

"Well then, let's hear them," he continued.

I began reading the journal I kept about the good things each of the kids had done. Trevor had more on his list than either of the girls.

"That's very good," he said, "I'm proud of all of you."

He continued by saying that he knew he had good kids. I was relieved. I thought it would be better not to bring up the problems with Trevor, at least, not yet.

"Does Amber have a bad list?" Karl asked.

"No," I said.

"Paula?"

"No."

"What about Trevor?" Karl spoke calmly.

Trevor started biting his nails and looking really scared. Karl had never laid a hand on any of the kids. It was agreed upon from the very start that we would not use corporal punishment to discipline the kids. I am of the opinion that if we'd backhanded Trevor a few times he wouldn't have had such a sassy mouth. Karl had other ways of making his point. Karl pressed me about the bad list, and so I read the infractions I had recorded on the list, including the incident of bad language. Karl listened and said nothing.

"Very well," he said. "Paula and Amber, you can have what is in the big box."

They excitedly opened it and unwrapped a darling miniature Delftware tea set for when they played house together. It matched my blue china set. The girls were thrilled. Next, Karl took out a small, slender box. Inside was a watch he brought for Trevor. It was gorgeous. Trevor's eyes lit up. His deep blue eyes sparkle when he's happy.

"You didn't keep your agreement so you can't have the watch," Karl explained.

Trevor looked stunned. Next, Karl walked over to the vanity drawer where some tools were kept. He took a small hammer and smashed the crystal on the watch. He put it back in the box and dropped it in the garbage. I took a deep breath. I had no idea how much he had paid for the watch. I'm sure it wasn't cheap. Why didn't he call me, I thought, before he bought the watch? I would have told him that Trevor had misbehaved.

Trevor immediately started his screaming episode. Karl told him to go to his room and to stay there. The girls started crying. The happy homecoming turned sour. Trevor went up to the top of the stairs and threw his cap down. He threw it right at Karl. Next, Trevor threw the T-shirt over the stair banister and screamed at Karl.

"You can keep these because *I won't wear them!*"

I went into our bedroom, took some medicine and stretched out on the bed. Trevor went to his room and his crying could be heard throughout the six-thousand-square-foot house. I warned Karl that Trevor had been wheezing and was using the inhaler. Karl said he would take care of it once Trevor settled down. Meanwhile we just left him alone until he ran out of steam.

Thirty minutes later, Karl went upstairs into Trevor's room carrying the cap, T-shirt and a shopping bag. Trevor was on his bed reading. Karl closed the bedroom door, put the T-shirt and cap on the dresser, and sat on the edge of the bed. He spoke Dutch. Trevor understood most of it and tried to answer. Karl kept speaking in Dutch but Trevor didn't comprehend everything Karl was saying.

"Did you say horse?" Trevor asked.

Karl, reaching in the bag, took out a box containing a solid glass horse and gave it to Trevor. The glass horse, Karl explained, had nothing to do with the bad list. It was a gift. Karl explained how he was away too long and how much he had missed Trevor.

Trevor snuggled up to his dad as if nothing had happened and told him about the book he just read. It was his third since Karl was away. Trevor was rewarded for every book he read. Karl told Trevor how much he loved him and that he had missed him while he was away. He reassured Trevor that he could earn another watch and that they would pick it out when we all were in Amsterdam during the summer. Karl gave him a big tight hug and the two of them came down for supper.

[Four years later]

I had just dropped Paula and Amber off for their music lessons. After four years of weekly piano lessons, Paula had become quite the pianist. Likewise, Amber was showing talent on the violin, an instrument Karl chose for her to learn. Trevor had studied guitar intermittently for six years, and according to his instructors, he had a cord vocabulary larger than those who had been playing twice as long. However, he played too much by ear and tended to not follow the music. He wouldn't learn the blues scales the last instructor tried to teach him. The instructor thought it would add a nice bluesy touch to his playing. Karl thought he might need a rest from guitar, so we were looking for a voice instructor. Some we talked with wanted him to wait, but Karl said he was ready for Trevor to start learning how to sing.

The last stop today was at the dance studio where Trevor was finishing with his ballet lessons. It was almost by accident that Trevor started ballet. It wasn't part of the original plan. Karl wanted Trevor to do gymnastics, martial arts, and eventually to play a contact sport. Dancing was supposed to be for the girls, Karl thought. One day, more than four years ago, I left Trevor at the dance studio with his sisters, who were to have their lesson. He wanted to read his book -- something he couldn't do in the car while driving because of his inclination for motion sickness.

It seemed convenient to leave him there where he could quietly read. Unsupervised, he laid his book aside and followed his sisters into the studio and participated in their class. The instructors were amused and they treated him like he was a class member. Already performing well in gymnastics, he displayed a definite talent for dance. When I came back for the girls, the instructors begged me to enroll him. It was also convenient, as I didn't have to schedule something different for Trevor while his sisters were in ballet. Karl was reluctant, but finally agreed.

When I arrived today at the studio, the parking lot was jammed with cars. After parking at the far end of the lot I walked into the mezzanine level of the studio and looked down onto the floor. The studio was buzzing with activity. There he was! Trevor was dancing down the side of the huge floor with Emma Brown, the owner of the studio. He was spectacular. I stood there transfixed along with dozens of other students and parents as they watched Emma and Trevor work through their routines. As I watched, I was wishing he had put on a better pair of jazz pants and nicer T-shirt. Although, to be honest, the outfit that he wore didn't detract much from the grace and style of the performance. Emma told me that he was coming along well, but she didn't say he was that good. She never did brag too much about her students. No matter how well you danced with Emma, she tried to push you to a higher level. I didn't think Karl realized that this kid was going to be a dancer.

"Now that is what you can get when you really push your kids into this," voiced a lady standing next to me just as Trevor did a series of perfect pirouettes, turning his whole body and pivoting off the ball of one foot. I looked at the lady who made the comment, smiled and left.

The lady didn't understand that it was a lot more than pushing your kids. Trevor had worked very hard, constantly practicing, stretching, and conditioning his muscles for ballet. He wanted to be better than everyone else. That was what pushed him forward. If he didn't want to do something, he couldn't be pushed to do it.

Unfortunately, he was the only boy at his particular ability level. He didn't like that, and Trevor decided to quit ballet. He told Karl, who was taken by surprise. The two sat down and discussed it. Trevor was determined to quit. It was Emma Brown who urged Trevor to remain. She took him as her private student for ballet. She also convinced him to study Latin dance, adding to his already-attained knowledge of Spanish. It was also partner dancing, and he was teamed up with other kids. It changed everything for him. Emma was very sly; she made him also commit to continuing with her as a private ballet student. His lessons got very pricey but he wanted to study both.

When Trevor was fifteen, he began kickboxing as his contact sport. He stayed with the Kensington School after earning his black belt in karate. Karl and I almost parted company over kickboxing. It was such a rough sport. Trevor had a temper. If he blew a fuse at somebody, I wouldn't put it past him to use some of the defensive tactics he learned. Trevor looked more like a Roman gladiator than a ballet dancer when he donned the kickboxing trousers, hand wraps, mouth guard, boxing gloves, groin guard, shin pads and kick boots. In the end Karl had his athlete and I had my dancer.

Trevor Jensen (age seventeen)

Did you ever try giving a horse a pedicure? It isn't easy. I shouldn't have started this job because I didn't have the time to finish it. I struggled with the pick as I tried to remove a rock that was lodged between the hoof and the right rear shoe of Mr. Jed, my nine-year-old quarter horse. He was a pretty chestnut color with a thin white streak down the forehead. The name Mr. Jed was a take on "Mr. Ed," the talking horse in the hit TV series from the '60s. I bought a collector's series of reruns and I still watch them. Unfortunately, Mr. Jed can't talk. I wish he could tell me exactly what is causing his lameness. I had to discontinue the rides in the state park adjacent to where we live. Tomorrow, a professional farrier will come to assess the situation and probably change his shoes. I wanted to take him up to Snoqualmie Pass, but he wouldn't be able to scale the steep rocky trails until his hoof healed.

"Yahoo!"

I hit a tender spot when I dug into the center of that hoof with the pick. Mr. Jed kicked me hard, sending me head over heels, while the pick went flying in the opposite direction. I was able to cushion my fall with a partial back flip, thus avoiding the full force of his hoof into my crotch. That would have been a painful kick. Suddenly a voice echoed over the intercom perched above the barn door.

"Trevor! We need to leave shortly. Please don't put me through this. We will be late for your dance recital."

This was mom's third and last warning. I needed to stop and get ready. I put the tools aside, untied Mr. Jed, leaped over the corral, and ran for the house. After a quick shower, I dressed, grabbed my ballet ensemble and we all dashed down to the studio. It was an important recital. The audience, in addition to pompous parents, included producers looking for fresh talent to cast in their upcoming theatrical productions. This recital would feature a few of us who were considered to be the epitome of Emma's work.

I wore black jazz pants and a blue, tight-fitting T-shirt. I didn't like a bunch of fancy stuff attached to me when I was doing an active routine like the one Emma had choreographed for this recital. She allowed me to incorporate some of my gymnastics skills. I didn't allow enough time for the wardrobe crew to completely make me over, but I did let them mousse up my hair to give it a stand-up, wet appearance. When it was my turn on the floor, I was ready. I like fast, active routines, and this one fit the bill. This routine was a mixture of every technique I knew, but mainly ballet. Afterwards, I felt pretty good about the quality of my performance. I could feel that the audience was a discriminating crowd. Emma never criticized your performance in the recital; she said the audience would do that. You knew soon enough what part of the recital you messed up, because that was what she would make you work on in future sessions. If you didn't continue to make progress she dropped you. You couldn't walk on a plateau with her. There were too many eager students on her waiting list.

After the recital, a couple of people asked me to come to some production tryouts and audition. I thanked them, but made no commitment. I had gone about as far as I wanted to with dance. I wanted to study voice and keep up with guitar. I didn't want to end up like Emma at age fifty, with two arthritic hips that needed replacing.

I loved going to the teen clubs with my sisters. We practiced together and danced competitively. Together, we out danced just about everybody there. One time, Amber's friend Tina had her mom take us downtown to a teen disco. Amber and I danced the jive and really impressed the crowd. The disc jockey kept playing fast Latin songs, and Amber and I kept dancing to them. Pretty soon Amber and I were the only ones dancing. Everybody stood around and watched. This kid assumed that Amber was my date. When I told him she was my sister, he didn't believe me. I insisted she was my sister and not my date. I didn't think there was anything weird about dancing with your sister, but apparently he did. He said some hurtful things to me, and I told him to shut up or I was going to shut him up. The jerk kept up the insults. I grabbed him, spun him around in a handcuff position, and the two of us marched towards the wall. We knocked over a few chairs on the way. I slammed him up against the wall and asked him if he was going to take back anything he said. I didn't hurt him. He shut up in a hurry, but the manager kicked Amber and me out of the club. We were told never to come back. It was embarrassing for Tina's mom. She told mom that I needed an anger-management counselor, because my fuse was too short!

Dad was spending more time at home expanding his venture capitalist pursuits. He continued working part-time as a lawyer for the law group, but he no longer did the international circuit. He had a small staff of analysts that helped him by appraising new start-up companies. He was on a couple of corporate boards. Between his board meetings, law office, and looking over financials in his study, he might just as well have been in Europe. I didn't complain because he gave me everything I wanted. He paid and I played. He and mom finally agreed to send us to public school here in Kirkland. It was a good school. I didn't make many friends due to extracurricular activities outside of school. Dad was still the man with the carrot and the stick. He was a control freak. He held the carrot on a very long stick. It was out of reach most of the time. I backed off from asking him for much in the way of material goods. I just didn't savvy that approach. I did what I did for my own gratification. I didn't need his carrots anymore. I worked it the opposite way. I had to make an appointment to see him.

"Trevor!" He began. "I'm entertaining about thirty of my business associates in two weeks. I want you, Paula, and Amber to entertain. If you can, I'll tell you what I'll do."

"Stop dad. I'll do it. Okay? I don't want anything for it. The three of us can put something together."

"Thank you, son. The next weekend, why don't you guys invite several of your classmates over for a dinner party? Let me know how many and I'll have my secretary print up the invitations and you can give them out at school. You can hire a disc jockey if you want."

Generally that is how it all came down. I'd play the guitar, Paula played the piano and Amber played the violin. Amber was turning out to be the multifaceted musician in the family. She played the violin in the high school orchestra and the clarinet in the band. We could all sing, too. I was happy to see my old man's head swell with pride when we did things his way. Our friends preferred our live performance to the disc jockey. We also did a lot of karaoke, too. We didn't have to get smashed to have a good time. Singing always made people happy.

During one of dad's conferences recently, we had a discussion about my future plans for college. I want to pursue a liberal arts degree in music. After that, I'd like to apply to graduate school, but beyond that, I didn't know. Dad expects a definite commitment. The words "perhaps" and "maybe" aren't in his vocabulary.

"So how's the application process going with UW?" Dad asks.

"I submitted all the forms for them to request my high school records. It's all in."

"Have they accepted you?"

"Not yet."

"When are you planning to visit them?"

"I don't know."

"Mom says she thinks you applied to other schools. Is that right?"

"I did."

"Why? UW is the best and they are right across the lake. Why would you consider going away from home?"

"I'm looking at a private liberal arts school in Spokane, and Washington State University at Ellensburg. They both have good music programs."

"We want you kids at home for school. If you left home, you would have to leave your horses. Dorm life is not easy Trevor. Your asthma could kick in. What can I do to get you to stay home and attend UW?"

"Dad, look. I'm just considering it. I keep all options open. How long do you want me to live at home?"

"Trevor, you have the best possible environment right here at home to work, play and study. You know the rules, and as long as you play by the rules, you are welcome to live at home as long as you want."

"Yes, dad. I know all the rules. So, then I'll just be comfy here at home until I'm fifty. Let's see. You will be about seventy-four then. You'll work yourself to death and pass away about then leaving me the keys to your kingdom. I won't have to do a darn thing around here, just keep myself clean and ride my ponies."

"Are you kidding me? Nobody's going to live here until they are fifty and just ride ponies. You kids are welcome to stay here as long as you are embarking upon a career. I want you and the girls to live here until you graduate from college and then get on your own. If you want to stay on here while you go to graduate school, that's fine, too. I would say, Trevor, that by the time each of you reach age twenty-five you should plan on flying out of the nest. You should have a career that you can support yourself in. That's all I'm saying, Trevor."

"Thank you, dad. I'll keep that in mind. I won't get into the doping, raping, tattooing, piercing, smoking, boozing, or popping a baby routine. I guess I can plan to hang around for another eight years or so?"

"I love you son."

I'm glued to those horses. If I left home to go to college, I didn't know a single person that I could get to take care of them. I would have to board them out. Mr. Jed couldn't stand out in the wet corral all the time. He had to be put in the barn at night, and let out in the morning. His feet had to be cared for. We put in a covered concrete floor for them in the corral, but those stupid horses stayed out in the rain, and they would not stand where they could keep their hoofs dry.

Once you turn eighteen, most kids want their independence. Dad was our cash cow, and we could milk him pretty hard. He never complained about my credit card bill, but he wouldn't let me draw out cash with it. Cash had to come from him with conditions attached. It was the stick and carrot routine again. When I approached dad about getting a job this summer, he gave me a resounding no. He wanted me to stay home, take the girls dancing, to concerts, have parties at home, and relax. I had my whole life to work, he said. He didn't understand why I wanted to go out and work for minimum wage when I could stay at home and have fun. But I needed the cash. It would provide some self-fulfillment and independence.

Dad gave me a new Volkswagen Cabriolet for graduation. He didn't ask me what I wanted. He had some favors he owed to people, so that had to figure into the equation. I picked it out and I love it. It's just that it was part of some convoluted business deal that involved other people. Everything he did had a hidden agenda lurking in the background.

Dad believed that jobs requiring menial labor were for the working class. He thought I would be much better off studying music or joining up with a summer band. One afternoon we had another heated discussion about me working away from home. He wasn't listening.

"Dad," I said. "Can I talk now? You aren't hearing me. I'm looking for a job."

"What are you looking at?"

"I don't know. I'm looking through the papers. There is an online job center."

"You could put yourself on the roster for entertaining at parties. You could audition for a dance company. I could have someone help you set up a website and advertise yourself. Why not try that? All I'm asking is that you use your artistic and intellectual talent. Don't waste it doing something else."

I pondered dad's suggestions and made an appointment to see Emma Brown. She helped me sort through the weekly casting call list for the Seattle area. Emma encouraged me to gain experience by auditioning for every part I could. She emphasized that the key to success in obtaining any role was to audition, audition, and audition.

The first problem was that the casting for the summer shows had already been completed. Most of the shows were ready for production. The second problem involved auditioning for shows scheduled for the fall when I, theoretically, would be in college. The music auditions, for the most part, either for chamber music or choral groups, were usually unpaid positions.

Discouraged, I almost decided to give up working and just enjoy the summer. Just when I had given up, though, there was a breakthrough. I had auditioned as a tour guide in Seattle's historic old town district, referred to as Pioneer Square. I received positive feedback so I knew I did well in the audition but as with the others, they promised to call if I was needed. I had dismissed it as a possibility. To my surprise, they called me to come back and learn the tour. They had a place for me. I could earn tips and there was a lump sum amount for each tour I gave. The more tours I was available to do, the more I could make. I was ecstatic. I set up an appointment for the next afternoon.

I'm not that familiar with the lower downtown district of Seattle. I knew where the main attractions were located. Anything else? Forget it. I missed the exit to Pioneer Square and had to go another couple of miles south before I could get off the freeway on South Spokane Street. I knew if I took Fourth Avenue South past Safeco and Qwest Field, I could easily get there. The route was parallel to the railroad tracks. Suddenly, off to the left, I spotted a parked train. It didn't appear to be an Amtrak train, as it wasn't decked out in the silver, red, or blue colors. I parked the Cabriolet on a side street and walked over to where the train was parked. I was fascinated with it. There were several cars coupled together along one track. They were all two stories tall. They were of a sleek streamlined design, painted a dark crimson and green trimmed with black. There appeared to be more of the train in a second section on the other side, hidden from full view.

It was a beehive of activity. I stood and watched the action through the high chain-link fence. It appeared that the crews were loading supplies onto the train. I was only twenty feet from where a girl was sorting through something on a cart. She looked at me and made eye contact.

"Where does this train go?" I yelled.

"Chicago," she said.

"When?" I asked.

"Tonight," she answered. "We leave at 7:30 p.m. Are you applying for a job?"

"Yes I am."

"You don't apply here," she said. "Our offices are in the Pacific Northwest Towers downtown on the forty-fifth floor."

She came over and introduced herself as Wren. She was a petite little thing with a really cute smile. Her name matched her build, as she was small like a bird. She told me that she was a passenger representative and worked on one of the coaches. She also told me that they were hiring. She encouraged me to apply.

"What's a passenger representative do?" I asked.

"Everything," she said. "We mostly ride the train from here to Chicago and have a lot of fun doing it," she continued.

"What does it pay?"

"Fourteen an hour or more plus tips. Good benefits too," she said.

"Does the whole train have two complete floors?" I asked, bewildered.

"Yes," she said, "it's referred to as a double-deck train with two open gangways on each car. It's the only real double-deck train in America right now."

I thanked her. I didn't know what she meant, but it looked really sleek to me.

I walked back, got into the Cabriolet and sat there a minute. I took out my cell phone and called the number I'd been given for the tour office in Pioneer Square and informed them I had an unexpected conflict and wouldn't make the two o'clock appointment.

I drove north on Fourth Avenue past Amtrak's King Street Station and kept going north until I was opposite the Pacific Northwest Towers, one of Seattle's tallest office buildings. I found an underground parking lot and walked down Seventh Avenue to the main entrance. Inside, the security guard asked my purpose for the visit.

"I wish to apply for a job on the train," I answered.

"The *Mountain Daylight*?" The tall, heavily built black security guard asked in a course voice.

"Yes," I answered. "I think so."

"Your name?" The guard asked.

"Trevor D. Jensen."

"Over there!" The guard pointed.

I passed through a metal detector and stood opposite the elevators that would take me to the forty-fifth floor.

I opened the double glass doors on which was written "Intermountain Rail Inc." The view was stunning. For a few seconds I was spellbound as I became immediately immersed in the wrap-around picture of Elliott Bay and the Seattle waterfront. It was a crystal-clear day and I saw all the way across the bay to Alki Point. The reception area was spacious and nicely furnished.

Judy, the receptionist behind the counter, introduced herself. She told me I could apply online. I sat down at a computer workstation and submitted the online application, wrote a statement in long hand, and turned it in to Judy. After she asked me a few more questions, she took the application into another room and asked me to wait. I hope I passed muster with her. Hey! Why not? I'm squeaky clean, devoid of offensive tattoos; I don't have a single body piercing, an extreme haircut, baggy pants or any offensive innuendos on my shirt. Besides, I'm also good-looking. Why wouldn't they hire me?

In a few minutes, Judy came back and asked if she could take my picture. She pushed a form in front of me to sign.

"Why, thank you!" I said as I smiled into her camera. "In which magazine will this appear?"

"It's not for sale. We keep it with your file. I want you to talk to Rudy. He's busy just now with a train that just arrived in Chicago. He is our manager. When he is through, he will speak with you."

In a few minutes, Judy introduced me to Rudy. I was cautious not to say too much. I spoke only when spoken to. It was a technique we learned from a high school class that covered the job interview. They told us not to blow your cover the first instant. If you said too much, it opened you up to more probing and questions.

"Your handwriting is done in some type of calligraphy style. It's very unique," he said. "Are you an artist?"

"I like to draw," I said.

"We need someone to work with the night crew from here to Minneapolis-St. Paul. I need five people right now to work the Twin Cities leg. I don't have that many coming up here applying.

The ones that do, I can't put them on the train. It's hard work. The crew is slinging bags all night long. From what I can tell here, you have never worked away from home. This usually isn't a good first job for anybody. Did you just graduate from high school?"

"Yes sir. I graduated in the top ten percent of my class," I bragged.

"I would expect a guy like you to be enrolling in college this fall."

"I want to work and earn some money first."

"Are your parents happy with that decision?" Rudy asked.

"I need some independence from them. I don't know exactly what I want to study, so I need to work awhile first. I'll enroll in a year or two. I have plenty of time for college."

"Will you sign a one-year work contract?"

"A whole year?" I asked.

"Yes. You will have to make that commitment. It takes about three months to fully learn the job so you can work independently. It's not that easy, but I think you can do it. Now, you aren't afraid of hard work, are you?"

"I'm a hard worker. I want to do it."

"Are you pretty savvy with computers?"

"I am. I'm very technically inclined."

"Good. We have a rather complicated 'work around system' we devised for keeping track of our onboard inventory, including the passengers personal property. It's been difficult for some of the crew to use. I'll put you with Dean. He's one of our stronger guys. He's very knowledgeable."

"When can I start?"

"I can start you right away. Do you think you can pass a rugged physical? It's a real thorough exam. You also need a healthy back to do this job."

"I'm never sick. I stretch and do calisthenics for my back every day. I'm in good shape. I'm a healthy young man."

"I wouldn't expect that you had any brushes with the law. Did you? You have to be finger printed and we have to do a background check. Is that okay?"

"No problem," I said as I sat on the edge of my chair. I was so excited; I nearly pushed the chair out from under me as I tried to scoot my butt further back on the chair.

"Very well, Trevor. Congratulations and welcome to the *Mountain Daylight* family. This offer is conditional on getting you processed through our hiring system. You have to follow through with everything that we require."

"I'm hired?" I asked.

"Yes."

Rudy stood up and shook my hand. I couldn't believe it. That was easy, I thought.

"I'm going to introduce you to your manager. Her name is Reyna Jefferson. I just spoke with her in a videoconference in Billings. Let me work on it. Meanwhile Judy can give you more particulars about what you'll be doing on the train."

Judy started scheduling my appointments on her laptop. I sat there in a state of shock, not believing what I was about to do. I almost backed out. For a few seconds I shook with fright. I didn't really know what I was getting myself into here. What a quirk of fate this was. In a few minutes, Rudy had made contact with Reyna, the train's night manager on the Billings-Twin Cities segment. Reyna was a well-put-together, middle-aged African-American who spoke with authority. My first impression was that she wouldn't be easy to get along with. Reyna was in her hotel room in Billings, Montana, getting ready to reboard the eastbound train.

Rudy said Reyna ran a tight ship. She didn't allow anyone to slack off. He assured me that as long as I did my job, I'd get along well with her. He said she was a very competent lady and he was happy to have her on their management team.

Judy took me out to the front and printed everything I needed in order to complete the appointments. My orientation schedule included more testing at another HR office, health and safety orientation, emergency procedures and evacuation training, criminal background check, drug testing, and finally, selecting my uniforms. Unfortunately, the train would deduct a uniform and meal allowance from my paycheck. Judy told me too much. My mind was a blur and I couldn't retain it all. I hardly knew what the job, Material Handling Clerk, entailed. I guessed I would be loading and unloading luggage and supplies, and helping where needed. I didn't understand how it all worked, but I would soon find out.

Back on the elevator that was rapidly descending, I hung on to the envelope stuffed full of papers. It finally sank in. I had a job and it was on a train doing something. Right now I couldn't have told anyone what I actually would be doing. I was overcome with a feeling of elation. As I walked out on the street, there was a homeless lady carrying an overstuffed plastic bag. She smiled at me. I pulled out a twenty-dollar bill and gave it to her. She dropped her bag on the sidewalk and tried to hug me. In order to stave off this unwanted affection, I took her hands, held them up, and started to do a dance with her. She caught on and the two of us danced a little jig together in the front of PNW Tower. She was pretty good. She started to stumble so I let her go, and I did a couple of not-so-perfect pirouettes, to everyone's astonishment. I continued dancing the rest of the way to the parking garage, where I had stashed the Cabriolet.

As I drove east to the human resources office, I swallowed hard. What was I going to tell dad? He would be furious. He might even disinherit me. It was four o'clock and there was heavy rush-hour traffic. I called mom to tell her I had appointments until six. I wanted to run the horses and shower before dinner. Everyone was home so mom planned a more formal sit-down dinner.

She thought we would eat about seven but she would check with everybody and let me know. I loved the sit-down evening meals we had as a family. We hadn't had one in a while because everyone had been running in different directions.

The procedures at human resources were very involved. I took a personality test, intelligence test, and volunteered for the computer skills assessment. Last, they scheduled the physical for early Friday morning. I was stuck on the 520 bridge when mom sent a text message saying "supper is ready, where R U?" I lost track of the time. It was late.

When I'm perplexed and nervous about something, I'm not good at faking it.

"Is something wrong, son?"

Dad asked the question in his usual inquisitive way, expecting a specific answer.

"It was a long day," I answered evasively.

We were eating supper in the dining room. I wished dinner had been served on the patio, as it was such a nice evening. Had I been home earlier I would have suggested it and ignited the gas heaters for the ladies, whom were always cold regardless of how warm it was. Paula and Amber were nowhere in sight, and I thought they should be more helpful in the kitchen. I thought mom had raised two spoiled daughters. Mom was rushing around like crazy. She had waited until I was home before she did the finishing touches. It was a simple menu of stir-fry, rice, and chicken almond salad. We finally sat down and began eating. Amber chatted away. I didn't say anything. I decided it was better to let her talk. The less I said the better.

Dad sat there. He never interrupted his kids' conversations. Amber had been with her two girlfriends all day. Amber had tinted her hair a slightly darker color and bought some new shoes and purse to match. She was fair-haired like me, but for some reason she always dyed her hair black. Tonight she had a fresh cut that was short in the back and longer in the front, with chin-length side bangs. She had the left bang pinned back and let the right one hang on the side of her face. I winked at dad as I teased Amber about her hair.

"It sounds like Amber. Is it really you, sis?"

Paula was always sedate and proper. She was never extreme in anything she wore, said or did. Paula looked like dad and carried all of his mannerisms. Our hunger won out over speech, and the conversation stopped until everyone's hunger pangs dissipated.

"So Trevor, how did your interview go today?" Paula asked.

Then it snowballed. They all fired the usual what, where, when, how and why at me. I think they had actually forgotten about me going out for an interview until Paula brought it up. I would have preferred that she not mention it. That said, there would not be a good time to discuss it, so the sooner the better.

"No. I didn't go to Pioneer Square!"

Everybody stopped eating and focused on what I would say next.

"I thought they called you back, Trevor," Mom said.

"They did, but I didn't go. I was hired on the railroad."

I laid it right on the table. Boom. Down came the lead balloon. Dad set his fork down on his plate. Mother wiped her mouth on the linen napkin and glared right at me. There was a deathly silence.

"Who?" Dad asked.

"I'm starting the orientation tomorrow."

I couldn't talk in full sentences. Everything was garbled. My speech was slurred like I had an impediment of some kind.

"Trevor!" Dad started, "who did you say hired you?"

Before I could answer, I had to stop and think. I hardly knew myself. I went blank. I asked myself what was the name on the glass doors I entered on the forty-fifth floor of the PNW Tower? I couldn't remember.

"Oh! I have it right here," I said.

I jumped up from the table and walked over to my shoulder bag and dug out the cover sheet from the HR folder. I handed it to dad. He read it.

"Who is Intermountain Rail Inc.?"

I started to explain but was abruptly interrupted by dad.

"Is this that new double-decked Talgo train that runs out of here to Chicago? It's in competition with Amtrak?"

He knew. Being a venture capitalist, dad knew just about every business that operated in the metropolitan area of Seattle and King County.

"Yes sir. The name is the *Mountain Daylight,* but I don't go all the way to Chicago," I said, thinking that might soften the blow. I knew Chicago was a rough place. Dad wouldn't want me to go there. Dad kept the questions flying and with each answer I gave, mom looked more distressed.

"Do they know you are going to school in the fall?" dad asked.

"I signed a one-year contract."

"How can you do that when you are going back to school?"

The atmosphere became very tense. Paula and Amber looked down at their plates. Nobody liked what was unfolding.

"Dad! I signed a one-year contract."

Dad took a deep breath and didn't say anything more. I lied. I hadn't signed the contract yet. The HR office wouldn't have it ready until late tomorrow, pending the results of my physical, background check, and other things they needed to confirm. I was expected to sign it tomorrow just before I was given the uniforms. I fully intended to sign it. I could see dad's cheeks turning red. He was steaming. Dad doesn't lose it often, but when the pressure starts building inside him like it was now, I knew what to expect. It was either duck under the table or take a direct hit. I decided to do neither. It came down to "fight or flight" and

I chose the latter. I excused myself, saying I needed to run the horses before dark. Mother sweetly announced that for dessert, she had prepared tiramisu, a light Italian cake and family favorite. I declined, saying I would have some later.

I saddled up Mr. Jed and rode down the equestrian trail into Bridal Trails State Park. I rode him hard. In twenty minutes, I returned for Sal and pulled her down the trail behind. Last was Ned. I could hardly believe I was leaving my horses. I had planned to ride them every day this summer. It was nine o'clock and the forest was getting dark when I rode back to our barn. I fed and currycombed the horses and went up to my room. I had a lot of information to read. There was a policy and procedure handbook for passenger services representatives. Included was a book on railroad safety. The HR clerk had marked the sections I had to read now and would be tested on tomorrow, to make sure I had read it. I had a password for a safety video on the HR website that I was to download and watch. Also included was a government pamphlet on the responsibility of railroad employees to watch for and report suspicious persons and activity that could be connected to terrorists. I thumbed through that first. I didn't relish the section where it outlined how the railroads are soft targets for terrorism. There was a long checklist of things I had to do before tomorrow if I wanted to go out on Saturday.

There was a knock on my door. Dad came in and was obviously still upset.

"Trevor? Do you really intend to work on that train?"

"Dad! Please," I begged.

"Trains kill people. You're going to get hurt on that train. Did you know that train travels 110 miles per hour?"

"Dad, could you please take it easy? Nobody told me that."

"What if they hit a car going that speed? What are you actually doing for the train? Mom thinks you are working at the train station in Seattle. Do you even know?"

"I'll know more about the job tomorrow. I think I'm on the train."

"Why would you delay your education a year just for a job you don't need? I don't understand you, Trevor. Son, this is crazy. You've lost your focus."

"Dad, just be patient, okay? I don't know the answers to all of your questions."

"I didn't spend thousands upon thousands of dollars to provide the very best tutors, teachers and schools for you, Paula and Amber just for you to blow it on some stupid job working on a *train*!"

The longer dad talked, the more red-faced and upset he became.

"I'm not going to talk to you when you are this mad. I'm not," I said.

"Don't tell me you aren't planning on continuing your education. *Don't*!"

"Of course I'm planning on college, dad, but not right now."

"I'm afraid for you, Trevor. Everyone smokes on the train. That won't be good for your asthma. Trains in the USA are dirty. You won't tolerate the heavy stale air. Did you even consider the fact that you are very susceptible to motion sickness? Trevor, the few times I've been down to King Street Station, it has been full of riffraff. Classy people don't ride trains anymore. You will become part of the riffraff."

I got mad and blew up at dad and told him to stop it and lay off. We both started shouting at each other. When dad and I get into these confrontations, the whole family suffers. I guess I was pretty stubborn. The more he yelled at me, the more determined I was to defy him by going out to work on my own. I told him to get out of my room and leave me alone so I could study my orientation materials. He went downstairs and out to the patio and started in on mom about my stupidity. I could hear dad yelling at mom. Paula and Amber went downstairs to get in on the fracas.

Shortly, Saint Paula, the peacemaker, knocked on my door and came in.

"You really upset daddy," she said.

"Oh really. I hadn't noticed," I quipped.

"Trevor, I don't want you to go away. I was looking forward to going places with you all summer. I was planning so many things to do with you."

"Oh sis. I'll miss you too, but I won't be on the train all the time. I have days off between every trip I take. I'll still be around."

I hugged her tight. She began to cry. She didn't want me to leave. Paula doesn't cry often and when she does it touches me deep in my heart. She really let it go. She told me how much she loved me and what a good brother I was. She just wanted me to stay home. I told her I loved her but I was going through with this and that was that.

The next morning I was up at six. No one was up yet. I checked on the horses and left for Seattle. I arrived at the clinic early, where I filled out a three-page medical history questionnaire. After waiting fifteen minutes in the icy cold office, I started to have second thoughts about this expedition I was on. I hated it when the family was upset with me. Just then, there was a knock on the door and a lady wearing a white coat introduced herself as Doctor something or other. I didn't catch her name. She went over my job description. She knew more about the job than I did. She explained that her job was to determine my physical and mental competency. She reviewed the medical history. She noted two conditions I checked on the questionnaire: asthma and seasickness.

"I guess you're not fond of deep-sea fishing."

"That's right, doctor. I don't go out on the water."

She wanted to know if I routinely took medicine for my asthma. She asked when I had the last attack and did I know what caused it.

"Do these attacks ever require you to be hospitalized?"

"No," I answered.

She explained that I would be exposed to diesel fumes and exhaust, especially when the train passed through a couple of the longer tunnels. She explained that the croplands during the summer season produced many pollens and allergens that could trigger asthma. She explained that the air in the Midwest was very dusty in the fall during the time of harvest. Had I ever been around grain when it was being harvested? Did high altitude bother me? She explained that the train crossed the Continental Divide and climbed up two mountain passes in Montana. Had I ever been to Chicago? Chicago's air quality, particularly now in summer, was very polluted. She sat down at the computer and filled out an action plan for me to use in order to prevent an asthmatic attack. She printed it and gave it to me to keep. It included a prescription for me to fill and carry in the event an attack occurred aboard the train. Since I was well controlled and seldom had to use an inhaler, I probably would not have a problem, but I was to be aware of the possible triggers and always have the medicine and inhaler with me.

"Do not leave town without it," she warned. "We don't want you to get sick on the train."

"I'm allergic to cigarette smoke. Do people smoke on the train?" I asked.

"No, the passengers are not allowed to smoke anywhere on the train. They have smoke detectors in the restrooms and first-class accommodations. The crew will put them off the train if they do," the doctor said.

She further explained that it was not uncommon to suffer from motion sickness when aboard the train. After the first couple of days, it usually stabilized where you could easily work on the train without suffering the ill effects of it. She asked if I had ever been on any Amtrak trains. She explained that the *Mountain Daylight* cars were designed to allow the cars to naturally tilt into the curves. This allowed for faster speeds on curves, but without the unpleasant sensations the passengers experienced with conventional equipment. Also, a prescription for motion sickness was prescribed that I was to carry at all times. I was instructed to first use over-the-counter remedies, and if they didn't work I was to replace it with the prescription. In fact, she instructed me to wear the patch the first two days on the train regardless.

"You will get your sea legs in a couple of days." she laughed. "Beware of mosquitoes," she cautioned. "The train travels through an area highly endemic for West Nile Virus and this is the prime season for it." She looked at my schedule. "Oh! I see. You work nights."

"Nights? I work during the night?" I interrupted. "I guess I didn't catch that."

"You didn't know that? I'm sure they told you," she insisted.

"When do I sleep?" I asked.

"Trevor, those are questions you should be asking the HR office. Not me. The second night the train goes through North Dakota. You'll be off the train in North Dakota where there could be potential exposure to disease-carrying mosquitoes. It is very important that you review this information about West Nile Virus. Did you know the new uniforms that you will be wearing have been treated with an insect repellant effective against mosquitoes? I still recommend that you use the topical application, as well. The disease is preventable if you avoid contact with mosquitoes," she explained.

She poked me hard in the abdomen just above the right groin area.

"Last week a new hire became ill on her first trip out, ending up with an emergency appendectomy in Spokane," she said.

Next came the chest X-ray and she referred me for some breathing tests. She wanted to know what sport I did.

"Ballet!" I answered.

"Oh, I thought you might be a swimmer," she countered.

Ballet obviously wasn't the answer she was expecting. I said I did swim but not competitively.

Finally, she gave me a sheet of paper with the phone number of the train's Command Center in Seattle to use in the unlikely event I needed medical assistance while aboard the train, during layovers back East or in Seattle.

"Just call this number day or night and someone will instruct you as to what hospital or clinic to use. Good luck on your new job. I hope you enjoy the train."

"Did I pass?" I asked

"You did, but before I sign off on this I want to see the results of your lung capacity tests and chest X-ray. I'm sure the tests will turn out fine."

She then said I was free to get dressed and leave.

The orientation went well at HR. There were about eighteen other employees in attendance. They were all friendly and nice people of various ages. Most of them were there for their annual health and safety training. We went out for lunch and they were all upbeat about the train. They knew Dean and Reyna and spoke well of them. They said I would get very tired and to make sure I rested when I had the opportunity. Contrary to what dad said about the riffraff in King Street Station, the crew told me that their clientele was middle to upper class because the fares are too pricey for the riffraff. They laughed, saying dad was probably at the bus station. The fares they charge are outrageous, they said, a lot more than Amtrak charges, and way more than plane tickets. I shivered when they told me how brutally cold the winters were east of the Cascades. And nobody as yet, had come down with mosquito-borne fever.

I signed the nonunion contract that specified my commitment to work twelve months. I noticed that the railroad had leeway to cancel but the employee didn't. There was no probationary work period. I could be fired any time after three written notices that documented failure to perform my duties, any type of misconduct, and failure to show up for work when scheduled.

Next, the HR lady went over my two-week work schedule. I was to leave on the evening train, Saturday at 7:30 p.m. I was hired for the night shift and would turn at the Twin Cities and come back to Seattle. The lady had memorized my schedule.

"You sleep all day tomorrow before you leave. You work Saturday night; you sleep in your assigned bunk in the crew quarters during the day Sunday, and work Sunday night until you arrive in the Twin Cities about 10 a.m. Monday. It is your responsibility to rest sufficiently in a hotel room provided until you reboard the westbound train in St. Paul at 6 p.m. You then work that night and the following night on the return trip back to Seattle. You are off until the following Thursday, when you go out again that night."

Everything was in the computer. I was issued a password to gain access to the work schedules in the employee section of the train's website. A copy of the schedule was printed off for me to carry.

I could use the downtown hotel in Seattle to rest if I wished, but I would have to meet my work partner, Dean, before 6 p.m., which was the time we were to begin loading the passenger baggage.

No personal cell phone use was allowed. When aboard the train, you could use only the train phones that would be issued at the warehouse. Each employee had their own private phone, number, and a unique code for inter-train communication. The phones had special features like intercom, allowing the managers to be in constant contact with the employees. It was a high-tech system of communication. Long-distance calls home were allowed and free as long as they weren't abused to the degree that it produced a distraction in the workplace. Last, I was given an identification badge, train card, and approval papers to select my uniforms.

"Don't lose that card," I was warned. "It costs you fifty dollars to have it replaced."

The card took you everywhere on the train you were authorized to go and bought you anything on the train not covered in your meal allowance. The passengers were issued cards with their tickets tied to their credit cards. No one carried cash on the train. You were issued a paycheck for each trip, and deductions were made for all train purchases with your card. Employees received a special discount.

I tried to digest everything I was being told, but it was impossible. It was all totally new. Soon, I was standing in a changing room at the warehouse on Industrial Way near South Spokane Street. I was given a catalog that contained some really cool things I could purchase. It was the online train store that the passengers ordered their train memorabilia from. They had some really neat clothes, cups, hats, videos, books, luggage, bags, purses, umbrellas and anything else you could think of.

"You get to wear the sporty stuff," the clerk said in envy as she mulled through the papers I brought. "You work with Dean! He's one neat guy." She kept up the prater. "He was in last week. We just received these new summer duds. They were supposed to be here weeks ago."

She excused herself and left to get the samples. She brought back several items for me to choose from and then try on.

"Too thin! Too tall! Too big!" She gasped as she took the measurements again, in an attempt to see if an alternative size would work. "I don't have a thirty waist. I only go as low as thirty-four. We'll have to take it in. Your legs are too long; I'll have to take the cuffs down. No size twelve but I have thirteen. By the way, how do you stay so slim and trim? I bet you don't eat a lot of Oreos!"

I couldn't get a word in edgewise. I wanted to explain that I could wear a thirty-two waist in some styles. I was really closer to a thirty-one. She didn't listen to me. Size thirteen was too big for my feet so she gave me a voucher and instructed me where to buy similar leather and suede boots that were approved for the job.

"Cool," I said. "New boots on the house."

The clerk called and verified the boots were in stock. I liked the uniforms. I picked out two pair of long cotton pants, one burnt orange and the other dark green; with several Velcro pockets for tools and a zippered security pocket. She said they stopped issuing shorts for summer wear due to the mosquito threat.

"Those little skeeters carry a fever. They come out at night and they drink your blood." the clerk snickered. "Dean said they're really bad in Dakota this year."

I picked out two double-stitched matching polo shirts, two T-shirts and two long-sleeved jacket shirts to be worn over the T-shirts. All the clothes had either embroidered insignias or sown patches that depicted some image of the train. All were very cool. I liked the patch on the front left pocket of the pants that showed a train car with a mountain in the background. I picked out rain gear and a summer jacket. My activated train card was scanned for each item I ordered, and that determined the uniform deduction from my paycheck. I used my credit card and purchased new luggage decorated in the train's colors and emblems. I also purchased a seventy-five dollar, ten by fourteen-inch photo essay book of the train route and a sixty-dollar, two-volume video series of a narrated tour of the route. I took the new phone and immediately started studying the manual and entering my phone numbers. It was the coolest phone I had ever seen. I grabbed my stuff and left to get the boots. I got myself a job -- a real job!

I headed the Cabriolet in the direction of Kirkland. It was 4 p.m. when I returned a call back to mom. Mom said dad would soon be home and they were eating late at Yarrow Bay. I drove in the driveway just ahead of dad, went for a quick ride on Mr. Jed, showered and was invited down on the patio for some pre-dinner snacks. I brought a big armload of stuff down, plunked it on the patio table and showed off my shirts, jacket and boots. It was tense for a second or two until I told everybody that I was sorry about last night. I don't like to remain at outs with anyone very long. Dad set his beer down, stood up and the two of us hugged. I gave a hug to my sisters and also one to mom.

Amber grabbed the train catalog and started paging through it.

"Just what this house needs," dad said, "another mail-order catalog."

Within minutes Amber marked several things she wanted to order. Dad thumbed through the photo essay book. I played with the new phone and started explaining all of the features to dad. Suddenly, there was a message from Dean.

Dean welcomed me to the crew and told me how to make contact. I called his cell phone and Dean answered. He was on a train traveling through western Montana. They were almost to Missoula. Dean was explaining how to meet up with him after his arrival the next morning in Seattle.

"Why don't we meet him for breakfast somewhere?" dad suggested.

Obviously dad wanted to be there, too. I saw my mother wince. I knew what she was thinking. She would think I should go by myself and meet this guy Dean, but dad was not about to stay behind. I don't think dad wanted to let go of me. He wouldn't trust this guy, anyway. He would have to know with whom I was working. Arrangements were made for us to meet Dean upon his arrival at the hotel downtown. We would then head somewhere for breakfast.

Raising Trevor

The next morning dad and I were up early, packed, ready to leave, and having a muffin and coffee when Dean called me on the cell. The train was on time, Dean said, but due to the large volume of Tacoma passengers leaving the train in Auburn, most likely they would not arrive in Seattle until 8 a.m. Dean showed up at the hotel about 8:45 a.m. Dean checked in, as did I, and the three of us took the bags up to the room with two twin beds.

"Ever sleep with a guy before?" Dean asked.

Dean teased, saying they rarely had to bunk up but sometimes the hotels overbooked and didn't reserve the sufficient number of beds. At first impression, Dean looked like a nightclub bouncer. He was a stocky fellow, medium height, with a military haircut, outgoing and likable. I realized immediately that he was much older than me. We walked down the street to a tiny café for breakfast, preferring that to the continental cuisine offered by the hotel.

We visited nonstop. Dad hardly said a word. I wanted to know what Dean did to work out, as he appeared to be a weight lifter-body builder type.

"How much do you bench press?" I asked.

"On an average day without any help, three-sixty-five, and on a good day with help, over four hundred. I'm not trying to be competitive."

Dean described his workouts and diet.

"I don't eat much of the train food," he added.

Dean said there were two other guys assigned to our crew for tonight's departure.

"Any women that we work with?" I asked.

"Oh for sure," Dean said.

Dean fished around in his pockets and pulled out the crew roster for tonight's train.

69

"It's mostly women tonight. Let's see," he said, "yeah we got Helen. She's forty, fat and bitchy." Dean laughed. "By the time they all get to Chicago after three days of eating the high-carb, high-fat food they serve us on the train, the women are all so bloated you can't get near them."

Dean and I laughed but dad wasn't amused and changed the subject. Being a businessman who analyzes business models, dad was very puzzled about the inner workings of the train.

"So the train makes money?" dad wanted to know.

"I think the train makes a lot of money but they never tell us that. If you listen to management we're broke," Dean said.

"Amtrak doesn't make money," dad added.

"We're different than Amtrak. Passengers sometimes go to Chicago one way with us and return on Amtrak. They tell us that we have the more scenic route, better equipment, more entertainment and really good service."

"So you compete against Amtrak?"

"No. By law, we can't compete with Amtrak on any route they run. We work together. We couldn't survive without Amtrak because over fifty percent of our passengers originate somewhere with them."

Dean continued going through the list of women that would be on tonight's train.

"All are too old for you, Trevor." Dean said.

"Who is your boss tonight?" dad asked.

"Oh!" Dean swore. "Tonight it is Jack. He is a total jerk, but we'll lose him at Sandpoint, Idaho, in the morning. Nobody likes Jack."

Dean explained that from Sandpoint they would have Eugenia as manager and finally Reyna from Billings to the Twin Cities.

"How can you work for so many bosses?" Dad asked.

Dean said he didn't. Reyna was the one in charge of the night crews. She did their scheduling, approved their days off and wrote their performance evaluations. They went directly to her with any workplace conflicts and problems. Reyna then worked with the other managers to solve the problems. That said, Dean explained, they were always in subjection to the conductor no matter which train manager was aboard. The train managers were responsible for the well-being of the passengers and crew. The conductors ran the train.

"Who do the train managers report to?" dad asked.

"Rudy, the miracle man," Dean answered. "Rudy sits on his great white throne in the Command Center in Seattle and makes everything happen. I don't think he ever sleeps."

"Who does Rudy answer to?" dad asked as he pieced together a mental organizational chart.

"The higher echelons of Intermountain Rail. They also own about seven hundred miles of our track. They are into a lot of things including natural resources." Dean went on to say it was a pretty good company.

He turned to me and said that I would like Reyna.

"She's tough but good. No one messes with her," he said.

"Do you know a girl named Wren?" I asked.

"Wren?" Dean looked really surprised.

I just blew my cover. I knew immediately that I shouldn't have asked him that question. I never told dad how I stumbled onto this job in the first place, and how a girl named Wren had told me through a fence where to apply.

"You know Wren?" Dean was completely baffled.

"I met her briefly," I said.

"So you don't know her personally," Dean wanted that confirmed before he continued. "She hits on all the guys. She's okay, but in my opinion it is best to avoid her if you can. Besides," Dean said, "if they catch you in any improprieties with the oppo-site sex on the train, they'll throw your butt off at the next stop.

Believe me, there isn't any place this train stops during the night that you want to be put off. How old are you, Trevor?"

"Eighteen," I said.

"I didn't know they would hire anyone that young. You must have made a very good impression on somebody up there."

"What's wrong with being eighteen?" I asked.

"Nothing. Sometimes life can be rough on the train. It helps to have thick skin and some experience. That's all. I'm glad they hired you. We need the help."

"How old are you?" I asked.

"Twenty-seven," Dean said as he turned and looked directly at dad. "Mr. Jensen, I'll look after Trevor. I'll take him with me. I'm pretty much into staying healthy. I don't drink. I'll watch out for him. He won't get into trouble. Some of the guys we work with like to party at night. The people they hire to work on the train are pretty responsible. Our crew consists of working moms and dads who need to support their families. Most of the time we behave ourselves. If we don't, they terminate us. They strap you to a code of conduct during layovers. They consider that as being on duty, more or less."

"Thank you Dean. I appreciate that," dad said.

He went on to say that tonight we would have Cory and Jarred working with us. Cory was married and didn't carouse around but Jarred did.

"When we get to St. Paul Monday morning, I'll keep Trevor with me, and Cory can share a room with Jarred because Jarred always drinks. He has his favorite hangout there in St. Paul."

"All your help is older than Trevor?" dad asked.

"Yeah. Mostly my age and older," Dean said.

Dad said it was time for him to go. I told him goodbye. He thanked Dean again about looking out for me. Dad said he would park the Cabriolet in the hotel's garage Tuesday night for me to use when I returned Wednesday morning. I knew he was still uneasy. He had that look about him. I knew he carried a premonition that something bad was going to happen to me. I didn't know why dad would think trains were so unsafe, so I began to be worried about it myself.

All Aboard

Trevor Jensen

It was a day any normal person would hate leaving Seattle. It had been one of those crystal-clear summer days when Mount Rainer became the dramatic focal point of the "Emerald City." Dean thought it would be hot, sticky and buggy on the Northern Plains. But at 5:45 p.m., Dean and I took the hotel's shuttle to King Street Station a few blocks away. Stuck in the logjam of traffic trying to gain access to the station, we exited the van, Dean tipped the driver, and we walked the rest of the way.

We met Jarred and Cory, the other two from the night crew. The uniforms they wore stood out in the crowd. Cory was as tall as me, blond and bashful. He didn't look at you when you shook hands. Dad always taught me to do that when I met someone for the first time. If you fail to do that, it's a sign that you are nervous, backwards and unsure of yourself, dad would say.

Earlier, Dean told me that Cory fell on some hard luck, lost his apartment, and he, his wife, and infant girl had been living on the street in their car. Dean said he was good on the job but had to be told how to do things. He said Cory was a clean-cut, likable guy.

Jarred, on the other hand, was of medium height, rugged, and looked the type that had been around the block a time or two. He was discharged from the Marines after he was wounded in Iraq. He had a huge gouge missing from his lower leg, but it didn't appear to slow him down. Jarred had a strong, confident handshake.

I felt like a million bucks in my new uniform. The colors blended in with the train parked on two tracks, stretching endlessly on the south end of the station.

The security guards checked our bags, drivers' licenses, train I.D. badges, and then checked our names off the crew roster. We reported in at the manager's kiosk and obtained our boarding assignments. We each picked up the assignment sheet and looked it over. I was clueless. Jack was behind the kiosk talking on his phone but motioned for me to stay. Jack spent a few minutes explaining some procedures to me while Dean, Cory and Jarred pushed the luggage dolly with our bags down the platform to the train. I thought Jack was nice. I picked up on the fact that he was a bit effeminate, but nothing more than that. Jack said Dean was a good teacher and to stick with him. Jack explained the bed assignments, their policy for meals the night of departure, and said any spare time should be spent reading the manuals. I kept looking at where the boys were going because I didn't want to lose them in the mobs of people boarding and servicing the train. I wanted Jack to stop talking so I could go. I wasn't listening, anyway because there was way too much to remember. I was too excited to try and stuff any more information in my head. I had to let things happen. Jack instructed me to familiarize myself with page thirty-eight of the PR Manual.

"PR Manual?" I asked.

"That is the Passenger Representative Manual. We refer to it as the PR Manual," Jack said.

He told me to memorize the scripts I was to recite while I was boarding and detraining passengers. I was to have it learned and to start using it by Spokane.

"Just remember," Jack said, "clean up your own messes when using the crew's dinette, showers and restrooms. We don't have any moms that come in and clean up after you. Do not lift more than seventy pounds by yourself. More than that takes two people," Jack instructed. "Did you sleep today?"

"Not much," I said.

"You can sleep after you leave Sandpoint, Idaho, sometime after 5 a.m. tomorrow," Jack said.

"Dean has pretty much explained all of that," I said.

"Fine then. Welcome aboard."

I started walking down the platform in the direction I had last seen Dean and the others when I spotted Jarred walking toward me. Dean had sent him back to find me. Jarred and I walked down the platform along several cars so tightly coupled together that they appeared to be a single unit. We found Dean in the lower level of car six, where he was jamming his stuff into an employee locker. Dean showed me where the four of us would sleep tomorrow. The crew of eighteen occupied the lower level of two coaches and one sleeping car. The lower level of one coach had a neat lounge and kitchen area solely for the use of the crew.

I wasn't sure that I could fit in any of the four small bunks, but Dean assured me that I would be so tired I wouldn't care. I was told that the dining-car crew would sleep in our room tonight. They would change the beds for us when they got up just before 5 a.m.

Dean took me on a quick tour of the train. The bottom deck had open, step-less gangways the full length of the train for crew access only. We walked through twelve cars of the coach section on the bottom deck. In the middle was the coach section's diner and lounge. I was told to put on my shin guards and back brace.

I started loading on the baggage that was transported by a small-wheeled cart.

"So it's just the crew that has access to the bottom deck?" I asked.

"The crew and the mice," Dean answered.

"Mice?"

"Mice." Dean said. "Keep the entry doors shut at night or else the mice will hop on for a free ride and free food. All the mice from here to Chicago know that we have the best pastry chefs on the railroad. They will take advantage of any access you give them."

Passengers boarded through one of three cars with entry doors, two in the coach section and through one first-class sleeper. They were equipped with elevators for handicapped passengers. It was about 7:40 p.m. when I realized the train was moving. The train moved forward, stopped, backed up and hooked up eight cars of the first-class section sitting on the opposite track. Slowly we pulled out onto the main track and our twenty-car train with two sleek-looking locomotives rapidly accelerated. It was after 8 p.m. when we stopped in Auburn. There were hoards of people and piles of luggage. I wondered where all these people were going.

Dean said for the crew to just load it and not bother to scan it curbside. Dean said they want the train out of there by eight-thirty or we will lose our slot on the pass. Dean said the conductor would let us know the situation. Some nights there isn't any traffic ahead of us so we can take our time. Tonight there was a mixed freight train waiting ahead, and if we didn't get there soon, they'd put the train ahead of us and make us late into Ellensburg. The boarding procedure went like clockwork and the train pulled out in twenty minutes, made a sharp left turn onto a different track and traveled due east.

I sat at the dinette table in the dorm section and looked out the window as we followed the Green River up into a canyon.

Jack described some of the highlights along the route as the train started to climb up Stampede Pass. I was wishing for a top-deck window so I could see above the heavy brush along the track. As we sped around some tight curves, I thought for a second I was on a carnival swing ride. The faster we did the curves, the greater the centrifugal forces, the more we swung out to compensate.

"The name *Mountain Daylight* is somewhat of a misnomer," Jack told the crowd as he laughed. "The name applies to the Rocky Mountains of Montana, but not the scenic Cascades of Washington. Thanks to the crew and their quick work here in Auburn," Jack continued, "we will have daylight almost to the summit."

The narration continued with Jack reminding everyone that the train was beginning our two-thousand-eight-hundred-foot ascent to the summit. In the process, the train would cross the Green River eleven times and pass through seven tunnels.

"There will be a panoramic view of the valley at milepost 47 when a bridge, one hundred sixty feet high and twelve hundred feet long, is crossed over the Green River Valley. At milepost 56, opposite sides of the mountain would be traversed using a double horseshoe curve necessary to maintain the 2.2 percent grade. Then at milepost 57, at the summit, the train enters Stampede Tunnel, two miles long at two-thousand-eight-hundred-thirty-seven feet elevation. From there, the train will descend thirteen hundred feet to the next station stop of Ellensburg, Washington."

Next, Jack spewed forth his litany of rules. He reminded everyone that the bottom deck of the train was a work area for the crew, and was off limits to passengers except when they entered or exited the train from the three entry cars. No one would be allowed off the train during the brief stops at Ellensburg, Yakima and Pasco. Smoking would be allowed on the station platform at Spokane, as there would be a twenty-minute stop at 3:30 a.m.

and the next one after that would be at Missoula, Montana, the next morning at 9:45 a.m. Passengers must sleep in their assigned seats. All unoccupied seats had been sold and would be occupied down line at a future station. Passengers leaving the train during the night at Ellensburg, Yakima, Pasco, Spokane and Sandpoint should be in their seats thirty minutes prior to arrival. The passenger representative would accompany you to car nine where you would pick up your checked luggage and make your exit. All food and beverage services would end at midnight one hour after departure from Yakima. Upon departure from Sandpoint at 5 a.m., watches should be advanced one hour to Mountain Daylight Time. Food services would resume at 6 a.m. With that bit of information, Jack thanked everyone for their patronage and wished them a restful night and pleasant journey.

It was break time. Jack had pizza delivered and the dining crew had just re-warmed it in the lower-level kitchen. I ate a deli sandwich about 4 p.m. but it wasn't sticking to my ribs, and I was mighty happy to see the pizza. There was a lot of it, too.

Jack said the pizza was for meeting the new crewmember. Then Jack introduced me to the crew and also another crewmember who had transferred from another train.

The female crewmembers, much older than me, were friendly and helpful. Several gave me their phone codes and said to call them if I had questions. I was busy entering their names and codes into my phone when Dean caught me and accused me of breaking rank with the men. The party ended about as quickly as it started as the day crews were preparing for their short night's sleep.

Dean showed me how to print off the passenger lists for each stop during the night. The train arrived in Ellensburg at 10:30 p.m., ten minutes early. I had a feeling of self-importance as I asked the first passenger to see their ticket and photo I.D. I sensed that Jack was watching me, but I already knew the script for performing the check-in procedures. I took each bag, tagged it and then scanned it. Dean and Cory loaded it. Jarred helped with the prescreening of passengers, making certain they had their photo I.D. and tickets. The train pulled ahead, loaded the one first-class passenger, and we were on the way to Yakima.

One of the passenger representatives named Helen asked us boys if we wanted something from the lounge. She offered to get it. Dean told me to go with her and bring back the food.

"Do I buy it with my train card?" I asked.

"They won't charge the night crew. You can have whatever you want from the lounge. No booze, of course," she said.

I thought Helen was really kind and not "fat and bitchy" like Dean had accused her of being. She might be old enough to be my mom. Helen and I walked through the lower deck to the lounge car, where the lounge crew was preparing the orders. They had an espresso bar and I had ordered a latte.

I carried the food back and downed my latte. Dean told me to go up and walk the full length of the train's top deck. Dean said, excluding the locomotives, the train's length was one thousand feet. He said he would call me on my phone if he needed me or for me to call him if I got lost. He laughed, saying most likely I would call him to get directions back. I thought it was weird when Jarred tied a string to the table leg and handed me the ball of twine.

"Undo the string as you walk," he said, "and when you run out of twine you're at the end of the train. It's easy to find your way back."

Everyone laughed at me. For a minute I thought he was serious.

I walked through five coaches through the diner into the lounge. It was teaming with activity. We were passing through Yakima Canyon. The train made several wide turns as it followed the river. It was really cool to watch at night. It was a weird sensation as the train floated along, naturally tilting on the curves. We were going fast around the curves. The train's unique pendulation feature was in full operation. Outside, it was pitch black. The train's headlights were bouncing off the cliffs. I didn't know if it was the flashing strobe lights on top of the lead locomotive or the beams of light that kept curving from side to side, but I started feeling dizzy. Suddenly the train reversed direction. It looked like the engine was going to pass us going the opposite direction. I felt disoriented. The two locomotives looked, for a few seconds, like they were disconnected from the rest of the train as they passed us in the opposite direction. We were now traveling west. In about five minutes, the train locomotives turned to the east and the front of the train passed the back of the train. I didn't know if it was the sensations of movement or if it was something I ate, but I was ready to heave. It was going to happen. I got up out of the seat, and for a second I didn't know what direction to go. I was totally lost.

"Restroom?" I squeaked, half afraid to open my mouth.

A passenger directed me to the right. I found it vacant not a minute too soon. I stepped inside, closed the door, and up came the latte, up came the pizza, and up came the deli sandwich. What a mess I made. I sprayed all over the seat, and puked on the floor. How can food that tasted so good going down taste so rotten in reverse?

Just then, I had a phone call. It was Amber. She, Paula, and Tina were driving home from the concert and wanted to know how I was doing.

"Umm, not so good right now." I said. "I just threw up my last two meals."

"Oh no!" The girls gasped. "Are you carsick?"

"I think they call it trainsick," I answered. "Please don't tell mom or dad," I pleaded. "I better go. I'm kind of in a mess here."

I ended the call and tried to do my best at cleaning up the restroom. I was wishing for my mom to come in and do it, but Jack had already warned about there not being any moms aboard that would clean up messes. Only a mother would clean up the mess I just made. I used up all the paper towels. The smell was nauseating. I stepped out of the bathroom and closed the door. Pity the next passenger who would open it. I made my way to the crew car where I told Helen what had happened. I wished I had complied with what the lady doctor had recommended about wearing the transdermal patch the first two days aboard the train. Dean told me not to because nobody ever had gotten sick riding the train. Helen recommended that I not use the patch now, as it was ineffective once I was sick. I was glad I had the pills the doctor prescribed.

Dean told me to sit it out at Yakima. Helen said she would clean up the restroom. I sat there with my head on the dinette table, wondering whatever in the world had I got myself into here? I had missed the concert at home I really wanted to see. In addition to being seasick, I was also homesick and this was only the first night away.

It was about 1 a.m. when the *Mountain Daylight* crossed the Columbia River and stopped in Pasco, Washington. Dean told me to stay back while he, Cory and Jarred worked the small crowd that was boarding through the middle coach. I stepped off the train to get some fresh air, but the air was hot and heavy. I still wasn't feeling very well.

Fifteen minutes out of Pasco, the train came to a sudden stop and stayed there for about ten minutes. Dean opened the small side door to see what was happening. In the distance, a train whistle was heard. It was fast approaching. All of a sudden it came. It passed with such force and speed it blew the door shut, almost slamming it against Dean's arm, but Dean miraculously pulled himself inside to safety. Dean swore. The cars rocked as the train sped by. It scared me plumb out of my wits.

"Was that us?" Jarred asked.

"Yep," Dean answered, "that was us, Number 1125, heading west. Trevor? Don't ever do what I just did. You can lose a limb or an eye. Between here and Spokane they go like gangbusters. Fast-moving trains can throw rocks, metal or other debris into our train. During wintertime, the trains throw ice that will impale you."

"Could the train ever hit us?" I asked.

"Yes," Dean laughed, "if some idiot dispatcher put us on the wrong track."

"Or the engineer falls asleep at the controls and runs a red light!" Jarred said.

"But they don't go to sleep while operating a train," I said.

"Trevor. What time is it?" Jarred asked.

"I got one thirty," I said.

"Are you sleepy?" Jarred asked.

"I'm a little sleepy," I admitted.

"I bet that engineer that took Number 1125 past us at ninety is a little sleepy too!"

I didn't know whether to believe him or not. I didn't like the way our train shook when the other *Mountain Daylight* passed us. This stuff was all new to me. I needed reassurance that everything was okay. I couldn't grasp that we could be on the wrong track and be hit head-on by an oncoming train.

"But," I insisted, "wouldn't there be a light or something to tell us we were on the wrong track?"

They all laughed.

"Oh sure. Yeah, so the light is red. Good for us. We stop. Bam! They still run into us," Dean said.

Then Dean told another story where a train he was working was instructed to cross over to the same track they had overheard the dispatcher assign to an on coming Amtrak train. Dean said it happened just a few miles south of Spokane. The Amtrak engineers overheard the conversation and immediately stopped their train. Dean said that apparently the *Mountain Daylight* didn't catch the error and proceeded forward without questioning the dispatcher. The dispatcher was immediately called on the radio by Amtrak and told of the impending collision if our train moved over onto their track. The dispatcher corrected the error and we never actually crossed over to their track. The dispatchers control several of our switches. One engineer was disciplined for not immediately recognizing the error and the dispatcher, who had a history of making such errors, was fired.

"So if Amtrak kept going and we crossed over," I paused.

"We're going, let's say seventy, and Amtrak keeps going at seventy; I just bet they'd never be able to unscramble the two trains. It would be like hitting a brick wall at one hundred and forty! There would be just one heap of burnt metal. We could never be extricated. They would dig a deep hole right here in the Palouse and bury the whole stinking mess," Jarred said.

"Palouse?" Cory asked?

"That's what they call this country we're passing through now. It's Palouse country. Read your route guide," Dean admonished.

Before long, we passed a fast freight train. We were blasting down the track right past them. Our two trains created a gale-force wind. I thought we were going to lift right off the track.

"These stack trains are really moving through here tonight!" Dean said.

"There's some big power pulling them babies," Jarred said.

"How big?" I asked.

"Four of them SD-70MAC's at four-thousand-plus horsepower," Dean said.

"And, if they ever hit us?" I asked.

"We're all dead men!" Jarred said. "A mile-and-a-half train, four hundred fifteen thousand pounds of engine each, pulling sixteen thousand tons of cargo running sixty miles per hour

our direction isn't going to make you real happy if you get in the way.

"What happens if we hit a car?" I asked.

"Nothing," Jarred answered.

"Nothing? How can nothing happen when you hit something as big as a car?"

"Nothing. You can't even feel it. We keep going right down the track."

"How can that be?" I challenged.

"Simple." Dean said. "The weight ratio of the average freight train to the car is the same equivalent of a car running over a tin can. A big percentage of our weight sits in those two big four-thousand-horse MP40's up front. At three hundred eighty five thousand pounds each, the locomotives are an effective car grinder."

"Have we ever hit anybody?"

"Not any time I was aboard. Hopefully never!" Dean finished. "Trevor, you don't look good. Are you okay?"

I said I was a bit better. I thought the medicine might be working.

"Can you eat anything?" Dean asked.

I thought I would throw it up again if I tried.

"You can't be on this train two days and not eat," Dean said. "You look like you need to lie down, but we don't have any empty beds now. After we leave Sandpoint, you can go to bed and maybe get well for tomorrow night, when I really need you. That's why they assign the dining-car crew to our room. They are the first up and our beds are ready early."

I was sitting at the dinette with my head on the table when Helen walked in. She sat down next to me and put her hand on my shoulder the way a mother would. She said not to let Jack see me like that or he might put me off at Spokane. She said they don't let them stay on if they are sick.

"Whatever it is that you have, they don't want it spread to the other crewmembers and passengers," Helen said.

"You mean they just throw my freaking butt off the train and I'm stuck there?" I panicked.

"No," she emphasized, "Jack would call the Command Center in Seattle and they would make the arrangements. They might transport you to a hotel where you could rest, or transport you to a hospital if they thought it was serious. Either way," she explained, "they would see that you went home either by train the next day or by plane. We will take care of you," she assured me.

"What I have is not contagious. I've had this before when I've traveled," I said.

"But we don't know that," Helen argued.

Helen said that Jack smelled the vomit in the bathroom and asked if a passenger was sick. Helen went on to say she was cleaning the bathroom but didn't inform Jack about any specifics.

"I didn't want you to lose your job the first night out," she laughed. "Trevor," she continued, "your uniform is a dead giveaway. It smells like you barfed on it."

I told her that I had a clean one. Helen told me to shower, change my uniform and see if I felt better. She gave me a sealed bag to put the soiled clothes in and went back into the train. I showered, changed, and when I went back to the crew dinette, Helen brought me some juice and told me to sip on it.

We arrived in Spokane at 3:15 a.m. Feeling much better, I stepped off the train to assist with the boarding. In Spokane, there was a change of operating crew consisting of two engineers and two conductors. I wanted to know if I could ever ride in the cab of the locomotives. One of the engineers told me that I couldn't legally, however, they invited me to go with them into the engine cab for a tour. I received a thorough education about operating the train. These two guys would be operating the train the next three hundred seventy four miles to Helena, Montana, arriving there later that day around 12:30 p.m.

I was still feeling somewhat weak. I curled up on the cushioned, circular bench that wrapped around the U-shaped dinette table and fell asleep. At 5 a.m. there was a flurry of activity as the crew awoke, preparing for the busy day that was ahead. I awoke with a start, sat up, and peered out the window just as the train made a dramatic approach into the town of Sandpoint, Idaho, as it entered an eight-thousand-foot deck bridge built over the mouth of the Pend Oreille River and lake.

The crew had made coffee and it tasted crisp and strong. When we arrived in Sandpoint, Dean said they didn't need me and to stay back. I didn't like the fact that I wasn't doing my job. I was sorry to see Helen leave. She really saved my life, but she was turning here and would return to Seattle on the next westbound at 10:30 p.m.

The girls, who were up and ready to work the train, stopped and talked to me. They were the permanent day crew that went through to Chicago. Most of them looked like the product of a bad night.

"How are you feeling? We heard you were sick last night?" They asked.

"How did you guys know?"

"Oh you can't do anything without the whole train knowing about it," they said.

"Are you ready for bed?" they asked. "The cooks are up."

"Not yet. I want to see some of the country," I said.

"Sweetie," she called me, "you better get some much-needed sleep. The country will always be there."

They all excused themselves, saying they had to go to work and prepare for the breakfast service.

"Passengers get breakfast?" I asked.

"They have to order it and we bring it to their seat or they can eat in the diner," she said.

"So what do they eat?"

"Eggs, toast and potatoes," she said, "it never changes but they constantly invent new names for the same items."

I was handed the breakfast menu and told that I could order anything I wanted. After everyone decided on their orders, Dean phoned them into the dining car. I was hungry but hesitant to eat much since my episode of nausea. In the end, I ordered what I really wanted: Bacon, eggs, toast and steak potatoes. Before long, the orders were delivered just as promised. The food was piping hot. One gal also brought me two bottles of OJ and a giant muffin hot from the oven. I thanked her, reached in my wallet and tipped her five. The guys razzed me, saying they never tip anybody for anything.

The food portions were generous. Dean ordered hot cereal and fruit but Cory, Jarred, and I ate like truck drivers. I was starved. When Cory and Jarred finished their breakfast, they hit the sack. Dean gave me the bottom bunk, saying it was a bit longer and if I was sick again it was easier to make a quick exit.

"You make the bed up when you get up just like you found it with clean sheets tightly tucked," Dean instructed. "Basically, we sleep until five, just before Billings."

Dean said he would sleep about three hours and then be up and down during the day. I was sitting on the bunk thinking that the bed looked very tempting. I had never been to the Big Sky Country of Montana, and I didn't want to miss out on the scenery. Dean said we would have some daylight on the trip back. I wanted to be awakened when the train crossed the two long bridges in the mountains above Helena. The engineers had told me they were the biggest on the route.

"If I'm awake, I'll get you up," Dean promised. "We hit those high trestles just before noon. But they aren't the tallest or the longest on the route. The tallest bridge is in North Dakota. We'll cross the Dakota High Bridge early tomorrow morning just before daylight. You'll see it."

Dean pulled down the window shade that darkened the room, threw off his clothes, swung up onto the top bunk and fastened the safety net. I did the same and crawled into the bottom bunk just as the train entered the Cabinet Gorge Tunnel on the Idaho/ Montana border. It was 7 a.m. Mountain Daylight Time. I just lost an hour.

[Crossing The Continental Divide]

Dean

For a few seconds, I didn't recall whether or not I had set my watch ahead before I went to sleep. Suddenly the train entered a tunnel. I heard the sound coming from the ventilation fans located inside the nearly four-thousand-foot Mullen Tunnel that cut through the Continental Divide. The tunnel created a deafening roar as each sound of the train echoed off the concrete walls and ceiling. It could awaken a light sleeper, but not here. My three pals, asleep for over five hours, were clearly in stage four of their sleep cycle. I looked at my watch and it was set correctly. It was twelve noon. I wanted to open the window curtain and look out, but using the knowledge from my psychology degree, I refrained. Light could stimulate the eyes, sending a message to the brain that nighttime had ended and curtailing the release of the Dracula hormone melatonin. It didn't matter. I didn't need to look, because on this side of the train our lower-deck window would only have a view of rock walls and sheer cliffs as we clung to the steep mountainsides descending down into the Helena Valley. My ears popped, signifying a change in altitude and air pressure. A wide yawn corrected the problem. This was the first high pass we crossed at fifty five hundred feet above sea level.

There were a series of jerks as the engineer applied the dynamic brakes, converting the engines from a propelling force to a retarding one. These engineers weren't taking any chances. They also exhausted some air to the wheels to help absorb the downhill momentum. They didn't release much. Let's release ten pounds more only if we need it for the big curve ahead. Please, you guys, don't run out of air before we get to the bottom. Please don't lose control of our train. It won't look so pretty if we go end over end down into the gully. Some engineers dropped us down using just the dynamic brakes from the engines, but today the engineers are a bit more cautious.

Shortly, I heard the unmistakable squeal of the wheels as we negotiated the ten-degree curve on the five-hundred-foot long Austin Trestle, the first of two high bridges that crossed over two deep ravines, less than a mile apart on the east side of the divide. I dangled my legs over the edge of the bunk and looked at Trevor sleeping. Only the top of his head was uncovered. It looked like some of those big downhill curves coming into Missoula off of Evaro Hill caused his body to slide farther down in the bunk and forcing his feet over the edge. He needed to be stretched out more in the bunk in order to make him look more comfortable. Trevor didn't get his pictures of Austin and Greenhorn Trestles this trip. There will be another time. Common sense dictated that he slept.

I looked across to where Jarred was sleeping on the top bunk. The first hook of the safety net was disengaged, allowing one arm to extend over the edge of the bunk. I've warned that guy about keeping both hooks secured to the ceiling. Several months ago a female crewmember fell out of the top bunk during the night. She broke her collarbone, right arm and tore up one knee. She was in extreme pain until they took her off the train in Jamestown, North Dakota, at four in the morning. After that, the train managers became irrational about enforcing the policy of securing both hooks. I never let new hires sleep up on the top bunk their first few nights on the train. Jarred had survived Iraq and had no fear of anything.

I judged our distance from Helena to be about twelve miles west of the city. Helena was Montana's capital and the "Queen City of the Rockies." We sliced through Iron Cut Mountain. As the train moved out of the cut, it made a wide two-degree, four-hundred-fifty-foot curve to the right, coasted down a thousand feet of tangent track and made a wide four-degree, five-hundred-foot curve to the left where it reached the bottom of the 2.2 percent descending grade. This was Class Two track, and our speed shouldn't exceed thirty mph. The train's event recorder would tell management if the train was fully in compliance during the steep decent. A stack train, one hundred cars in length, was sitting on the passing track below called Austin siding. I could see it stretched out for a mile. It slowly moved forward just as the *Mountain Daylight* passed.

I set my watch alarm for 2 p.m., went to the restroom, and then stood in the vestibule stretching while I peered out the window. We had another seven miles of almost tangent track into Helena. They called this stretch "the seven-mile grade." As the train continued to accelerate, the force created a sudden breeze along the right of way, putting a strain on the chokecherry bushes bent low under the heavy weight of their long, white, flowering spikes.

We had just come over a dangerous pass. I was always glad when we passed Elliston, Montana, a tiny railroad berg located on the west side of Mullen Tunnel. Eastbound trains were sometimes delayed for hours when there was a problem getting a train up and down the spiral curve. I refrained from telling Trevor more stories about train wrecks. I also told Jarred to cool it. Trevor was good, and I didn't want him to quit us. He was still a puppy, green as grass and very gullible.

There were thirty tri-level automotive transport cars that had come off the track here last April. We were stuck at Elliston for hours while they cleaned up the mess. The sixty-eight-car train was leaking air at the rear, caused by some valve problem. The engineers, not being able to send down enough air to maintain control of the train, overapplied the dynamic brakes to compensate. They shouldn't have done that. It was a colossal error. That mistake caused the rear of the train to move faster than the cars closest to the engine. As a consequence, the force concentrated on the nineteenth car, sending it over the edge of the rail right on the curve. Fortunately, they were going slow and the cars remained upright. Nobody's new auto was totaled on that one.

The story I loved, but didn't tell Trevor, was when a well-meaning crew, twenty years back, decided to uncouple five head-end locomotives from a forty-seven-car tank train parked exactly where we just passed that stack train at the bottom of the spiral curve. They didn't set the hand brakes on the unattended train. Gravity did its work. All forty-seven cars started moving slowly down the seven-mile grade. The engineers opened up their engine throttle and started chasing their runaway train. Faster and faster went the train cars, rolling backwards downhill into Helena with the engines in hot pursuit. At the first major intersection in the city, next to the college, the runaway train collided with a couple of helper locomotives resting on the track waiting to help another train up the grade. Fortunately, the crew in the engine cab wasn't asleep and saw the train coming and bailed. Fifteen cars derailed; of that number, three were tank cars loaded with hazardous materials: hydrogen peroxide, isopropyl alcohol and acetone. *Boom! Double boom!* The surprise explosions and fire woke the city up at four in the morning on a cold winter day. There wasn't a window left in the college buildings. In fact, several campus buildings received so much damage they were uninhabitable for over a month. There were train parts strewn everywhere around the campus. The toxic cloud of carbon monoxide forced thousands from their homes on a bitterly cold winter day. An axle and rod from an exploding train car went airborne over the entire campus and landed on a house, narrowly missing a lady asleep in her bed as it fell through a five-foot hole it made in her roof. That lady received a rude awakening. I was glad we weren't following it, either. All the red signal lights in the world couldn't have stopped those unmanned missiles from coming down on top of us. After a yearlong tedious investigation, federal officials came to one conclusion. The crew didn't follow procedure when securing their train at the foot of the spiral curve. Oh really?

As we pulled into Helena, I let the day crew work and crawled back in the sack for a nap. I knew the route from here to Bozeman. It was worth staying up for if you had never seen it.

I awoke while the train was parked somewhere close to Bozeman. Soon, an unmistakable sound was heard from an approaching train's horn that could only come from a passenger MP40 diesel electric locomotive. The westbound *Mountain Daylight* was passing us here at full track speed, and even if I were up, dressed and standing at the door to wave them by, I wouldn't dare expose myself by opening the door. If we were late, then we would pass in the Missouri River Canyon. The slower speed through the canyon would permit a safe and friendly exchange with the other crew as we passed.

The population of Bozeman, Montana's third-largest city, was booming. Bozeman was one of the most popular destinations on the route summer and winter. The center for outdoor recreation, the Bozeman lifestyle endorsed the state's reputation of being the "Big Sky Country."

The heavy turnover of passengers on today's stop will be a challenge for the crew. Passengers from two tour buses coming from Yellowstone Park would board the train. I noticed from the manifest that had been emailed to the crew that ten mountain bikes had to be loaded, fifteen backpacks, two kayaks, and one hundred seventy five pieces of luggage. The crew had thirty minutes to do it. It will be hustle time in Bozeman. I want to make sure the scanners are correctly programmed, and I want all the pieces to be uploaded in the system. When I wasn't watching, I knew the tendency of the day crew was to manually load the luggage as fast as they could and ignore the computer system, in the process losing some pieces when they were placed in the wrong bin. Today we have to get it right. I needed help. I woke Jarred and Cory but let Trevor sleep.

We had everything aboard the train in twenty minutes. We left Bozeman on time. I regretted that Trevor wasn't involved.

Trevor Jensen

The boisterous activity during the stop at Bozeman woke me. Dazed from nearly seven hours of sleep, I was startled when no one else was in the bunks. I quickly dressed and found the crew in the center entry coach, where the last items of luggage had been loaded at Bozeman. I stood there bewildered.

"Why didn't you guys wake me?" I asked.

"In just a few, you can call up the reconciliation reports and see how we did," Dean yelled back.

"Don't treat me like I'm sick, because I'm not," I said as I helped one of the guys push up a bag on top of its bin. "So where are we?" I asked.

"Check your schedule. We're OT," Jarred said. "Always carry a schedule in your pocket. Once you are familiar with the route, you can look out the window and know."

I walked over to the tiny window and looked out.

"We're still in the mountains."

"Not for long," someone answered, "another twenty miles and we're out."

"You mean I've slept all day and didn't get to see the Rocky Mountains?"

"You're seeing them now," Dean said as he laughed.

The train was winding its way up through Rocky Canyon to the top of Bozeman Pass. There were huge boulders and outcroppings scattered along the mountainside. The locomotives utilized their powerful tractive effort as they pulled the long consist forward.

I was in urgent need of some coffee, so I walked through to the lounge.

"Comin' right up," Dig said as he handed me a steaming cup of Columbian brew.

Dig Baker, as they called him, had slept in my bed the previous night and wanted to know how I had made out.

"What time are you turning in tonight?" I asked.

"Little after midnight," Dig replied.

I said I was out of there for the day and I would see that his bed was ready. I handed Dig my train card to pay for the coffee. Dig wouldn't take it so the coffee was on the house. I walked back as the train reached the summit of Bozeman Pass. I stood in the vestibule area looking out at the magnificent country. The train slowed and stopped. We were on a passing track. There was a tunnel ahead. In a few minutes a freight train emerged from the tunnel and passed us. I used my phone camera and caught the moment. It was a cool scene. Slowly the train began moving toward the tunnel. I noticed a large sign on the right commemorating the passage of Captain Clark in 1806. The sign read:

*On July 15, 1806, Captain Clark, ten men, a woman, one child,
a black servant, forty-nine horses and one colt crossed Bozeman
Pass.*

At the east portal of the tunnel was an expansive view of the mountains to the south. My ears popped. One of the crew announced over the public-address system that the train was at its highest elevation on the route: five thousand five hundred sixty-two feet.

Indeed, twenty-five miles out of Bozeman after descending Bozeman Pass, the Rocky Mountains were fading in the distance. The major scenic attraction now, for the next three hundred forty miles, was the Yellowstone River. Except for a few wide curves along the banks of the river, there was no shortage of straight track and the *Mountain Daylight* rushed along at full speed. As long as I didn't look out the window I didn't suffer from further motion sickness.

It was hot in the Yellowstone Valley. The thermometer yielded a ninety-degree reading for the outside air. At 5 p.m. an announcement was made that we were soon to arrive in Billings, Montana's largest city. Billings would be a thirty-minute service stop for refueling the locomotives and loading supplies. Passengers were allowed to step off the train if they wished. Passengers were warned that the train would leave as soon as the bags, supplies and Billings passengers were aboard. Anyone failing to obey the boarding whistle from the locomotives would be left, and the next train to the east in twenty-four hours was completely sold out.

Upon departure from Billings, the passenger representatives were busy serving up the evening meal. On the outskirts of Billings the train crossed the Yellowstone River for the third and final time but we would follow the river for another two hundred twenty-five miles to Glendive.

Reyna boarded the train and congratulated us on our success so far. It was immediately apparent that she was a take-charge person, a quality that earned her respect from the crew. She gave me a pep talk, saying that we played an extremely critical function in passenger satisfaction and the punctuality of the train.

She told me that I would help the passenger representatives with the dinner service as needed.

"Wear your earpiece and keep your phone on at all times tonight," she instructed, as she liked to keep in close contact with the crew during the night.

Dean said Reyna was a registered nurse who had worked most of her career in a Minneapolis trauma unit and was board certified in just about every facet of nursing. She was burnt out with nursing and wanted to try her hand at something different. Even though the job was sometimes stressful, working on the train had been a rewarding change from the pressures of being overworked and understaffed in a big-city trauma unit.

In about two seconds, Reyna called for me to help Rene. I found Rene on the lower deck of the coach diner, preparing her trays. The menu was oriental steak on a bed of rice. The smell of the meat and sauce was everywhere throughout the train. Rene was a nice lady of thirty-something and had fallen behind in her dinner service. She worked feverishly, loading each tray with the steak, rice, stir fries, salad, and the other table condiments necessary to round out the meal. My job was to deliver the trays all arranged by car. All I had to go on to locate the right customer was a meal receipt with the car and seat number. I was really slow. I took a stack of trays. It was harder than it looked. In the hustle and bustle of delivering the trays, I became mixed up and handed out trays of food to passengers who didn't order them. But, when offered the food, they took the tray and ate. One elderly lady handed me a ten-dollar bill that I thought was a tip. It caused a bit of confusion for Rene when she ended up being several trays short. The tantalizing smell started messing with my gastric secretions. I was starved. If Rene messed up the presentation of the food on the trays, she started over and set the steak on a platter. I couldn't stop myself. I gobbled down a steak with the same speed a heron swallows a frog. The meat was so succulent and tasty. I took more. Bing, one of the Chinese cooks, yelled at me.

"You like?"

I gave him a thumbs up with my left hand as I scooped up more meat with the right hand. Bing usually worked in the first-class diner but tonight the coach passengers were eating like royalty. Bing stepped over, took my meat, dumped some rice in a dish, and placed the meat on top and poured sauce over it. It was yummy!

An announcement was made for everyone to look out to the north side of the train. The train was approaching Pompey's Pillar National Monument. It was a sandstone outcropping two hundred feet high at the edge of the Yellowstone River where Captain Clark had inscribed his name. The rock figured prominently in Indian folklore. If your imagination ran wild, the rock might take on the shape of a lion's head. I tried to look as we sped by, but I wasn't too impressed. The passengers sitting on the right side almost tipped the train over getting to the left side to see it. One lady, sitting by the window on the opposite side, jumped up, lost her balance as the train swayed and fell over on the gentleman sitting next to her, knocking his tray of food off the seat table onto his lap. It wouldn't have been so bad if his hot coffee hadn't tipped over and scorched his crotch. I rushed him some ice to ease the pain. He was in some serious hurt. He was more than a little mad! He slipped the ice down his pants and sat there with his arms stretched above his head. I thought I should lift his tray up off his lap or something but he yelled at me not to touch him. Only the whites of his eyes could be seen as he rolled his eyeballs up into his head. Instead of apologizing, his seat partner reprimanded him for removing the plastic top on his coffee, but he scolded her back saying he couldn't drink out of the little tiny hole. I thought for doing what she did to him, she was certainly rude about it. She turned out to be his wife.

It was almost dark when the train pulled out of Glendive, Montana. I set my watch forward and wished for a nap.

"I hope it isn't like this all night," I said as the train tilted from left to right as it rounded the corners.

It started to feel like Yakima Canyon, but on fast-forward. I didn't want to lose my dinner.

"We're in the Dakota badlands now," Dean explained. "This crew in the front locomotive ignores the curves. It will go like this for another hour or so. Wait until winter when we hit the snow drifts. It's like riding on a bucking horse."

"Now that we're in North Dakota, do I start worrying about the mosquitoes?" I asked.

"Yeah worry. Worry a lot because the fever they carry ... well, it fries your brains," Jarred said.

"Are you serious? I won't get off the train in North Dakota."

"Just use the repellent," Jarred said with a laugh, "and try not to breathe."

"How can you not breathe?" I asked, not believing a thing he said.

"Mosquitoes are attracted to carbon dioxide. That's how they find you. Just take small shallow breaths." Jarred tried to look serious.

"But not all the mosquitoes carry the virus," I said.

"No of course not," Jarred said, "just the cross-eyed ones."

Reyna came through about then and sensed I was being teased.

"Trevor," she said, "welcome to the night crew!"

It was about 2 a.m. when we crossed the Missouri River over a long bridge from Mandan into Bismarck, the capitol of North Dakota. We stopped at the newly built station located near the downtown section of the city. Tonight there were forty coach and nine first-class passengers leaving the train and about the same number boarding. The night crew had twenty minutes to load or the train would be late out of Bismarck. The dispatchers scheduled and prioritized the movements of the rail traffic somewhat based on when the *Mountain Daylight* left Bismarck. A short distance out of Bismarck the train slowed to a stop. A nervous chill tingled down my spine as the speeding westbound *Mountain Daylight* passed us at full bore, blowing its high-pitched horn.

"I guess they're on time tonight. If not, they soon will be," Jarred said.

"They're not OT," Dean said, "they're twenty minutes early!"

"Jamestown is next!" Cory informed.

As the train left Jamestown, Dean told me to get some coffee and relax.

"The Dakota High Bridge is thirty miles ahead. It's pretty cool," he said.

It was 4:20 a.m. and there was a hint of daylight in the east as the train passed through a low cut in the hills and slowed to about fifty mph. There was a hollow clanging sound as the train glided across the bridge to the other side. We passed right over a town. Once on the other side, the scene quickly faded when we passed through a cut in the hill. The train quickly regained its track speed as we raced across the flat prairie to Fargo.

"How do you get down to the town?" I asked.

"You bungee jump," Jarred answered.

"And what is the name of the town again?" I asked.

"Cheneau Valley," they said.

Reyna Jefferson

When I first saw Trevor, I couldn't believe Rudy had sent me a kid. Rudy didn't say he was so young. Had I known that, I wouldn't have been so quick to add Trevor to my crew. This job was not easy for anybody, much less someone who had never worked away from home. Most could not adjust to sleeping on a train during the day in between working two nights. I'll withhold my judgment of Trevor until I see how he performs on the trip back. I won't be there, but Dean will let me know.

I was pulling Jarred off the crew. I could use him on Thursday's train and he wouldn't mind laying over two days in the Cities. I told Dean to get Jarred off Trevor's back. It was bad enough adjusting to the schedule, but being taunted and harassed by a fellow crewmember at the same time was unacceptable.

Jarred doesn't like taking orders from a black woman. He has a bit of a racist attitude. Jarred is a good worker, and he will fit in with the other crew that has two women. They boss him around but he doesn't seem to mind. I don't want to lose Trevor in St. Paul.

I called everyone to come to the crew quarters. I served up some cold dessert. Then I had to ruin everyone's morning with some bad news.

"We have trouble ahead," I said.

We had received an urgent bulletin from the dispatcher. The railroad was questioning the condition of the track south of Fargo to Breckenridge. There had been a torrential downpour, creating a lot of surface water. They had one report of a drainage ditch flooding the track.

The track followed the bottomland in the Red River Basin, which was a network of small ponds and sloughs that fed into the Red River. A loaded coal train ahead of us had been rerouted through Detroit Lakes and St. Cloud, Minnesota, just as a precaution.

"If we continue on the regular route through Breckenridge and Willmar, we might have to deal with slow orders along the Red River, putting us into the Cities late," I explained. "A decision will be made when we reach Fargo."

After we arrived in Fargo, we waited for our orders. I went inside the Fargo station and told the passengers before they boarded that we wouldn't be leaving right away. I said we might have to sit awhile until the conditions of the track were evaluated. Once they were on the train, it was like they'd never been told. They kept the passenger representatives busy answering the same question again and again.

We were given two options. One option was to wait until daylight and proceed under slow orders on the regular route, or we could be rerouted on the freight's mainline through the north, where the dispatchers would have to wedge the *Mountain Daylight* around the freight traffic, resulting in further delays. Meanwhile, the railroad had dispatched "maintenance of way" vehicles from Breckenridge to check the track. We waited. We sat for over an hour in Fargo, waiting for our go orders. At 6:50 a.m., nearly one and a half hours late, we crossed over the Red River to Moorhead, Minnesota, and turned south on our regular route to Breckenridge. We had ten miles where the train was ordered to travel at no more than forty mph. There was no flooding anywhere along the track. I sent the night crew to bed because it would be the only sleep they had before their departure out of Midway Station in St. Paul later this evening.

It was 11:30 a.m. when the *Mountain Daylight* made its way through the suburb of Wayzata, Minnesota, on the north shore of Lake Minnetonka twenty-three miles from the Twin Cities. Dean, Trevor, Cory and Jarred sat in the crew dinette and voraciously devoured the generic breakfast of scrambled eggs, sausage, toast and home fries. They would lay over only five hours before reporting back to Midway Station.

No one was happy about Jarred getting busted to another crew. The *Mountain Daylight* operated five days a week, resulting in two-day layovers for some crews. Jarred would enjoy two days off in the Cities before going back out on the next westbound.

Soon the steel and glass skyscrapers of Minneapolis were in view. The train passed through the heart of downtown before crossing the Mississippi River on Nicollet Island in view of the St Anthony Locks and dam. Now on the St. Paul side of the river, the train turned sharply to the right and passed several large rail yards before pulling into Midway Station, named for being midway between the downtown districts of St. Paul and Minneapolis. It was noon Monday, thirty-eight and one-half hours since departing Seattle on Saturday evening.

I told Dean to head for the hotel, but he insisted helping the day crew unload. Trevor was glad for the opportunity to grab more tips as the bags were handed over to the arriving passengers.

Before long we were all standing on the curb waiting for the shuttle van that would take us to the hotel, where I had left my car parked.

"Well?" Dean asked. "Are we ready to get back on the train in five hours?"

"Dunno," said Trevor. "I haven't stopped swaying. Is it the same distance back?"

"It can be longer," Cory said.

"Longer?" Trevor questioned.

"Depends on what kind of a mess we get into," Dean said.

"Mess? What kind of mess?" Trevor wanted to know.

"Trains can get messy," Cory interposed.

"Especially the 'Train from Hell,' " Dean said.

"I'm not getting on that one," Trevor vowed.

They all laughed. Nobody wanted on the "Train from Hell." Trevor reached down and felt the wad of cash in his cargo pants pocket.

"Does the 'Train from Hell' pay? If so, maybe I do," he said.

"Trevor! How did you enjoy your first stint working on the train?" I asked.

"It's different. I didn't know what to expect. I liked it," he said.

I wished them all the best of luck going back to Seattle. I was tired and in need of my two-day break. I told Jarred to behave himself the two days he was here in the Cities.

Westbound Adventure

Dean

After we checked into the hotel, Trevor and I took the shuttle to the gym.

"By the way," I asked, "how much did you make in tips?"

"How about three hundred seventy dollars," Trevor said as he tallied up the last few bills.

"Wow! You didn't move that many bags. Don't tell anyone and don't leave it lying around or it will be gone. I don't trust anyone with cash," I responded.

I hoped Jarred wouldn't find out about Trevor being a dancer. He would notch up the teasing. I called for the hotel shuttle to take us back, and as we waited outside I felt the urge to light up. Trevor was shocked when he learned I smoked.

"Oh! I don't smoke many of them. I know what you are thinking, it's out of vogue to see a man, engrossed with maintaining his well-sculptured body, engage in something so unhealthy. Everybody says that when they see me smoke."

We didn't sleep. I never did on these short turnarounds. At 5 p.m. the shuttle took us back to the Midway Station. Trevor caught on fast. Considering he was a rich spoiled kid, he wasn't afraid of hard work. He would soon be able to do this job alone. For such a thinly built man, he is pretty strong. He doesn't do heavy weights, but I guess his strength and endurance comes from throwing his two sisters around in those dance routines.

We were considered to be orphans tonight. There was no onboard manager from here to Billings. Technically, our manager tonight would be in Seattle, as the Command Center would staff an extra body to assume that role. It was much easier to work with a real live manager you don't like than a disembodied voice over the phone.

I liked working nights with Reyna. Thanks to her, they had boosted my pay to that of an assistant manager in order to keep me happy. She did it on the grounds I'd make the inventory program work for tracking the luggage. As I glanced over the passenger manifest, I saw that we would have a special guest tonight. The crew would be entertaining Aunt Mattie. The official name on the manifest was Matilda Q. Smeek, but to the train crew that knew her, she was affectionately known as Aunt Mattie. When we asked her about her middle initial, she told us it stood for Quincy. It was her father's name.

"When I was in mother's womb, I kicked like a boy, so they named me James Quincy. So, when I was born, they decided to keep the middle name of Quincy."

She was a ninety-plus-year-old lady who was shuttled back and forth between two daughters, one living in Willmar, Minnesota, and the other living on a farm near Dickinson, North Dakota. She traveled with us frequently, sometimes as often as twice a month. Stricken with dementia, she had only half of her marbles. During previous trips, Reyna had been very kind to her and never complained about her traveling alone since it was a night journey both directions, and for most of the trip she slept in her seat. Well, she usually slept unless she fell victim to Sundowner's Syndrome and thought she had missed breakfast.

In that case, the crew brought her some Cheerios and milk, which usually satisfied her. On one trip she thought she should get ready for bed. She unbuttoned her blouse. The lady sitting nearby buttoned it up for her, but in a minute, Aunt Mattie unbuttoned it again. Finally, she took it off and demanded that someone get her nightie. Reyna was onboard that trip. She put the blouse on backwards and buttoned it from behind. Aunt Mattie couldn't reach it to take it off again. As a token of their appreciation for the crew's attentiveness, each daughter always sent a sack of home-baked goodies as a reward for the crew that so faithfully looked after her. Between the train crew and the watchful eyes of a few perceptive passengers, Aunt Mattie always survived the trip without serious incident.

I told Trevor that she wasn't our problem and not to worry about her. The night crew would see that Aunt Mattie had a safe journey, and they would get her off at 4 a.m. in Dickinson. We dare not lose her checked bag.

Reyna had a discriminating palate, and she claimed the home-made pastry Aunt Mattie brought was the best she'd ever had. It was most unfortunate that Reyna would miss out on tonight's culinary delights.

It was strange, I thought, when Trevor approached one of the Chicago crewmembers and spoke to her. She recognized him and they embraced. Oh! I said to myself, I know that girl -- that's Wren. Trevor isn't shy about meeting strangers, particularly if it is a girl.

The *Mountain Daylight* departed the Twin Cities on time at 6:30 p.m. and headed west. I told Cory and Trevor to eat and then hit the sack until we hit Breckinridge at 11 p.m. I planned to stay up.

Among the handful of passengers standing in front of the old station, as the train pulled in to Willmar twenty minutes late, was Matilda Smeek. She was standing between two of her family members, holding a shopping bag presumably stuffed with our treats. Aunt Mattie was ready to be handed over to the train crew, who for the price of a coach ticket would provide seven hours of respite care for the family.

Trevor Jensen

When I woke up, it felt like I'd been on a month of fatigue duty with Jarred in Iraq. His stories of the war were starting to mess with my psychology. I was feeling the stress of sleep deprivation. Wren passed me in the corridor just as I stepped out of the shower with my bath towel wrapped around me. She looked at me and smiled.

"You're defenseless," she said as she stood on her tiptoes to offer me a kiss.

"I can't let my package get unwrapped," I told her as the two of us made our way back to our rooms.

As a permanent day-crew person, she was turning in for the night.

"Keep us on time tonight, okay Trevor? I have plans when I get to Seattle."

"I'll do my best," I said.

I needed a cup of coffee and some of Aunt Mattie's sweets, but the night crew said she was sleeping and to let her be. So far, there had not been any time for a break.

Bismarck was sheer bedlam. A drunken man tried to board the train but was arrested by the Bismarck police assigned to patrol the station. That was no big deal until we were confronted with a family of five ticketed to Spokane but not listed on the passenger manifest. There were no seats together. They had three small children who could not sit alone. The father became extremely irate when he was told there were no seats for them, as somehow they had fallen through the cracks of the computer system. The problem was that the computer had issued tickets prematurely, when they were only wait-listed. It was an uncommon but serious glitch in the software. Such errors were supposed to be caught by suspicious eyes watching for such devious problems.

So, the train was delayed further while the Command Center figured out a remedy. Rather than wake people up and switch seats around, something you never wanted to do in the middle of the night, the disgruntled family was allowed to ride in the first-class section to Bozeman. After that, they would be moved to coach seats for the remainder of the journey to Spokane. And they would be given vouchers for the evening meal. They were happy with this remedy. Now the train was over an hour late when we finally pulled out of Bismarck.

Preparing for the next stop at Dickinson, the crew made a horrifying discovery. Aunt Mattie was not in her seat. Her handbag was missing, but the sack with the sweets for the crew was sitting on the floor underneath the seat. When the crew could not find her they notified Dean and requested his help. Dean, Cory, and I searched every nook and cranny on the train. Using our flashlights, we looked around every seat and each restroom. I mistakenly awakened an elderly lady who I thought looked like Aunt Mattie. The poor lady was furious. We looked behind the service counters in the lounge and diner. Being a coach passenger, her train card would not grant her access into the first-class section, but we searched there anyway. We checked downstairs and walked the entire lower deck.

When the train stopped at Dickinson, we were still searching. Dean said it was the first time they had ever lost a person. The train stayed in Dickinson while the Command Center was notified about the missing passenger. The Command Center wanted to know if there was any evidence she might have jumped from the train when it was moving. The conductors investigated that possibility. Dean insisted that he had checked each entry door while doing the search, and there was no evidence that she had exited the train while it was moving as the three main exit doors were all in the locked position. No one had noticed her missing until about a half hour out of Bismarck. The timeline of her exact disappearance was debatable. Who would deliver the bad news to the family that was patiently waiting for their aged mother?

"It's hard enough," Dean said, to tell someone in the middle of the night in Bismarck that you couldn't find the bags they handed you in Seattle. "How do you tell them, 'Here is her bag but I lost your mother!' "

Then Dean said they never had those problems when Reyna was aboard. He said Reyna, with her proactive disposition, snooped through the train looking for problems before they surfaced. She would have kept her eye on Aunt Mattie so nothing like this could have happened. Cory said he had a premonition that we were going to be hit with bad luck. Meanwhile, the train sat in Dickinson awaiting the outcome. If she couldn't be found, the train would become part of a crime scene said Tim, the conductor.

"If that happens, we'll never get out of Dickinson," Tim lamented.

He told about a lady, couple years back, who had a heart attack on the train. The crew found her dead in the restroom. Law enforcement was overly zealous and held up the train for hours while they did their crime-scene investigation.

Ten people left the train in Dickinson. We unloaded the bags and set Aunt Mattie's one checked bag aside while we handed the others off to the passengers as they stepped off the train. We waited, hoping for a miracle. Maybe, I thought, she would suddenly realize we were in Dickinson, come out of hiding, get off the train, and run down the track into the arms of her caring daughter, who was standing there waiting for her to appear. Dean set her bag on the platform and we checked in the boarding passengers. The daughter approached and picked up Aunt Mattie's bag. We ignored her. Dean said to let Tim deal with her.

Tim was in no hurry to face her, either. Tim wanted to give the family something more than nothing regarding the specifics of Aunt Mattie's disappearance. Tim and Maggie, our lead person, were now talking to the police at the Command Center trying to piece together when Maggie thought the crew last saw Aunt Mattie. Maybe they would just take her bag and leave, I hoped. Finally, we had to confront somebody with the facts.

"Hello. My name is Wilma. I'm waiting for my mother, Matilda Smeek," she said as she held Aunt Mattie's bag.

"Well, that is her bag," Dean said hesitantly.

"She didn't get off the train. Is someone with her?" Wilma asked.

"The conductor will talk to you. He's not here right now, but he'll come soon," Dean said as he looked up and down the track wishing he would spot Tim somewhere.

"Did something happen to my mother?"

"I can't discuss that with you right now," Dean said.

"What do you mean?" Wilma asked. "Where is my mother? My sister called and told us they put her on the train in Willmar last night."

"I don't know where your mother is. We can't find her. She's missing." Dean said.

"Missing? How can that be?"

"Ma'am, I'm sorry, but she's *missing!*"

"I don't understand how she could be missing." Wilma was now very distraught.

"I don't think she is on the train. We did everything we could to locate her."

"How could she not be on the train?"

"We searched the train when we discovered she wasn't in her seat," Dean said.

The poor lady stood there speechless, looking up and down the track as if to look for her mother who was not there. She put her hands to her face. I thought she might cry. We loaded the luggage and stayed on the train. We continued to sit in Dickinson.

Then came a break in the case of the missing Aunt Mattie: the Command Center wanted to know if the policy of locking the entry doors during the stop at Bismarck had been followed. This was the policy any time the crew was away from the train. This was an absolute requirement in Bismarck unless a crewmember was left behind to watch. Once the arriving passengers detrained the doors were to be shut, preventing an unauthorized person from boarding. Tonight, however, everyone had to work inside the station, leaving the train unguarded. During the confusion and mass hysteria of the Bismarck stop, no one could say definitely that they unequivocally had shut the one train door used to disembark the passengers. The Bismarck coach passengers exited the train from Aunt Mattie's car. If the door was left open, was it possible that Aunt Mattie could have left the train in Bismarck without being noticed? She didn't appear to have mobility problems. When she boarded, she didn't want to use the elevator.

The operating crew at Bismarck was busy with their internal briefings, as they usually had to review the new train orders. Assuming then that the train door had been left unsecured, the Command Center notified the Bismarck police about the missing lady with dementia. Other than jumping off the train, which was highly unlikely, the Command Center in Seattle was under the assumption that Aunt Mattie had somehow left the train in Bismarck.

We waited. We were told that we could not leave Dickinson until the case was resolved. Meanwhile, we sat in the crew dinette and ate Aunt Mattie's treats packed in plastic freezer bags that were labeled "train crew." We ate the lemon squares, oatmeal crisp, and the brownie nut bars. Maggie found some ice cream in the diner and served it up as we talked.

"Do you think Aunt Mattie is dead?" Cory asked.

"If she jumped out of the train she sure is better than dead," Dean remarked.

I was beginning to lose my appetite for the brownie nut bars as I sat thinking about Aunt Mattie being strung out along the track in a kajillion pieces.

"And, after she is ground to powder by that coal train that had been following us, only the crows could find her!" Dean finished and then he continued, saying, "the lemon bars that Aunt Mattie brought were to die for."

Maggie asked if anyone had seen the movie *Throw Momma From the Train*.

"So what happens," I wanted to know, "if they don't find her in Bismarck?"

"Then we're all suspects or material witnesses to her disappearance," Maggie said.

"Why would they think we had anything to do with it?" I asked.

"Well, somebody did. You are eating her food. Isn't that a motive?" Maggie teased. "Food is always a motive for killing, at least in the animal kingdom, of which we are members."

"Maybe a passenger did it," I reasoned.

"Maybe," Maggie said. "I don't think she could figure out how to unlock the train doors herself without some help."

"What do you think really happened to her?" Cory wanted to know.

"I think she is still on the train somewhere. Maybe when we unload in Seattle, we'll find her squashed in the bottom of one of the luggage bins," Dean said.

"Do you think she might have crawled in bed with someone in first class, and they haven't noticed yet?" another crewmember, Rose, suggested.

"It's always nice to ride with the more affluent clientele," Maggie said.

"Could we be blamed?" I asked.

"Of course," Dean responded, "Everything is always our fault. It always is."

"And will we get in trouble?" I asked.

"Who knows?" Maggie said. "I might, but by the time they get this all sorted out, I'll be off in Billings."

"Did you hear about that big lady using the walker that we left in Bozeman last week?" Rose asked. "That was a challenge for the Command Center."

"Oh yeah, I did hear about her," Maggie confirmed, "She left the train to use the bathroom because she couldn't squeeze her big butt into the one on the train?"

"No, I think she was told by one of the crew to take her time as the train would be there for half an hour, but whoever told her that didn't realize how slow she moved," Rose said.

"She was on oxygen, too! Poor lady," Maggie said.

"Yeah! The train left her standing on the platform pushing her wheeled walker and oxygen tank. When she saw the train pull out without her, she had a panic attack. The station agent called the Command Center to see what he was supposed to do with her."

"What did they say to do?" Dean asked.

"They said to call 911. All of her medicine was left on the train."

"Couldn't they have stopped the train and let her on?" I asked.

"By then the train was halfway up Bozeman Pass!" Maggie said. "It couldn't stop anyway ... railroad rules."

"We're out of here!" Dean exclaimed as the train moved ahead.

The train pulled out of Dickinson at 6 a.m., now two hours late. In a few minutes, Tim called Maggie on her phone to say they had found Aunt Mattie and she was very much alive. The

Bismarck police found her in front of the shopping mall down on South Seventh at four in the morning. After the police learned she was missing, they started looking for her. She was in front of the mall waiting for the stores to open, Tim explained.

"You know," Rose started, "Aunt Mattie was awake at Fargo. She asked me, just as we stopped, about 'zipping in and doing some quick shopping' but I told her there was nothing in the Fargo station to buy. She seemed fine with that."

"So, Rose." Dean said. "You should have also told her that the shopping mall was still closed."

Maggie went on to say that the Command Center would hire a private shuttle that would take her to Dickinson.

"Boy, we lost money on her fare," Dean said.

I was in serious need of some sleep. I wasn't hungry, because we had all overdosed on the sweets Aunt Mattie had brought. Tim said we had thirty miles of fairly straight track before twisting through the badlands of western Dakota. I was torn between sleeping and gazing out the window at the never-before-seen landscape. This morning, it was far from the dark abyss it had been on the trip east.

Before long the train passed through the historic town of Medora, crossed the Little Missouri River, and made its way between the numerous scenic buttes, the geographic trademarks of the Dakota badlands. I loaded my camera up with pictures. Finally, I couldn't stay awake any longer. In the last day and a half I only had seven hours of sleep and a short nap.

Wren

Trevor is only eighteen and I'm twenty-five. I guess we'll have to be friends. I'm glad he was hired because he is one cool guy. I wish he worked the day crew, where I could get to know him better.

I was thrilled to see that our favorite celebrity passenger was getting on in Forsyth, Montana. We all loved this little kid, but his life is sad. Little Jamie Rosenthal and his mother Mona were on the manifest, ticketed in coach to Seattle. Jamie, who was barely eight years old, had leukemia. The Seattle Children's Clinic enrolled him in an experimental treatment program that so far has helped restrain his bone marrow from producing an overload of cancer cells. He always gets first-class treatment. His mother was a big loser but Jamie was always such a sweetheart. His doctors didn't think he could survive if this treatment protocol failed.

When Reyna was on board the last time Jamie was, she talked at length with Mona about Jamie's condition and care. Reyna was somewhat dismayed about Mona's laissez faire attitude that she sometimes demonstrated when riding the train.

Mona's live-in boyfriend, who was not Jamie's dad, worked for a local rancher. He, Mona, and Jamie lived in a travel trailer on the ranch property a few miles out of Forsyth.

Jamie's dad was a tough guy, drank a lot, and worked construction jobs wherever he could find them. Jamie told us his family history, some of which would be better left untold. Jamie was an alert and very bright little kid but he had not been in school for the past year. Life had been tough for little Jamie.

We arrived in Forsyth at 10 a.m. We continued to be two hours behind schedule, thanks to heavy freight traffic and Aunt Mattie. Mona and Jamie were assigned to my car. I didn't have any passengers to put off, so I waited until they spotted my entry coach opposite where they had Jamie in the pickup. I went over to help gather up all the stuff they brought. He was on oxygen now. He looked really bad. My heart sank when I saw him. This doesn't look good, I thought. Mona's boyfriend carried him over to the door and one of our guys lifted him onto the train and carried him upstairs to his seat. Yep! It was Jamie all right. He still had his spunk and spirit. I started teasing him right away and he ate it up.

He was such a happy little kid in spite of being thrown such a raw deal. He was happy to see me and started asking about the others he remembered from a month ago, when they last rode.

I helped them settle in. Jamie had the window seat. Mona wrapped him up in his blankets and I brought him some cold juice to sip. I predicted that everyone aboard, almost everyone anyway, would know about Jamie by the time we arrived in Seattle. On one return trip that I worked, wellwishers made their way through the train to where Jamie sat, promising him that he would be in their prayers and thoughts. On that trip he was given gifts galore, even cards with money from some passengers as they learned about his illness and ultimate fate.

I noticed that Mona was well-dressed in her expensive boots, jeans and western shirt. Jamie, however, had on a pair of ragged sneakers, jeans and a plain T-shirt. I think the study group in Seattle pays for the train tickets.

Jamie loved hot dogs and ice cream. If he could eat, we would buy him his food from the lounge car. We used our crew cards to pay, and depending on who was working the lounge, they sometimes didn't charge us. If Mona drank too much and overshot her debit card, the train manager gave her enough meal vouchers to get her back to Forsyth. We didn't let them go hungry.

Today, however, the crew was a bit perplexed when they saw how much ground Jamie had lost since his last time on the train. He was in urgent need of another exotic mixture of chemo drugs in order to bring the white blood count down. Once we started moving, he went right to sleep. He was so cute wearing his baseball cap and wrapped up in his cowboy blanket.

Trevor Jensen

It was 5:30 p.m. when I was awakened. I couldn't believe I had slept that long. The manager woke us up to help with the evening meal service. The train was packed. We had just left Helena when Dean told me to hurry and bring my camera. The two trestles were just ahead. I took some good shots of both Austin and Greenhorn trestles. I opened the window while taking the pictures. Opening the windows and sticking your fool head out is a real no-no, but I was careful to make sure no one saw.

I was barely awake and still somewhat groggy when I handed out the food trays for the evening meal to the passengers. I paid little attention to Mona and Jamie when I delivered their food. It was Jamie who noticed me when he saw my brass guitar belt buckle. When I passed through the car again, I heard this shrill little voice call me.

"Do you play the guitar?" Jamie asked.

"Why yes," I said, "I do, how did you know?"

"Mister, I liked your buckle," Jamie said.

I stood there and looked at this little kid wrapped up in a blanket with his meal tray on his lap. He looked sick. I unbuckled my belt, snapped off the buckle and handed it to Jamie for him to see. Jamie grabbed it and cupped it in his hands, admiring it.

"This is awesome!" he said.

"Hi. I'm Trevor. What is your name?"

"Jamie Rosenthal."

"Do you play the guitar?" I asked.

"I want to play the guitar but I can't right now because I'm too sick. Besides, I don't have one, anyway."

"I see," I said.

"My mom says I'm too young anyway. I have to get older," Jamie said.

"Well, how old are you?" I asked.

"Eight."

"I obtained my first guitar when I was six. You can start learning the chords on a child's guitar and when you grow, you move on to a larger size," I said.

Jamie gave the buckle back to me and I left to help with the arrival in Missoula.

Wren said I really impressed Jamie with the belt buckle. She wanted me to go back and see him again. She told me his whole story. When I went back to see Jamie, he appeared to be sleeping. There was an oxygen clip in his nose. His mother was away from her seat so Jamie was alone. His eyes were closed. I sat down in Mona's seat and put my hand on Jamie's shoulder. Jamie opened his eyes and when he saw it was me sitting there, he broke out with a big smile. We talked for a few minutes. Jamie talked about his plans to play the guitar. He wanted to know what I sang so I quietly sang some of my folk songs. I sang one of my own I wrote about Snoqualmie Pass. I told him that this was where I sometimes rode my horse, Mr. Jed. I also snowboard up there in the winter, I told him. The song "Snoqualmie Pass" was a clever song with a catchy tune and Jamie loved it. I got my laptop and showed him some pictures of Mr. Jed and me.

I immediately was attached to this little guy. He became my little friend. His magnetic personality made me forget that he was sick. In the course of our conversation, his mother returned. She told me that Jamie would receive his chemo on Wednesday afternoon on the same day they arrived in Seattle, and that if everything went okay, they planned to go back on Thursday night's train, the same train on which I was scheduled to work.

"I'll bring my guitar and we'll sing together," I promised.

I could tell that his mother had been hitting the booze pretty hard.

Upon arrival in Seattle we were free to leave, as the day crew would be unloading the train. Then, just when I spotted dad at the gate, Cory hit me up for some money that he said was needed to pay some bills. I dug into my pocket and grudgingly gave him one hundred dollars.

When I jumped into the car, dad pelted me with one question after another about the trip.

"Dean smokes, I made over five hundred dollars in tips, and you meet some really interesting people!"

I took out the wad of cash from the security pocket and showed him how much I made just on my return and explained that another three hundred was deposited in an account I opened in St. Paul.

"What, if anything, did you learn your first time away from home?"

"Well, for one thing dad, it's a crazy world out there. I have to learn when to fold 'em in poker and I have to learn to hold on to my tips."

"Did you lose money?" dad asked.

"I sure did," I answered. "I lost eighty in poker and let Cory make off with a hundred of my tips."

"Well son, fifty percent of a man's success is making money and the other fifty percent is holding on to it after you made it."

"Well said, dad!"

The Red River Monster

Trevor Jensen

I was feeling somewhat fatigued and hoarse, plus the fact that my repertoire of songs had been sung at least twice; I had to stop. I excused myself from the crowd that had gathered in the coach lounge car, which had seating only for twenty-four, but at least twice that many were standing around watching and listening. They came to hear me play the guitar and sing. I was accustomed to performing before a live audience, so I felt right at home with the crowd. Mona brought Jamie and sat him down in front of me. He sat there quietly for an hour and listened to me sing. He didn't say a word. He just looked up and drank it in. I thought the kid was daydreaming about playing the guitar just like me someday. I loved it. He inspired me to keep singing. No announcement had been made about my act over the public-address system of the train. I was told to perform as long as I wanted, and the crowd would come, and that they did.

I needed some more sleep since I was going to be up all night. Jamie was also tired but appeared to be feeling better than he had on the trip into Seattle two days previous. I assured Jamie I would be back before we arrived in Forsyth. I told him that I would help him off the train. Wren had asked me if I would please do it.

It was astonishing to see Jamie so happy when there was so much wrong with him. The blood transfusion he received at the clinic in Seattle had really perked him up. There was a black cloud looming, though, and it had a sobering effect on the crew. Jamie was dismissed from the experimental study protocol. His leukemia had become worse. The experimental chemo drugs were no longer working. Mona and Jamie would not be returning to Seattle. Whatever could be done from here on out would be done in Billings. There were few, if any, options. There was a noticeable difference in Mona's demeanor this time around. She was much more attentive and considerate in providing the care needed for her son. She stayed at his side the entire trip home.

The crew let me sleep through the Billings stop. At 7 p.m., forty-five minutes before the anticipated on-time arrival in Forsyth, I was up, showered, fed, and ready for the night. Forsyth, located eleven hundred miles from Seattle, was about half way to Chicago.

Jamie had been on the train for twenty-four hours and he was still going strong. When I went back to his car, Jamie was engrossed in watching the waterfowl that were flushed from the banks of the Yellowstone River when the train rushed by. Jamie knew the common names of some of the birds, and excitedly told me as they flew in different directions. I told him I didn't know the difference between a goose and a duck.

"Now, Trevor! Tell me. What was that?" he would ask.

"A duck," I said.

"No! What kind of duck?" he asked.

"I don't know. A duck is duck," I said.

"A mallard duck," he insisted.

As the train pulled into Forsyth, I helped Mona gather up their belongings and we moved downstairs by the door, ready to hop off when the train stopped. I could not believe it; we stopped a mile past the platform so they could conveniently unload a first-class passenger from the rear of the train. Reyna would have never allowed that if she'd been on duty tonight. Because of the very short station platform, we would have done two stops here. It would be a long walk back to where Jamie's pickup was parked.

"Are we all ready to go, bud?" I said as I repositioned Jamie's baseball cap sideways.

I lifted down their one suitcase, a canvas shopping bag, and the oxygen apparatus. Mona trudged off down the gravel side road, pulling her suitcase and carrying the rest. It was a huge load but she handled it well. Jamie and I followed behind. I carried Jamie since it was too far for him to walk. We had a long walk down to where the pickup was waiting to meet Mona and Jamie. I walked as fast as I could. It was uneven terrain and I didn't want to stumble. It was always a short stop at Forsyth. When Mona was out of hearing range, Jamie started talking to me.

"Trevor?" he asked. "Did you know that I'm going to die soon?"

I didn't know what to say so I just kept walking. Jamie kept talking. Then he let go with a little whimper. It broke my heart.

"I can't go back to Seattle. They don't want me anymore."

I still couldn't come up with anything to say. I kept walking.

"Trevor?" Jamie gave a big sigh and immediately began to sob. "I'm toast," he said as he cried.

I stopped walking.

"Give me a second, Jamie. Hug me around my neck so I don't drop you, okay? Hang on now."

I bent my leg and reached low into the zipped pocket where I kept the tip money and pulled out a wad of cash. I had thought that it was mostly five-dollar bills, but when I handed it to Jamie there were a few twenties mixed in the batch. I didn't mean to give him that much. I quickly counted the money. It totaled out at one hundred and fifty. Shoot. Why not? I gave it all to Jamie and told him to have his mom buy him something that he wanted.

"And make sure she spends it *all* on you," I insisted as I stuffed the cash in Jamie's shirt pocket.

I put Jamie in the cab of the pickup. As I turned away, I looked back and saw Jamie sitting there with big tears streaming down his face, but he also had a big smile on his face. How could he be so happy? I turned and walked back over to the pickup and the two of us did a couple of high fives.

"Oh!" I said, "I almost forgot."

I pulled off my belt, removed the guitar buckle, and handed it to Jamie.

"You keep this. If you are ever scared, Jamie, hold this buckle, and remember that I'm there with you. I'll always love you, Jamie."

He gave me another hug. There was a loud blast from the horn of the front locomotive, warning that the *Mountain Daylight* was ready to depart. I made a beeline for the closest open train door. I jumped aboard and waved to him as the train slowly pulled away from where the pickup was parked. Jamie kept smiling and waving.

Coach Rodger Epperson

I was ecstatic upon learning that Cheneau Valley High School would get two new recruits for basketball this coming season. Both boys, Joey Carlson and Kyle Hickles, were coming in as seniors and would add considerable strength to the varsity basketball team. I had heard rumors about Kyle coming, but I usually discounted what the kids told me. I was totally shocked when I heard that Joey planned to transfer from nearby Taylor High. Publicly, they said their decision to transfer was for personal reasons. Behind the scenes, rumors were flying that the boys wanted to play ball with Travis Olsen. They thought there was a good chance that the three of them could come up with a championship team in the Eastern Division. However, Kyle and Joey both claimed they didn't consult one another before they made their decision. I didn't know if I should believe that story or not.

From what I learned when I talked with their coaches, these boys, Kyle especially, were two of the best high school basketball players in North Dakota. The coaches were not very happy about losing Kyle and Joey to another school, and their attendance at Cheneau Valley High was not without controversy. Although it appeared shady on the surface, both boys had a parent living in Cheneau Valley. I assumed that the transfers would be legal and ethical. The last thing anybody wanted was for the North Dakota State Athletic Association to launch an investigation that would expose an illegal transfer and create an eligibility problem. If there was a transfer-rule violation, you could bet on the fact that Jamestown and Taylor High would not have looked the other way.

When I talked to Travis, he claimed he didn't know either of these boys. They knew about him, of course. Travis was pretty famous, at least throughout eastern North Dakota. Travis was somewhat ambivalent about sharing the glory with these two other guys. Well, that's the impression I got after I talked to him. Travis had never played against Joey, but Kyle, he said, was a force to be reckoned with on the court. Better that their presence on our team was a result of serendipity, opposed to a deceptive scheme that they all had contrived together. If we could vouch for the fact that Travis had no prior contact with these guys before the transfer, it would help make the transfers cleaner.

Joey's mom, Lana Delaney, has worked for the Cheneau Valley School District. She manages the superintendent's office. She has agreed to his coming and has carefully worked out the details, studying each move carefully and making sure no policies or procedures were violated. The last thing she wanted was for Joey to become ineligible after he enrolls, due to some rule violation. Other than some eyebrows being raised, she didn't think there would be a problem with Joey's transfer to Cheneau Valley High under the existing rules.

Kyle was in a similar situation and would have to live with his mom, Sharon Hickles, who rented a small one-bedroom apartment, which was all she could afford. During the school week, Kyle has to sleep on the sofa and would likely spend weekends with his dad, who lived in Jamestown. Kyle's transfer appeared, on the surface, to be more dubious. As rumor had it, he wouldn't be living in Cheneau Valley, because his mom didn't have room for him. The truth of the matter was that Kyle lived anywhere he could between Cheneau Valley and Jamestown with anyone who let him in their door. Kyle was reportedly one of the best ball-handlers in the state. He was short, standing five feet, eight and a half inches, but what he lacked in height he made up for with speed and adroitness. In addition to his basketball skills, Kyle was a talented artist. Yes indeed, Kyle and Joey's departure from Jamestown and Taylor High is a huge loss for those schools.

Sunny

My boss suggested that I attend a two-day leadership conference in Minneapolis. I was given a small stipend to help with expenses. Ordinarily I would not spend that kind of money on a trip. My son Ace and daughter Shona had never been that far from home. If I drove, I speculated that the trip could be done for that amount, but my old coupe was in need of some work and couldn't be trusted on long trips. Ace drove a beater of an old pickup, which had so many different brands of spare parts on it that the make and model of the truck was in question.

Shona came up with the brilliant idea of taking the train from Jamestown to Minneapolis and back. The fare was not cheap and would consume a big chunk of the stipend. However, flying out of Fargo was more than double the train fare. I had planned to share a room with another employee. A room with a double queen would allow Shona to accompany me for a three-day vacation in Minneapolis. All the pieces were falling into place. Shona was thrilled over the possibility of going. We didn't own a single piece of luggage, so I borrowed a nice piece from a co-worker.

Hardly sleeping that night, when it was time to leave Shona and I drove a few blocks and parked under the lighted kiosk beside the track, where the old Jamestown train station once stood. The train arrived at 4:10 a.m. It crawled to a halt, looking like a long dark string of sausage links. Neither of us had actually seen the *Mountain Daylight* before, and hardly knew what to expect. In spite of our excitement, we settled into our seats and promptly went to sleep. We slept most of the way to Minneapolis.

I broke away from the conference, skipping the evening banquet, so Shona could see the town. We hopped on the hotel shuttle for the mall. We were like two little kids on the loose. There was so much to see and do as we checked out the amusement park, shopping, and restaurants.

During dinner, we foolishly discussed moving to the big city. I imagined that I could transfer with my job. Shona didn't think she could leave Jamestown High before her senior year. As we talked, we settled on the fact that Shona didn't want to leave her newly acquired boyfriend, who was Jamestown High's star point guard. She was really taken with this guy, who was also a brilliant artist.

"I think my point guard is going to leave me," Shona said. "He intends to transfer to Cheneau Valley this fall. But I guess I'll just enjoy it while it lasts." Shona sighed and giggled.

I even skipped the last afternoon of the conference so we could see more of the city. By unanimous agreement we headed back to the mall for another few hours of shopping.

We were pretty tired and pushed for time when we caught the hotel shuttle to the Midway Train Station for the return trip. It wasn't a minute too early, as the *Mountain Daylight* had arrived and was ready for boarding. In fact the train was more than ready. There was no one at the boarding gate when we arrived. All the train doors were closed. I had this sick feeling that the train was going to pull out without us. I told Shona to run and get somebody's attention while I followed behind, dragging our suitcase. Shona panicked.

"Are you ladies on this train?" asked a tall, handsome young man in uniform.

The man came out of nowhere. I think he was behind us. He looked at our tickets, checked our ID's and called someone on his phone to verify that our names were on the train's manifest and that no one else had used our names to check in. Then he told us that they had seats available for us. We all stepped on the train and followed him to our assigned seats. He checked our luggage and said he'd give it back to us in Jamestown. We were seated just as the train pulled out of the station.

"Mother! Did you notice that guy that helped us on the train?" Shona asked.

"Honey, I was so out of breath trying to catch up to you, I wouldn't have noticed who anybody was," I answered.

"Mother! He was totally awesome," Shona said.

"Did you get his name?"

"No. I wish I had."

"I think you are spoken for, are you not?" I questioned.

"I still like to window shop," she said.

We were plum exhausted from the hectic afternoon at the mall. We passed on the dinner service and relaxed as we watched the Minnesota landscape race by. We brought a snack back to our seats and soon fell asleep. I was awake when we arrived at Fargo a little after midnight. As we started moving again, I settled back in my seat and began to dose. Shona was asleep, as were most of the other passengers.

At first, I didn't believe it. In the darkened car, illuminated by the tiny aisle lights, I thought I saw the shadow of an animal moving toward me in the aisle. From my reclining position, I stretched my neck to the left, looking down the aisle to see if what I saw was real. The animal kept coming toward me. It was about the size of a house cat. In an instant, it leaped on my lap; it jumped on Shona and for a second looked curiously at her sleeping with her head on a pillow propped up against the window. It wagged its head from side to side as it rested on Shona's lap almost in a hypnotic stance. Just as I was getting ready to whack it with my pillow, it turned, opened its mouth, and grabbed Shona's rubber coin purse that was on the drop-down snack table and ducked under the seat. Shona stirred and mumbled something.

"Shona!" I cried, "A huge weasel creature jumped on your lap and stole your coin purse."

Shona wasn't aware of it. Shona didn't know what I was talking about. I tried to find a crewmember. I walked back, where I found two of the crew kibitzing in the service nook of one of the cars. I was so excited that I started hyperventilating.

"There is some kind of animal in our car. It has my daughter's purse," I said.

They both looked at me like I was nuts or something. I repeated what I saw to them. The name badges they wore read "Trevor" and "Maggie."

"We've had mice on the train," Maggie explained. "They come aboard if the Chicago yard crews leave our doors open when we are parked during the night. Do you think it could have been a mouse that you saw?"

"That must be a pretty big mouse if it took your daughter's purse," Trevor said.

"Oh no!" I said, "It's more the size of a big rat!"

"A rat?" Maggie shuddered. "I don't think we've ever had a rat on the train."

"Does it have a long tail like a rat?" Trevor wanted to know.

"Yes," I said," It has a bushy tail."

"Does a rat have a bushy tail?" Trevor asked, saying he didn't have a clear picture in his mind of what a rat even looked like. "You mean a bushy tail with hair on it?"

"Yes," I said, "and it is shaped more like a weasel than a rat."

"About how big is it?" Trevor asked.

"About two feet in length," I answered.

"Isn't that big for a rat?" Trevor asked.

"No! No!" Maggie said as she took in a deep breath. "It's the Red River Monster! It must have come aboard in Fargo when you guys had the doors open. The Red River flooded Fargo this past spring, and all kinds of weird animals have been seen running around the city."

"Don't be ridiculous, Maggie!" Trevor said.

Trevor accompanied me back to my seat, and with his pocket light he set out to find the Red River Monster that was the size of a cat, in the shape of a weasel, and with the tail of a rat. It was all the evidence he had to go on as he diligently searched for the invader. He didn't have to look long. As he paraded up and down the aisle, looking in each dark corner, the animal ran out from under a seat and headed right for him. It stopped right at Trevor's feet. Trevor reached down with his bare hands and grabbed the animal by the nape of the neck and midsection. The animal bared its fangs but couldn't reach Trevor's hands, which were fastened onto the animal's hide with the tenacity of an eagle gripping its prey. He asked me to come and help him. Trevor took the animal to the nearest exit door, with me following behind. He instructed me to open the top half of the door. The train was moving very fast and the wind about blew me over. Trevor threw that poor, defenseless what-ever-it was animal off the train out into the cruel blackness of the night.

"Well, I guess that takes care of that, whatever it was!" he said as he rubbed the palms of his hands together as if to say, "It's all in a night's work!"

With that episode over, I returned to my seat and tried to settle down for the remaining hour ride to Jamestown. Maggie came and said they would try and find Shona's purse and return it. She confirmed our address, apologized for the inconvenience and left.

Within minutes, a lady wrapped in a blanket was pacing up and down the aisle looking for something. She appeared to be a bit disheveled but I thought she probably had been sleeping. I asked her if anything was wrong. The woman was very distraught.

"I can't find my pet ferret."

"A ferret?" I said. "Oh my gosh! That's what it was." I spoke out loud. "You had a ferret?"

At first we spoke in rather hushed tones, but soon began to attract the attention of some of the other passengers who had noticed Trevor carrying the animal out.

"Did you have it in some sort of cage?" I asked.

"I brought it in a zipped canvas bag," She said, "I'm off at Glendive early this morning and my ferret sleeps most of the time, anyway."

Just then another passenger nosed into the conversation, saying he saw a crewmember carry it out.

"What? Where?" The woman became very excited.

I told her, in a very calm and collected way, that we threw it off the train. I explained how it jumped on my lap, and also on my daughter while she slept. It really startled us. I didn't know what it was. I didn't think I had ever seen a ferret. The woman started to cry.

"How could you throw it off the train? Oh no! My poor baby! *Bandit* was my baby."

The lady demanded to speak to someone. Maggie came and tried to calm her down. Maggie phoned her manager, whose name was Reyna. Reyna talked to the conductor, who came and calmed the lady down. He explained that animals were not allowed on the train unless it was a service animal designated as such on the ticket. The woman became more and more distraught and wanted to talk to Trevor. Trevor was warned not to talk to her. The conductor informed the woman that if she made any further disturbance about it, they might force her off the train in Jamestown. He came and talked to me about it. He said that she shouldn't have been allowed to board the train with it.

Shona was smitten with Trevor when he handed her our bag. He promised to get her purse back. He left before I could tip him.

Trevor Jensen

Reyna was on the eastbound train, trying to work out some problems with the crew. She told Dean she might have to terminate someone and she needed to fire the final shot. If we encountered any problems on our train, Dean was to call Reyna by phone and she would help him resolve it. Likewise, Maggie was to do the same. In theory, Reyna was our omniscient commander. It was a "slam-dunk" for a trouble-free night riding the rails across North Dakota.

I was looking for some fresh coffee when I found Maggie just as this lady, Sunny, approached us about the ferret. I guess it was her daughter sitting by the window. Earlier this evening, we were getting ready to leave when I helped Sunny and her daughter on the train. I'm glad that girl didn't miss our train. She is one hot dame. I wonder how old she is? As soon as it was daylight, I planned to search that car and find her purse. I would like to deliver it to her personally. Dean said I'd better wait until Lola Hollingsworth, the lady whose ferret I killed, got off in Glendive. She had it in for me.

When we arrived in Bismarck, Reyna was there waiting. She got off Number 1126 and waited in Bismarck for our train going west. Oh boy! Reyna was not a happy camper. Apparently she had already had her fuse lit on the eastbound train. It was about to blow when she saw me. Until now, I had withheld judgment about Reyna being the bad-tempered woman I thought she might be, given the right circumstances. Tonight, however, she earned the distinction of being the bitch goddess. We had completely mishandled the incident involving the pet ferret. She said that we all had forgotten our training and professionalism as outlined in the PR manual. The modus operandi we followed was seriously flawed.

"In the first place," Reyna said, "how could the ferret be smuggled aboard the train if you guys had done your job in checking the contents of the carryon?"

Reyna continued on, saying the crew had to be particularly thorough in the Cities. They always tried to bring contraband on the train in St. Paul.

Reyna lit into Maggie for taking it on without involving the conductor at the start of the crisis. Reyna wanted to know why Dean wasn't involved. Dean said I didn't tell him about it.

"Did you happen to realize that sneaking a wild animal on the train was grounds for being expelled at the next stop?" she asked.

Dean said the animal could have been caught and put in with the luggage, where there was a small portable cage to hold the animal until the outcome was determined.

"What if she refused and didn't cooperate?" Maggie asked.

"Then it was a law-enforcement issue," Reyna snapped.

Reyna looked right at me.

"If you don't know what to do in any situation, how do you find out?"

"I guess I could ask someone," I said.

"And what if they didn't know?"

"Look it up in the PR manual," Dean interrupted.

Next, she lit into me about picking up the animal with my bare hands.

"If you had been bitten," Reyna stopped and changed the statement into a question. "Were you bitten by the animal?"

"No, it didn't bite me but it sure tried," I said.

"Any animal bite would need a rabies follow-up, Trevor. It could be a serious medical issue. How would they check the animal for rabies if they didn't have the animal?"

In the end, it was a learning experience for everyone. Lola Hollingsworth left the train in Glendive threatening to sue. When I arrived back in Seattle, dad met me at the gate.

"Did anything interesting happen on this trip, Trevor?" he asked.

"Dad, I think I need a lawyer!" I said.

"What in the world for?"

"Some lady in Montana is going to sue me!"

"Why?" dad asked.

"I killed her ferret."

Team Effort

Travis Olsen

Today is Sunday, September seventh and my eighteenth birthday. I had a good sleep. No bad dreams. I really spooked
my psychic grandma when I told her about one of my dreams
a while back. I would not do that again. In my dream, I didn't
know if it was day or night. There was no wind but lots of water.
I couldn't cross the water because it was big, like the ocean.
Actually, I've never seen the ocean, but I think I might have been
at the ocean's edge. I heard Laser barking in the distance but I
couldn't see him. My teacher was crying, or at least she was very
sorrowful. I smelled fumes that were drifting towards me. I tried
to run but I couldn't. Some people were water-skiing farther out.
I couldn't reach them. It was weird.

My Granny is more into the out-of-body experiences. I am the
opposite; totally physical focused. I'm not moved by the psychic
phenomenon like Granny. I don't know where she gets it. My
dad is not akin to it, either.

"Dreams are honest expressions of the body and spirit,"
Granny told me.

I wanted to know what it all meant. Granny thought my dream
could be a foreboding of something bad in my future. Granny

said dreams by themselves were not precognitive, but rather a reflection of the inner feelings, fears and anxieties. If we believed something would happen, then it might happen, she explained. She thought this dream carried several messages. The fact that I heard Laser bark but didn't see him was expressing a fear of losing what was familiar to me. The teacher was crying because I failed to realize the goals that she was hoping I would achieve. The fumes that came towards me were due to a fear of catastrophe. My inability to run from the fumes indicated a fear of losing control over situations that came in my life. Granny's interpretation was as weird as the dream itself. Today, on my birthday, my experiences were in the physical realm.

"Good morning. Happy birthday," Terri said.

My little sister is the singer. She sang happy birthday to me. She has a beautiful voice. The rest of us can't sing. Tanner and I are completely tone deaf.

"Travis, what is so great about being eighteen?" Terri asked.

"Now that I'm eighteen? All opportunities are open to me. I can do anything!"

"Travis?" Dad interrupted. "You can't do anything you want as long as you live in this house."

Okay! I guess Dad made his point abundantly clear. Tanner sat there at the table and gulped down his sticky bun. So far he had ignored me. Suddenly, Tanner moved away from the table and came around to where I was sitting; Tanner gave me a one-armed hug. Tanner was holding his second sticky bun with the other hand. As I pulled him over, Tanner lost his balance and drizzled the gooey icing down his white T-shirt. That kid is so messy. He is a bit like Laser; he can't keep himself clean.

After breakfast, dad and I walked the soybean fields. It was our next and last big harvesting project of the year. If my predictions were right, they would be ready to harvest in two weeks. Dad disagreed. With the leaves gone from the plants, we still had to wait for the pods to mature. The lower pods were ready but the upper pods needed more time. Most of the upper pods were already starting to turn. I say, two more weeks if the weather cooperates. No more rain, please.

Today is perfect for a birthday barbeque and basketball practice. The weather around here can change in a minute, but hopefully it will stay calm throughout the afternoon. I've a short guest list for the party today. I put in a request for mom to cool it for the company this afternoon. I want to practice with Brad, Aaron, Joey and Kyle. I need more time to acquaint myself with Joey and Kyle. This would be our first time playing together. We're the starters on this year's varsity team. We're it. If Coach Epperson wants to pull out a "W" each game, we have the cards. Play us or the team doesn't win. Coach may have other ideas. He'll want to play the other kids, too. The other guys are all milk-drinking puppies when it comes to the game of basketball. When we walk out of here next spring, the Dakota Eastern Division will walk all over the guys we have left behind on the team. This year we will put Chencau Valley on the map. All the sportswriters will be talking about us.

Aaron will need to move up to first string. We have to get along and play together. I told him that the other day. I told him that when these two new guys joined the team, we couldn't be fighting each other. We had to play as one team and put our egos and differences aside. He agreed.

I asked Aaron what it was that I did last year that ticked him off all the time. He said I excluded him and wouldn't chill out with him. On the team trips, he told me that I ignored him and didn't talk to him. I didn't treat him like he was a useful part of the team. He said the other guys also felt that way about me. They said that I monopolized Brad, and the two of us were good buddies, but not with the rest of the team. The team felt that they had to constantly pass the ball to Brad or me so we could score.

They executed the plays, but we made the points. Oh man. He went on and on about me. So finally I told him to stop and not go there anymore.

I wanted to tell him a few things, too, like how he almost killed me driving his dad's grain truck last summer. He was so obnoxious with that air horn when he came fully loaded, busting down those township roads. I was sure he was going to kill himself or somebody else the way he drove through those intersections. He will be eighteen in a couple more weeks. You aren't allowed to drive those trucks unless you are eighteen. Dad never let me drive his grain truck, even when he was along. For the sake of the team, I chose to bury the hatchet.

"Let's put all that behind us and see what we have now," I said. "Look, Aaron. You are a good player. You have strength. You're good at screens, guarding and rebounds. You are as good as any of us. You are not a good ballhandler and you're not an accurate shooter. You've got to get away from trying that jump hook and do what you can do, and let what you can't do be done by someone else. We can't have a championship team if everybody tries to be everything. Shooting is not your game. I'm good under the key. I'm not that good playing on the outside. If you can get the ball into me, I'll score. I'm good defensively, on rebounds, and guarding my opponent."

It was unfortunate that Coach Epperson couldn't come today because of the rules. Basketball practice didn't start officially until November and his presence today could be misconstrued as a preseason practice. I did invite him, but he declined. He told me that if he came we couldn't play basketball. I told him my birthday barbeque is all about basketball. I suggested that he remain in the house with the adults and watch us play from the window. I guaranteed that he would be impressed. The coach is too hung up on rules and policies. He says that because Kyle and Joey transferred from Jamestown and Taylor, the whole state is watching him. Jamestown and Taylor are upset because we have their players. Just you wait. We'll give them something to get upset about.

It's so stupid and darn funny. People are such idiots. My Granny. She comes over to the house one day and out of the blue she wants to know if I had anything to do with Kyle and Joey transferring to Cheneau Valley High. Of course I didn't. It was the great white basketball spirit that brought us together for this last great hunt and ceremonial rendezvous so we can all three ride together over the great divide into the sunset. It was a force greater than me, I told her; once it started, I couldn't stop it. She wasn't real pleased with that answer, so I just let it cook on her burner for a while.

I like to go up to the Buffalo Mall in Jamestown, where I can always meet up with some other kids, take in a movie, and just hang out. People recognize me up there and they come around and talk.

"Aren't you Travis Olsen from Cheneau Valley High?" they ask.

"You bet I am!" I answer. "I'm Travis Olsen. *The* Travis Olsen!"

One night, I was up with my folks in Jamestown having dinner at Aunt Betty's. I got bored, so I left and drove over to the mall just to see who was there. I wanted to do some shopping. I walked by the theater just as the movie finished. I pushed my way through the crowd, disgusted that I even had to tolerate it. I bumped right into Kyle. This little weasel came up to me, didn't say a word, and we did a chest bump. I knew who he was. I had played against that little wimp a time or two.

"Too bad we kicked your ass so bad last season. Do you guys down there have anything different up your sleeve for next year, or are you just going to take the ball away from me and throw it back out to O'Connor and hope he makes his one out of three from the outside?"

I took a deep breath as I looked down at him. He had an evil little smirk on his pimply little face. I didn't know what to say to counteract his insults, which turned me into a bad-tempered German Rottie. I didn't know if I should poo on him first, then stifle him, tear him into pieces or leave him intact after I knocked him flat. He stood there like a stubby-nosed Pekingese talking out his back end with that tail of hair flopping from side to side. So I challenged him to move to Cheneau Valley, where he could find out for himself what I had up my sleeve.

"Are you serious?" he asked.

"Serious."

"I might just do that," he answered. "I can use my old lady's address down there and still live in Jamestown with pops."

I gave him my cell number.

"Call me anytime," I said.

So he did. He was fed up with everybody at Jamestown. Nobody could play with him. His center couldn't articulate with him and instead of the coach hitting on the other players to improve, the coach was blaming Kyle for their messed-up plays.

Then he called me one day to set up a lunch appointment with Joey Carlson. Until Kyle told me, I never even heard of Joey Carlson. Joey played a mean game of basketball. How could such a little place like Taylor have a guy like Joey playing on their team and I not know about it? Kyle took me out to meet Joey at the elevator where Joey worked for his dad. We ate lunch with him. Joey's dad was moving into Jamestown and Joey wanted to stay at Taylor, but he didn't have a place to live out there, so he planned on transferring to Jamestown his senior year. Kyle wanted Joey to transfer to Jamestown, but we discussed other possibilities. I don't discuss publicly what we talked about. Joey's mom lived in Cheneau Valley. You figure it out.

So today, after everybody arrived for my birthday barbeque, we all went into a huddle and started discussing girls, hoops, and farming, in that order. My sister, given to flirting, courted triflingly with Joey, who brushed her off like a fly. Whenever we were on the subject of farming, Kyle tried to change the subject. This guy doesn't know beans from a haystack when it comes to agriculture. We sat patiently and listened to Aaron brag about their corn crop and how much of it was selling at a premium for ethanol production. The shortage of corn used for feed was going to drive prices higher. This year's crop was the best he'd ever seen. Joey was more laid back and slower to speak. He was thoughtful with his answers and always grabbed his chin with his right hand, rubbing his beard with the index finger before he spoke. Joey has more farming packed into his head than most people I know around here. Tanner tried to wedge into the group, like the family pet that wasn't needed or wanted. I told him to come over and sit down on the floor by me. I gave him a flat-handed swat on the top of his head. After that he knew the proper pecking order in the pack. It was a token of my approval. He was a good little brother and he worshiped me.

Mom was doing her slow-cooked beef in barbeque sauce, served open-faced on a bun. I also ordered mom's homemade fries. I ordered Granny's chocolate sheet cake with the chocolate icing. Dad was making homemade ice cream.

The other thing I ordered, which I'm not getting, was some beer to have with my friends. Dad said no beer. Aaron brought over a couple of six-packs, which he left in his pickup. I tried to get dad to let us drink at least two beers on my birthday. Dad agreed to the beer, but only if it were non-alcoholic. That stupid Aaron; while I was inside trying to convince dad to let us drink Aaron's beer, Aaron goes and gets it and pops one open for himself. Dad wouldn't let him drink it, so Aaron put it back in his pickup.

We dropped that subject and hit the half court and did some serious shooting. Kyle stood up there with Brad and the two of them dumped in one three-pointer after another.

"What's your scoring average?" I asked.

"I'm about forty-five percent from the three-point arc and seventy-five percent from the line," Kyle said.

"Let's try some alley-oop plays," I said as I positioned myself under the basket.

Kyle passed to me and I slammed them in. We were great together. Joey was a good shooter and a solid player. He pumped them in from the outside and from the line.

During games, Brad often scored in double digits. Kyle immediately got the picture as to why you hand the ball back out to Brad if you can't get it up. Aaron tried to impress us with his performance under the key. He did several slam-dunks. He was very good. That guy is putting out. He needed to swallow his pride and serve up more assists. However, compared to the rest of us, Aaron's shooting skills looked pathetic. Aaron's strength was defense and rebounding. Last season Aaron was good offensively at drawing fouls, but defensively often found him in foul trouble. I seldom fouled out. A good player never wants to be benched. More than once last season, Aaron had expressed his displeasure at being benched so he could be my backup while I rested during the third quarter. Aaron's pride didn't like to take second place. I was the same.

Trevor Jensen

It was still dark this morning before we reached Glendive, when they let me hit the sack. I was so wasted. I didn't know about the commotion I caused in Forsyth this morning when we stopped there at 8 a.m. We were almost to Livingston, Montana, when I woke up and saw a note on the floor of my room instructing me to contact Jiggs about a package that was put on the train for me at Forsyth. He is so officious, this guy Jiggs. He's working toward becoming an assistant manager and has been doing a two-week stint working with the baggage crews. He hated the computer program we used. The guys said it took him a long time to learn it. So far I've avoided him. I was puzzled about his message, so I called him right away on his phone.

"Trevor!" he began, "what's the idea here of arranging with this woman to deliver a package to you? It would have been polite to inform me in advance. We're not supposed to take packages unless it is from a ticketed passenger who is on board the train. We don't want to get ourselves blown up here."

"Could I say something, please?" I asked.

"Yes. Please explain," Jiggs insisted.

"I don't know what you are talking about. I was not expecting a package from anybody anywhere," I said.

"Who then, is Mona Rosenthal?" Jiggs asked. "Someone must know her, she knew you were on this morning's train!"

"*Mona Rosenthal*!" I exclaimed. "Is that who brought it?"

Apparently the train was delayed a few minutes while they called the Command Center for advice. The Command Center told Jiggs to accept it after they talked to Rudy. Jiggs demanded that I come up and get the package. Jiggs said Mona told them it belonged to me. They opened it before they would take it from her. I told Jiggs I just woke up and wasn't very together. He brought it to me.

"How did you lose this in Forsyth?" Jiggs said as he handed me the package.

He shut the door and left. Inside the envelope was my brass guitar belt buckle. There was also a picture of Jamie holding a guitar. He looked horrible. He didn't look anything like when I carried him off the train. There was a note.

Dear Trevor,

I'm so sorry to not have contacted you sooner. I have been overwhelmed the past few weeks. We lost our Jamie on August tenth.

He died peacefully in Billings. He wore your buckle on his belt. When he would rally, which he did off and on for several days, he would reach for the buckle to make sure it was still there. He felt your presence with him clear to the end. I am returning the buckle for you to keep in memory of Jamie. You brought him so much happiness the last few weeks of his life. It was all he talked about. We spent the money you gave him on a child's guitar. He was too sick for lessons but he strummed on it by the hour. A man in town came and played it for him a few times. I want to thank you for your enormous generosity.

Gratefully,
Mona Rosenthal

I had wanted to contact Jamie one more time. I had completely forgotten. The letter caused the tears to flow. For a few seconds I thought I was seriously going to cry. I can't even remember the last time I cried. I begged myself not to do it now. I sat on the edge of the bunk until I got hold of my emotions. Regrets filled my head. How could I be so wrapped up with work and my own life to forget about Jamie? I'm not into writing letters or sending cards. If I'd known he was in Billings, I could have done a turnaround there and visited him. Reyna always wanted us to do that from time to time. I really could have done it. We all knew he was sick and wasn't going to make it. I knew it was over for Jamie. I guess maybe I didn't want to face it. Subconsciously, I didn't want to see him on his deathbed. Maybe that's it. I hate regrets. I was so tormented.

Wren was in Chicago. I hadn't seen her in a while. I left her a message that Jamie had died. I hated to do it through a message. I called Reyna. Dean was on vacation. I called home and talked to mom. Dad was busy so I told her not to bother him.

"Bless his heart," she said. "Bless his little heart!"

I tried to think who else was on the train that knew him. There wasn't anybody. I was alone with this sadness the rest of the way to Seattle. I wore the guitar buckle. I was glad to have it back. I took my guitar and sang "Snoqualmie Pass." I sang it quietly for Jamie. I could see him singing as I strummed out the melody.

Up, on a Pass in Kittitas County, A young man on his horse takes a high country ride. Up a trail that is rocky, with hanging vine maples, and hemlocks so wide.
The gentian is quiet. The stillness is heard. The creek still laughing, but can't say a word. The woodpecker no tapping. The thrush has no song. The cones, they fall silent. The squirrel sees no wrong. The scat of the black bear is seen on the trail.
The tracks of the coon where no people prevail.

Snoqualmie! I love you. People of the Moon. No longer you live here. You all died too soon. I never did meet you. I never could say. This place that you left me. I cherish today.

Up, on a Pass in Kittitas County, A young man on his horse takes a high country ride. Up a trail that is rocky, with violets so blue, chipmunks that chatter and hide. The freeway cuts through it with thousands of cars. Closed in by the traffic, a jail without bars. As I climb towards the sky, I'm free from all that. The trail, it gets steeper, hang on to your hat. Climbing higher, away from machines, Mr. Jed doesn't whinny. I'm lost in my dreams.

Snoqualmie! I love you. People of the Moon. No longer you live here. You all died too soon. I never did meet you. I never could say. This place that you left me. I cherish today.

Up, on a Pass In Kittitas County, A young man on his horse takes a high country ride. Up a trail that is rocky, with both legs astride, chickadees call as my guide.

BRIDGE *Over the* VALLEY

Down gentle comes the rain. Like tears shed from the sky. The wetness softens even me, a guy who hates to cry. I come in winter for the snow. The dangers then I even know. In an avalanche be carried. Down the mountain 'til you're buried.
Lost forever, never found. The snow protects you from the ground. Mother Nature's children are, from her bosom never far.

Snoqualmie! I love you. People of the Moon. No longer you live here. You all died too soon. I never did meet you. I never could say. This place that you left me. I cherish today.

As we wound around the foothills climbing up Bozeman Pass, I looked out to the south, where there was a cross-stitch of craggy mountains towering in the distance. They stood there like an impenetrable wall protecting the vast wilderness behind it. The granite peaks were already snow-covered. What is it about a mountain that makes a person feel so weak and small?

[Later that same autumn]

The scene was somber and the weather was foul. The date was October twenty-seventh, my nineteenth birthday. I had just spent a hectic night working the eastbound train, which was running three hours behind schedule. The trouble started in Spokane, where it was snowing lightly and freezing cold. The platform was slick and when I stepped off the train I fell, spraining my wrist. At Spokane, the locomotive had mechanical problems that took almost two hours to fix. When the train did get out of Spokane at 5:30 a.m., a passenger in one of the coaches became sicker than a dog and thought she needed some nitroglycerin for her chest pain. She didn't have it in her purse, so she asked for her checked bag. It took forever to dig it out of the bottom of the Chicago bin, where it was buried. No nitroglycerin was found,

146

and she finally remembered that her medicine bag had been left at home. The train stopped at a place called Post Falls, where we waited for an ambulance to come and take her off. When the ambulance couldn't get to where the train was parked, the railroad had to get special track authority to back the train up to where the ambulance could get access to the train. The backup maneuver caused a snafu with the local dispatchers trying to keep the heavily traveled freight line moving.

The cold was damp and penetrating when Dean and I comlpeted the night's work in Sandpoint, an hour and a half north of Spokane. When Jack, the on-duty train manager, left the train in Sandpoint, he told me that we came pretty close to being on the "Train from Hell." He hoped we would have better luck on the rest of the trip east.

I had just finished icing my wrist when Dean came to wrap it with some athletic wrap he had obtained from the first-aid box. Dean didn't mention my birthday. I was pretty sure Dean would remember it was my birthday if he'd had a chance to think about it. Dean said nothing. I was in a glum mood, staring out the window and watching the train kick up some of the snow that had fallen during the night. So far, the only recognition that I was born today had come from dad in a text message. Birthdays were always a big celebration at home. As a kid, I lived in anticipation of my birthday for months. There was a certain loneliness about being stuck on a very late train with a sore hand on my birthday. I had decided that I wouldn't mention my birthday to anybody. As we all sat around the dinette having breakfast, I didn't say a word about it. No one else did, either. I crawled into my bunk without a single birthday wish. By the time I awoke later in the day, it would be nearly dark and my birthday would be over. I lay in my bunk, cuddled up with my disappointment and soon fell asleep as the train pushed its way along the Clark Fork River further into Montana.

I woke up suddenly. I needed to use the restroom. It was a minor inconvenience to pull on my jeans. I skipped the jeans. It was urgent. I wrapped myself in a bath towel. The first bathroom was locked. As a matter of fact, it was intentionally locked. I tried the second bathroom. I opened the door. It was packed to the brim with birthday balloons. On the verge of losing control of my bladder with the excitement, I desperately tried to remove as many balloons out of the stall as possible so I could squeeze enough of me in to relieve myself. My bath towel fell off as I frantically tried to squeeze myself inside. "Pop! Pop! Pop!" There still wasn't enough room for me amongst all the balloons as I tried to stand facing the toilet. I couldn't get the door closed. "Pop! Pop!" The popping continued as if a new star was being born in the cosmos. This was like a bugle calling for the troops to assemble, ready to wish me happy birthday. The troops watched me emerge from the restroom. As I stepped out towel-less, they were there pointing their cameras right at me. They escorted me out to where they sang happy birthday, snapping pictures of me standing there in my boxers. The cooks had made a big cake for me and stored it in the refrigerator. From then on, it was one continual celebration. I received the funniest cards and a burst of emails from the crew. It started off slow, but my first birthday on the train was one of the best birthdays I ever had.

Coach Rodger Epperson

My dream team had turned into a nightmare. Travis, Kyle, Joey, Brad and Aaron had become a clique on the court and were not playing as a team with the others. It was clear that a wide gap in ability separated the starting five from the other kids. The atmosphere among the other players had turned sour. I knew I had to play the other kids as well as the starting five. I tried making it as competitive as possible by splitting up the five into competing groups with the others for scrimmage and drills.

Kyle was terrific at the fast break and he worked well with Travis. The two were doing great. Unfortunately, the other kids didn't play well with Kyle. They didn't anticipate his moves. They did if it was a cookie-cutter play. If Kyle changed direction suddenly, they didn't. Travis, Kyle, Brad, Joey, and Aaron had played together all fall out at the Olsen's half court. The other players weren't involved in those practice sessions. When they all practiced together in the school gym they didn't mesh with each other. It was going to take a lot of work to get the team together.

Another issue erupted concerning Kyle's eligibility. Originally, he said that his mother had custody. If that was the case, then his transfer to Cheneau Valley from Jamestown was allowed under the bylaws of the High School Athletic Association. Unfortunately, word circulated that Guy had custody. As far as Kyle was concerned, it didn't matter who had custody. He had always lived with his dad, but now he was living with mom. He flipped it off as being unimportant, but it was Guy who had custody. That made Kyle subject to the one-hundred-eighty-day rule in transferring to a second school, in accordance with the eligibility rules that applied to high school athletes. If enforced, he couldn't play at the new school until he had attended classes there for one hundred eighty days, the equivalent of one school year. Since he was a senior, his high school basketball career was over unless Guy also moved to Cheneau Valley. The only way to resolve it was for Guy to share custody with Sharon, something he did not want to do. That way, Kyle's eligibility would not be questioned and he was free to transfer once during his four years in school as long as he lived with a parent who had custody. It was messy, and the last thing we needed at the start of the season was for our school to get caught with an ineligible player. If Kyle was ruled ineligible, he was finished. This became a nail-biter, and I didn't know from one day to the next whether Kyle was on the team or not.

About five days into practice, Travis and Aaron had a disagreement that ended in a pushing match between the two of them. Some said it was Travis who started it over a comment about a girl they had both dated. Travis didn't want Aaron's "sloppy seconds." It started first as an exchange of innuendoes back and forth but progressed to where Travis pushed Aaron away when he confronted him in the locker room. I never saw it, but I heard about it later.

I could see that Travis had a mean side to him. It was a flaw in his character. It was okay for Travis to show this rapacious side under the basket, grabbing offensive rebounds, but not with his own teammates off the playing floor. Aaron had resented Travis the year before, but I chalked it up to jealously. Aaron's game wasn't up to speed. Beyond that, there hadn't been trouble between the two of them. They kept apart and didn't hang out together. This recent event was very troubling; I couldn't tolerate such incorrigibility among the players. Joey and Brad were both saints. Joey's transfer from Taylor High was clean. Lana had dual custody. Besides, Joey's dad had changed his residence, opening the door for Joey to transfer to a different school of his own choosing.

I went to work rebuilding my dream team. Although I had my opinion, I stayed neutral as I attempted to settle the rivalry between Travis and Aaron. I first talked to Travis.

"Did you push Aaron in the locker room after practice Monday?" I asked.

I looked directly at Travis as I spoke, trying to detect any guilt. Travis evaded the question and began to justify his actions. "Just answer me yes or no." I demanded. "I'm not interested as to why you did it, only if you did."

Travis acknowledged that he did push Aaron first. Aaron pushed him back and he retaliated with a harder push that knocked Aaron across the bench, although Aaron caught himself and didn't fall. Nothing happened after that, Travis claimed. Travis again tried to tell his side of the story but I refused to listen.

"What would happen if you were groin-jabbed by your opponent in regulation play and you pushed the offender?" Travis looked down as I spoke.

"They'd kick my ass off the court. I'd be benched for the remainder of the game and draw a technical foul." Travis hung his head as he answered.

"Did you ever get elbowed last year where it really hurts?" I continued the questioning.

"Yeah, that guy from Senior did it a couple of times last year," Travis admitted. "They tried to block the offensive rebounds I made."

"Did you ever hit him?" I asked.

"No." Travis said. "You talked to his coach, who benched him."

"If you aren't allowed to strike out at an opponent, Travis, why do you think it is okay to push your brother? Aaron is on your team. This conference is too big for you. You aren't going to win that way. Everyone looks up to you. You just set a terrible example. Aaron is going to protect you when you are in the key so those groin jabs don't happen. He'll also be the one that sets the screen for you, allowing you to score. You need him. He is on your team. Think seriously about what you did."

Travis apologized and said he was sorry.

Aaron was repentant when I talked with him, saying he didn't know why Travis reacted with such hostility to what was said. Aaron said Travis had been very temperamental about everything. When Aaron walked out of the room, I picked up the phone and called David Olsen. I asked David to talk to Travis about his attitude toward Aaron and the other team members. David agreed to try. That night, David followed Travis upstairs. They went into his bedroom and talked. They talked late into the night. Later, when David talked to me about it he said Travis needed an attitude adjustment. David said he laid all the cards out on the table and some of them were not pretty. David's a good man and I know he'll work hard with Travis. David is going to get some other parents involved and host a dinner for the entire team at their farm.

In the first basketball game of the season, the Bridgers had to duke it out with Jamestown. It was a non-conference game because Jamestown had just been moved to the Western Division. It was an important game nonetheless, as this was the first time Kyle had to face the Jamestown teammates that he had deserted. It was a hard-fought win for the Cheneau Valley Bridgers. It was standing-room-only in the Jamestown High gym to see Cheneau Valley outscore Jamestown 56 to 50. It was Travis who won the game. Jamestown threw its entire defense at Kyle, stopping his fast breaks and guarding him heavy from the three-point arc. When he could he passed inside to Travis, who scored again and again and again. Other than when Aaron fouled out, I stuck to my first string in order to win the game.

Overall, aside from a few mistakes, I was very pleased with how things played out. Back in the locker room, I ballyhooed the victory.

"We won this game playing four guys! Kyle," I said as I put my arm on his shoulder, "we also won by what you didn't do. You didn't get flustered and turn the ball over like they thought you might. Between Brad and Travis, you made fourteen assists and seventy percent of your free throws. Good job! Just think what we can do next week with five guys!" Soon the conversation changed to lighter subjects.

"Hey Kyle!" Travis teased, "Was that your girl yelling for Jamestown?"

"Yeah, I heard her, too," Kyle said. "She was sitting in their cheering section. She goes to school here. She's still mad at me for leaving."

"Aren't you going to dump her?" Travis asked.

"Naw! I like her that way. She's no wimp," Kyle insisted.

"Any time you can't handle her disrespect, I'll try her." Joey added to the comments.

In future practices, the team worked out their offensive strategies for penetrating whatever defensive strategy the opponents would throw at them. Without exception, the strongest play was for Kyle to break the screen, go for the key and then pass to someone on the side that was open. It was obvious from their first game that the two top magnets that drew the opponent's defenders were Kyle and Travis, Cheneau Valley's top scorers.

Kyle was the type of player who knew where his teammates were on the court the instant he took possession of the ball. Therefore, he was able to think on his feet and make good decisions. This helped him execute the plays. Something strange happened to Kyle when he took hold of a basketball. He changed from being an artist with a paintbrush into a top athlete. Travis and Aaron did their best in practice to draw an offensive foul off of Kyle's fast breaks. They seldom could. He was masterful at darting around them and scoring. When Kyle saw that the bucket was open, he dribbled his way into the key on all four cylinders. Without dispute, he was an impressive ballhandler.

Joey and Aaron were good at setting screens. Joey was eighty percent from the free throw line but he was seldom fouled. His shooting from outside was about fifty percent. It would be higher, but he concentrated too long and his shots were frequently blocked. Defensively, Joey was a strong player.

Aaron was becoming a team player. I continually stressed the importance of scoring, but not at the expense of the other players. Aaron made some nice assists in practice.

Next was strategy number two, where they played the shot clock down, if necessary, in order to penetrate the opponent's defense. Kyle would do the pick-and-roll to get an opening for

Travis, Brad, or Joey. Kyle would signal to the person he would roll to. If they didn't score, Travis rebounded; they brought the ball out and started over. Aaron was always to be there for the rebound or to tip in shots that Travis missed. In the event that Kyle passed to Brad or Joey, Travis was always under the basket for an offensive rebound. Aaron's road to glory was to tip in shots that Travis missed.

I pigeonholed everyone into one slot. I didn't let them choose where on the floor they wanted to play. When they messed up, it was easy to recognize and correct the mistake. When they took a bad shot, I made an issue of it. There was no reason to throw the ball away. We practiced and drilled the same plays over and over again. Travis told me he never thought basketball could become boring, but it had. Everyone could learn it, and learn it they did.

I appointed Kyle as the team captain. It was his role to decide what offensive play was to be made. His eligibility was finally resolved before the conference season started. He found himself in the principal's office more than once before things got cleared up, but it finally happened. After a bitter argument with Kyle, Guy finally agreed to share custody and had his lawyer amend the original divorce papers. Jamestown gave it a wink and nod but they weren't happy when Kyle showed up in Jamestown with his girl at their school events. They also knew he was driving back to Jamestown and pretty much staying with his dad most of the time. Guy wouldn't let him on the roads during bad weather, so by the time basketball season arrived in November, he was living with Sharon full time.

Winter Hoops
[Westbound, late January]

Trevor Jensen

Tim was the conductor on duty out of Fargo. His shift finished in Glendive, Montana. Along with the engineers, he knew every inch of track across North Dakota.

On some trips across the state, he wasn't always optimistic. Tonight was no exception. There was a high-wind advisory, blowing and drifting snow was possible and highway travel was not advised anywhere in the state due to the dangerous wind chill. We had a frozen switch and report of possible broken rails ahead. Depending on the wind, Tim said the engineers might decide to park the train before crossing over Cheneau Valley on the Dakota High Bridge. They don't like to cross if there are wind gusts of forty-five mph or higher. Those were the major concerns on Tim's list for this trip. He laughed it off, saying the track bulletin for tonight's journey was typical for this location on the continent in January.

Tim told us the frozen switch was at the West Fargo junction, where we diverged off to connect up with the lower line to Bismarck. A special road crew had been dispatched to fix it, but there would be more delays.

It had already been quite a night. A few hours earlier, east of Willmar, a 15-year-old kid ran into our train with his snowmobile. He survived without serious injury. He bailed just on impact. That delayed us two hours. Fortunately Reyna was aboard tonight. She intervened and refused to hand the kid over to authorities. We took him onboard with us because it was so cold outside. It got pretty interesting there for a while. She was afraid they wouldn't take him to the hospital right away because he didn't appear to be hurt. When they couldn't get an ambulance to where we were because of the icy roads, Reyna convinced the Command Center and the railroad investigator in Willmar to bring him there on the train. When we got to Willmar the paramedics came and took him to the hospital. I don't think there was a thing wrong with him other than being scared half to death. Man! Some of these Swedes they breed here are tough!

We sat at West Fargo for another hour until the road crew fixed the switch so the dispatch center could open it, allowing the train to travel a couple or so miles across to the lower line. As if that wasn't bad enough, I lost my pants in a poker game while we waited. Dean really cleaned me out. From this time forward, I would always hate this section of track and any mention of West Fargo. I was beat that badly.

It was 5 a.m. when the *Mountain Daylight* finally accelerated to track speed on the Jamestown Subdivision, taking us on our route west. The day crew was stirring and didn't believe we had just left Fargo. I asked Reyna if I could switch over to the day crew. She answered me with a silent glare. I was just kidding, but it looked tempting.

"You need some sleep, Trevor," Reyna said as she left the crew quarters to take a nap in a vacant room in the first-class section. "You guys can hit the sack after Jamestown. The day crew can handle Bismarck."

Once we left West Fargo we started going. I mean like going fast!

"Are we traveling at track speed through this blizzard?" I was nervous as I talked to Tim, who had just come back for some coffee. He looked nervous as he shuffled through all the train bulletins and orders.

"We are," Tim confirmed.

"The engineers can't see ahead, can they?"

"I don't think they can see five feet in front of the train," Tim said.

"How can we go this fast when they can't see ahead?" I asked.

"As long as they can see the signals as we pass we are good to go, my friend. So far they are all green. After we passed that container freight at Casselton, we were clear all the way into Jamestown."

"We could kill somebody tonight," I said.

"We sure could, if they get in our way. Trevor, you need to think of it differently. Trains don't kill people. People kill themselves when they don't keep off the tracks."

"Do the engineers know where we are?"

"Hope so!" Tim chuckled. "Engineers are paid to know where they are, but tonight it is more by feel than by sight!"

"Do the dispatchers know where we are at in this blizzard?" I asked.

"Nope!" Tim answered. "They only see a blank screen for this territory. This is 'poor man's CTC' territory. They know only from what we tell them. We are on Track Warrant Control on this subdivision. We follow our train orders and watch the signals. They respond to our movements."

"So what's your greatest fear on a night like this? Getting blizzard-bound?"

"Nope. We'll turn those snowdrifts into powdered sugar. We can plow through three-foot drifts. I have only one worry when I'm working this train or any train summer or winter," Tim continued. "I hope that no one falls asleep while they are oper-ating their train, or gets distracted and runs past a red signal, hitting us head on."

"That would do us in?" I asked.

"We won't survive a head-on collision going this speed, if another train hits us."

"So where's the safest place to be in a head-on collision?"

"There isn't a safe place, but the further from impact, the better."

"So we're all dead if we're asleep in the front dorm?"

"You'd be mincemeat!"

"We would survive a derailment, but there would be mass casualties in any kind of head-on collision," Tim confirmed.

"Is that why the first-class sleeping cars are on the rear of the train, because they also pay more for their safety?"

"No! We could be stopped on the main and have someone pile into us from behind. Each train has to watch the signals on their route and obey them."

"But head-on collisions never happen, do they?" I asked.

"It happens, my friend, but not that often," Tim replied.

Just as we spoke, the train lurched forward suddenly, then backwards. Then it did it again, and a third time.

"Relax, Trevor," Dean laughed, "it's just snowdrifts."

Everyone was tickled to death over my anxiety.

"How many crossing accidents have you seen?" I asked.

Tim didn't respond to my question because he was listen-ing to the engineers on his radio. They reported that the impact felt throughout the train had been caused by furrows of snow deposited by snowplows clearing the streets. We had just passed through a small town that had three crossings. Tim refocused his attention on answering my questions.

"Figure we have any further delays ahead?" I inquired, not really wanting to know Tim's true feelings about the current situ-ation.

"So far so good," Tim said, "I don't have any negatives from the dispatcher on the High Bridge."

Tim went on to explain that the railroad had been really picky about sending trains across those long, high bridges during gale-force winds.

"After they put all those containers in the lake, twenty miles to the north of where we are now, management started getting real picky. That bridge to the north carries wind sensors that sort of tell us what the wind is doing in Cheneau Valley."

I was awakened after a few hours of sleep by the sound of hail pelting the train. We had traveled three hundred eighty miles from Fargo. I looked out the window of my room just in time to see an impressive statue of a man standing atop a hill on the west end of Wibaux, Montana, eight miles from the North Dakota border. It was the statue of a nineteenth-century cattle baron, Pierre Wibaux, whose ashes had been scattered on that very hill. This section of our route was always in darkness, so I had never seen the statue before. I was familiar with it, because it was featured in the route guides that I had read. What was more amazing, as I gazed over the rolling prairies, was what I didn't see: snow. The land was bone dry. It was like we were passing through a different world. The train, coated in ice and snow, began shedding its frosting. Chunks of ice and snow were falling off, pelting the side of the train, and disintegrating on impact with the roadbed. The temperature outside was thirty-nine degrees, nearly fifty degrees warmer than what we had just come through during the previous hours of darkness.

As I sat on the edge of my bunk trying to wake up, the events of the previous night weighed heavy on my mind. Everything that happened was surreal. I was in a stupor as I reflected back, reliving the collision with the snowmobile, the stuck switch at West Fargo, the disastrous poker game and blizzard. Never play poker with Dean when you are tired, that's the lesson I learned. It was too much to experience all at once. Dad said not to play poker with Dean, period! He's right.

My laptop had a good wireless connection to the Internet. An email from dad was asking why the train was late. Dad was overly anxious about me being on the train in such bad weather. He was consumed with tracking me every mile along the route. He wanted to meet me when I arrived back in Seattle. On each trip back, he wanted to know everything that had happened. After each trip, I had some new adventure to report on. Dad suggested that I keep a diary and write a book someday. My email back to dad was brief. "We ran into some bad weather in Dakota."

David Olsen

One night Travis received a call on his cell from a girl he vaguely knew whose name was Katie Russell. He had met her at some previous 4H events. She was a senior at Rollinsville High, a small class B school about an hour southeast of Cheneau Valley. She had a favor to ask. She wanted him to come down and help her pick out a steer for her new 4H project. She had to have it by March in order to qualify for the coming year's competition.

Joey and Brad were with Travis when he received the call from Katie. For some reason, which I never heard explained, Joey knew her, and told Travis she was a hot chick. I don't think Joey really knew that, but Joey teases about everything. If he had that little smirk on his face, you knew Joey was not telling it straight.

Katie had two or three animals in mind and wanted Travis to help her decide. Travis asked if she had pictures of the animals she was considering. She did. Travis asked her to send them to him, and he would look at them. Over they came. Katie displayed herself along with the cattle in two or three of them.

"*She is a hot chick!*" Joey exclaimed as he looked over Travis' shoulder at Katie's pictures. "How is it," Joey wanted to know, "that you and Kyle can get these chicks eating out of your hand? I have to work hard to get them to just look at me!"

Travis decided this project needed his personal attention. He didn't waste any time before going down to Rollinsville to execute on his talent for judging cattle, and checking out Katie to see if she was for real. The minute he saw Katie, he almost forgot the purpose for the trip. It was new territory and a new conquest.

Katie Russell didn't have a chance. Travis fell head over heels in love with her. None of us at the Olsen residence liked her, and we hadn't even had a chance to meet her yet. Our negative feelings about her hinged on the fact that we had never seen Travis go completely over the top like this for a girl. Travis tossed all logic aside in any decision involving Katie. It wasn't that far to Rollinsville, where Katie lived with her parents and five siblings on a small family farm, but I wished it was at least a day's drive, making it less convenient for Travis to travel there in his spare time, of which he had very little.

It seemed that the Russells kept a tight rein on their kids and, due to being somewhat isolated, Katie didn't have opportunity or the money, to come to Cheneau Valley. Maybe it was her lack of accessibility to the real world that made her so appealing. She was innocent and unspoiled. Travis said her life was very uncomplicated and simple. Travis said that the dad, mom, and the five kids lived in a small wood-frame house with one bathroom. There was also an outhouse one could use if needed.

"I'm impressed," I said as I interrupted Travis.

Katie loved animals and, Travis said, inside and outside their place smelled like a zoo. The kids kept sheep, Angora goats, miniature potbellied pigs, farm pigs, chickens, turkeys, geese, ducks, and two Shetland ponies. Mr. Russell earned his living by working in an assembly plant that manufactured small machinery.

"I wouldn't like my house to smell like a zoo," Lynn said. "So is the house clean?"

"Well…not real clean." Travis justified that statement by saying with so many people living in such a small space it wouldn't be possible for the house to be clean.

"Excuse me, but there are a lot of people tracking through this house. I keep it clean." Lynn argued that she could keep five kids pretty busy cleaning house if she in fact had five kids. "I have three kids and that is enough!" She laughed.

"What's Katie's room like?" Terri asked, as we grilled Travis with one question after another.

"It's small," Travis said.

"You mean, you hardly know them and her parents let you go into her room?" Terri asked.

Travis explained that since the house was so small, it was kind of like being in every room at once. Katie shared a room with another sister. Travis said there were no closets in her bedroom, and they kept their clothes in boxes that were on top of the bed. He assumed they put them under the bed at night before they got into bed.

Travis proceeded to show everyone his pictures of Katie. While not glamorous, she was attractive. Actually, she was cute. She was very cute. We couldn't deny that. She was a tall girl, but nevertheless, Travis stood two heads taller than Katie. She sported a crop of thick, long brown hair. Then Terri teased Travis about him not liking long hair on a girl.

"How can they afford to feed all those animals?" I asked.

"Travis, the kids all look bony thin. Do they have enough to eat?" Terri asked.

Poor Travis continued to get barraged from all four sides. Terri heckled him about Katie storing her dresses in a box. Dresses have to hang, she said. Travis didn't think she even owned a dress.

"Then I guess you won't take her to the prom this April if she doesn't have a dress." Terri said.

We stopped our interrogation and harassment and decided to let nature take its course, and it sure enough did.

Coach Rodger Epperson

By the end of February we had racked up a stellar record. We won eighteen of twenty basketball games and all but one conference game. Our team was crowned top seed for the Eastern Division Tournament.

We took the division championship, but not before nearly losing to Devils Lake. It was a real nail-biter. It would have been a major upset because we had handily defeated Devils Lake in the two regular-season conference games.

Travis' Granny wasn't able to attend the championship game in Grand Forks because she had been nursing a cold and was saving her strength for the state tourney next week in Bismarck. She had already punched her ticket for the big one. She called me to say that she wasn't settling for anything less than us being number one! To help us along with that, she was planning to listen with one ear while she prayed the Rosary for Travis and the team with the other.

Devils Lake had been a better-than-average team during the season, but it was astonishing for them to upset Fargo's Dakotah High the previous night, earning them a spot in the championship game. Devils Lake was on a roll and they wanted to win. We had a commanding lead at the half, but went stone cold during the first ten minutes of the second half. That was very out of character. We turned the ball over, we fouled, we took bad shots and Travis ended up on the bench after suffering some back spasms. Point by point, the Devils cauldron boiled over and it burnt the Bridgers. There was one foul after another called by the officials, who didn't want to be labeled as partial to either team. The atmosphere in the crowd turned sour. It started to look ugly; there was a complete absence of any sportsmanship. The Cheneau Valley fans were not going to be cheerful losers. We were number one and we didn't want to be anything but!

With a minute left in regulation play, ahead by three, we drove down the court. I expected to run down the clock until we could make the final two- or three-point attempt that would seal the deal. The officials hit us with an offensive foul just when we drove in underneath and scored, but the basket didn't count. Three points behind, with less than a minute in regulation play, Devils Lake controlled the ball. Next, we were charged with a blocking foul underneath the net. It was in the act of shooting and the basket counted. Devils Lake made the free throw and tied the score. The game went into overtime.

Kyle, Travis and Brad were on the floor. Joey and Aaron had fouled out. The first ball in overtime play was tipped to Devils Lake, who got in underneath their net but didn't score. About four players went up for the rebound and three came crashing down on the floor. There was much at stake and the game became physical. Travis lay prostrate on the floor for a few seconds. The crowd became quiet. Travis stood up on his own and insisted he wasn't hurt, but I replaced him. The foul was called on Travis, his fourth, but Devils Lake missed both free throws. Devils Lake was playing tough defense. I told the team to keep it simple and to keep doing what they knew worked. Brad shot a nice floater that put us ahead by two.

Devils Lake brought the ball down and took a wild shot from far out that was supposed to be a tip-in by their center. Brad rebounded the ball, but gave it up to their big center, an Indian kid named Johnny Big Elk from the local reservation, who put it in the bucket to tie the score. This Indian kid had committed several reach-in fouls, but the officials didn't call them. He would reach in and pull the ball out of the hands of his opponent. If he took hold of the ball, you weren't going to keep it. He was more than an irritation; he was absolutely predatory in his greed to get the ball. He was the one that landed on Travis in the last pileup. He was one of the most physical players in the league.

Brad took another shot from the arc and missed. The ball was rebounded by Devils Lake. At midcourt, Brad and Kyle attacked the dribbler. Brad forced the opponent to the sideline and then went around him from behind. When the dribbler turned in the opposite direction, Kyle grabbed the ball out of his hands, slipped and went down on his tail but handed the ball off to Brad, who ran downcourt with it. The crowd became unglued at the officials for not charging Kyle with a foul. The opponents swarmed around Brad, who tried to get a shot off, missed and rebounded his own ball but in the process committed an offensive foul, Brad's fourth, against Big Elk. Brad went over Big Elk's back and knocked him down flat on the floor. Unscathed, Big Elk stood up and went to the line. The first free throw was good but the second rimmed out.

Travis came back in. Devils Lake used a strong man-to-man, full-court press. Kyle tried to get into the basket. He had been cold all night from the arc and I told him not to throw the ball away on long shots. Kyle signaled to Travis and then positioned himself to shoot toward the basket. It was a clever head fake. He routed the ball to Travis, who was there for the stunning alley-oop. Cheneau Valley was up by one.

With forty seconds left in overtime, Devils Lake drove downcourt, penetrated without a screen, but missed the shot. The ball was rebounded by Big Elk, who tipped it in for two; in the process he was fouled by Travis. It was Travis' fifth foul and he was gone. The basket was good and Devils Lake could win with a free throw. Big Elk scored, putting Devils Lake ahead by two. Kyle called timeout, our last one, for final instructions from me. I felt our only hope, with Travis, Joey and Aaron on the bench, was Brad. I had no other plan to win this game without my fabulous five on the floor. Get the ball to Brad.

They pressed us hard. Devils Lake almost took it away from us. With about five seconds to go Brad ran to the outside behind the arc. Kyle watched, and when Brad was in position Kyle did his head fake and threw to Brad. Devils Lake was sure Kyle would drive in and try to tie the score. When Brad got the ball, he positioned himself just as Devils Lake came in to block him. His quick release and high, arching shot wasn't blocked. He pushed the ball off his fingertips and the ball received the perfect back-spin that floated it in for a triple. Game over. Cheneau Valley won by one point. It was a heartbreaker for Devils Lake. They stood there in total disbelief.

The police looked the other way as the unrestrained crowd piled onto the floor to congratulate our team. In seconds, Brad was hoisted up on Joey's shoulders and carried to the center of the floor. It was wild. I was real happy when Kyle received the Eastern Division MVP Award in the ceremony that followed the game.

[Bismarck Arena, a week later]

The entire town of Bismarck was captivated by basketball the three days the tourney was played in town. The girls' championship game, now just over, had stunned the crowd after the Cinderella team from Grand Forks upset the top-seeded lady Scouts from Bismarck Capitol to earn the state championship. Could the sellout crowd that filled the arena endure a second tense game between Capitol and Cheneau Valley, another Eastern Division team? The Scouts from Capitol were number one in the Western Division. It was destined to be a tight game. If Cheneau Valley could pull it off, it would be our first state championship in decades.

The earlier defeat on Capitol's home court back in December weighed heavy on the minds of the starting five. I told the team that they would have to do whatever it took to win. I warned them to get ready to play the entire game. Their respite from substitutes would be brief at best. I was riding this one-trick pony as far as it could go, and so far it had been a good ride.

The crowd was ready. There was tension between the teams. The crowd was eager to raise the roof. Let's play ball! The noise level intensified as the lights went out for the announcement of the starting lineups. One by one, each player had their moment of glory as they ran to the center circle and stood in the spotlight after their name was announced:

"Kyle Hickles, *guard*; Brad O'Connor, *guard*, Joey Carlson, *forward*, Aaron Richards, *forward*, and Travis Olsen, *center*!"

But before the team hit the court, we reviewed what the strategy would be from the opponents. Thinking we might have to face Capitol in order to win the state championship, we studied the Capitol defense intently as they swept over Fargo Senior in Friday's semifinals. Capitol was going to try to do the same as any other team we played, and that was to shut down our scoring with tough defense.

"Don't fall in love with the three-point arc," I warned. "No matter how deadly we are from the perimeter, remember that we can't win the game shooting triples."

"*Kyle*! Capitol will step in and take charges off of you," I yelled as I started screaming passionately at the team.

"*Travis*! Capitol will foul the crap out of you. What are you going to do about it?"

"*Make free throws!*" Travis got right in my face as he screamed back his answer.

"How many?"

"*All of them!*" Travis screamed.

"You have to want that ball really badly or they will take it away from you," I yelled. "Are we going to be out hustled?"

"*No!*" The team yelled.

"Aggressive!?" I yelled.

"*Yes!*" Yelled the team.

"How!?"

"*Rebound, block, deflect and steal!*"

I drew them into the final pregame huddle. I asked them if they wanted to win. I wanted to know if *EVERYBODY* on the team wanted to win.

"*Yes! Yes! Yes!*"

It was 8 p.m. on the dot when one official stood between Travis and Capitol's center, Tyson Andersen, and threw up the jump ball. Travis easily accomplished his thirty-inch vertical leap and tipped the ball to Joey, for first possession.

"Get the ball first and score, so they know you mean it!" I preached.

Joey passed to Kyle, who, without hesitation, ran right through the Capitol defense and floated one off the rim. There was immediate follow-through from Travis, who tipped the ball in for two. Less than a minute into the game, Capitol called a timeout. Capitol's coach was obviously not happy. They had to stop Kyle's fast break and the follow-through by Travis. It was a deadly weapon that we used in every game.

Travis described Tyson Andersen as a big sandbag. Tall and made for football, he was a big kid who had at one time weighed over three hundred fifty pounds. He had lost about one hundred pounds of beef. He was a good shot blocker and good at grabbing rebounds, but he was not a great scorer. Travis, however, with his superior athleticism, could easily outplay him. Before the game, when asked about Tyson, Travis said that what he feared most about his opponent was what would happen if Tyson went down on top of him.

"Big Elk was a lightweight compared to this guy," Travis said with a worried look.

From the start, all appearances indicated a low-scoring game. Travis wanted to accumulate double digits in points and rebounds. It would be his last game playing high school basketball. He wanted it to be one of his best games.

With fifty-two seconds left in the first half, Bismarck shot from the perimeter and missed. Brad rebounded and passed to Kyle, who brought it down court. They ran down the clock, which had a three-second differential from the shot clock. Travis stayed wide, hoping Kyle would pass to him so he could sink a last-second triple. Kyle continued to stall, passed to Joey, to Brad, back out to Kyle who, with eight seconds on the clock, pushed in and floated a deuce just inside the arc. Capitol threw the ball downcourt as the horn sounded. At the end of the first half it was twenty-six to fourteen, Cheneau Valley.

Inside the locker room, I told the team to hang in there and push harder into the offensive glass. We had to keep up the hustle. The team, already tired, needed a rest.

"Be selective, be patient, execute your plays and keep doing what we know works. Keep pounding the glass. The closer to the glass we get the ball, the higher the score will be."

I felt really good about the game so far. We made a few mistakes but I didn't mention most of them because my guys really needed encouragement. It had been a long season. They had worked hard. I knew they were tired, nevertheless, I wished for a larger lead. The Capitol Scouts were scrappy and they could fight. Capitol was not an easy team to beat in their hometown. I also knew what was being said in Capitol's locker room on the other side of the arena. They knew we were tired. They knew my second string was weak. They were going to run us hard.

"I don't have a thought in my mind that this game is going to get away from us," I told the team. "Don't prove me wrong."

The team, anxious to get on the court, stood at the perimeter watching the last of the Cheneau Valley girls' dance team complete their flag-twirling routine. The CVHS pep band excelled at playing the fast-paced number *Hold That Tiger.* The girls were an obvious crowd-pleaser as the onlookers stood, cheering their every move and giving a standing ovation throughout the entire performance. They were quite the attraction as they marched together in perfect formation wearing their revealing blue and crimson velvet majorette costumes and white-tasseled boots. Until now, the guys had missed seeing the dance teams perform. It was the perfect halftime entertainment for a state championship game.

The moment the second half was underway we exploded. Once we took possession of the ball, we burst downcourt making good transition plays. It left Bismarck in a fog. In five minutes we had increased the lead to twenty points. Bismarck became completely discombobulated. They started throwing the ball away, giving us more opportunities to score. The crowd was subdued. Bismarck fought back, but they didn't play their best ball. Kyle got hot from the perimeter. He banged them in one after the other. It turned into being like a scrimmage game from the perimeter. Everyone wanted in on the action, so when each player had the ball, they shot from the three-point arc. Travis shot three in. I split up my five starters with some substitutes and everyone had their chance to play in the championship game. No one expected this. Bismarck's game went south.

Granny told me afterwards that she kept her Rosary close by, but other than tip-off she said she didn't use it. I told her to hang on to that Rosary because next year's team would be a different story.

I finally took Travis out. That kid can get so cocky. Travis was getting all the rebounds from Tyson, who was exhausted. On this particular play, Travis rebounded and passed the ball to Kyle, who kept ahead of the opponents and laid it up. Kyle did a fancy behind-the-back layup like they might do in the pros. It didn't go over with the crowd and I didn't want this championship game to turn into a circus. Immediately Travis ran down-court and did a chest bump with Kyle and then Kyle jumped on Travis' back and flexed his biceps. The crowd booed. They didn't appreciate such theatrics. I called timeout and chewed them all out for being cocky showoffs. That said, when Travis left the game for the last time, he was given a standing ovation from most of the crowd. He played a scintillating game and everybody knew it. In the end, we reined supreme, winning sixty-three to thirty-nine. Travis achieved his double double with twenty-seven points and twelve rebounds. Thanks to Brad and Kyle, he also pulled down ten assists.

The awards ceremony that followed the championship game added to the excitement. Travis earned the Coaches Trophy, given to the outstanding senior athlete. It was based on votes cast by the coaches in each Class A school. The state's sportswriters voted to honor Travis as North Dakota's "Mr. Basketball." The two trophies were not often given to the same athlete.

David Olsen

Last fall I let Travis plant five hundred acres of winter wheat. I never plant winter wheat. I prefer to do all the planting in the spring. Too many farmers in this part of North Dakota have suffered heavy losses with winter wheat. The weather in early spring is too unpredictable. Travis had time in his schedule and needed something to keep him out of trouble. He used an old soybean field. It was good for the ground, he argued. We'd had such a mild fall and he's not happy unless he can be on a tractor doing something. John O'Connor discouraged him from doing it and Aaron laughed at him. Very few farmers here plant in the fall.

He did all the seeding himself. We had some late fall rains and good snow cover. It was Granny's land, and the snow usually lies full to the stubble in that section. Of course, Granny was all for it if Travis wanted to do it, and she agreed to take on the loss.

I expected that we would have to replant this spring, so we would be out the price of the seed and seeding costs. I even budgeted for it. Winter wheat isn't insurable until the following spring, when there is a guarantee of a crop. The crop broke germination the instant the weather warmed in March. Then we had a cold spell, but hardly any of it died off. There is nothing more beautiful in North Dakota in the spring than a lush green field of winter wheat. Nobody appreciated it more than Travis. It was a county showpiece. Everybody was talking about it. Farmers were calling, wanting to know the particulars. It made the Fargo paper. Travis couldn't get his hat on any more because his head had swelled up too big.

I hate prom night. This is the third one for Travis, because he got asked as a sophomore. It gets worse every year. The costs keep going up. I have to survive at least four more, two each for Tanner and Terri.

On prom night, Katie arrived early with her dad, Jim Russell. He had to return back to Rollinsville in time to take the younger sister to her prom that was scheduled the same evening. Katie didn't have access to a car to drive here herself, but even if she did, her dad insisted that he bring her. Lynn wanted the Russells to come for dinner because we hadn't met them yet. They declined because of the prom conflict and their desire to chaperone their other daughter as best they could. I like the fact that Katie's parents have kept a tight rein on the kids. I don't think Mr. Russell trusts Travis that much, either.

We liked Katie's dad. Katie is just like her father. Almost as tall as Travis, Jim Russell sported a thin, well-groomed mustache. I could tell he liked Travis, but it all seemed to hinge on the expert help Travis had been with Katie's 4H steer. I could see that Katie had her dad's shyness.

I could see why Katie would appeal to Travis. I immediately noticed what Travis had said about her eyes. What she didn't say with her mouth, she said with her eyes. If you watched her eyes you could read her like a book. She had big beautiful brown eyes. She had Lynn's eyes. By the time they left, I was convinced that in her own quiet way, Katie was a charmer, and she was charming my son like nobody else had.

Travis was not going to agree to have Katie picked up by her dad at 6 a.m., the time when the all-night party at the bowling alley ended. Travis informed Mr. Russell that he would bring her home, but it wouldn't be early as they might go out for breakfast afterwards. Travis said he needed to work the steer with her in the afternoon. Katie's dad did not want Travis to drive her to Rollinsville without any sleep. When Mr. Russell left to go home, Travis walked out with him and had a rather terse discussion about it. I saw the point that Travis was making, but I wasn't so sure I liked the way that Travis stood up to him. I'm afraid Mr. Russell thinks Travis, at eighteen, owns and runs our farm. Well, Travis doesn't run Mr. Russell. Jim said for Travis to call him as soon as the prom activities ended and he would be there to get her.

When Granny called over telling us to hold dessert because she was bringing her famous deep-dish apple pan cobbler over later, I should have been suspicious. I could never stay ahead of her craftiness. Travis was mysteriously absent from this affair, staying in his bedroom and studying. Normally, he would be right here hogging the conversation.

"I know what Travis really wants for his graduation present," she said with all the authority of the pope. And I suppose that I don't know? I thought to myself as I listened. I was totally befuddled as to why she was involving herself in this matter.

"Did you hear what Aaron got from his folks?" She acted like she was the first person to know and tell it. Aaron was getting a hot-rod truck. Travis had told me all about it. It was getting a lot of aftermarket stuff put on it, and Aaron was supposed to get it sometime next week. She kept on about the gift I'm supposedly getting for Travis. I knew what she was getting at. We're talking price here. I knew she wanted it to be big, but I didn't know how big. Certainly she didn't expect me to spend the price of a new truck!

"I know exactly what he wants," she said, "but it is too expensive for you to buy it without any help."

Oh no. Here we go again. So it turned out that Travis had picked out a five-thousand-dollar Rolex watch he wanted, and Granny wanted to know how much I was willing to contribute toward it.

"Mom, who picked this watch? You or Travis?"

"David! Good taste runs in the family. You know that," she said.

"If Travis has developed a taste for expensive jewelry, mom, I blame you!"

Poor Paul sat there stone-faced. He didn't hand money like that out to his grandkids, and neither did they expect it. Yeah right. That will be a good one when Travis goes around the Norlund clan flashing his bright chrome Rolex.

So, in the end, I agreed to pay two thousand dollars for the watch. I think Travis had earned it. He had worked hard with me on the farm. He's been a good student and athlete. He's accomplished a lot during his eighteen years on earth.

Granny ordered it from her jeweler in Fargo. When she brought the watch over the next week, I looked at it and almost kept it for myself. I'll give it to him on grad night, but not a minute before.

Aaron came by the house to show off his new truck. The Richards were good farmers, so they could afford it. The truck was impressive, to say the least. Aaron took us for a ride across the open prairie. It had a six-inch lift on the chassis and oversized tires capable of off-road travel. In short, the metallic red, six-passenger XLT, with eight cylinders, 4x4, turbo-charged diesel with a high-performance cold-air intake proved to be a viable monster truck. Travis tried not to act enthused. This kid is hard to read, but I think he was a bit jealous of Aaron.

The graduation ceremony went off without a hitch. Katie's graduation at Rollinsville was scheduled the same night -- thank goodness. Travis was so completely engrossed with the night that I don't believe he even missed her. She is still his girlfriend but his interest in her is fading.

Travis and four of the other ten honor students spoke at the graduation. Travis spoke last. After Travis sat down, I couldn't have been more proud of him. He spoke about what there was yet to achieve. He talked about shooting from the three-point line on the basketball court. The most he had ever done consecutively was eight out of ten. He wasn't pleased with that, because his goal was to do ten for ten. He's never been able to do that. Then he had learned that the best in the nation won first place by doing seven out of ten. He suggested that we set high goals for ourselves and do our best at achieving them. We might surprise ourselves by what we could achieve, he said.

He is quite happy with the watch. I tussled with Granny over who should give it to him, but she refused to be swayed. She said that I should give it to him, so I did. Before the procession commenced with its pomp and circumstance, the parents were standing in the lineup with their grads, taking pictures. Lynn was ready with the camera when I gave it to him. A look of shock turned to extreme pleasure. It was a priceless picture of him wearing a mile-long, ear-to-ear smile. A week earlier, Travis asked us if it would be all right for him to have Granny march with him in the processional. I knew Lynn was hurt when he asked that, but she was the first to give her approval, realizing how much it would mean to Granny. Travis and Granny went arm in arm, right to the front of the auditorium until he had to mount the platform and take up position with his class. Travis will never know how much that meant to his Granny.

Lynn Olsen

I pulled the Suburban to the front of Greer's market and left Travis alone in the car. He had developed a headache from the anesthetic he was given when the dentist ground down a back molar. He sometimes reacts to the Novocain. They tried it without, but Travis couldn't handle the pain. He doesn't have a high pain tolerance. When I came out to the car with the basket full of groceries, Aaron's truck was parked next to us and Aaron was in the car talking to Travis. They kept talking as I unloaded the groceries. It was raining, and I could have used some help but I just let them talk because I was listening to what they were saying.

Aaron wanted Travis, Brad, Kyle and Joey to all go out some night and raise hell together one last time before Aaron gets busy with harvest and other farm work. Travis is getting too chummy with Aaron. I prefer Travis being with Brad or Joey. Kyle is sort of shiftless but he doesn't have much of an influence on Travis or the others. Aaron isn't going to college because he plans to stay on the farm and work with his dad and two stepbrothers. I don't trust Aaron, and I don't want Travis to hang with him. I have a mother's intuition about some things. Aaron's stepbrothers have taken him places and done things with him that most young men his age don't engage in. Aaron grew up fast, and he's a lot more street smart than Travis. I don't want to see Travis involved with the same things as Aaron. I know Aaron drinks. Travis, as an athlete, has a standard and reputation to uphold. He's going to have that over his head the next five years at NDSU. Aaron's life is on a different trajectory than Travis'. In another month, the friendships will drift apart as everyone gets busy with the crops. I don't think Travis will have a lasting friendship with Aaron. I hope not.

Travis wants Aaron to take him out in the new truck to Kindersley, where there is lots of range country to drive over. Travis is itching to get that off-road monster of Aaron's in those hills. Aaron's truck is built for that range country out at Kindersley.

[Saturday, May the twenty-ninth]

David left early for Fargo, where he had an all-day Farm Bureau meeting and banquet. I urged him to take Travis but Travis had other plans. So far, Travis could care less about farm politics. David thinks that political blood doesn't flow in the veins of a farmer until later in life, when frustration finally sets in with the local leadership. David said there would be nothing in the meetings that Travis would be interested in at this point. The kids and I will drive down to Fargo in the evening and attend the banquet with David.

Aaron came by in his truck and the two of them left at 9 a.m. They were hauling some supplies out to Kindersley as a favor for some guy who is pasturing his cattle out there. They want to do some mud running in the hills. I was home alone when Aaron and Travis returned later in the afternoon. I was furious. Aaron had apparently driven that truck all over the rangeland pasture. That truck would tear up the country. It was plastered with mud. The windshields were grimy. Aaron and Travis were laughing it up, talking loud, and every once in awhile I saw Aaron, not Travis, reach in through the driver's window and pick something up and drink from it. It could have been a soda pop. It could have been beer. I couldn't be sure. I kept watching them through the kitchen window.

Travis put his wading boots on, pulled off his shirt, grabbed the hose, connected it to the pressure washer, and started hosing off Aaron's truck. Aaron tried to grab the nozzle out of his hand in an attempt to get Travis wet, but he didn't succeed. Instead, Travis turned the hose on Aaron and drenched him. Then I saw it. Aaron stumbled hard and fell down. Travis laughed his head off. Aaron picked himself up and leaned against his truck. He appeared weak in his knees. He was unsteady on his feet. He wobbled a bit. I had the immediate notion that Aaron was drinking. I kept watching. When the truck was washed, Aaron drove off and Travis came in the house for a drink. I confronted Travis.

"Has Aaron been drinking?" I asked. Travis looked surprised. "If he is drinking and driving on our local roads here, I'm calling the sheriff right now."

Travis was stunned. He didn't know what to say. "Answer me, Travis! Has he been drinking? Is he drunk? Shall I call the sheriff?"

I was so upset I was shaking. I didn't want to call the sheriff. I didn't know what to do when David wasn't here. I can't call David. He won't have his cell on when he's in the meetings. What was he going to do, anyway?

"Mom, relax. Nobody's drunk. Yeah, Aaron had a couple of beers with him that he brought from home. I drank a couple. Man, it was hot down there. We drank the beer with our lunch. We bought some sandwiches in Kindersley before we went tearing through the hills. A man was there and he took us around. We dumped the salt where he said."

"I'm calling the sheriff and let's see what he thinks. Aaron's breaking the law, and if you are in the truck with him you are breaking it, too."

"Mom. Nobody's drunk!" Travis was yelling at me now. "Do you want me to lose my basketball scholarship over two freaking beers?"

I took him by the shoulders and I could smell the booze on his breath. I broke out into a cold sweat. Travis stood there looking at me.

"Travis, I'm going to tell Dad, and the two of you are going to sit down and have a long talk. Neither one of us is going to tolerate this type of behavior. You can plan on going down to Fargo with us tonight and have dinner with your dad and we'll discuss this tomorrow."

"Mom! I'm not going to Fargo tonight. I have other plans."

"Like what?"

"Joey, Brad, Kyle and me are going to Jamestown to a movie."

"What are you driving?"

"The Mustang. I told dad. Dad knows all about it. Call him and ask him."

"Katie, too?"

"Forget Katie. She's not in the picture right now."

I let him worm his way out of that one. Travis went upstairs and showered. I asked him to take his jeans off on the porch, so he wouldn't track the mud through the house. He ignored me. When he came down, he was nicely dressed and looked like a different kid. He looked clean and handsome. I gave him a hug and a kiss. I told him I was sorry I was so upset with him. He took the Mustang and left. I picked the kids up in Cheneau Valley and drove to Fargo. Travis ruined the whole evening for me. I couldn't bring myself to tell David. He would have been so upset. I just buried it for now.

The Train From Hell
[Midway Train Station, St. Paul (May twenty-ninth)]

Trevor Jensen

When Dean and I arrived at Midway Station in St. Paul, a place much too small for the number of passengers it served, it looked like a disaster scene. Reyna was behind the boarding gate talking with Homeland Security. She gave us an angry look as we walked into the station. It was 5 p.m. It was not like we were late to work! The train wasn't due in until six and departure was not until 6:25 p.m. Dean would have had us come down to the station an hour ago had he known the passenger volume. It was going to be just Dean and me on the night crew. People and luggage were everywhere. Dean hadn't bothered to check out the manifest for the Twin Cities, like he usually did beforehand. I never thought about it. It was what it was. As a result, we didn't know that we were boarding one hundred and twenty people. It looked like half the train was turning here in the Cities. This was unusual. We weren't early enough to handle this load. Homeland Security did an occasional sweep through the station at train time. You never knew when or why they came. They did their thing and we usually just ignored them while we did our work. They never bothered us.

We sprung into action and began the check-in procedures. Homeland Security was down our backs about everything. They wanted to know what documents we were using for identification. They asked Dean about the questions he asked the boarding passengers, as if they didn't already know. We followed their guidelines. The railroad had bent over backwards for them without ever getting the extra funding promised from Homeland Security. They wanted to know how we made the decision to search deeper through a passenger's handbag and what that decision was based on.

I was suspicious that something was going on, as they didn't usually have the bomb-sniffing dogs with them. Maybe they were sniffing for drugs. I didn't know. This was more than just a routine surveillance. It made me feel really creepy. Then, I noticed there were two border patrol agents, but they can show up on occasion. Sometimes the government doesn't make any sense. They don't show up for the longest time and then, like tonight, they all come at once.

Reyna didn't tell us, maybe she didn't know, but they had a plant in the crowd who had a weapon in a carry-on. Reyna kept talking to two other guys, who we soon learned were with Drug Enforcement. The two drug agents had windbreakers on over their vests on which was written "DEA." They had done background checks on some of the passengers and they were ready to make an arrest. Actually, what we learned later was they had pinned down two drug runners coming in from Chicago, who were leaving the train carrying only hand luggage filled with money. Next, two different thugs ticketed to Spokane boarded, carrying two bags filled with drugs. It was pretty easy to slip the money and drugs through our check-in system. Don't worry, we wouldn't have found the money as we don't check those kinds of bags that closely and they knew that. The whole process slowed us down, and before we knew it, the train arrived and things became real tense as we were working with the incoming crew, trying to keep the bags separate for the DEA and get everything loaded/unloaded on and off the train.

I kept thinking about what I heard the others say about the "Train from Hell." It usually starts off bad and then gets worse. Once things start in the direction of Hades, unless you can change course, everything you do goes to Hell in a hand basket. I've never actually been on the "Train from Hell," but at times I've been suspicious. I hope I never am. That is one train we all want to miss.

We finally got the luggage loaded. The DEA went on the train and took a male and female passenger off; handcuffed them, and led them off to a parked car in front of the station, where they had the other two who had just arrived locked up already. You could tell right away that the passengers started feeling a bit uneasy about their traveling companions. That immediately left us with two vacant seats on a sold-out train.

The dopey agents let us load the bags from the two passengers they had just busted, knowing full well they would be arrested. Now, we had to find their checked bags and take them off. It is now 7 p.m., and we are already over thirty minutes late. The passengers haven't eaten and they can't start the dinner service until we leave. The idea here is to feed them as soon as possible so they soon forget about everything else that went wrong. Leave them hungry too long and they will be mad at you for the whole trip.

The bakery fouled up on where they were taking Wren's birthday cakes. Apparently, the driver didn't know that the Minneapolis train station was in St. Paul. We always say, as do the passengers, that the train goes to Minneapolis. Wrong! Reyna ordered two ice cream cakes and they looked tasty. Maybe we will get a chance to eat them tonight.

Homeland Security became unglued when a man, who was on the train, told Reyna that I had checked him off for boarding even though he had a gun in his bag. He was the plant from Homeland Security. What was I supposed to have done? I didn't have an X-ray machine. It was impossible to go through every handbag and carry-on when there were so many to check. There was only Dean and I from our crew checking people in. Reyna put the other three from the night crew on board the train to get people seated. She thought Dean and I could do it all. We did bust our fannies tonight. We tried to get it done without delaying the departure. Wren and her crew coming from Chicago were busy with the first half of the dinner service and helping the arriving passengers off the train. We had too much work without enough help.

I was chastised by everybody, written up, and signed my life away with the government. It was really nothing. I had to sign off on the report they turned in after they did these practice exercises. Reyna said I shouldn't worry about it. She understood how a gun could get smuggled onto the train. She said that the railroad believed security was a law-enforcement problem and the crew should not have to take on that responsibility.

Bernie, tonight's conductor, had us out of the Cities at 7:15 p.m., about fifty minutes late. We left St. Paul, crossed the Mississippi River into Minneapolis, busted through the downtown district of the city, and were soon highballing through the suburbs. We're definitely not on the "dog train" tonight.

[A restaurant in Jamestown, that same evening]

Sunny

It was busy at the restaurant where I was working my second job trying to earn more college money for my two kids. Saturday nights were always busy. I had them all wait until I could get a table for seven in my section. Finally, when I secured the space, in they came: Travis, Kyle, Brad, Aaron, Joey, Ace and Shona. They were noticeably showy and conspicuous as they gathered around the table all talking at once. I was happy that Shona brought them here to eat. They put in a huge order. It took half of the kitchen to cook and deliver it. Ace, in a hurry to get to work, swallowed his chicken crisps and left. Travis ordered the steak and shrimp, not the combo, but as separate orders. He wanted more jumbo shrimp. I had the cook put in some extra for him, thinking he might share some with the others. I brought him out a huge pile of shrimp. As luck would have it, one of the other tables wanted to know exactly what he had ordered. They wanted the same. I had to tell them that what Travis had wasn't on the menu. Travis kept one potato and sent the other sides back to the kitchen. Travis put the plate of shrimp on his lap so nobody could snatch it.

"Travis? That your last meal?" Joey teased.

Travis paid for Kyle, who only had enough money for his and Shona's movie tickets. The others paid with their own money. I always pay for Ace, as that poor kid works too hard to throw his money away here. I keep warning Shona that if she moves in with Kyle, he won't support her.

I sat down for a few minutes and introduced myself to everybody. I had never met Travis or Aaron. The night their team played here, I had to work. I was real pleased to finally meet Travis, as I had heard so much about him. I keep telling Shona that he is the one she needs to catch this fall at NDSU. She doesn't share my point of view on that. She says there will be a big flock of chickadees standing in line for Travis. Shona just doesn't care for that kind of lineup. Well, Travis is certainly the leader of this pack.

"This pie is better than what Granny makes! Please don't tell her I said so," Travis laughed as he scooped up the last of the apple caramel pie. "Made with fresh Michigan apples!" Travis recited what was written about the pie on the plastic centerpiece flip file, listing the pies. He turned to me. "Sunny? Are the apples actually from Michigan?"

"Not this time of year, Travis," I said. "I think they come from Washington but I really don't know. Well, I think the box says Washington apples."

By that time, everyone in the restaurant had noticed the ruckus erupting from our table and I was wondering what the manger was thinking.

"Fraud!" Travis yelled. "It's all a fraud! I want Michigan apples. False advertisement -- money back!"

When they left I gave a big sigh of relief. Travis tipped me twenty-five dollars.

Shona was supposed to get dates for the guys. Kyle was always asking Shona to do things that he should be doing. Shona got a few girls together who knew Kyle, but that was the best she could do. Shona assumed the boys would each have their own cars, but that didn't happen. They came with Aaron in his truck. They planned to all meet at the theatre and see how things went. The girls weren't very happy when the so-called dates weren't furnishing the wheels. Plus, there were going to be more girls than boys. In the end, Shona told me she wanted no part of it and planned for her and Kyle to go back home for the evening. Shona didn't care to be around the girls who were to be part of the group. One girl she knew fairly well, the others she didn't.

According to Shona, after the movie, the girls decided to go with the boys out to Sanders Lake and party. One girl obtained several six-packs of beer. Shona insisted that Kyle come home with her. Kyle wanted to go with the boys, but he also wanted to stay with Shona. He didn't know what to do until Aaron informed him that he didn't intend to drive back into Jamestown to get him. Sanders Lake was about fifteen miles toward Cheneau Valley. Kyle could have gone over and stayed with his dad, but I don't know why he chose not to do that. Kyle decided he'd better stay with the guys. She was home alone, mad, when I arrived about 11:30 p.m.

[Aboard The *Mountain Daylight* near Breckenridge, MN]

Trevor Jensen

It was a swell birthday party we had for Wren. I played the guitar and we turned it into karaoke style. It got pretty zany. I was surprised with some of the lyrics we created. We made up a song called "On The Daylight Tonight." It goes something like this:

We're all riding the Daylight *tonight.*
The Twin Cities are just out of sight.
The riders they're crappy and we aren't too happy,
riding the Daylight *tonight.*
One bathroom has already plugged;
one sink, they think doesn't drain.
The front coach is hot, the next one is not,
but that's just life on the train.
A couple ole biddies got on in the Cities,
their food was too cold and not really a lot
The crew, they correct it, they re-inspect it,
but the biddies claim a lot is too hot.

We're all riding the Daylight *tonight,*
and now, Willmar is out of our sight.
The track, now quite bumpy;
the next town is dumpy, please don't stop there tonight.
We're still in Minnesota? Why not Dakota?
Didn't you know that the Daylight *is slow?*
Go take a short snooze.
You got time to lose. In Dakota, they got forty below!
A coal train behind us, a grain train in front,
a mixed we just passed got sprayed with our grunt.

The Train From Hell

The signals, they're clear, no yellow, or red.
Throttle it down before we're all dead.

No mountains or streams? Asked the passenger forlorn.
It's Minnesota. You see only corn!
Ever see light through Dakota at night?
The moon, give or take, silhouettes on a lake.
During the day, you might see widgeons.
At daybreak in Bismarck, I only saw pigeons.
When in Dakota at night, it's those skeeters that bite.
Don't leave the train is our policy plain.
When it's cold in Dakota, and the wind blows a gale,
the worst that can happen is a broken rail.
When it's hot in Dakota, we'll speed right on through,
trying to miss a sun kink or two.

We're all riding the Daylight *tonight;*
Minnesota's gone out of sight.
That horn, it's annoying, it just keeps on a blowing
while riding the Daylight *tonight.*
We checked every bag like we're blind.
We paid the Red River monster no mind.
A big lady from Glendive, richly endowed,
brought Bandit on board when it wasn't allowed.
Soon someone reported, "I'd like to complain!
A bushy tailed rat is loose on the train!"
I caught him. I threw him out on the track.
Whenever in Glendive, I watch my back.

We're all riding the Daylight *tonight;*
it must be Fargo that's now in our sight.
The Red River, it flooded, and Fargo's a mess.
Oh! That was last April I guess.
Amtrak's a shack; I think that's a crime,

beside the Great Northern lit up like a shrine.
The neighborhood's dicey, the tickets too pricey,
the hour too late for a train now to take.
Ahead is West Fargo, a switch that froze shut;
a poker game last winter cost me my butt.
The high bridge is calling. Look out below.
It's Cheneau Valley. Oh! What a good show.

The faster we go the more rocks that
we throw riding the Daylight *tonight.*
At speed 99 our train you can't beat.
Stay out of our way or be dead on the street.
If you have been drinking instead of thinking,
and at the crossing gate, you can't wait,
When we come through, and you in the car do too,
life will be over for the car and for you.
We will stop and find your scrambled behind,
and gather your brains and remains underneath.
Any parts we can't find, the crows they will dine.
The rest of you, to the coroner bequeath.

Tonight's the train we cannot tell. The dispatcher
has warned us: "it's the train from Hell."
How does he know? Well it's only a guess.
Cause it started in the Cities as a great big mess.
The Daylight *was heavily booked you see,*
but a man and his gun got through some security.
The gun was only a plot and fortunately nobody's shot.
The feds caused all of the trouble we got.
We'll all be re-tested. Four thugs got arrested.
We'll put into practice all things they suggested.
No whistle post, no warning, not a whistle or bell,
this is the Devil's train, the one from Hell.

My three best friends are my two sisters, followed by Wren. She is a sweetie. Nothing romantic here, but we do love each other, as friends. Wren is perceptive of my feelings and she knows when I'm upset and tries to dig into my soul and get to the core of my unhappiness. She's my sub-mommy. We hug and kiss a lot and everybody thinks I'm making out with her but I'm not. There's a difference between a kiss and sensual kissing. I have missed my sisters so much. I kiss her the same way I do my sisters. I've set boundaries for myself with Wren. I don't violate them. She understands me and doesn't try to cross them. It is a complex relationship and everybody understands us by now, I think. When we get going, we can be quite a comedy team.

Dean is a good friend. Dean puts out a certain façade that is lacking in softness. He's the type of friend you can lean on during the day. He always has the right answers. He will give you the shirt off his back during the daytime, if you needed it; then at night kick your ass at poker, take all your money, and not even flinch. He's tough and impenetrable at times, with no room for weakness. If there is a weak spot in him, he guards it ruthlessly. He does well in a crisis. He doesn't come unglued. That's good. He has a new girlfriend. He is happy now, and that's good also. He's the alpha male of our crew. When he wants his own space, he hunches over like a gorilla, curls his fingers in and flexes his huge biceps. That means don't approach.

We made up some of the time the train lost earlier in the Cities. The train has kept a pretty good pace traveling through the flat farmland of southern Minnesota. The corn looks like it is waist high already. Bernie said we might lose some time at Breckenridge. That's nothing new. There are not enough passing tracks of sufficient length to accommodate a long coal train between Breckenridge and Fargo. Somebody has to wait, I guess.

Bernie was right. When we arrived at Breckenridge our train orders went south. The dispatcher put a mile-and-a-half long, very hot stack train on the route that was coming toward us down from Fargo. That was not the way it was written on the original track warrant Bernie carried out of the Twin Cities. Because we were late, the dispatcher put the hot freight through first.

We put on a few passengers in Breckenridge and waited. The air was heavy, humid and cool. It was hard for me to breathe. This country has been saturated with rain. We heard that the Red River was flooding near the Canadian border. Dean walked up to the head unit and started talking to the engineers. He needed a smoke. He felt like it would be a long night. In about twenty minutes, the hot stack train pulled through Breckenridge and we were on our way north to Fargo, now later than ever. It was just after midnight when we made the tight turn on the west edge of Wahpeton, North Dakota, and headed due north, through the Red River Basin, on forty miles of fast track. Dean said the engineers thought we'd make up more of the lost time. Lots of traffic tonight they said, but we're shooting straight through.

[A county road near Sanders Lake]

There wasn't a plan. There were thirteen kids and three vehicles. Five boys packed inside a six-passenger, four-door pickup, and eight girls between two cars, trying to find a private spot to hang out for a while and drink a few beers. The girls didn't know the boys that well and what better way to get acquainted, they thought. There were a few obstacles. The girls didn't know exactly where to go and it was muddy. Aaron wasn't that familiar with the country, so after the girls couldn't figure out where they were or where they were going, Aaron took out the geographical map of North Dakota and located a small road to a pond on the north end of Sanders Lake. The girls followed Aaron to the next junction, where they parked their cars, jumped into the pickup bed with their beer, and headed down to the pond, but Aaron's truck became stuck in the mud. It was too wet even for a four-wheel drive.

He spun mud all over the bed of the truck and one of the girls, so they stopped there and decided to have the party and worry about getting unstuck later. They consumed most of the beer.

Aaron paired himself up with a girl he really liked, and when she complained of being cold, he put her in the cab of his truck and sat inside with her. Soon the other girls were chilly and wanted to get in the truck, but Aaron wouldn't open the doors. When Aaron wouldn't let the other girls in the truck, the girl sitting by Aaron became mad and got out of the truck on the other side, slammed the cab door shut, and started walking back toward the main road, where the girls had parked their cars. The other girls went with her. The party, as far as the girls were concerned, was over. The boys polished off the rest of the beer. They threw all the cans in the bed of the pickup. You don't litter North Dakota, and you don't leave telltale tracks of a party behind.

The boys worked for about half an hour getting the truck unstuck. Aaron had shovels in his toolbox and they were able to dig around the tire and shove brush under the one wheel. Four of them climbed in the pickup bed and the combined weight provided the necessary traction. In a flash, they were up on the road and out of there. Aaron decided to go further north, to where there was a township road that cut across the lake, on a dike to the other side. He had been across it before, he said, and it was a well-maintained road. It was pretty far up. The road they were on was gumbo clay. It had hardly been traveled since the rains. He almost slid off into the barrow pit more than once. Finally, they crossed the dike. Aaron took the first right turn south, which should have taken him into the town of Sanders, where he could get onto the old highway and back to Cheneau Valley. What he failed to realize was the road into the town from that end of the lake had been closed for over two years due to flooding. He was a few miles west of Sanders on a seldom-used, poorly maintained perimeter road.

This road was worse than the one coming north. Besides, it had a lot of huge puddles. Once, Aaron almost lost it in some high water flowing onto the road from an overflowing ditch. They kept going, and going, and going. Aaron missed a couple of turns and once he almost rolled the truck over. They didn't really know where the road, if that's what you called it, was taking them. It continued south so they kept going. If they were in fact lost, at least they were headed in the right direction.

There also was an annoying problem. They were out of wiper fluid. Thick, muddy water covered the windshield after every puddle they hit. This made it difficult for Aaron to see the road, but he kept going. Aaron hadn't realized that the dealer only put a tiny amount in the reservoir in his new truck. They had pretty well used it up, he and Travis, running the hills in Kindersley earlier that day. Joey was in the front passenger seat with the window down, looking out, trying to see ahead on the road. Joey said he enjoyed mud running but not under these conditions. Travis, Kyle and Brad were in the back without their seatbelts on.

Travis told Aaron that he needed to get home or else his old man would kill him. They all teased him about being eighteen and still on a curfew. Aaron convinced him that he'd have to stay over with him for the night because he was drunk. Aaron said that David would kill him for sure if he went home drunk. Best plan was not to go home!

Suddenly, a miracle happened. The wagon trail they had been on was transformed into a gravel road. It was a well-traveled road. Aaron put the pedal to the metal. The road went straight south.

[Aboard *The Mountain Daylight* Sunday May the thirtieth (1 a.m.)]

Trevor Jensen

We were banging through each little town like a white tornado. We were making up time. It was neat to have Tim back on board, as our conductor, out of Fargo. We hadn't seen him for a while.

Tim was telling us that our trip tonight was a product of good dispatching at Fort Worth. What's to hate about having a lady engineer who loves to drive? She also has an assistant engineer aboard. I'd never seen her before, but apparently Delaine had worked several of our trains from Fargo to Glendive. Her assistant's name is Mick. We had a lot of traffic scattered along the route from here to Bismarck. We passed an empty coal train at Tower, a few miles east of Cheneau Valley. Another westbound train was ahead of us, just west of Cheneau Valley at Brower. There was a trail of green signal lights, positioned about two miles apart, up the track as far as you could see.

"Clear! Clear! Clear! Clear!" Delaine and Mick blasted over Dean's radio as they shouted back and forth to each other as each block signal was passed.

Most of the time, unless we were on a curve, three and sometimes four signals could be seen in the distance. The sea of green confirmed a clear right of way through the night into Jamestown. This train was hot tonight. It was smoking. It was that hot. This lady loves an open throttle. She's a real rail banger. We continued to make up more time. Tim started a dialogue with Delaine on the radio.

"That's a monster train ahead us." Tim said.

"Yes sir. It's over eight thousand two hundred feet, and pulling eleven thousand four hundred tons," Delaine confirmed.

"Is he going to be able to squeeze in that siding at Brower so we can get around him? How long is it?" Tim asked.

"How long is the siding? At least eighty-three hundred," Delaine answered. "Maybe it's eighty-four. I'd have to look it up."

"It's got four AC units on the front and two AC units pushing from behind."

"Yeah! It isn't too fun to fit all of that in a siding eighty three hundred feet while being pushed by that much tonnage," Delaine said.

"If they go past that red signal, it's adios!" Tim said.

"Sure is. I see a yellow ahead. We'll slow down and make sure he's out of our way," Delaine said.

"Please make sure," Tim said as he laughed.

It seemed we didn't slow down that much on the Dakota High Bridge as we passed over Cheneau Valley. The bridge girders went clank-clank-clank-clank, one after the other, as we sped across. The recommended speed was fifty, but I think we were doing more than that tonight. Once on the other side, we pulled up out of the valley and Delaine opened up on the throttle again. Just as planned, she slowed the train through Brower, where we passed the monster freight. The nose of the lead cab unit looked like it bumped up against the red signal light that protected our right of way.

"I'd say that siding was just eighty-three hundred," Tim joked as we passed by at about forty mph.

"Right on!" Delaine said, "That crew did a magnificent job of spotting that train."

Just as she engaged more tractive effort, to accelerate back up to track speed, Tim reminded her about the maintenance of way equipment scattered along the track in the area. They reconfirmed that there were no slow orders along that stretch. Tim said the equipment was still there the day before when he came through. She kept accelerating, until Tim asked if she overheard the dispatcher warning the train behind us. So Delaine began to decelerate down to the maximum allowable speed of sixty, as recorded on the railroad's timetable, for crossing the Sanders Lake dike and bridge, two miles ahead. Tim didn't think it was a good idea to be doing full track speed when there was equipment along the track. Tim explained that some of the equipment had long extension arms that could come in contact with our train if not fully retracted and properly secured by the track crew at the end of the workday. The digging wheel of an undercutter, if not fully retracted and locked in place, could potentially derail the locomotives. It's scary stuff out here running through Dakota in the dark!

Jamestown was next, in about twenty minutes or less. All of the Jamestown passengers were awake, accounted for, and in their seats. If we were able to get them off and everyone loaded in less than ten minutes, we'd make the planned meet with our eastbound sister train, comfortably avoiding delaying her at West Lagos Junction. We were counting on Delaine to get us there in time for the meet. Tim said he expected to be home on time, around 6 a.m. in Glendive.

The engineers noticed vehicle headlights off in the distance. This time of the night, in such a remote area, it was unusual to see headlights here. Tim didn't think there was a crossing nearby. The train passed through a small cut through a hill. The headlights disappeared. When the train pulled out of the cut into open country, just before the lake, it happened. The headlights were there. Almost instantly, there was a tremendous thud as a large object bashed into the side of the train. There was a clatter of metal for several seconds like something was being torn apart. Then it was quiet as the train barreled down the track.

"*Something hit us!*" Tim screamed into the radio.

Without giving a warning, Delaine immediately placed the air-brake handle in the emergency position, exhausting the full hundred and ten pounds of air from the brake lines throughout the train. This action nullified the throttle, causing the train to rapidly decelerate. The engineer brought the six-hundred-fifty ton, fifty-million-dollar train with its two hundred forty passengers to a quick but fully controlled stop in less than thirty seconds. The stopping distance was roughly one-third of a mile. The fast stop was inconsequential for the majority of passengers asleep in their seats. Delaine was sitting on the right side, across from Mick, and appeared to be visibly shaken after stopping the train so abruptly. Mick picked up the radio and called to the dispatcher.

"Emergency! Emergency! Emergency!" Mick's voice was transmitted to the Fort Worth, Texas, dispatch center where the call took top priority.

It was not something they wanted to hear in Fort Worth, where a supervisor and his two trainees were struggling to keep high-priority traffic moving through Minot to the north. There had been a burst of trains dispatched out of the Moorhead Yards in Minnesota into the Dakota Subdivision, all headed to the west. The situation had the full attention of the supervisor, who was closely monitoring the CTC train occupancy indicators on that subdivision. Their task was to get as many trains moving out of Minot as possible, one behind the other, into Montana, where they could spread out, keeping more distance between them. Dispatching two *Mountain Daylights* -- speeding toward each other on the lower line, two hundred miles to the south, darting around five freights -- had involved earlier effort and had been moved off their task list. The dispatch center did not want or need an emergency on that route that would unravel previously arranged meets.

"This is Fort Worth, what is your emergency? Over."

This is the *Mountain Daylight* train 1125. Something hit our train at milepost 76, over."

"Eleven twenty-five what did you hit? A vehicle? Over."

"Something hit us." Tim took over the radio and began to describe what had just happened as best he could.

"There was a sizeable side impact to the front-end coach directly behind the locomotives," Tim reported.

Instantly, Reyna called us, saying she and the crew were going to make a sweep of the train to check on the passengers. She wanted to know if everybody was okay and what, if anything, did we see. The impact startled an elderly lady who jumped up, lost her balance and fell, hitting her head and bruising her leg. She was sitting in the front-end coach. We continued to listen to the conversations coming through on Dean's radio.

"This is dispatcher 24 calling the *Mountain Daylight* 1125. I show you over water there. Is that the case? Over."

"We have water on both sides of the train. It is Sanders Lake, over."

"Eleven twenty-five, what can you see behind you? Over."

"Nothing. It is pitch black, over."

"Eleven twenty-five, you are on a bridge, correct? Over."

"Dispatcher 24, we're on the Sanders Lake dike. We have already crossed over the bridge, over."

"Eleven twenty-five, do you know if the bridge is walkable? I don't have that information here, over."

"I believe the bridge is open underneath, but we're not sure. We prefer not to walk back to the scene from here, over."

"Please hold there, 1125. I'll stop the traffic coming behind you. You are protected by the signals. We don't want anybody off the train there. I'll try for authority for a reverse move, so nobody walks across the bridge, over."

"This is the *Mountain Daylight* 1125, holding on the main, at milepost 76 on Sanders Lake dike until further notice, 1125 out."

"Dispatcher 24, out."

"This is dispatcher 24 calling Train 5490 west. Did you over-hear my conversation with the *Mountain Daylight* regarding their emergency? Over."

"This is 5490 west. We did overhear your conversation with 1125. We have an advance approach on the signal. Do you want a stop here, dispatcher 24? Over."

"Fifty-four ninety west, what's your milepost reading? Over."

"We just passed a signal at 69.3, over."

"Fifty-four ninety west, can you stop within eighty-four hundred feet? You might have a hard yellow advance there. Hold there until we get the emergency sorted out, over."

"Fifty-four ninety west, stopping on the main within eighty-four hundred feet. Holding on the main until further notice. Train 5490 out."

"Dispatcher 24, out."

"This is dispatcher 24 calling Train 8450 west, over."

"Go ahead this is 8450 west, over."

"Are you across the Dakota High Bridge yet? Over."

"We are crossing now, over."

"I'm diverting you in at Brower, due to the emergency ahead at milepost 76, with the *Mountain Daylight.* What signals are you getting, 8450? Over."

"The approach diverging signal is within sight, dispatcher 24, over."

"Very well 8450. We'll give you a clear signal when we're ready, over."

"Train 8450 west will divert to the Brower siding and hold. 8450 out."

"Dispatcher 24, out."

In a few more minutes, the dispatcher came back on the radio.

"Dispatcher 24 calling the *Mountain Daylight* 1125, over."

"Go ahead dispatcher 24, this is the *Mountain Daylight* 1125."

"Is it possible that you hit some maintenance of way equipment? Apparently there is still some along the track on your territory? Over."

"We don't think so, dispatcher 24. We saw headlights. Over."

"Very well 1125, the State Emergency Dispatch Center will be notified of a possible grade crossing event. Keep us up to date on your findings. Is there any train damage? Over."

"Dispatcher 24, we can't make an assessment of train damage now. It's too dangerous for us be off the train here. We don't see any evidence of a problem up front.

We need to back the train up across the bridge and off the

dike. One of the cars took a pretty serious hit. We need to back up closer to the scene if possible, over."

"Okay 1125, I'm faxing over authority for a two-thousand-five-hundred-foot reverse and if you don't receive it shortly, you can move on my verbal, over."

"Eleven twenty-five cleared for two-thousand-five-hundred-foot reverse, over"

"That is correct 1125. I also need the DOT number from the crossbuck if there is one there. Dispatcher 24 over."

"Dispatcher 24. I have the assistant conductor on the rear and we're ready to move, over."

"Any passenger injuries to report as yet 1125? Over."

"We're accessing that now, dispatcher 24. Eleven twenty-five out."

At that moment there was a call from the train directly behind us.

"Train 5490 west, calling dispatcher 24."

"This is dispatcher 24. Go ahead 5490."

"Our signal is dark."

"You have no block signal 5490?"

"That is correct."

"I'll dispatch a signal crew for you, 5490."

"Dispatcher 24 out."

"Dispatcher 24, calling train 1125."

"This is 1125. Go ahead dispatcher 24."

"Did you lose your signal there at milepost 76, 1125?"

"Looks like we did, dispatcher 24. I don't see it now."

"You mean it's not there, or it isn't working?"

"We're backing up now, dispatcher. The signal is destroyed by whatever we hit. The signal is laying on its side, perpendicular to the track, straddling water."

"Thank you 1125. I'll report that information. Dispatcher 24 out."

We crept backwards across the dike. The assistant conductor was on the point, guarding the movement from the rear end of the train. We pulled out the emergency equipment box, one of several stored throughout the train. In the emergency storage, there were hand shovels, wrecking bars, a pickaxe, high-intensity spotlights, fire extinguishers, heavy-duty gloves, first-aid equipment, blankets, portable oxygen and an automated external defibrillator.

All crewmembers participate in emergency drills and we are supposedly trained for different types of emergencies. They teach us how to handle onboard fires, hostage situations, derailments, heart attacks, how to deliver a baby, how to handle and carry injured passengers, terrorist threats, and everything else you can think of. It is a thick and all-encompassing book that we have to read and understand. Next edition, they'll have a whole chapter on ferret removal. I can teach that course. But, as I stand here in the vestibule of the entry coach moving slowly backwards, I can't think of a thing I'm supposed to do in an emergency. I guess we're in some kind of an emergency, so I hope something pops into my head pretty soon. Tim and Dean are looking out each vestibule door trying to spot what we hit or what hit us.

Shortly, the engineers called back to Tim, saying that we were across the bridge and off the dike and did Tim want them to stop or keep going. Tim said to stop and we'd do a preliminary check. We stopped just on the edge of the lake. There was still water on my side of the train. We heard muffled screams. Then it was quiet. More screams. In the distance we saw a flash of fire. It wasn't too far down the track, but it wasn't on the track. There appeared to be a depression filled with water between the track and the bank. No emergency personnel had arrived, but Tim seemed to think they had been dispatched.

Tim couldn't talk to the Fort Worth dispatchers directly from his handset, so he had to depend on the engineers to do that. By now Tim was at the rear with his assistant. He stepped off the train and walked the track, making sure it was safe to continue the backup move. We continued to move as he directed. The track was clear of debris. Tim responded by saying whatever we hit took the signal out. It was snapped right off of its support. Tim thought it was safer to move the train further past the downed signal, further back from the site of impact. He wanted the passengers to be out of site of the accident scene. We continued to back up. We passed whatever it was that we hit. We went right by it. It was thrown across a little inlet to the lake, but landed out of the water. When we passed, we saw the fire again. I started to get frightened. I chilled with fright. We came to the crossing and pulled through it. Tim said to keep it clear for emergency vehicle access. He told both the engineers and his assistant conductor to remain on the train. Someone of authority needed to remain with the service crew and handle passenger issues.

Reyna called us and said that other than the elderly lady, there were no other injuries. Reyna said she would come out and help if there were survivors.

Dean and I carried some emergency supplies off the train and set them down on the edge of the track. It was a dark and moonless night. It was damp with a slight chill in the air. We had road access, even though we didn't know where the road came from. There was another scream. Tim heard it. He came up to where we were and told us to stand by.

Tim took his spotlight and walked in front of the locomotives up the track, searching for evidence of what we had hit. There were bits and pieces of debris scattered along both sides of the track. He instructed us to wait by the train while he went down to make an assessment. Tim said he would take decisive action in the absence of law enforcement and emergency medical personnel.

Also, the dispatch center and five other trains were waiting to hear his findings. His report would impact their movements. Dean assured me that the two trains behind us were stopped and wouldn't be running into us. I could just imagine a huge train wreck, on top of whatever else had just happened.

Just then someone hollered for help. Dean, without hesitation, asked me to grab onto one end of the emergency box. We placed the fire extinguishers on top of the tools. We started running down the road to where we could get around the water, which petered out, there at the crossing. We negotiated a slight incline. It flattened out and we kept moving in the direction of the screams. I started to shake all over. Every scream cut like a knife. From the top of the incline, we could look down onto the accident scene.

Dean grabbed the fire extinguisher, wrecking bar, and pickaxe, and told me to follow him. The box was light so I dragged it down the hill behind me. Dean said to put in my earpiece so we could talk to Reyna. Dean informed Reyna about what we were doing. She said to be careful. I think she was too strung out to compute in her brain what he said. We ran down the steep hill to the wreckage. I nearly fell in the goopy, slippery mud. This sticky prairie clay clings like glue. You get it on you and it doesn't come off. There was water between the wreckage and the track. I couldn't believe this vehicle was so far away from the track, on the opposite side. It looked like a giant discus thrower had picked it up and tossed the vehicle across the water.

The driver was yelling. He had tried to untangle himself from the wreckage but couldn't get out. He was thrashing his arms. His legs were hopelessly trapped. The dashboard was shoved up into his lap. He was in agony.

"We're here! We're here!" Dean yelled into the cab.

"Get me out of here. I'm hurt. I'm hurt really bad. I can't move! Don't let me burn man! Don't let me burn! My friends are in here too! Please get us out!"

It was a pickup or what was left of it. I could see that it was a young man inside, when Dean shined the light into his face. I would guess him to be my age. I could see other occupants in the vehicle, but they weren't moving and they weren't talking. Dean didn't ask the victim any questions and like a drill sergeant, Dean started barking orders at me.

"Discharge the extinguisher, Trevor. Get the fire out first. Hit it underneath. Stop! That's enough. *Hit it again.* Don't use it all. We may need more. *Hit it!*"

I knelt down and pointed the nozzle under the vehicle. I actuated the extinguisher. I sprayed the chemical underneath the vehicle, stopped, and waited for more flame before discharging more retardant. The fire would go out but then flare back. I kept applying the retardant until I ran out. In the end we did extinguish the fire, at least what we could see of it. It appeared to be out. Dean went to work trying to pry open the doors. There were four doors, all badly smashed. If we do get them out, where are we going to put the victims? We were mired down in gumbo clay. The mud was accumulating on the bottom of my shoes like lead weights. When he couldn't get the doors off right away, he told me to get in the truck bed and see if we could pull someone out the top before the vehicle caught fire again. There was a smashed-in moon roof. I looked over my shoulder and saw Tim running with the spotlight down the track back toward the train. He couldn't get to us from where he was standing because of the water. Tim was yelling something to us. Dean yelled back to him that we had survivors. I couldn't hear everything Tim said. I thought he said that he would get Reyna and they would come to help.

The truck landed right side up on the edge of the water with the cab pointing up the hill on a thirty-degree angle. The tailgate was partly submerged in the water. I hoisted myself up into the bed of the truck. A victim, a body, somebody, was partially ejected out the rear window. The body was folded in half. I could tell it was a very young man. It looked like if you'd pulled on him, you might pull him apart. The upper torso was hanging limp, with head and arms dangling onto the pickup bed. It was like a battle scene from a war movie. It was horrifying.

"Pull 'em out of the truck and lay 'em on the hillside!" Dean kept telling me everything to do.

Dean stopped what he was doing and hoisted himself up far enough to see me. I stood with one foot braced on the wheel well and the other braced on the cab body. It was the only way I could stand and not fall down backwards into the water.

"Pull on 'em! Do it! He's dead. You can't hurt 'em. Drop him over the edge and we can get the others out the back," Dean said. Then he jumped down and tried to get the driver out.

I didn't think I could do it. Someone in the back seat began to moan.

"Hurry Trevor! We have another live one."

I pulled on the boy. I knew he was dead considering the gross injuries I saw on his head. I pulled and pulled. I needed better traction so I straddled the stream of blood that had flowed out of the victim's neck. I braced both legs against the wheel well. I pulled hard. My hands were bloody and slick. Nothing gave. His hair was peeled back off his head, like he had been partially scalped. I moved up close, placed my arms underneath his shoulders, and pulled with all my might. I pushed his head into my chest. I didn't want the head to roll off. It seemed to be loosely attached. Suddenly, I got this wrenching pain in my chest and in the process I lost my balance and slipped on the blood running down the bed of the pickup. Both of us slid down the pickup bed backwards into the water. On the way down, I scraped my ribs against something in the truck bed. We did a big splash. The water was waist deep and icy cold. It felt like the ribcage on my left side was on fire. I worked to keep myself upright. I didn't know what end of him I had in or out of the water. There was better footing behind me so I kept stepping backwards, pulling him with me. I soon stepped back to where there were big rocks piled against the track bed. I tried to climb up out of the water. Some of the rocks were huge. Some were jagged blocks of concrete. My right leg went down into a hole between two of the rocks. I hurt my leg and shinbone really bad, but I held onto the boy I was carrying. I hoisted him up out of the water. My boots were full of water. I could hardly walk and it was hard to maintain any traction as I drug us both up the rock-strewn bank to the top of the track.

Dean seemed oblivious to what had just happened to me. I didn't know where to lay him, so I continued to carry him up, over, and off the track. He was a much smaller man than me; otherwise I couldn't have carried him so far. I didn't want to lay him down in the mud. For sure he was dead, but I couldn't just drop him in the muck. I had to walk a ways out into the field that was illuminated by the locomotive's headlights. It seemed drier there so I gently laid him down in some thick grass. I tried to position him in a dignified manner. Fortunately, my pocket light still worked. It was then I discovered his skull was cracked open. The back of the head was mushy, and there was brain matter oozing out of his head. This stuff was all over my hands and shirt. I pulled his hair back over his head. I supported the back of his head with his left hand and put his right hand over his heart and left him there. I shined my pocket light into his face again. He looked right at me as if to say, "thank you sir, I feel better now." He looked serene and comfortable laying there in the darkness, in spite of the empty stare coming from his eyes.

I couldn't think of my own pain. There was too much of an adrenaline rush. My heart was racing and the only medical attention I craved was a Dr. Pepper to soothe my dry mouth. I was totally frozen in the icy water. My pain had lessened, but my teeth were chattering with the cold. I made my way back over to the track and wreckage. Dean was frustrated. He was calling for me. I didn't bother walking down the track to where I could cross over on the road. I was already cold and wet, so it was quicker to ford the moat again over to the wreckage. I made my way carefully down through the rocks to the edge of the water and leapt as far across as I could, where I landed knee-deep in water again. Dean needed my help. He had one rear door off and had laid another young man in the mud. I assumed he was dead but I didn't ask. Dean called for Reyna. She and Tim came with more extinguishers, blankets, portable oxygen and the defibrillator.

The engineers relayed a message to Tim from the dispatch center that rescue units and law enforcement were on their way. All we knew at that point was that we had hit a pickup truck with five occupants, some dead and some alive. Tim couldn't use his cell phone to call out. We were in a dead zone, no pun intended. The only communication was by radio. He had been trying to call 911 but couldn't get a signal on the phones. My phone was waterlogged and out of commission. Tim's modus operandi was to always call 911 locally and not depend on Fort Worth to do it. Since there was no signal, he said we would have to rely on the railroad dispatcher to do the proper notification. After all, this was rural North Dakota in the middle of the night.

Reyna went right to work, trying to determine who was hurt the worst among the remaining victims. She asked the driver his name. He said his name was Aaron. The one next to him in the front was Joey. The three in the back seat were Travis, Brad and Kyle. Brad and Kyle were dead but Travis was still alive. Joey was unresponsive but alive. Reyna talked to Travis. He couldn't move. Reyna told Dean and me to try and get Travis out. The truck was getting hot where he was lying. He couldn't stay there much longer without suffering burns. His body was pressed together in a heap. Before Dean pulled Brad out, Brad was on top of Travis. The guy I pulled out the back window was Kyle, who was on top of Brad. It was obvious that they were not wearing seatbelts.

We finally pried both rear doors off. Dean was on one side and I was on the other. We stretched Travis out. Reyna worked to immobilize his cervical spine by using several blankets, the best option available in the absence of a backboard, something the paramedics carry. She was afraid there was a possible cervical spine fracture. We would be dealing with worse injuries, she said, if we didn't get him out. She and Dean each took him by the shoulder and I was on the other side holding his feet. I crawled through the wreckage and helped ease him out onto a bed of blankets. As I crawled across the seats in the back, I scraped my right thigh and shin again on something sharp. Something gashed my leg and upper thigh. I felt a wet burning sensation down my thigh. I did another number on my right leg.

Dean and I took the shovels and scraped out a flat place to lay him on top of the hill. I tried not to limp but Dean noticed and asked if I was okay. Reyna wanted Travis away from the foot traffic and his dead friend, who had already started to slide down into the water. It was Reyna's opinion that Travis was more stable than Joey, who was unconscious. The three of us carried Travis in the blankets. Reyna positioned him to eliminate any pooling of blood from internal injuries. I covered him with two blankets. Other than being cold, he seemed to be comfortable and didn't complain of pain. Reyna told me to stay with him and to call her if I needed help. She assured me that he would be fine until help came.

Reyna thought Joey was the most critical. Aaron, she reasoned, should be left in the truck. From what she could tell most of his injuries were to the legs. She said both legs appeared to be broken. At least one was a compound fracture. She said the rescue squads would have to handle him. She was afraid to lay him out flat, or even try to transport him, without the necessary leg splint equipment. She told Dean not to pull on him unless the fire flared out of control. In that case, she thought they could get him out if we all pulled on him. But if it came to that, where we had to pull him out, it would put him at a huge risk for making the injuries worse. At this time, the fire barely smoldered. Reyna, prepared for the worst, always carried a pair of high-top rubber boots. Tonight they came in handy.

It was a horrible scene. What made it worse was Aaron. When he couldn't stand the pain any longer, he would scream until he couldn't scream anymore. He's fighting, Reyna said, and that was a good sign. He didn't cry. When he was too exhausted to holler, he groaned. He was one tough dude.

"You hang in there. We're helping your friend Joey. He's bleeding bad, Aaron. You hang together for us. Help will come." Reyna kept reassuring him.

When he wasn't talking on his handset to the assistant conductor and engineers, Tim kept putting out the fire that smoldered under the car. He was mostly preoccupied doing that.

There was diesel fuel everywhere. Best guess was that one of the dual tanks had ruptured, spilling out the fuel. Some of it leaked inside the truck. It was fortunate for all of us that the interior of the truck didn't ignite. The truck looked like it had passed through a viselike device, applying force onto each side of the doorposts and separating the front and rear doors. Next, the vise was positioned front to back and squeezed inward. Aaron and Joey were saved by seatbelts and airbags, but their legs remained entangled in the wreckage. The truck must have rolled several times. That was the only logical explanation for the damage.

Dean and Tim still couldn't get Joey free. Dean tried to work from inside the cab, but he was too wide and clumsy. They called me down to help. Joey had a large amount of blood around his legs. Reyna said he was slowly bleeding to death. His heartbeat was getting weaker. She said his breath sounds were so labored that he could die any minute. She thought there were undoubtedly chest injuries, even a collapsed lung. They had to get him out, find the source of the hemorrhaging and apply the necessary pressure. She thought he was a goner, even if we got him out. I was afraid the truck was going to explode into a ball of fire and kill both Aaron and Joey.

Reluctantly, I left Travis and came to their aid.

"Who vomited?" Reyna asked me.

It was all over my shirt down to my waist. I told her it was Travis. He vomited twice. I told her I held his head up when he started to gag so he could discharge the vomit. She said she would be up to check on him as soon as she could. All she told me was to make certain he doesn't drown in his own vomit.

"He's been talking to me all the time. He's breathing okay," I told her.

I was terrified to get into the cab. I'm young, limber, agile, athletic, and thin with long arms. I was qualified for the job. It was dangerous work. Tim directed the spotlight across Aaron that allowed me to work getting Joey's legs free. I wormed my way in the back, hoisted myself over the front seat and practically stood on my head in order to work. Dean had removed all the debris from the moon roof. We couldn't get the front passenger door off. Reyna said it would require the Jaws of Life, special equipment that firemen carry, to accomplish such a task. Dean stood on the mangled rooftop. He pulled out the cargo straps that were strung along the sides of the pickup bed. I was able to free Joey's legs from the wreckage. Dean pulled him up through the roof, with the aid of the straps. I pushed on his butt with my neck as Dean pulled and lifted. The long hours Dean had spent strength training on the bench press paid off. Joey was no lightweight. His left leg was so twisted I wondered what would happen to it. I questioned whether he would ever walk again. We laid him down just as he quit breathing. Reyna was expecting it and she was ready. She used the defibrillator. His body jerked up off the ground when she shocked him. It was scary, but he started breathing again. Reyna started mouth-to-mouth resuscitation. He needed to be bagged but she didn't have the necessary airway equipment. In a minute or so, she had Dean continue the mouth-to-mouth. Reyna was completely winded. She couldn't do it anymore. Suddenly Reyna detected a good pulse.

She listened with the stethoscope and said the heartbeat was getting stronger. Next she focused on his leg, where there was evidence of blood. She cut his jeans off. She stopped the bleeding by applying pressure. She took his belt off and made a tourniquet. Reyna told me to go back and stay with Travis.

When I returned back to Travis, he seemed weaker, at least in his voice. He assured me he was fine. Then he said,

"Trevor, will you stay with me from now on? I don't want to be alone here."

"Yes sir dude, I'm right here and I'm not leaving."

Travis asked me to check to see if he had his watch on. He said it was his graduation present. His arms were numb, he said, and he couldn't move them. It was there on his left wrist and I told him so. He told me to take it off of him and keep it. It was expensive and he was afraid someone would steal it. I removed the watch and put it in my cargo pants pocket. I told him I would see that he got it back. If I have to, I'll mail it to you, I said. He told me I had better insure it.

I asked him if I could use his cell phone. I took it, it was on and it lit up. There was a signal for a connection.

"I should call your mom and dad."

"No, my parents will be sleeping. What time is it?"

"It's 2:15 a.m.," I said.

"I don't want you to call them."

"Where do you live?"

"East of Cheneau Valley."

"That's not too far. I have to call them, Travis. They need to come."

"No!"

"Why?"

"I'm drunk."

I dialed 911.

"Nine one one. What is your emergency please?"

"We're waiting for help. When are you coming?"

"What is your name, location, and what is your emergency?"

"This is Trevor calling from my friend's cell phone. I'm with injured people by the train track. We have a truck on fire. I need help now!"

"What is your location sir?"

"The conductor said we're at Sanders Lake. I'm east of Jamestown. A truck carrying five boys hit our train."

"Are you injured?"

"No. What's taking so long? Can you just send out the fire department and paramedics to our location? How far away are you?"

"Trevor, this is Cheneau Valley. My name is Julie. I am the emergency dispatcher for Valley County. I'm less than a half hour to the east. You say a train hit a vehicle with five occupants? Any fatalities?"

"Please. Just send us some help here. Forget the details. I don't want to do a survey. We have people that are hurt. We have five people, all in bad shape."

"Are you saying this was a passenger train that hit the vehicle?"

"Yes the *Mountain Daylight* headed for Seattle."

"Any passengers hurt?"

"Maybe. I don't know. They hit us pretty hard. We stopped fast. Could you please hurry and send help before everybody's dead?"

"Sir. Please stay calm. I'm dispatching you help as we talk. I have to have specific information so I can dispatch the appropriate help to the right location. I have to know how much help you need. I had no prior knowledge of your accident. I'm sorry, but you are in my jurisdiction, but nobody phoned until now. I'll investigate that problem, but now I'm making available the necessary emergency medical services needed to help. Trevor, I have the North Dakota State Patrol on the line. Will you talk to him, please? Go ahead, trooper."

I was so mad and so upset and so cold that I was about to cry. There was a chilly wind blowing. I didn't want to talk too much in front of Travis. Two of his buddies are dead. I needed to be positive. I tried to remain calm but by now my voice was shaking.

I continued talking to the patrol officer. I stepped away from Travis so I could talk more frankly with the trooper. I explained our situation. He asked to talk to the conductor or someone in command. I told him that they were either fighting the fire or assisting with the injured. He wanted everyone's name. The trooper was calling from Bismarck and would dispatch an officer, but the closest trooper was thirty minutes away on the interstate. No one had told him what had just happened. He checked with somebody in Jamestown to see what was going on. I listened. It was the railroad that screwed up, from what I could tell. They did nothing. Somebody was waiting for somebody else to tell somebody, somewhere, what to do and where to go. Then, when the officer hung up with Jamestown, I didn't really know what had happened, or who had screwed up.

Julie from 911 came on, saying she had the Cheneau Valley Fire Chief on the phone. I restated everything that I had just told the trooper. He said the Sanders Fire Department would be the first to respond, and they would extinguish the fire and provide basic medical support until the paramedics from Cheneau Valley arrived. He said his force would be on their way soon and would bring the extrication equipment. I told him about the water that I guessed to be about fifty feet wide. I told him I thought the truck was sitting maybe a half a city block over some steep terrain from the road where we crossed the track. He said they would bring a boat. Julie wouldn't let me hang up. She went on to assure me that the Cheneau Valley Police were on their way, as well as a sheriff, and three ambulances. She told me the name of the lead paramedic and the Cheneau Valley fireman who would take on the role of commander once he arrived. The names flew right over my head. I didn't remember anything she told me, five seconds after she said it.

"Trevor?" Julie kept up the dialogue. "Your closest fire house is right around the corner in Sanders. I've activated the fire whistle in Sanders and sent a page to each of the fire crew. They will bring you an EMT. She can stabilize the victims. Stay with me now, please, just a few more minutes and help will be there. I'll tell you when they report to duty at the fire station in Sanders. They will check in with me."

Sanders had an all-volunteer force, but Julie said they would respond quickly, that within seven minutes there would be ample crew to man one fire truck. Next, she put me in touch with the state dispatcher in Bismarck. It was then I learned that the railroad called the state's emergency dispatcher in Bismarck, who was still in limbo waiting for the railroad to provide specifics. They weren't sure which of the two trains had the problem. Was it 1125 westbound east of Jamestown or 1126 eastbound now approaching Jamestown? They didn't know. They needed clarification lest they send help to the wrong train.

"Trevor! The first unit has left the fire station in Sanders. They are on their way. They are carrying a thousand gallons of water to extinguish the fire. The medical unit will be on the way shortly."

She explained that Life Flight in Fargo was on standby and would come if directed by the paramedics. The weather in Fargo was unsettled, but the equipment and crew were ready if they were granted permission to fly. Julie also notified St. Catherine's

Hospital in Cheneau Valley to expect multiple victims. I wanted to hang up and get back to Travis. I was uncomfortable about stepping out of earshot from him. Julie kept talking. She kept repeating everything again.

I heard the first siren. What a relief to hear the howl of the sirens! I've never heard a siren that sounded so good. Julie insisted I hang with her in case they couldn't find us. I couldn't get free from Julie to tell Dean and Reyna what I had done. I guess it didn't matter as long as we got help. Why would they need to know that it was me that finally got through to 911?

The fire truck couldn't get to where we were. My attention was diverted away from Travis as I talked to Julie, explaining how to get to the wreckage from the train. I went berserk screaming into Travis' phone. I could see the flashing lights, but they stopped as if they didn't know where to go from there. Julie kept telling me to calm down.

"Take a deep breath, Trevor! Please. I've sent you a lot of help. They are all coming at once. They will need your assistance. We will find you. You have done very well so far. Please stay with us. Don't panic. When they get there, they will take over. You are almost done!"

Tim started yelling at Delaine over the radio, to get down out of the unit and direct the fire crew over to where we were. The locomotives had backed several hundred feet down from the crossing. This confused the fire crew, who started driving over the open field toward where the train was stopped. The fields were so wet they couldn't drive off the road without getting mired down in gumbo clay. Realizing this, the fire truck backed up onto the road, stopped at the crossing, and waited for Mick, who was running toward the fire truck to direct them. They turned and drove onto the track. They straddled the track and came toward the wreckage. They stopped. They got out of the truck just as the fire flared up. In seconds, it seemed, two firemen came down to the wreckage carrying extinguishers. The two on the pump truck pulled the hose down to the water's edge. Immediately a heavy stream of water landed on the pickup bed from the hose. They shot it fifty feet over the water. Again and again the water came. The fire kept burning. They didn't have a boat. They got down into the water with the hose where they could direct the spray underneath the truck. They shot the water under the truck. The fire went out. The others standing by the truck used their extinguishers. They were on top of the truck and the fire was completely extinguished in seconds. They weren't a second too soon or Aaron would have been fried. It created a lot of smoke. Next to their equipment, our extinguishers were about as effective as squirt guns.

There were more sirens. A crew of four carrying medical equipment came. A lady, I didn't catch her name, said she was the EMT with Sanders fire. She looked at Travis.

"He's doing fine." I said. "They've got two more over there alive. One is almost dead and the other guy beside him is dead," They ran toward Joey and Reyna. They went right to work helping Reyna.

Julie wanted to know if the county extrication team had arrived. Just as I told her no, a couple more trucks drove down the track. A bunch of men got out. They had a boat. They started loading equipment onto the boat. It had an engine. In seconds they were at the pickup. I could tell that everyone was talking to someone on the radios. It was crazy. I stood there by Travis, hoping he didn't get terrified like I was. I wanted him to stay calm. He remained quiet. I kept him covered, which protected him from the water spray and smoke. The boat went back to the trucks. They pulled out an additional hose, laid it on the boat and strung it through the water to the truck.

There was a huddle around Joey. They soon had Joey laid out on a board. He had on a facemask and they were pumping air into the mask. I could tell that he was still alive. The Sanders EMT removed the tourniquet on Joey and applied new bandages to his puncture wound. She got the bleeding stopped. They moved him out of the way.

They started a gas-operated generator. They were all over Aaron. They cut the roof away from the truck. The driver's door came off. A hydraulic pusher moved the dashboard off of Aaron's lap. He was soon free of the wreckage. He was out in about five minutes. It must have really hurt when they moved him, but he was quiet. He didn't make a peep. I heard them say he went into shock. They started to apply a traction splint on his legs, but stopped when the commander gave the order to move him out of there. The EMTs picked him up and carried him to the boat, which crossed the water to the trucks. He was carried away out of sight.

Julie wanted to know if any of the three ambulances had arrived. I didn't know. I couldn't believe that more people could be coming. Julie said that each ambulance would have two EMTs and a paramedic and it would be their job to transport the victims to the hospital.

Julie asked the names of the victims. I told her I was with Travis --Travis Olsen. There was silence.

"What is his status? Can I speak with him?"

She didn't say, but I think she knew who he was.

"Travis! Travis? Julie from 911 wants to talk to you. Can you talk to her? If I hold the phone up to your mouth, can you talk?" There was no response. I immediately ended my call with Julie. I started talking to Travis. "Hey dude! Are you okay? Talk to me Travis. Do you need something? Can you talk? Talk to me bro. Talk. Do you want me to get Reyna? Are you asleep? Help is here. Did you hear all the sirens, bro? Everything is going to get better from now on. Dude! Everything is okay. Are you okay?"

I stood up. I was shaking like a leaf. Travis's phone rang. It was Julie calling me back. She wanted to know what was wrong.

"I don't know," I told her. "Help us!" I hollered. I think something is wrong here. Travis won't talk. "TRAVIS! TALK!" I screamed into the phone, thinking Julie could do something.

Four strobe lights were set up on the field in front of the locomotives, where Sanders Fire had prepared a landing spot for a helicopter. In a few minutes a copter dropped out of the sky. It came from nowhere. I heard them say that the helicopter could carry only one critical victim. Who would be the lucky one to get the passport to life? The helicopter landed. It was so surreal.

But I kept hollering for help. Finally Reyna realized I needed something and she yelled something back. She said to wait a minute. So I waited a minute. Travis wouldn't talk. In about three minutes they all came. There were medical people everywhere. They came down the hill and stopped to examine Brad. I yelled for them to come over to me.

"He's been dead for an hour," I said. "Come over here. I have somebody alive. I hope."

They ignored me. They turned him over and knelt down and stayed there for what seemed to be an eternity. I heard them yell something. I didn't understand it. Then someone picked up their handset and said that Brad was pulseless and apneic. I didn't know what that meant other than he was dead. They finally came over and I moved out of the way. They stampeded right on top of me and went to work on Travis. Suddenly a tall, coarsely featured woman appeared out of nowhere. She was talking on a radio to somebody. She looked at me like I should know something.

"How long has he not been breathing?"

"How long? He's not breathing?" I asked. "He has to be breathing. I was just talking to him. Oh no," I said. "Do something. He has to be breathing. He's not dead."

She turned her attention to Travis. They cut away his shirt. He didn't flinch or move. I knew what they were going to do. I had just seen Reyna do it to Joey. They zapped him once and they zapped him twice. They did it a third time. I couldn't breathe. I started to get emotional. I knew that wouldn't help. I didn't want to look. How could this be happening? How can they just keep doing that? I wondered if all that electricity finished him off. That's what I thought. That woman is going to either save him or kill him. It looked like she swooped in for the kill. I jumped every time she applied the electricity. I hoped the jerking was not the result of any pain he was feeling. But then, I wanted him to feel something. I wanted him to live. I wanted the shocks to bring him back. I wanted to hear him scream with pain like Aaron had. I had to hope. This dude can't be dead, I thought. Hope was fading. There was nothing. He didn't move, he didn't flinch, and he didn't talk. I wanted to call his mom and dad. I was too afraid. They discontinued the shock treatment. I sensed that it hadn't worked. I wanted to pray but I didn't know whom to pray to, or how.

The crew didn't look up. They put a tube down his throat and started pumping air into this chest. This looks really bad, I thought. She put an IV line in his arm and pushed in some medicine to get the heart going again. They didn't talk to one another. They kept working. It was like something they did every day. It was effortless. It was routine, like there was nothing to it. I stood there looking at them, at Travis, at Brad lying sprawled out on the hill, at the fire crew working. There were about eight or so flashing lights around on the field, on the other side of the track. It looked like the airport. The helicopter sat there for a while. Suddenly, it lifted off the ground. There goes somebody, I thought. Somebody's getting out of here alive, I hope.

I still had my hands on Travis' phone. I was wishing I had called his folks. A guy in his kind of trouble needs his mom and dad. He told me about his parents. He's a lucky man to have a mom and dad. I thought he said he had a brother and sister. My leg where I scraped it felt wet and bloody. Dried blood was caked to my uniform. It hurt to stand. I couldn't bend my right knee.

Reyna came up to where I stood watching. She said that Life Flight took Aaron and one ambulance took Joey. They are taking Joey to Cheneau Valley in hopes of stabilizing him. He can't wait. He needs blood and they have some there they can give him. Joey needed a doctor or he wasn't going to make it. They needed to fly Aaron out. They need to get him to surgery. Reyna explained that Joey was the most critical, but it was the right decision to fly Aaron out. They didn't think Joey would live through the flight if he didn't get some replacement fluids and receive the necessary treatment for his chest injuries. If he can get some blood and survives the next hour or so, they will fly back to Cheneau Valley and take him to the trauma center in Fargo.

"Trevor, our work is done here. We've done all we can do. Come back to the train with me. You need to get those clothes off and shower. Dean says he thinks you are hurt. The quicker we all get back on the train and give our statements to law enforcement, the quicker we'll get out of here. We have over two hundred people waiting for us."

"No," I said. Reyna acted like she didn't hear me and kept talking.

"You need a great big hug and I'm going to give you and everybody else a big hug. Trevor, you smell so rotten I can't hug you now. You need to clean up. Come with me. Let's go."

"I'm not leaving Travis. I promised I would stay with him."

At that moment the woman, the same one who asked how long he had not been breathing, was talking to the doctor at St. Catherine's hospital by radio. I was stunned as she asked permission to discontinue the resuscitation procedures. The doctor told her he couldn't come to the scene and instructed her to transport Travis there for him to examine. She looked up at Reyna, who by now had become very distraught over Travis. It suddenly dawned on her that he was dying or dead.

"I'm sorry, but I think we lost him. He will be DOA at the hospital. There is nothing more we can do here for him."

I don't recall just how she said it. I knew that it meant that he had passed away. I stood there in complete denial and shock. How can someone you just talked to just up and pass away? She said they would take him and Brad to St. Catherine's in Cheneau Valley. By now the EMS crew had the decency to put a sheet over Brad.

"The doctor there tonight is also acting as the county coroner," she said. "He will pronounce him dead at the hospital."

I turned and looked north away from the carnage into the blackness of the night. I don't believe this, I thought. I was standing right here talking on the phone when he up and freaking died. I let him die while I was talking to Julie. Why did I talk to her and let him die? I couldn't talk. I couldn't swallow. I couldn't move. I turned to stone.

Then she began to take a tally as to how many were in the truck.

"Were three victims in the back seat of the truck?"

Reyna was so distressed she couldn't think. She went blank. The stress and emotion of the scene was finally getting to her.

"I was told we had five victims! Who is the fifth victim?"

"He's lying over there in the field. His name is Kyle," I answered as I turned back to face reality.

"How'd he get way over there?" she wanted to know.

"I carried him," I said.

Reyna acted like she didn't know anything about it.

"Have any of us examined him?" she demanded.

When I told her no, she used the radio and reported back to the commander. She made it sound like I carried him away from the scene and dumped him. The commander couldn't believe we had another casualty at the scene he didn't know about. Apparently in the confusion, Dean didn't mention it and they had completely overlooked it.

"Take us to where his is. Now!" the commander insisted on his radio.

"I don't want to leave Travis," I said. "He is over there across the track on the other side of your trucks, lying out of the mud in the tall grass. He is straight out from where you are standing."

I shined my spotlight over toward the spot. I knew exactly where it was. I didn't want to see him again. They acted like I had done something terrible in taking him so far away from the scene of the accident.

The commander dispatched his crew, who followed my light over to where they found Kyle in the grass. The lady paramedic got into the boat with her equipment. The boat transferred her to the other side of the water. They disappeared behind the trucks and dropped down on the other side of the track. I stood there in despair. I wondered if I had broken some law. I asked Reyna if she knew about a Good Samaritan law in North Dakota that would protect me. She said not to worry. I don't think Reyna believed me that I had put a dead victim so far away from everything.

In a few minutes they all came back. They left Kyle where he was. They said nothing more about it.

"I'm Joanna, the lead paramedic," the lady said. "Sorry to be so late with the introduction."

She called a Mr. Simmons in Cheneau Valley. He'll help, she said. I'll have him come out and pick up Kyle. He'll be working with us tonight. He's from the Simmons-Kline Funeral Home in Cheneau Valley. That is where the bodies will be taken after the doctor examines them. They picked up Brad and carried him off. I felt sorry no one stood by Brad. Dean just threw him out onto the mud and left him. That's not right.

"I'm sorry," she said as she turned to me. "Was he your friend?"

"Yes," I answered.

I didn't know if she was talking about Brad or Travis. I still don't think she got it, as to who I was or where I came from. She tried to put her arm around me but I flinched, saying I fell on my side and hurt my ribs. It was very painful when she touched my ribcage. At first she thought I was in the truck and escaped somehow. Mentally, by including me, she had accounted for the five. Nobody noticed my train uniform, not that you could distinguish it from anything with all the brains, vomit, and blood all over it. She asked how I got hurt, so I told her how I fell down in the truck bed. She asked me if I would go in to the hospital. I said no. She said to think about it.

They let me stay with Travis. I had a few minutes with him before they came back for him. As I sat there by Travis, I told him I was sorry. He wasn't supposed to die. I was sorry I left him for any time at all. I was sorry I didn't call 911 earlier. I was sorry I didn't call his folks. I sent the first EMT to Joey. She had equipment. She maybe could have saved him. I shouldn't have done that. I was sorry I stayed on the phone with Julie so long. That's it. I'm blaming Julie. This whole mess is her fault. I asked him what he wanted me to say to his folks if I ever met them. Then I asked myself; well what would he want me to say? I answered my own question: the less said, the better.

My thoughts were interrupted when they came back with the stretcher. I walked with them as they carried Travis to the ambulance. When I walked down the hill behind the stretcher, I stepped on a can. I picked it up. It was an empty beer can. I threw it in the water. Then I noticed several more beer cans lying around. This is an odd place to have a party, I thought.

Mr. Simmons was nice. He explained that the hospital gave him permission to pick up a body that I rescued from the burning truck. He was very professional, saying he would go look for Kyle if I told him where to look. I wouldn't have to come if I didn't want to, but he would appreciate my help.

"I want to," I said. "I need to finish my job."

He was very gracious and thanked me. He said the emergency crews were already talking about how courageous we all were.

I didn't feel that way, I said. We just did the best we could. A highway trooper came with us. The three of us walked and walked and walked. I had a spotlight and both men had big flashlights. I stood and looked and looked and looked. I lost touch with where I was. Delaine had cut the ditch lights on the front locomotive. It seemed like the field was twice as big as it was originally. Where was he? I was tired. I hurt. It was three in the morning. I stopped. Mr. Simmons said to relax and take my time. I pivoted around, shining the light everywhere. I could not see the clump of tall grass where I knew he would be. Everything got tramped on. The landscape had changed. I was completely disoriented. I couldn't get my bearings. It was dark and nothing looked familiar from my vantage point.

"He's not here. I can't find him. The firemen must have moved him. Did they take him already?"

"No, I don't think they took him. We'll find him," Mr. Simmons assured me. "I was told they marked where he was laying."

My side was raw. I could hardly bend my leg. I stank to high heaven. Even I could smell me now. It was making me sick.

"The wolves got him," I said.

"We don't have wild wolves in North Dakota. Nothing took him. He is still there where you left him, and the rescue squad saw him." Mr. Simmons remained calm as he talked to me.

"Trevor," he asked, "how old are you?"

When I told him I was nineteen, he said that was too young to see such carnage. He said this was one of the worst accidents he had ever been called to.

"Train-vehicle accidents are the worst," he said. "When dawn breaks in Cheneau Valley, the community will suffer untold grief and pain over what happened here tonight. These were our boys. They were good boys. I know this is hard," he said.

The trooper suggested that we call off the search for Kyle and walk back to the train. Daylight will come in less than two hours, and it would be much easier to find where I had put him. The trooper explained that law enforcement would remain at the scene through the night. Nobody is going to bother any of the evidence. None of this, he told me, was my responsibility. Mr. Simmons suggested that I get back on the train and take care of myself.

I told Mr. Simmons that I was totally disoriented. But if I could get my bearings, I'd be okay, I thought. I didn't want to leave Kyle in the grass. Suddenly, I took hold of myself. I saw the fire crew still working at the scene. I could focus on where the helicopter had landed. I could visualize where I had stood, pointing the spotlight. I realized I was turned around and needed to walk further east, toward the train. That's it, I said. I know now. I went right to the spot. I told Mr. Simmons how I laid Kyle down and how I placed one hand on the back of the head to hold in his brains that were falling out. He thought that was very considerate. He said it was a very good idea to have pulled his hair back into place. The crew had staked the location. It was clearly marked. I don't know why I couldn't see it. I stood there while they worked. The trooper didn't touch him, but he went over some papers and made some check marks. Mr. Simmons took off Kyle's watch and removed the wallet from his jeans pocket. Mr. Simmons checked all the pockets. There was a bracelet around his wrist but his arm had swelled. Mr. Simmons left the bracelet attached. The trooper noted it on the papers. Next Mr. Simmons put Kyle in a white vinyl pouch while we watched. I guess it was a body bag. It unzipped like a garment bag. He pulled the front flap down and gently laid Kyle inside and zipped it up. He told the trooper it was Kyle Hickles. The trooper confirmed it by the driver's license. Mr. Simmons took out a marking pen and wrote his name on the outside of the bag. They put the wallet and watch in a bag and sealed it with some tape. Next, he slid a plastic buckboard underneath the bag. We picked it up, placed the bag on a portable cot and carried him back to the road. I helped. I limped and stumbled along, hardly able to walk. It was the least I could do. I wanted to lay him in a safer place. The cot was placed inside the van. Mr. Simmons closed the rear door. He took my hand, held it a second, thanked me again, got in the van and drove off. I stood there stunned, disbelieving what had just taken place. I watched until the van disappeared around a clump of trees, out of sight.

I trudged back and reboarded the train from Hell.

The Tragic Aftermath

Trevor Jensen

Dean was sitting in the crew quarters giving his statement to law enforcement. He was sure acting like a big shot. He was up front and saw the truck hit the train. It startled the passengers, who were asleep in their seats in the front coaches. The very front coach took a serious hit. Dean was making himself out to be the expert witness.

You could smell my putrid stench a mile away. When I walked by, everybody moved out of my way. The day crew was up and ready to work. The sirens awakened them. The passengers were getting impatient and anxious, so the Command Center suggested that everyone be served complementary breakfasts as soon as the cooks could get it ready.

Would the train be deemed road-worthy? Would the train be evacuated? Would we be able to continue on our route to Seattle? There were many questions but few answers.

Reyna took me into one of the dorm rooms. I was really a mess. I took off all my clothes and stuck them in a biohazard bag. Reyna had to cut my pants off the bad leg.

"I'm your nurse now, and not your boss," she said as I laid a bath towel over my crotch while she tried her best to clean me up.

226

I wanted her to stick me in the bag, tie a big knot in it, and throw me out the vestibule door when the train achieved track speed, like I had done to the ferret. Right now, the way I felt, that would be just dandy with me. My shoulder and ribs were throbbing. There were some pretty bad scrapes on my right leg from the thigh down to the foot. It looked like huge gobs of skin had peeled and separated from the flesh. I still don't know what I did to myself. She was shocked to see the extent of the bruising that occurred over my chest. She listened to my chest and thought she heard some wheezing sounds. Maybe the best and fastest way out of here would be a killer asthma attack.

Reyna's phone kept going off. They were trying to reach her from the Command Center in Seattle. They left messages. Reyna was getting perturbed at them.

"Seattle wants to know why we are still sitting here, Trevor! What should I tell them?"

"Tell them the train ran out of fuel," I said, "and the tank truck broke down."

I hobbled into the shower. I became upset when she said that I had to go to the hospital. She said there were possibly broken ribs, maybe a dislocated shoulder, and the leg lacerations needed treatment. I declined. She said that I had to go. I said no. She said yes. She said I needed a tetanus shot. An ambulance had been called for the injured lady with the head and leg wound. She was on a blood thinner. She had developed a huge hematoma on her leg and might have bleeding complications in her head. Reyna was trying to fix me up, talk to Tim about this lady, and answer the cell phone all at the same time. I kept telling Reyna that I couldn't lie down on the rigid backboard that they used to carry Joey and Aaron. It would be too painful to stretch out and bounce along on a hard surface. She said I wouldn't have to lie down on a gurney, but that I could sit in the back of the ambulance beside the lady. They could take both of us together.

"I'm not riding in an ambulance with a wounded old lady."

Tim had been working with the state dispatcher in Bismarck, who had arranged for an ambulance to come from Jamestown to help because St. Catherine's Hospital in Cheneau Valley was overloaded with the dead and wounded from the accident. Reyna kept insisting that I was going into Jamestown and I kept insisting that I wasn't. I wrapped myself in some blankets. I couldn't pull my jeans up over the injured leg. I had to sit with my leg stretched out. If I bent the knee at all, it would dislodge the blood clots that had formed on the skin and start bleeding. I looked like a stretched-out, stiff Dutch mummy.

Wouldn't that be something to write home about? I could just see my picture in the morning papers. Here I am wrapped in a blanket, limping into the hospital alongside a gurney with an old lady on it. The headlines read "Big Freaking Train Accident." Out of two hundred forty passengers, two injured: a nineteen-year-old man and an elderly lady. The next morning, dad would see my picture in the paper, on the Internet and TV. He would totally freak out.

I used Travis' cell phone and called Julie back at 911. She answered right away. I explained the situation.

"Do you think you could send that tall ambulance lady back with some bandages to clean up my leg wounds? She knows what she is doing. She told me her name, but I don't remember it."

"I had so many units out there. Can you describe her, Trevor?"

"Let's see here, she has thin, stick-like legs, tall, skinny, and her thick black hair was double-braided. I think she could be a Native American. She walks with her toes pointed in."

"I got it. That must be Joanna, Joanna Night-Horse, our lead paramedic. Let me work on it."

In about two seconds, Joanna called me back. She thought I was coming to St. Catherine's. The doctor was told there were people hurt on the train. I let her talk to Reyna. She told Reyna that the doctor would be available to see me if I came into Cheneau Valley. Life Flight had come back from Fargo and they took Joey. They were able to stabilize him and pump in some blood. He was still alive when they put him on the copter.

Joanna came in about twenty minutes with her crew. I received first-class treatment. Joanna called St. Catherine's and I talked to a Dr. Martin. He wanted me to come back on the ambulance, but again I said no. He gave me a full medical exam over the phone. He put me through all kinds of maneuvers and asked several questions. He thought I had bruised ribs rather than broken ribs. He said there wouldn't be much they could do anyway for the ribs, and I'd likely have to see a specialist for the shoulder. He had me do several arm maneuvers. No, he didn't think the shoulder was dislocated. He wanted to know if it hurt to breathe. I lied and said no. I didn't want to go to the hospital. It did hurt to breathe. The doctor thought the ribs and the shoulder could wait until I arrived home. They brought pain medication, which I refused initially. Reyna insisted I keep the medicine. When the doctor finished talking to me, I hung up and Joanna took over.

She opened her red toolbox, flipped her black braids back over her shoulders, and went to work. She gave me the tetanus shot. I screamed when she started cleaning the leg. They scraped hard to get the dirt out. They took off all the dried blood. It really hurt. I couldn't look, but it felt like she was using a tomahawk on me. My leg was literally being scalped. They pulled off all the crinkled skin. I felt like a peach that was scalded with boiling water and then peeled. She said it was debridement, but I called it flayed. The Apache Indians used to do that as torture. It's still torture. She painted my leg brown from the groin down to my ankles, and then neatly bandaged me up. She put me in a foam contraption that immobilized my shoulder but also doubled as an arm sling. It lessened the pain on the left side over my ribs.

When she was done with me, I asked to talk to her privately. The death of Travis was eating on me pretty hard.

"Thank you for coming, Joanna. There is something I have to say, or I can't live with myself. When you came, I didn't know that Travis was in trouble. I didn't just sit there with Travis knowing that he wasn't breathing. When he quit talking, I let him rest. I wasn't that alarmed that he didn't talk. I was busy talking to Julie. I had to go help them get Joey out of the truck before it exploded. They couldn't get him out. I had to go and help. I didn't want to leave him. I can't be in two places at once. When I realized he wasn't talking, I yelled. I called. You were the first to come. You were there when it happened. That's when he died, not when I was with him. The whole time I was with him he was alive. I don't just sit around and let people die. I'm a whole lot better than that."

She knelt down. Her head was the same level as mine. She took my hand and held it. She rubbed my hand and squeezed it tight. She smiled sweetly. That did it. I let go with a monster cry. I let it all out. I probably hadn't cried like that since I was eight years old when my dad wouldn't give me that new watch he had brought back from Amsterdam. I ran out of tears, I cried so hard. Everybody heard me. The meltdown was huge. It must have reverberated throughout the entire train. I erupted like a superheated kettle. This idea of so many people dying was really getting to me. She didn't say anything until I ended my fit of weeping. She just knelt there looking sympathetic. Then she spoke.

"Don't blame yourself for what happened to Travis. As a professionally trained first responder with fifteen years of experience, I have never left an accident scene feeling like I've done enough. Every accident presents its own set of challenges. No two accidents are the same. In each and every call, we're confronted with different circumstances, different victims, different vehicles, different injuries, and sometimes even adverse weather. The methods you have used before don't apply in the present setting. We come equipped to do the best that we can with the circumstances handed to us on a second's notice. No training session could have prepared me for tonight. When I'm off duty later today, I'll think back on what happened. I'll wish I'd done this or that differently, in hopes that the outcome would have been more favorable. If I let myself get too entwined with regrets, eventually I couldn't function at a high enough level to perform my job. Tonight, for the first time in your life, you were a first responder. You acted courageously and successfully. In the coming weeks and months, when all the details of this accident are revealed, you and your crew will be the heroes of tonight. Trevor, please listen to me. In this business, I meet a lot of people who were on the scene before we arrived and the action they took was often the difference between life and death. I meet a lot of self-made heroes. Do you know what they all have in common, Trevor? They never feel like they've done enough or that they did it right."

Then she stood up and started to leave. Just as she walked out of the dorm room, she paused and said, "Trevor, it is going to take some time for you to heal. You will heal, but if you could get some counseling, I think you would benefit from it. Please get some counseling. It will help you deal with the emotional trauma. These accidents take a huge toll on the body and soul. We all need counseling after these types of accidents. This also takes a heavy toll on your two engineers. Don't feel like you are different because you need help. We all do."

I told her I'd look into it. She left. I really upset the crew by being so distraught. Dean came in and asked what I wanted him to do. I told him I needed some coffee. He brought me the coffee and then handed me his phone and suggested that I call home. I told him I wouldn't bother. It would be three in the morning there. What would they do in the middle of the night fifteen hundred miles away? I could hear dad say, "So what, you stupid kid? Told ya so. If you'd enrolled in college like I wanted you to, this wouldn't have happened to you. Don't come whining to me."

No, I'm not calling home. Wren was standing outside my room, crying. I really didn't need that. I told her to come in my room and cry. Wren came in and loved me up one side and down the other. That's what I needed. I told her I was so sorry her birthday was ruined. She said she was only worried about me. We both cried some more.

Reyna busied herself talking to the authorities. There were people with more fancy titles than you could imagine: Trainmaster! Roadmaster! Track Inspector! Road Foreman! Lead Mechanic! Claim Agent! Signal Supervisor! The dispatch center was slow to get us an emergency response team, but they sure gathered up every type of railroad hack they could find to come out and inspect their track. They were only worried about their train.

I heard Reyna tell somebody that I was too upset to give any statements. The claim agent insisted that he had to take a statement from everybody at the scene. Reyna said no. She believed that I was too emotionally distraught to talk to anyone.

The stupid media came on the train. The one entry door was left open so they came aboard. How quickly everyone forgot how Aunt Mattie escaped from the train through unlocked doors. They were trying to interview the passengers and get a handle on what had happened from them. The passengers were asleep. They didn't see anything. They didn't know what happened. The passengers in the front two coaches got quite a scare when the truck rammed the second locomotive and flipped into the first coach. That's what the railroad pundits are saying now. Tim told the media to go buy a ticket in Jamestown if they wanted to talk to anybody on the train. The train was sold out so that wasn't possible. The media monitors the state radio channels with their scanners. They followed the noise out to the crash site. Do they really pay somebody to sit up all night, listening to the airways hoping something like this happens?

I heard Tim discussing something with the engineers about how much longer they could remain on the train before they were classified as a dead crew. I'd never heard that expression before. That's all we needed was for the crew to die. I didn't like to hear that after what had already happened. If we didn't get to Glendive by noon, Tim said, they would have to stop the train and replace the engineers, including Tim and his assistant. It was some federal rule.

The engineers couldn't move the train anywhere until the Trainmaster downloaded the data from the event recorder into their computers. Then they all had to go into Jamestown and have their blood drawn for toxicology analysis. It would all take time. We weren't moving any time soon.

"Do they think the engineers are stoned?" I asked.

Reyna explained that everything had to be done in accordance with the Federal Railroad Administration regulations. Three fatalities, four injured: two in the truck, an employee (me), and the lady in the front coach. Add in the damage to the train, the downed signal, and the driver's truck, and it all made for an enormous chunk of money. The accident was big enough to warrant a full-scale investigation by every agency in the country's Transportation Department.

Lynn Olsen

I was dreaming about phones ringing. The phones kept ringing and ringing. No one would answer them. I couldn't understand why no one answered them. I was semi-conscious when I heard our phone. It was ringing. I lay there thinking I should get up and answer it, but it was on David's side of the bed. It kept on ringing. The message center was activated. The ringing stopped. The caller didn't leave a message. Then the phone rang again. When I did wake up, David was sitting on the edge of the bed. He had turned the night-light on. He was talking to someone on the phone. It was 4:30 Sunday morning. I didn't listen to a thing he said to the caller. It was a short conversation. He hung up, turned around, and looked at me. I was awake.

"That was St. Catherine's. They have Travis. He's dead. We have to go there now."

"I thought I heard him come in last night. David, go upstairs and check on him. I think he's there. This is some sort of prank."

"I don't think so, Lynn. That was Granny's friend on the phone, Sister Lisa Marie. She's at St. Catherine's now. She said Travis was brought into the emergency room."

We moved fast. We both dressed. It wasn't quite daylight.

"Are we taking Tanner and Terri?" I asked without thinking.

"Let them sleep," he said.

We walked outside, across to the garage. David backed out the Suburban. Laser came and sat next to me. I petted him. I started to get in the front and Laser jumped in. He never does that with us. Sometimes Travis would take Laser with him in the Suburban, but usually he doesn't. I started to pull him out.

"Let him be, Lynn." David sounded cross so I didn't argue.

Laser jumped in the back seat. We circled the driveway and drove by Paul and Granny's place onto the county road. Just as we turned left onto the road, a sheriff's cruiser came up behind us. He was coming to get us. He said to follow him into town and we could park next to him in the back of the hospital. David wasn't talking. He didn't tell me anything more that Sister Lisa Marie had said. David gets quiet when he is in a crisis. I just sat there fidgeting with my purse straps.

"Did Travis wreck the Mustang?" I asked.

"I guess so," he said.

The hospital was quiet. The receptionist recognized us and took us to Sister Lisa Marie's office. I'm not really sure what was said. I think she said Travis was "dead on arrival." Nothing penetrated. She called for Dr. Martin. In a minute, he came.

"I'm Dr. Martin, the on-duty physician. I examined your son Travis. He died at the accident scene before he arrived here. I'm sorry that I couldn't help him. They did everything they could at the scene to revive him. I'm sorry."

I was stunned. David didn't ask any questions and the doctor didn't volunteer anything about what happened. He took us to a treatment room where they had Travis. He was in a white plastic body bag, lying on a stretcher. Dr. Martin said we couldn't touch him until the autopsy was completed. After that was done, the state would release his body to the funeral home. His body was considered evidence in the investigation. I started to cry. David looked at me like I shouldn't, so I suppressed my emotions.

The doctor started to unzip the bag. There was his name, "Travis Olsen," written on the front of the bag. David made the doctor completely unzip the bag so we could see everything. He had his clothes on, except for his shirt. They had removed that, and there were some marks on his chest area around the heart -- I suppose from the equipment they used on him. His stomach was black and blue. It was horribly discolored. IV tubing was lying across his chest, still inserted in his arm. I kept staring at his right shoulder, where he had those black tribal swirl tattoos. It was one of the first things he did as soon as he turned eighteen. A new tattoo artist moved into town and Travis couldn't wait to get one.

David noticed right away that his watch was missing. There was a farmer's tan line where he always wore a watch. Dr. Martin assured us that it had been removed in the field by law enforcement and was part of the property held as evidence. Dr.

Martin seemed to be in a hurry. He told us as soon as we left that Travis would be transferred to Bismarck, where the state medical examiner would perform an autopsy. Dr. Martin said the entire accident scene was being handled as a crime scene. I was so stunned I couldn't think of anything to say. Did they think that Travis had committed a crime? Just as I asked myself that question, I began to feel faint.

"I need to sit down, David."

"Lynn. Let's leave."

David took me by the arm and led me out. We signed everything we had to sign. Sister said she didn't know exactly what happened. She thought he had come there about four or later. He was pronounced dead by Dr. Martin at 4 a.m., she said, checking the death certificate. Then she said it wasn't completely filled out yet. Sister called Simmons-Kline Funeral Home and we talked to Mr. Simmons. Sister walked out to the car with us. She opened the door for me. When I sat down, she reached through the door and patted me gently on my shoulder.

"I'm so very sorry," she said in a very soft voice, "may the Lord comfort and bless you. May the Lord be merciful and kind to you both. You tell Granny I'm coming out to see her today. Also, tell Granny that I called Father Fitzgerald and he came and gave Travis a blessing. Granny told me one time that Travis loved his Lord."

So, without knowing for certain what had really happened to Travis, we went back home. When we entered the house, there was a message on our phone from the state highway patrol. I made some coffee and waited for the kids to wake up. We sat there looking at each other in disbelief and bewilderment. David tried to call the highway patrol but there was no answer when he rang the number left on the phone.

"I'm going up to Bismarck, Lynn. I want to be with Travis. I think he would expect that."

Before I could respond he was dialing Mr. Simmons again, to get the specifics of where Travis was being taken. David hung up and said we wouldn't be able to be there, because the autopsy was done at the state correctional facility. The public wasn't allowed access. Mr. Simmons thought they might keep Travis until sometime Monday, but he said that they know we like to get the remains ready within eight hours. That is optimum.

The highway patrol called again. David answered. The officer wanted to know if Travis had a cell phone. We told him that he did. The officer explained that it would be important evidence. He wanted the cell number, so David gave it to him. The officer said it was missing. They were going to attempt to trace it. He said the officers at the scene would call it to see if they could hear a ringtone anywhere in the vicinity of the crash. David asked about the watch, but the officer either couldn't remember or was evasive about knowing anything about it. If he did, he said it would have been removed at the scene, inventoried and put in an evidence bag. He said all the paperwork and personal items were with the body. He said the accident scene would be thoroughly searched at daybreak, and they would likely find more items. The officer said he didn't know exactly what had happened, but a fast-moving passenger train traveling west, had hit Aaron's truck at a crossing near Sanders Lake. David was so stunned that he couldn't think of any questions to ask.

As soon as he hung up, the phone rang. It was Sara O'Connor. David put the phone on speaker so I could hear.

"Oh David! *David*. We lost our Brad tonight. He was killed. He is dead. Do you know where Travis is? Is Travis okay? I can't talk. I'll have you talk to John."

As soon as David told them Travis was dead, I could hear Sara sobbing in the background. I started to cry. I knew if I let myself go, I wouldn't stop and I wanted to be in good form for when we told the kids. I had no idea how I would deal with Travis dying. And now Brad is dead, too? David and John kept talking. It was like they were talking about farming or the weather or the latest scoop on the Minnesota Twins. I couldn't get it that they were so composed as they discussed the deaths of our two boys. David was in shock. The whole nightmare of Travis dying hadn't penetrated yet. John O'Connor started telling us what they knew, which was a lot more than we did.

One of the nursing supervisors on duty, who knew Joey's parents, Lana and Bob, was called to the emergency room to help after the 911 dispatcher notified the hospital of the likelihood of multiple victims. She overheard Joey's name mentioned on the radio. She immediately called Lana and Bob. They were there when Joey arrived. Lana looked at him and said she thought he was dead. Lana knew Joey was with Aaron, and she had been upset about it from the get-go. She was afraid that Brad and Travis might be involved. Lana pressed the ambulance driver, who told her that five people were in the truck, and it was bad for all five but he didn't know all the names or wouldn't tell her. It was Lana who called John and Sara because she thought Brad must be hurt, too, but she didn't know he was dead. So, when John and Sara showed up at the hospital, everyone was surprised because Brad hadn't been brought in yet. She said Joey's stepdad, Bob, was a basket case. He was real emotional and couldn't stand up and couldn't be in the treatment room with Joey. She said the emergency room staff was on Joey like vultures. They immediately took an X-ray of his chest. Lana said it was brutal to watch what they did to Joey. Bob collapsed. He couldn't watch. Joey arrived at the emergency room with a needle in his chest that the Life Flight Crew inserted when he stopped breathing again while they were loading Aaron on the helicopter. That procedure probably saved his life, allowing him enough time to get to the hospital where a doctor could work on his chest. The doctor cut into his ribs, separated them, and inserted a huge needle into the chest wall. After that the doctor put in a tube. They had to inflate the lung. They had to relieve the pressure building up around his heart. Three people were trying to keep him breathing. Two more nurses were attempting to start the blood transfusions on one side of him while another nurse was infusing some drugs into his other arm. She expected them to pronounce him dead. They kept working. They didn't talk. She said everyone seemed to know what to do without being told by the doctor. She couldn't believe how organized they all were. She didn't know how so many people could squeeze in and work on one person. Lana said that most of the time she couldn't actually see what was going on because there were so many of the staff pressed shoulder to shoulder working on him, including the paramedics who bought him in. Finally, she couldn't take it any more so Lana came out to talk to John and Sara.

John said Lana wasn't fully dressed. She came to the hospital in her housecoat, but she had on those blue, flat-heeled shoes she always wears to work. Her hair was still in curlers. When Life Flight came back for Joey, they went right out with him and drove to Fargo.

When John started in about how he was finally told that Brad had died, I couldn't listen anymore. Lana was standing out in the hall when one of the paramedics came out of the treatment room. Lana pressed him about who else was at the scene and what was their condition. He just shook his head and told her that they were all dead and that only two survived. "Names?" Lana wanted to know the names. "How many?" she asked. He looked very distraught and said "I can't" and walked away. In about two seconds the charge nurse came out and hugged Sara.

"We have a report that Brad is dead. He's still at the scene. I need to prepare you for the worst. They are bringing him in shortly."

That's how they heard about Brad. No mention was made about Travis. They were in such shock they couldn't even think to ask.

Finally, John said, they were sure Kyle was involved, but they can't find Guy or Sharon. John said Brad was also being taken to Bismarck for an autopsy. John said that they hadn't been able to reach Brad's sister, Dana. She had gone to Fargo on Saturday to complete her wedding plans. They had to make a final payment on the flowers and some other stuff. John went on to say they had tried to call Rod Sorenson, her fiancé, at Thief River, but no one is answering their phone. John thought it would be better to first tell Rod, and then have Rod go over to Morris, where Dana was supposed to spend the night with a friend. Instead of Dana's wedding on Saturday, they'd have to face having a funeral for Brad. John received another call, so he hung up from talking with David.

David called Mr. Simmons again, who, when asked about Kyle, said law enforcement hadn't been able to reach the next of kin. Until then, the release of any information was under tight wraps. Mr. Simmons thought the media might already know, but they were going to hold off on the reporting until all next of kin were notified. He said the police had gone to an address listed in Kyle's wallet and woke up the residents, but it wasn't Guy. David said Guy had moved. David told him that Rodger Epperson would have Kyle's address in Jamestown, where Guy would be. No one was at Sharon's apartment in Cheneau Valley. Mr. Simmons said he would share that information with the highway patrol.

At 5:30 a.m. we knew Travis and Brad were dead for sure, and probably Kyle. Joey was at Fargo in critical condition. Lana told the O'Connors it didn't look like Joey would make it. We didn't know about Aaron. It was a train accident. We didn't know the details. John O'Connor said he thought the Mustang must be at Aaron's place. That's all we knew.

I told David that he had to wake Tanner and Terri. We had to tell them before Granny, and I warned him that if we waited much longer Granny would hear. I knew that in this town, nothing this big is going to be kept secret for very long. The nurses are going to talk, and too many others know already. We both went upstairs. I woke Terri up. I told her to freshen up, not to get dressed, and come down as fast as she could. In about a flash, there she was coming down the stairs in her nightgown and robe. She had combed her hair. Right behind her came Tanner, wearing only his boxers. The poor kid was still asleep. David yelled at him to get his jeans on. David never talks to him that roughly, so he turned around and stumbled upstairs, half asleep, to get his jeans. Terri sensed that something terrible was wrong. She looked at me. She looked at David. By now, David looked like a truck had hit him.

"Mother!" she yelled, "What happened?"

I started to cry.

"Where is Travis? He didn't come home last night did he? *Mother!* Brother is not in his room. Where is he?"

My crying became uncontrollable. I shook my head no that he hadn't come home. David wouldn't tell her. He said to wait for Tanner. When Tanner heard me crying, he came flying down the stairs with his jeans half on and half off. He nearly fell head first down the stairs. I was hugging Terri and crying so hard that David had to tell them. I couldn't. I hugged her more tightly in order to muffle her screams. Tanner just dropped on his haunches to the floor like he does and stared off into space. He didn't cry. He didn't ask questions. He was speechless. In a couple of minutes, Tanner went out to the back porch, pulled on a pullover that belonged to Travis, went outside and sat down on the steps in the sun beside Laser. That's where I wanted to be, too. Just by myself with Laser.

In a few minutes I caught my breath, stopped crying, picked up the phone and called Granny. David could not do it. She answered. I told her as calmly as I could that Travis was killed in a train accident with some other boys sometime early this morning. I told her we would be talking with her about the funeral plans. I had no idea about what, where or when. I hung up. I felt so cruel to tell her in such a cold, calculating way. I didn't know how else to do it. I didn't want her to see us in the state we were in.

••••

Granny clutched the phone in her hand, turned around and told Paul, who was sitting at the breakfast nook.

"Paul. That was Lynn," she said. "Travis is dead. Paul? Did you hear what I just said? Travis is dead. Lynn just told me. What about his basketball scholarship? Paul! He won't be able to work on the farm any more! Oh my goodness. Poor David. What is he going to do without his boy? My poor, poor David. Paul? Do you think Travis is …?"

Paul rushed over to catch her just as her knees buckled. He managed to drag her over to where he could get a dinette chair under her for support. When she came to, Granny put her hands over her eyes. Paul steadied her arms and tried to hold her on the chair. She looked at Paul as the tears starting streaming down her face.

"Tell me it's not so, Paul. Tell me it's not so. Please tell me …"

Trevor Jensen

More railroad officials came from Jamestown to help Tim with the train. They brought a computer and downloaded the front unit's event recorder, which included train speed for the entire trip, dynamic braking records, throttle positions, and even when and where the engineers blew the whistle and for how long. The front locomotive carries a camera pack that videotapes everything the engineers do inside the cab and records the images in front of the train as it moves down the track.

I talked to the claim agent from the railroad. I told Reyna that I wanted to do everything I was supposed to do. If they wanted a statement I would talk to them. I sat on the edge of the bunk and answered one question after another.

"Who directed you to leave the train?"

"No one did. I went voluntarily," I said.

I just told them that I saw the fire, heard the screaming and went over to help get them out so they wouldn't burn to death. That sounded like a good enough reason to me.

I didn't tell them that I was so frightened; I couldn't have done anything unless Dean told me to do it. The paperwork is what is killing this country. It was pretty redundant. By the time I get back to Seattle, every government agency in the country will know my name. Reyna had to do a huge pile of paperwork that they faxed from Intermountain Rail. She brought Dean in and we helped her fill that out first. We tried to keep our stories straight. Not that we had anything to hide, but they want to talk to you separately, and then if there are discrepancies between the statements they play gotcha. We were all so tired that we could hardly think. Seattle wanted everything *right now* in writing.

The highway patrolman was very incriminating with his questions. He asked if Travis had talked or said anything that might indicate that they were drinking. I told him nothing. The officer wasn't as interested in questioning me further when he discovered I didn't actually see the truck's headlights. He had already talked to Dean. I didn't know how Dean could be so omniscient in his statements. I had this make-believe pact with Travis, and I wasn't talking. Nobody knew he was drunk but me. I kept it all to myself. Since I sat there and let him die, he wasn't here to defend himself. I decided it was my job to cover for him.

When I was left alone, I picked up Travis' phone and turned it on. Someone kept calling him. I started to feel really sick again. I was tormented about knowing who might be calling. Was it a girlfriend? Had she heard already that he was dead? I was holding it when it rang. I was afraid to answer it. The display showed the calls all originated in North Dakota. What would I say? Reyna came into my room so I turned the phone off. I didn't want it ringing. I put my hand over the phone just as she noticed.

"That's not our phone," she said.

She knew the train's phone I carried was ruined. Then she shifted the conversation. Reyna realized that the vomit on my uniform appeared to be bloody. Travis was vomiting up blood. She felt awful about not making a correct assessment of his condition. I was beginning to realize what Joanna had meant about the guilt trip. Reyna was traveling down the guilt-trip road. She looked like an old hag. She had deep, dark circles around her eyes. She never looked that way. She was always well-kept and bright. She had regrets about me being alone with Travis. Then she wanted to know exactly what I did to keep his airway clear while he was vomiting. It really got me going again, because I didn't know to do anything she said should have been done. I should have told her that he vomited. I didn't. Likely, we let him lie there and bleed to death right before our very eyes. I asked her if she was going to make a report of that, and she said it wouldn't matter because the autopsy would establish the extent of injuries and cause of death.

"Do you think Travis strangled on his own vomit?" I asked her.

"No, Trevor. No, I don't think so. I wish I had known when he vomited. I would have helped you with him, that's all. We should have rolled him on his side while at the same time stabilizing his neck and spine so that he didn't aspirate anything into the airway. I don't think that is why he died. We didn't have the equipment and drugs that we needed."

"Like what?"

"Like what the paramedics did for Joey when they arrived. The same needed to be done for Travis. He needed to be intubated, where an endotracheal tube is placed to keep the airway clear. The procedure stimulates the gag reflex. We give a sedative and then a paralytic drug to prevent vomiting during the intubation procedure. Once the bag-valve device was in place for Joey, his breathing stabilized. The endotracheal tube protects the airway."

"Why don't they have that on the train?"

"Only paramedics are trained to use that equipment. It's a miracle that we had the external defibrillator. We saved Joey. At least he didn't die at the scene. We didn't save Travis. Right now, I can't even think about it. I was too much involved with Joey to help you, Trevor. I'm sorry. I'm really sorry. We did the best we could, but we didn't do everything that should have been done. Trevor, all of this is going to end up being a legal juggernaut. You and Dean are going to be material witnesses for the railroad, and also for law enforcement. You are trapped in a legal powder keg. If you tell the truth every time you talk, you have nothing to worry about. If you are not consistent with your stories, they will rip you apart in court. You cannot lie. If they catch you lying, they can charge you with obstruction of justice. Just remember that. This is very serious. Also, we are not allowed to talk to the media. Within the railroad there is a culture of fear and intimidation between management and the employees. The railroad is very touchy about what we say that might pinpoint blame on them or disparage their public image. They care more about their public image than they do you or I. The press, the government, and everybody outside their organization are viewed as their enemy. Don't talk to anyone. Do that and you will be spared a lot of grief. If approached by the media, you need to respond by telling them that you have no comments."

Then she continued on by saying that I never should have been off the train.

"So could you or Tim get in trouble?"

"Yes indeed," she affirmed.

I didn't tell her about the watch and the phone. Then the thought hit me. What happens to me if I'm caught with this dead man's property? Then what? Why didn't I give the watch and phone to Mr. Simmons? That is what I should have done, but I didn't want it stolen and I had promised Travis I would return it directly to him. I decided the best approach would be to get his phone and watch returned to his parents as soon as I could figure out a way to do it.

The watch! Where was it? I was in such a dismal state of mind; I had forgotten to remove the watch from the cargo pants pocket. I had sacrificed my uniform and the watch to the biohazard bag. I had better not lose that watch or I'll have to plead guilty in the Devil's court. I'm really messed up now. My chest is bound up in some swath and my left arm is in a sling contraption. I can't lift it, and if I stand, I wobble like a rotten post. I have to use a crutch. My right leg is tightly bandaged. I can't bend my knee. I assume that the biohazard bag will be offloaded in Seattle. I used Travis' phone and called Dean on his cell. I told him to come to my room and help me. Dean retrieved my crappy uniform, contaminated with the dead victim's blood and body fluids, and retrieved the watch.

I stayed in my room. Dean kept me informed. He said the media was starting to gather in large numbers and law enforcement had posted guards. He said the area where I had laid Kyle was roped off. Dean said every inch of the crash site was being preserved and searched. Dean went on to report that they had collected a pile of beer cans that were being considered as part of the wreckage. He said they were all empty. They didn't know the source of the beer cans, but it was being gathered as evidence.

Dean said the media kept badgering the officers, but no one would answer their questions. Supposedly, a press conference is scheduled for later in the day.

The poor saps going to Jamestown have sat here for more than four hours. They were about fifteen minutes from home, but Tim wouldn't allow anyone off the train. One lady is upset. She called her husband, who came to the scene to pick her up, but Tim wouldn't let her off. He said it wasn't safe to walk along the track. Tim is talking to the passengers. They know basically what happened. The people on the left side of the train heard the sirens and saw all the emergency vehicles as they approached. It really alarmed them. It's a miracle that the signal fell away from the train and not into it. The metal fragments could have killed a passenger had they come in through the windows. Some of the passengers are local and keep asking about the victim's names. Tim tells them that the victims have not been identified. Reyna is staying in the background, too exhausted to handle the passengers' questions and concerns.

Aaron's truck was in pieces, hardly recognizable as a long-bed pickup. Large pieces that had been cut away by the firemen were strewn around, including doors, the front dash above the motor, and the roof. There must have been ten miles of yellow tape printed with "do not cross" every few feet. There were police cruisers on both sides of the road, and they wouldn't let any traffic cross the track.

Talgo Corporation, whose equipment was widely used in Europe, was also the manufacturer of the cars on our train. They planned to send out a crew of technical specialists from the assembly plant in Seattle by private jet to Bismarck in order to further check out the train. If we ever make it to Bismarck, we'll have to wait for their analysis before proceeding further west. Rumors are flying that the train may not operate further west than Bismarck. The train operates as a single unit. A mechanical defect with the wheels or axle of one car could disrupt the operation of the entire train. Fortunately for the train, and us, the truck struck the second locomotive before it sideswiped the five train coaches. Dean said the visible damage on each of the five coaches occurred below the windows. Fortunately there weren't broken windows. The equipment, unique in America, had never been involved in a side impact of this type. They had to make sure they could safely move the train. Hopefully, we could limp into Bismarck, about one hundred and twenty six miles from here.

The train passed the air-brake test. That was lucky. The flat-wheel test went fine, indicating the wheels weren't damaged from the sudden stop. The train's anti-slip system performed just as expected. Tim, with a group of inspectors, stood by as the train slowly pulled past them. Any car with a flat defect on its wheels could seriously affect our speed. It was a record-stopping distance. Each car was searched underneath for debris or damage. None was found. It was lucky the train didn't derail. The officials were flabbergasted over how well it handled after being hit by a six-ton missile coming into it with such force.

It was 8 a.m. when the *Mountain Daylight* was finally cleared to resume its westward journey. It was one thousand five hundred eighty-four miles from Seattle. We crawled slowly over the Sanders Lake Bridge and dike, and before long the hotbox detector positioned along the track audibly announced the train's speed of forty mph as heard on our scanner. That was the fastest they said we should go until everything was checked out by the technicians. I thought to myself that if I ever got out of North Dakota, I'd never come back.

At 6 a.m. the police were knocking on the front door of Rodger Epperson's home in Cheneau Valley. Rodger opened the door and was shocked to see a grim-faced officer standing there. Rodger was so shaken upon hearing of the deaths of his three star players that he couldn't think or find the address he had for Kyle in Jamestown, where they could find Guy Hickles. Thus far, neither of Kyle's parents had been notified. Rodger's wife finally came to his aid, and the Jamestown Police were soon pounding on the door of Guy Hickles' apartment.

Refusing to take the officer's word for it, Guy called David Olsen, who had the unsavory task of confirming that he and Lynn had just come back from identifying Travis, and Travis was, in fact, dead. Guy hung up from talking to David and immediately phoned Shona. Fortunately for Shona, she was not home alone. Guy blurted it out to her without asking if she had someone with her. She did. With tears streaming down her cheeks, she put one hand over her mouth so Guy wouldn't hear her cries. She handed the phone to Sunny, who stood there in shock. Her brother, Ace, had just finished working the night shift. Guy said he wanted Shona to go with him to St. Catherine's to identify Kyle's body. Sunny turned around with a scowl on her face and related Guy's request to Shona. As Shona stood there contemplating what she wanted to do, Sunny mouthed the comment *"That is Share-Ron's Job."*

Sunny then asked about Sharon and learned that they hadn't been able to contact her. Guy begged for someone to go with him to identify Kyle. He couldn't go alone. Shona said she would keep calling Sharon on the cell phone. According to Shona, Sharon had gone to Moorhead, Minnesota, to spend the weekend with her friend, and had Monday off. She thought they were at a lake somewhere, possibly out of cell-phone range. Shona said Sharon never turns her phone off and she never runs down the battery. Shona agreed to go with Guy to identify Kyle, but only if Sunny could go with her, Ace stood behind his sister, saying that he would go, too. When the initial shock subsided, Shona began to manifest some of her mother's strength. Guy was weak, and he would need someone strong with him. The trooper pressed Guy to come immediately to St. Catherine's, as they didn't want to transport Kyle to Bismarck until the next of kin identified him.

The officer instructed Guy to phone him immediately when anything surfaced regarding Sharon's whereabouts. Guy complied and within minutes the Minnesota Highway Patrol, along with Sharon's cell-phone provider, was tracing the location of Sharon's phone.

••••

Rod Sorenson was glad they had an early start at 4 a.m. milking their registered Holsteins. Rod was training his replacement, a high school kid who would work through the summer until a permanent milker could be hired. He could hardly leave his dad, even for a week, unless this kid was fully trained. He kept ignoring the cell phone, as he knew it wasn't Dana calling him yet. She would, the minute she opened her eyes, and he intended to take that call. It had been a stressful week at the Sorenson dairy farm. He and Dana had graduated from a small branch of the University of Minnesota just two weeks previous. In less than a week, they would be married. Right now it didn't much matter if he remained to work on the family dairy farm, where they milked one hundred Holsteins twice day, or relocated to the Twin Cities, where they could both teach. Hopefully, Dana at least could utilize her elementary education degree even if he stayed on the farm.

Now the distraction was Dana, the wedding, and the honeymoon. The closest to royalty he'd ever get would be riding into the ceremony with Dana on the horse-drawn carriage that a local farmer rented out for such purposes. Then he'd be thousands of miles from the farm in less than seven days, lying with Dana on a warm Caribbean beach. Sunday morning was a "hurry up" situation to attend the ten o'clock Lutheran service in Thief River. He planned to meet Dana there. Rod hoped to make a good impression by being in church the Sunday before their wedding.

His replacement was busy setting up the six milking units while Rod was getting the next batch of cows ready in the tie-stall barn used for the operation. The kid was from town, but he was good on the farm. It was working out. He didn't yet know the silly nuances you needed to recognize in order to forestall trouble. Because it was well past 6:30 a.m., an hour or more beyond what Susie could tolerate, she started bellowing about her fifty-pound udder of milk. Rod knew to bring her in with the next batch. She should have been first. That is hard for a newcomer to decipher.

The milking went fast, but it was the finish-up work that took time. His dad would soon come out to help with the clean-up chores, such as washing and sanitizing the milk lines. Rod would be free until 4:30 p.m., when the process repeated itself.

It was about 7 a.m. when Rod unclipped his phone from his hip and noticed about five calls coming from his soon-to-be-father-in-law, John O'Connor. The first call had been received at 4:30 a.m. That was an aberration. John would know Rod was up milking, but why would John be up at that hour? Without giving it further thought, he flipped the call back to John. The news of Brad's sudden death jolted him to such extent that he couldn't stand up straight. He braced himself between two Holsteins in the process of being milked, and flung his arms over their hindquarters in order to steady himself.

He turned to his trainee, who was removing a rubber milk hose from the milk line, and tried to explain what he had just

251

been told, but it came out like a mixed-up riddle. He was unable to completely process it.

"Something awful happened. That was Brad's dad. It's about Brad. He's dead. I have to tell Dana. Oh no! He wants me to tell Dana and bring her home. I have to leave. Can you?..."

The young man told Rod to go and do whatever, not knowing the full extent of the problem. Rod ran out of the barn and darted through the holding pen across the wide lot to the house, his long legs galloping and arms flinging about as though he was fighting off a swarm of bees.

Breakfast was ready, but his dad was standing by the kitchen sink eating an orange. Rod threw his hat on the table, sat down and struggled to speak. Thinking there might be a crisis in the barn and knowing that his son, when under stress, had a stuttering problem, his dad calmly asked him to take his time and tell them what was wrong. Rod unscrambled enough thoughts to yell out the news to his mom and dad. It didn't make any sense. Terrance Sorenson, not a man of emotion, took a hold of his son and began to ask serious questions that Rod could not answer. In a second, Terrance was on the phone to John O'Connor, asking him to repeat what Rod could not make clear. So, the plan was for Terrance and Rod to drive the thirty-five miles into Morris, wake Dana, and John would be on the phone to tell her. Her dad John would do it; Rod would be spared the awful job of telling her Brad was dead.

As they were knocking on the door where Dana had spent the night, Rod told his dad that he was afraid she would take it hard. He was right. Her friend Patsy opened the door. Dana was still sleeping. They did not disclose their business, but went into the bedroom where Dana was, closed the door and woke her up. Surprised to see them, Dana didn't sense anything was amiss. They got John on the phone, and he told her that Brad was dead, a victim of a train accident. She was not told about Travis or Kyle. Instantly Dana uttered the primal grief reaction. Rod and Terrance held on to Dana while she shrieked and screamed. Before Rod proposed to Dana, he discussed his ambitions with his parents. The only negative his dad could come up with was the fact that Terrance read Dana as having a short fuse. The news of Brad's death so shook her that she became hysterical. Horrified by what was happening, Patsy opened the bedroom door and watched while Rod tried to hold and console Dana. Dana caught her breath long enough to tell Patsy that Aaron had just killed her brother Brad.

••••

Authorities traced Sharon's phone to Maplewood Lake near Pelican Falls, about a two-hour drive into Minnesota. Shona told authorities that Sharon would have driven her beige Toyota Camry. The Minnesota Highway Patrol had her license number. A female trooper, trained in crisis intervention, had been dispatched to Maplewood Lake to look for Sharon's car. She found it parked in front of a cabin at about the same time authorities were on the phone with the other occupants of the cabin. Everyone was enjoying a mid-morning brunch of waffles, egg casserole and deer sausage on the screened-in back porch that faced the lake. The trooper walked between the summer cabins to the back and noticed some folks eating on the porch. Sharon had just told a new joke that Kyle had told her the day before. The group had reservations for a dinner show at the nearby Indian casino. The officer approached just as she heard someone in the group say that they hoped they wouldn't eat again until tonight. Everyone stopped talking and focused their attention on the officer standing at the porch door.

"I'm looking for Sharon Hickles," the trooper said. "Is she here? I need to talk to her concerning her son Kyle. It's an emergency."

Lynn Olsen

I was very glad to see all of David's step relatives walk in. They came immediately. They will be good support for David after they all recover from the initial shock of this tragedy. Right now, they are all too emotional to be of much help. They are taking this worse than we are. My two sisters are here working with Granny in the kitchen. Granny is in charge of the kitchen. That's the best place for her to be in a crisis. Cooking will be her outlet until she is able to reckon with reality. Granny is at the door receiving the food that people are bringing. Granny thanks them for bringing it and she thanks them for not bringing it. We already have more food than we can possibly eat, use or store. It takes a large staff in the kitchen to receive, label the bowls, and put it all away somewhere. The media is parked in front of our house. They asked us if they could cover the story from there and David said yes. We found out that they are an affiliate of CNN. CNN is covering the press conference that was scheduled for 10 a.m. at the accident site, but it was canceled until Sharon was notified. It is rescheduled for 2 p.m.

I can't think. I just sit here, looking out the window at the crowd gathering outside. There are flocks of kids bringing flowers and sitting around on the lawn. Granny said we'd have to feed them sometime. David turned his cell phone off. My sisters are answering our house phone as much as possible. Tanner is quite taken with all the attention. I don't think he has had much time to think about what happened.

The O'Connors don't want anyone there. They prefer to grieve privately with their family. They have their hands full trying to help Dana. John had several farm projects going, and they have to carry on. I want to talk to Dana but she doesn't need to feel any of our pain. She has enough of her own.

A florist just delivered a huge spray of white carnations. That was Travis' favorite flowers. It came from Joey. Obviously, Lana sent them. With all her worries, how could she think of us? I told them to put the flowers in Travis' room, on his dresser.

David won't go into Travis' room. He's closed the door. It's a mess in there. Travis threw his muddy clothes down over the chair. I haven't cleaned the bathrooms up there for over a week. I know the day we put Travis in the ground, a part of David will go with him that I will never get back. I'm afraid I'll also lose part of David in this tragedy. He'll have to connect with Tanner. Tanner is all he has now. I hope Tanner can resonate with him. Terri is resilient. She'll survive. She has her cousins and her friends at school. She will marry her prince charming when it is time. She appears on the outside to be the emotional basket case, but I'm not too worried about her once we get through this.

David has searched through everything, trying to find an extra set of car keys for the Mustang. Everything Travis carried is being held as evidence. Travis might have an extra set in his room. David can't remember. Some of the men took off and went over to Aaron's farm, where they thought the Mustang might be. The sheriff had the road blocked. The Mustang was there, but it was being searched or was to be searched. The state may want it hauled to Bismarck. They didn't know. Apparently they have a search warrant to search Aaron's room. What for, I don't know.

I know the authorities are going to question us. I haven't told David about Travis drinking the afternoon before he died. What if he was drunk when he was killed? What will happen to Aaron if he was drinking and driving that truck when that train hit them? What if I had followed up and called the sheriff? Maybe Travis would still be here. I can't bear to go there. I can't possibly tell David that I knew Travis was drinking down at Kindersley. This whole nightmare could be my fault. I can't deal with that now. The whole country will hate Aaron, and they will never know that it was really my fault because I could have had Aaron picked up by the sheriff. I will refuse to talk. That is the only way I'll be able to handle it. This regret will eat on my soul for the rest of my life. I know one thing. I will tell Granny, and she will help me get rid of this. I might have to go to the priest with her and confess.

The media is making the train out to be the bad guys here. They are digging up some fancy statistics concerning the number of people killed by trains in America.

"Dad! Dad! Dad! Someone answered brother's phone. *A man has his phone!*"

Tanner came running into the house, holding his phone and pointing to the number that was displayed on the screen. It was Travis' phone number. Tanner sat down on the floor and cried. It was the first time he cried. He said it again. David just stood there looking at him.

"Tanner can you calm down please? Who?"

"A man on the train. It's a man on the train. He wants to talk to my dad. He wants to talk to you. His name is Trevor."

It was clear that the call was coming from Travis' phone. Was it for real? David took the phone, took Tanner by the arm, and the two of them walked into our bedroom. I followed them in. David wouldn't put it on speaker. I didn't ask him to. He listened while the man talked. David broke down crying. It upset Tanner. I don't think Tanner has ever seen his dad cry. I don't think I have, either. David just sobbed as the man on the phone talked to him. I took the phone away from David. He couldn't talk anyway.

"Hello? I'm Mrs. Olsen. I'm Travis' mother. Who are you?"

I put the phone on speaker and listened to what he said. He sounded like a young man. He told us everything. He told us how he had used Travis' phone to call 911 because they had been there for almost an hour and nobody came. He told how Travis died and what he said. He said Travis had vomited up blood again and again. Travis gave him his watch because he didn't want to lose it. He wanted to phone us, but Travis wouldn't let him. Travis didn't want us to see him in that condition. He said that Aaron hit the train. He stopped talking for a minute. I was suspicious he might be crying. His voice sounded like he was breaking down in tears. I asked if anyone had been hurt on the train. He was hurt a little and they wanted him off the train in Bismarck, but there weren't any available flights out. He intended to stay on the train. Then he said that he might be in trouble with the law for evidence tampering because he didn't turn over the phone or the watch to the authorities. When he arrived home, he would send the watch and phone by overnight mail. We talked for about half an hour and then asked him to repeat everything he said. We couldn't absorb everything he told us. He told us again of the heroic rescue by Reyna and Dean. He described in detail how they had carried Travis out of the hot truck that was still on fire. He said the floorboard of the back seat was so hot, where Travis was, that he was afraid of being burned. He told the awful story about Kyle, and how he fell backwards into the water, dragging Kyle down the bed of the truck. He thought Brad must have been killed instantly. He wasn't supposed to talk to anyone, but he wanted us to know where the watch was and hopefully he could slip it back to us before he was caught with it. David told him he didn't want the authorities to get their hands on the phone and to turn it off and not use it. He warned Trevor about it being traceable. David gave him his cell number and asked him to keep us informed. Trevor said he would borrow a phone. David told Tanner to keep his mouth shut or he would get the man who had called in trouble. David told Tanner not to call Travis' phone again.

We hung up from talking to Trevor and David got on his phone and called NDSU. I don't understand why he thought he had to do that now. He was barely in control of his emotions. He had the cell number of the assistant coach that Travis liked. One time after Travis borrowed our phone, David discovered this guy's number that Travis had put in. I stood speechless as he dialed it. The coach answered. Well, they knew. The coaches had all heard it. They were all on campus for a big basketball camp. They were stunned. What could they say? They didn't want to believe it. Travis was their big fish. More shattered dreams. Their plans for shaping and molding their protégé into the champion athlete they envisioned had evaporated.

Trevor Jensen

I knew Travis' father cried as I talked to him. I didn't think I should sugarcoat it. He had to know eventually. It was better to lay all the cards on the table and be square with them. I was feeling pretty blue and glum after hanging up from talking to them. They sounded like nice people. I tried to imagine how my folks would feel if I had died in that truck. It made me tear up as I thought about it. They put their whole life into nurturing and training you, and then you go out one night, get hammered, and run yourself right into a train. I am hurting so bad and Travis isn't even my kid. I could feel their pain coming at me over the phone. It blasted me with more pain.

We pulled into Bismarck and through the downtown section. All I saw was pigeons, streets, and backs of buildings. I'd never seen Bismarck in the daylight before, and from my vantage point I hadn't missed anything. We pulled up past the station. There were people there. I saw a police car and I shivered. I wondered if they had traced the phone and were waiting to come aboard and arrest me. I could just imagine it: evidence tampering, five years; obstruction of justice five years. Dad always told me to never mess with the government, because the best defense attorneys in the world can't get you off if the government wants you down. We pulled a long way past the station and stopped by a brick building. I couldn't see anything. We sat for quite a while.

Just as I was sitting on my bunk, waiting to hear what was happening now that we had arrived in Bismarck, there was a loud knock on my door. I froze in fear. It opened. It was Rudy from the Seattle Command Center.

"Trevor!" he said. "I can't believe you! I can't believe what you, Reyna, and Dean did last night. You guys are real heroes. We're all proud of you. How are you feeling? You look great. Can I see your wounds? What happened?"

I was so happy to see him. He was so upbeat, jovial and reassuring. He flew in with the technicians and maintenance engineers who were here to inspect the train and hopefully give us the go-ahead.

"I thought you guys might need some support! That's what I'm here for, Trevor. Oh! And I brought you a new phone. Don't use it in the rain. It isn't waterproof. The new phones have some real cool features. You will enjoy using it."

I laughed. He laughed. He brought new uniforms and a gift box of candy bars, Bellevue's favorite chocolates. Soon we were both laughing so hard I told him I hurt too much to laugh anymore. It felt good to laugh. It perked me up. He said not to worry about a thing. They have the best lawyers and he'd see that I had the best one standing in front of me and second-best one standing behind me. They would take care of me the whole way.

"Besides, Trevor, your pappy is a lawyer, too! Right?"

Rudy said they are trying to get us off the train at Billings, where they could fly in a new crew. It is hard not knowing our exact arrival time. If we arrived late at night into Billings, there wouldn't be flights available, anyway. We sat on the main too long and we created a backlog of coal trains between Fargo and the Powder River mainline that wouldn't quit. Rudy said the railroad had a problem keeping ahead of the coal deliveries when things went smoothly, and most likely we would have to take our turn getting dispatched through the logjam. I told him that I preferred to stay on the train. I didn't feel like being strapped into an airline seat. Besides, I was being pampered. I was getting hugs and kisses and food and more promises of love. Everything was going to go my way if I could only thwart the black cloud that continued to gather around me during the moments of frivolity. Rudy said he had to go. He mainly came to help with the decisions. It will be up to Rudy to make the arrangements for everybody aboard if the train is annulled. So far the passengers are hanging in there with video entertainment and free food. The tray meals are complimentary for the remainder of the trip. Everyone seems satisfied to sit there and hope for the best, in light of the circumstances and faced with the fact that they have zero options.

"Rudy. Before you leave I need to tell you something. I used one of the victim's phones and talked to the family."

Rudy immediately stiffened. He turned and stood over my bunk with both hands resting on the upper bunk.

"You did? What did you say?"

"I told them the truth. Nobody there knows what happened. I felt obligated because the younger brother kept calling and sending text messages on his dead brother's phone. The messages were pathetic. He was trying to reach his brother. I couldn't sit here and let him keep calling, so I answered one of his calls."

I could tell that did not make Rudy happy.

"I would have preferred that you had not done that, but now that you did, it's done. Let's hope the media does not quote you. Look Trevor, the reason we don't like you to talk to the media is because, in their minds, they have already written their story before you talk. After you talk, they take what you said and twist it to fit their story. They usually have an agenda, and right now it is against the railroads. We don't need a whole lot of negative press. It just doesn't help our cause. Why did you have the phone in the first place?"

I explained to him all that had happened. He didn't know any of that. I told him about the watch I was carrying. He said Reyna's updates were piecemeal and incomplete. He took Travis' watch and phone to prevent me from being caught with them. He said the train could keep any evidence they collect and are not obligated to turn it over to local law enforcement. The railroads are their own little entity. He wasn't so sure about the phone, but he said the property manager would put the watch in over-night express and insure it. He said the Olsens would have it by Monday or Tuesday. He shook both my hands and prepared to leave just as the train moved out of the station. They weren't going to allow us to block the main track any longer. We had to pull over across the Missouri River into Mandan, where there is a large rail yard, to do the inspections and analysis.

Shortly after Rudy left, Reyna came in and chastised me about not using the ice packs. I could see that my leg wound was seeping fluid through the bandages. My leg felt raw. It started throbbing. I called Reyna again. She told me to take the codeine narcotic the doctor prescribed and lie down and see if I could sleep. The lounge-car attendant was going to sneak me in a couple of beers. I preferred that to a narcotic. News spread like wildfire that we were being cleared for takeoff, and the train would not be annulled here. It was 1 p.m., over nine hours behind schedule, when we pulled out of the rail yards in Mandan and continued west. Reyna went to bed and I drank my beer. I called my dad and gave him my new phone number. He hadn't heard a thing. He was glad I was okay. I didn't tell him much -- only that I had hurt my shoulder.

We lost another hour between Bismarck and Billings. We were stopped in Billings just at dark. I had slept very little and was awake when Reyna came in to say goodbye. She was getting off and flying to Seattle in the morning. She said she would drink about ten martinis that night. She made me take the pain medicine. Before I knew it, I was totally stoned and didn't hear a thing until the next morning.

What I didn't know was that when Reyna arrived at her hotel room, she immediately called my folks and gave them a more pessimistic report on my physical and emotional condition. My mother and sisters cried, but my dad sat there seething. She thought they needed to know that I was going to need a lot of help healing.

I slept for ten hours straight. We were rerouted along the Clark Fork River out of Missoula. It was a slightly longer route, but not as curvy. In case of some latent damage to the wheel axle set, taking a straighter course would be less of a strain on the wheels. More time was being lost because we were wedged in between two freights.

We arrived in Spokane just before noon. We should have arrived about 10:30 the night before. Intermountain Rail annulled the train. Everybody had to get off. Passengers were to be bussed the remaining three hundred miles to Seattle. They brought me a wheelchair. They didn't want me to fall, and believe me, I didn't want to. My comrades carried my stuff and Dean pushed me in the wheelchair. Reyna suggested to my folks that they come to Spokane and take me off. She didn't know that the train would be annulled, anyway. I was so happy to see my mom and dad waiting for me. I wished my sisters had come too, but they didn't. I told them not to hug me on my left side. As we waited in the emergency room to see the doctor, dad didn't say anything much to me about the trip or the accident. Suddenly, dad turned and looked me right in the eyes.

"You had a rough time of it, didn't you?"

"I was on the 'Train from Hell!' "

The Requiem

When daylight awakened Cheneau Valley that fateful Sunday morning, news of the accident hit the valley like a tsunami. The floodwaters of disbelief, shock, and finally grief completely overwhelmed the peaceful town and quickly spread to the rest of North Dakota and to the nation. The news that three star high school athletes were dead, and the lives of two others were hanging in jeopardy, was an incomprehensible tragedy. Because of the prolonged delay in reaching Sharon Hickles, authorities remained tightlipped about the details and who exactly was involved. That news came later, at 2 p.m. from the accident site, where a press conference was held. But most, living in Cheneau Valley, knew at daybreak after rumors spread from house to house like a wind-driven prairie fire.

Coach Epperson went into seclusion. He couldn't face anyone. The coach's phone was overwhelmed with students calling, hoping he could tell them that what they had heard wasn't true. Students phoned each other, they phoned teachers, and they phoned their pastors. There was a debate on where to go, what to do, what to say and where to gather. It started at the school, where they immediately changed the message area of the outdoor school sign from "Congratulations All Graduates" to

"Travis, Brad & Kyle R.I.P." School officials decided to re-open the school, even though it had been closed for the summer, but soon reconsidered, because many staff members were out of town for the summer holiday.

A small group of students began to gather on the vast front lawn outside Travis' house at the farm. The lawn was lush and green from rains, and Travis had just mowed it a couple days before. It turned into a giant tailgate party. A sheriff's deputy was dispatched to maintain order, but his services were not needed. David said to leave them alone in their grief. They cried, they laughed, they told stories, Terri took them out Travis' CDs and they played loud music. They danced and Granny made sure they didn't go hungry. People brought tons of food. They set up barbeques and some brought RVs, which were used as comfort stations. Granny put in an order to Greer's for paper goods and Greer's delivered it out to the farm. Laser was agitated at the crowd, and the fact that his master was missing, so Tanner took Laser up to Travis' room. Laser jumped up on the bed and Tanner left him there.

By four that afternoon, a rainsquall blew through, scattering the crowd and ending the party. As it continued to rain, they all left. The wind scattered the piles of flowers people had brought from their yards. Nobody picked them up. Everywhere you looked around the Olsen's farm, there were homegrown peonies, lilacs, daisies and dozens of supermarket bouquets, strewn here and blown there. They blew over to Granny's yard, over against the corrals where Travis had raised his steers, across the driveway and on the half court.

Meanwhile, that evening, another gathering took place between city and county officials. They started discussing what they could do to help the town recover, honor the dead, help the injured and heal the grieved. Randy Spencer was in the gathering that took place at the home of the mayor, who lived next to Cheneau River Park, along the still, meandering waters of Cheneau River. Randy kept his thoughts to himself. He would make his move at just the right time. City officials from Jamestown called the mayor and offered their condolences and help.

Lynn Olsen

Monday came and went. It was a complete blur. I had no privacy to grieve, so I cried all Monday night, when I should have been sleeping. I cried unselfishly for the world I would live in, which would be a much sadder place without Travis. I cried for my grandchildren, the children that Travis would never have. I cried for Katie. I wanted her because Travis had loved her. I wanted a daughter-in-law just like her. I cried because I didn't deserve her. I cried for Granny, and for the pain she would carry for the rest of her life. I cried for David, who would not cry for himself. I cried because I could never go to the Bison Arena at North Dakota State and watch another basketball game without being haunted by Travis' ghost. I cried because if we had dealt with some of Travis' bad behavior that surfaced, this would not have happened. I cried because I didn't call the sheriff on Aaron. The sheriff would have arrested him and he wouldn't have killed my son. I cried until I couldn't cry anymore. It was an ache that only I could feel.

Poor David. He put up with it. During the night he was at the side of the bed with his head in his hands, frustrated with me and with the situation we found ourselves in. David promised me that there would be brighter days ahead, but I couldn't see anything, but darkness.

"*Lynn!* Please. We'll be all right. We have each other. We have Terri and Tanner. It will get better. *Please*, I can't stand to hear you cry anymore," he begged.

My sisters are treating me like an invalid. I'm not allowed to work in my own kitchen. They cleaned my house at least twice, but I asked them to please not go into Travis' room. All I have to do is plan the funeral and I can't even do that. I can't come up with anything. I don't know what David is planning. He won't talk about it. People keep asking. The three boys are back from Bismarck, and that is all I know. The ball is in our court.

We are to meet with Mr. Simmons this afternoon. He wants us to bring the clothes Travis will wear as he lays in the coffin. I couldn't do it so I handed the task to my sister Arlene, who asked Terri to help her. Terri picked the outfit that Travis will wear.

"I don't want to see what you picked out," I said.

They put the things that Mr. Simmons asked for in a brown paper bag for us to take. When Sharon came over, I asked her what Kyle was wearing.

"Oh, I won't be able to open the coffin," she said.

Granny wants me to go with her to see Father Fitzgerald. I don't know why and I don't want to go. I'm trying to get up the courage to confess to Father Fitzgerald about my betrayal to David. I don't know if it will help me. Maybe I'll ask Granny first, to see what she thinks. If it turns out that Travis is at all culpable in this matter, then maybe I shouldn't tell Father Fitzgerald anything about it. I can't think clearly enough to make good decisions.

At 10 a.m. Granny pulled up in her Expedition and we both went into town to see Father Fitzgerald. We sat there in the rectory office, Granny and I, waiting for Father Fitzgerald to enter. He entered the rectory and took Granny's hands, held them together and kissed them. He made the sign of the cross as he spoke.

"In the name of the Father, and of the Son, and of the Holy Spirit. Amen."

He sat down behind his desk. I sat there, impassive, looking out the window at the cars passing on the street. I wasn't really listening as he told Granny about the blessing he gave Travis at St. Catherine's, and how Sister Lisa Marie had called him to come and bless Cecelia's dead grandson, who had just arrived. Father Fitzgerald explained that Travis was already dead and could not have his last confession. For that reason, he worried that Travis' soul could not travel confidently into God's presence in eternity. I trembled as Father Fitzgerald informed Granny that the baptism Travis had as an infant would have little, if any effect, on his soul, considering that he had never been to confession as an adult.

"Father, but what can we do now? How can we help?" Granny pleaded with him to give her some assurances that Travis' soul could be in God's presence.

I held back. I struggled to control my urge to weep by catching my breath again and again and again. Father Fitzgerald looked at me and then turned away just as I broke down sobbing. Granny put her hand on my shoulder but kept on talking about Travis' soul, wanting to know where it was, where it was going, and how to get it to where she wanted it to be. She was worried it was in limbo and that was why we came.

Father said he did say a prayer of the Viaticum in the presence of Travis' body, and that was the most he could do under the circumstances.

"Father, did you touch him? Did you touch his body when you gave this prayer?"

At first he didn't want to answer her, but then he was honest and told her no, because the doctor wouldn't unzip the pouch. Father explained that the doctor had to have a witness in order to do so and no law enforcement official was there at the time. He went on to say that under the guidelines of handling evidence, the hospital was not supposed to open the evidence until the next of kin came to identify the remains. When he said that, I knew it really upset Granny. She didn't question him any further. I was able to get better control of myself, just as Father Fitzgerald asked a question.

"Cecelia? Did Travis ever exhibit any animosity toward me or the church?"

I held my breath. Granny knew Travis had no use for the church. He went to Mass with her when he was a kid. When he was about twelve years old, he wouldn't go any more. He hadn't gone since. I don't know what Granny knew, but Travis talked against Father Fitzgerald's predecessor. She told Father Fitzgerald no, that there had been no dislike for the church. I knew that wasn't true.

If that was the case, Father Fitzgerald thought the blessing he gave would be of benefit and for her to leave it in the hands of God, Christ, Mary, and the saints.

"Surely, one of the saints would take him and care for his soul, would they not?" Granny said, begging again for some reassurance. When he couldn't give it to her, she began to cry and that set me off again.

"But *Father*, he was *a good boy*!" Granny insisted.

Father Fitzgerald agreed, but he said Travis didn't die in the perfect state. He didn't have that final chance to confess and now a time of purgation would be needed in order to cleanse his soul so it could move closer to God.

"There may have been sins that Travis committed that we didn't know about but God did," he said. "If he had committed sexual improprieties, sins against his family or anyone else, and these sins were not confessed, his soul could not be in a place of freedom from the pain and worry of the external world."

He told us not to think of purgatory as a place, but rather as a transition period whereby the soul was prepared to approach unto God.

"But what if he had been drinking Saturday night, what harm would that do to his soul?" Granny wept as she spoke.

I had no idea she had that on her mind. Father Fitzgerald restated what he had already explained. He finished by saying that Travis' spirit would see our grief and comprehend the immensity of his deeds. In the grieving of his spirit, the cleansing would come.

I couldn't accept that. I didn't want Travis to be anywhere grieving about what had happened to him or how we were reacting to it. I wanted him at peace. I cried harder. It was upsetting me so much I couldn't stay any longer.

"Granny, I think we better leave."

I shifted my straight-back chair sideways, away from Granny, so I could stand up. Father Fitzgerald ignored me and looked right at Granny.

"Cecelia? Are you having a funeral Mass? A Mass will help assist his soul through purgatory."

I knew what Granny wanted. I didn't know what to do. Just as I opened my mouth to say that I'd have to talk it over with David, Granny said she wanted a funeral Mass. The priest then looked at me.

"Lynn? Do you want Travis to have a Mass?"

My emotional state prevented me from speaking, but without further contemplation, I nodded yes.

"Fine," he said. "You let me know when."

We went on our way home, I kept up the sobbing in the car, with Granny driving, and now I had to confront David about a Mass that I knew he didn't want. Certainly, Travis wouldn't want it. I was a total wreck. I had not slept the past twenty-four hours. I soon had to go to the mortuary and pick out the coffin.

"*Lynn! Lynn!*" David tried to calm me. He was waiting to leave for town again. "So, we'll have a Mass. Is there anything wrong with that? Granny needs to have the Mass, so let her have it. It doesn't matter what Travis would want or say right now. He's not here. Let it be. Travis would want Granny to be happy. I'll let Granny plan it. It will be her Mass for Travis."

Granny was too exhausted to go back into town with us to the funeral home, so we took Tanner. David asked him if he'd like to go and help us pick out his brother's coffin. I guess I was all cried out, because nothing we saw or did or said at the funeral home seemed to affect me. Sharon said she wanted to display Kyle's high school jersey, so Tanner brought along Travis' jersey for the purpose of color-coordinating it with his coffin. Sharon met us there at the mortuary. She was a strong comfort. She knew the ropes already and had some suggestions. David and Tanner picked out a light-blue coffin. It was beautiful, but very expensive. Travis would not have wanted us to bury him in such an expensive coffin, but Tanner picked it out. It seemed important to Tanner, so David went along with it. It was a perfect match for the school's colors. It matched his jersey. On the way home, David reminded me that there was to be a meeting with city officials that same night. We had to give our okay for a public service that they wanted to conduct.

We all gathered at the mayor's house. When I saw Brad's sister Dana, I rushed over to her and we hugged each other tight. Dana didn't let go of me. We said nothing to each other. We just hugged. Dana looked just like I felt. Sara told me that Dana had cried nonstop for two days. They were beside themselves about what to do with her. Poor Rod. He had never seen his fiancée in such a condition. He didn't know how to handle her, either.

I listened, but I couldn't have repeated anything that was said regarding the public memorial service that the city wanted to plan. Jamestown offered to help. The Jamestown Civic Center was offered, since Cheneau Valley had no facilities to accommodate a crowd of the expected capacity. The mayor said both cities had some money in the budget they could use to cover the expenses.

Then the mayor suggested that the families talk privately and they all left the room, except for Randy Spencer. I was startled when he asked to bury all three together on his wheat field, which overlooked the valley. He was donating the land to us, if we would agree to his proposal.

"I was thinking, " he said as he cleared his throat, "the boys went to school together, they were close friends, they played basketball together, they all worked hard together and won the state basketball championship together, and they died together. I wanted them to be buried together." He had this priceless photo he took of Brad, Kyle and Travis arm in arm holding the trophy after they won the state basketball championship.

I knew Randy loved those boys. He never missed a game and was one of their staunchest supporters. Everybody was silent, it seemed, for the longest time. David said he would pay him something, but Randy refused.

"We would have to pay somebody to dig and cover the graves. The local cemeteries wanted a small fortune just to open and close one grave, according to Mr. Simmons."

David seemed to be going for it. I knew Granny wanted Travis buried in St. Xavier's next to her first husband, Arnie. She had already looked into it.

"I have that covered." Randy said. "There are a couple of guys with backhoes that want to do it. Everybody is so devastated; they all want to do something. They won't charge you. A couple other men will build the wood boxes to be used as the burial crypts. They wouldn't charge for the crypts, either."

"We can pay you for the lumber."

Randy shook his head no.

Just when he said that, Guy Hickles said it would be wonderful, because he and Sharon would have to borrow the money to bury Kyle. I could see Sharon was upset when he said that, but Guy was just being honest. David had just written Mr. Simmons a huge check and it didn't include any burial services.

Randy explained that he had already submitted a plot plan to be surveyed for future use as a burial place for him and his family.

He said they could push the paperwork through the county in time for the necessary burial permits. As Valley County Commissioner, Randy thought he could get it all ready by Friday. He would follow everything through, making sure it was legal and right.

John O'Connor said they originally wanted to bury Brad next to his grandparents up north an hour away, but they would reconsider. Then he turned to Dana and asked her what she wanted done.

"Do you want Brad over with Grammy? Or, do you want him buried with Travis and Kyle?"

"Travis and Kyle," she said in a halting, shaky voice.

By Tuesday night, we had almost everything arranged. Brad was to have a service at Good Shephard Lutheran on Thursday evening. Travis was to have a Mass at St. Xavier's on Friday at noon. Sharon and Guy were planning nothing religious for Kyle, but he would lie in state with Travis and Brad at the public wake held at the Cheneau Valley Civic Auditorium on Friday, from 3 to 8 p.m. Following the wake, at sunset, the boys would be buried on top of the bluff, on a corner of Spencer's wheat field, overlooking Cheneau Valley.

Saturday, at 2 p.m., there would be a public Celebration of Life service at the Jamestown Civic Center, where between six and seven thousand people would be able to attend. That is what it would hold. Following that, the various civic organizations planned a barbeque for everyone at Cheneau River Park in Cheneau Valley. The local bank set up a memorial fund for the boys. Donations would be used as the families deemed appropriate.

John O'Connor asked for the burials to be private, only for the three families, invited friends, and city and school officials. We all agreed to those arrangements. It was planned to have the announcements made public on the community's websites and in the paper the next morning. There were reporters following the officials around everywhere, wanting an update on what was happening.

Karl Jensen

Our home, located on the edge of the secluded forests of Bridal Trails State Park in Kirkland, had become a revolving door of reporters, grief counselors, lawyers and home health practitioners. The interrogation that Trevor endured from Intermountain Rail just about put him and me both over the edge. During the questioning, they tried to make Trevor look like a risk-taking idiot. He had to defend himself every step of the way regarding what he did and why he did it.

Trevor agreed to talk to a reporter who contacted him from the Fargo paper. Two reporters came in person and called on the intercom from the front gate. Susan did not know who they were. She thought they were railroad officials, but they did not tell her that. She let them in. The timing was unfortunate because we were expecting an official to come about that time. I was not home and Trevor did not communicate about their intended visit to me. He knew they were newspaper reporters from Fargo. When Susan found out whom Trevor was talking to, she called me. I was up at Everett in a meeting. There was not a thing I could do. They walked away with a million-dollar story, for which Trevor was paid nothing.

Obviously, when Intermountain Rail saw the story, they were outraged and two railroad lawyers immediately came, charged into our home, and took Trevor to task about it. They began to dissect the story piece by piece. They wanted to know who gave Trevor permission to leave the train. They made him feel it was insubordination in the worst degree, to have stepped off the train and get involved with any part of the rescue. I was proud of Trevor when he argued that he was trained and equipped to help in the rescue. They challenged that point of view, but Trevor then told them that maybe they should take the same training classes that he did. They chided him, saying the emergency techniques he was taught applied while aboard the train and only within those parameters. They went back and forth on the issue of why Trevor did what he did and how he was hurt and on and on. They cruelly accused Trevor of compromising the life of Travis by moving him when there was internal hemorrhaging. Somehow, they obtained information stating that Travis had bled to death internally. They even insinuated that because Travis wasn't laid in the proper posture, such negligence could have been a contributing factor to his death. The railroad could be liable, they said, for such incompetence. The questions continued.

"Do you know what the Trendelenburg position is and how to apply it?"

Of course Trevor didn't know any medical terms like that. He wasn't a trained EMT. Reyna was the nurse. She should have known and saw to it that Travis was laid in the proper position to safeguard his life.

"Well, then," they said. "Since you were so thoroughly trained to perform a rescue, did you initiate CPR immediately when Travis quit breathing? Did you even know when he quit breathing?"

When they asked how it was he went inside the wreckage and removed Joey without using the Jaws of Life, the conversation ended. They said that if Joey lived at all, he might never walk again because of how Trevor and Dean removed him from the truck. Trevor lost his temper, started screaming at them, and that is when I took charge. Trevor said they were not about to stand by and watch anybody burn. He didn't care how their railroad policies read.

"Get out of my room! Get out of my house. *Now*! *Get out*! *Both of you*! *Out*! Now!"

I placed myself between the two lawyers and Trevor. Trevor broke out in a cold sweat. He stood leaning on his crutch for support, hunched over with his injured leg half bent. He looked like he could fall over any second. I calmly as possible told them that there must be a better way to resolve this. They left immediately.

Trevor was so mad he was shaking. He sat down and I asked him if he was able to take this on by himself, or did he want me to help him? When he humbly told me that he needed my help, I sat there with him and we talked it over. I explained what they were about. I told Trevor not to talk to the media again. As long as he was employed by the railroad he was to follow their policies. Also, they could see what kind of witness Trevor would be for them and how they would have to groom him for whatever it was he had to do. Those two men will never darken our door again. They discovered Trevor's bad temper and ego.

The lacerations are deep, but they are healing quickly. His ribs are very tender, and they want him to wear the sling and to use the one crutch for walking. The physical therapist comes to the house every day and checks his leg movement. They want him to avoid a fall that could cause an orthopedic injury to boot. A nurse comes three times a week and changes the bandages and checks the wounds. Trevor doesn't want this, but they insist. They don't want any complications to develop.

When he feels good, he is a real tease and showoff. He poses for his sisters and their girlfriends who come over to visit. One time, he came down in his black silk boxers and the crazy kid let the girls photograph his wounds. He did all kinds of crazy poses for them. It cheered him up. Wait until the lawyers see those pictures displayed on the Internet!

Cards and letters have started arriving downtown at the Intermountain Rail Office, sent to him from unknown well-wishers from all over the country. This whole experience has had a sobering effect on all of us. His sisters realize that Trevor could have been killed in that truck while rescuing those boys, or at least been seriously hurt on impact when Aaron hit the train.

We've kept up on the news by reading the obituaries and announcements from the Cheneau Valley newspaper. It is all horribly sad. The news about Aaron and Joey has been sketchy at best. This has worried Trevor, but we know they are both alive. That means everything to Trevor.

Everything was going as well as could be expected until Thursday morning, when Trevor took a call from David Olsen. David asked if it was at all possible for him to come back to North Dakota for the Celebration of Life service that was to be held in Jamestown on Saturday. The family wanted him to speak at the service on behalf of Travis. David said all of Travis' cousins would be there and they all would want to meet him.

Of course he couldn't go, I thought. He is off work indefinitely. He walks with a crutch. Of course he can't. Why would anybody think he could? I didn't expect Trevor to ever get on that train again. His emotional state was improving but he was still quite fragile.

Tanner had called Trevor repeatedly. Tanner was calling to inquire about Trevor. We knew Travis' family was concerned about Trevor. I didn't comprehend that such a strong friendship was being forged between Trevor and the Olsens.

"Dad! I just talked with Rudy at Intermountain Rail. I'm going back to North Dakota for the service Saturday. If I leave tonight, I'll get to Jamestown at three in the morning the day of the service. Mr. Olsen said he would meet me. Dad, they want me to come, and Rudy found me space on the train tonight. I can leave tonight, but I can't drive. Can you or mom take me into Seattle?"

I didn't want to argue with Trevor over what appeared to be a totally senseless thing to do. He looked at me in such a sad, pitiful way; it was impossible for me to refuse. It broke my heart to see his deep sadness and determination to return back into the eye of the storm. What in the world did he plan to say on behalf of Travis, someone he knew for thirty minutes? It was unthinkable. It would certainly unravel his emotions.

When Trevor reviewed the crew roster on tonight's train, he didn't know anyone. Reyna went back to Minneapolis and Dean was off until Saturday. Paula wanted to know who would take care of him by putting the healing salve and cream on all the places he couldn't reach? We all laughed when Trevor assured her that most of the crewmembers were women and they would know all the right places to touch.

Susan and I left him at King Street Station at 6 p.m. We watched while an attendant took him in a wheelchair inside the station where he would board the train.

Suddenly, I had these thoughts spinning in my head. As we drove back across Lake Washington to Kirkland, they stayed in my head. I wanted to wind them around, like thread on a spool and put them in a drawer, someplace out of my head. I couldn't get rid of them. What so completely amazed me was the pull this had on Trevor. The instant they asked him to come, he was out the door without giving it a second thought. We were swept away in this giant hurricane. It was something I had no control over. The eye was in North Dakota and the gale-force winds were blowing our life away here in Kirkland.

"Susan," I started, "when we get home we have to pack. We're going to North Dakota. I have to be in the audience when Trevor speaks. I have to be there in support of my son."

"Karl? What makes you think Trevor wants us there? I don't think he wants us to go there. You could call him and ask."

"He doesn't need to know we're there. We can see him afterwards at the barbeque in the park. He'll be glad we came. I know it."

Susan immediately dialed Amber, because Amber had already made plans with her friend Tina for the weekend. They were going over to the island. She didn't think Amber would want to come.

"Tell her to cancel it. She is going with us. We're doing this as a family."

I called the agency at work that does our travel and told them to get started booking four round-trip tickets between Seattle and Fargo, plus car rental.

"When we are in Fargo, I will go and visit those two boys that were injured, if they are still alive."

Amber talked back to her mother. She was not about to change her plans. I couldn't believe that I had raised a daughter who was so selfish. I told Susan to tell her she was going and I would explain why later. She was too much into herself and her own pleasures. She needed to be more in tune with what was important for the family. She needed to be there for her brother, who was facing a huge crisis.

Lynn Olsen

When we arrived at St. Xavier's, I scarcely noticed the crowd of people gathered in front of the church. It was funeral number two for us, with Brad's being the first. Brad's service was small, limited to family and invited friends only. Sara told us that we didn't have to come. We went. We had to do it for Travis. Brad was his best buddy.

We had just viewed Travis for the first time and everyone had taken it pretty hard. He looked like he was asleep. He and Brad both did. Never in your wildest imagination would you have thought either boy had suffered such a violent death. I didn't read any of the newspaper accounts, but I did watch a TV broadcast in which the reporter explained the number of times the truck catapulted along the track, as it was pulled by the train to where it was finally hurled across the water. I couldn't imagine that anyone in the truck could have survived.

I was way ahead of everybody else because I had bawled my eyes and heart out for four days. I'm glad I had that head start. I was stronger for my family, where I couldn't have been a few days earlier. I sat in the car, looking through the tear-stained windows watching Tanner, his four cousins, and Jakey, Travis' good high school buddy, unload the coffin and carry it into the church. David wanted to help, but there was nothing for him to do. He wanted to touch the coffin and hold on to it, but there wasn't a spare handle to grab. Finally, Mr. Simmons let him crowd in and help. When everything was in position, they motioned for us to get out and we followed the coffin inside the church, past four hundred people gathered for the Mass. I was totally numb. I didn't know I had so many friends. I didn't know that Travis knew so many people.

Granny and Paul sat in the front row with us, next to my parents. My poor mother struggled to breathe. Her emphysema is at the stage where it requires her to carry oxygen. She doesn't do well in crowds.

During the communion, Dr. Yvonne Leslie, voice instructor from the university, using her beautiful soprano voice, sang *Panis Angelicus* "Bread of Angels." Granny asked her to sing it in Latin. Her voice completely filled the church. I know Travis would have enjoyed her singing.

Last December, the Cheneau Valley State University Music Department put on a Madrigal Dinner. Granny took a whole bunch of us. The price for admission went toward the music scholarships. Granny loves classical music and has made many generous contributions to the university. During the dinner, the students served several courses of food, and before each course, a choral group performed. Dr. Leslie sang an old carol in Italian. It really impressed Travis. When she finished singing, he said, "Wow! That lady can sing!"

Sister Lisa Marie took Granny by the hand and led her to where Father Fitzgerald served the communion. Sister motioned for me to follow. I took mother by the arm and followed. The congregation lined up behind us. There were too many in the line. The ushers cut it off. Everyone put their hands on Travis' coffin as they passed by it.

After the Mass ended we found ourselves at the local Eagles Hall, where the community put on a simple but wonderful meal for the three families and some invited guests. I was starved. We didn't feel like going home, eating and coming back into town, where it was expected for us to attend the wake. I knew it was going to be five difficult hours, but that would be the last hours we could stand by our boys before they were buried. I wanted to be there. I needed to be strong. I wondered what advice Travis would give.

"Go for it! Hang in there. Act like a winner. You can do it! Hit it! Harder!"

All his phrases popped into my mind. Travis was never for giving up or shying away from any project. I went for it. Hundreds of people had lined up to come into the auditorium for the wake. Mr. Simmons and his staff nicely arranged the viewing area.

"Do you folks want a few private moments with them, before we open the doors to the public? We can do it either before or afterwards."

"Both." We answered unanimously.

Poor Sharon, before the doors opened, had Kyle's coffin opened. It would be for a few minutes in case any of us wanted to see him. After what Trevor had told us, I didn't want to see him. For Sharon's sake, I felt obligated. She stood by Kyle, expecting us to come over and view him. David, Tanner and I went over and looked at him. It was Kyle, all right. His hair looked nice, in fact, better than the way he combed it. He looked dressed for church, although he never went to church. Beside the coffin was his basketball jersey. Everything about him looked like Kyle, but his face was terribly swollen, deformed, and discolored. He was covered in makeup. His poor dad couldn't look. Guy couldn't even approach the coffin. In a few minutes Sharon asked for the coffin to be closed. It remained closed.

It was arranged for the Cheneau Valley High School students to enter first for a few private moments with their dead friends before the wake was opened to the public. There were tables with tissues for wiping away the thousands of tears that were shed. I never knew that Cheneau Valley had such a nice-looking bunch of kids. Every one of them hugged us.

A lady approached us. She introduced herself as Joey's aunt from Iowa. She said that Joey was still very critical but the brain surgery he had on top of everything else was successful. He had a bad head injury and they had removed a clot. His chest was improving, but so far they had left his legs the way they were, for now. It was too painful for him to be awake, so they left him in a drug-induced coma. She reported that periodically they brought him back and he was responsive each time. She was looking for Trevor, because his name was in the paper as one of the people who rescued Joey before the truck burned. They were very grateful for that, and Lana wanted her to specifically find Trevor and tell him. We told her that we expected him for Saturday's service.

Katie Russell spotted me and she bolted over. She looked so nice.

"Pretty and plain," Travis would say. Then he would rephrase it with "plain pretty."

I told her that Travis loved her and that it was love at first sight. He had never loved any other girl like he had loved her. She smiled at me as I told her that. It pleased her. We held onto each other. She looked away as the tears from reddened eyes started streaming down her smooth, clean face. When she stopped crying, she told me Travis had told her the same thing. He also apologized about the way he had treated her by neglecting her for the past couple of months. He begged her to forgive him and asked if he could have another chance when they both got to NDSU this fall. That was hard to take. I loved the way Travis loved her. She was his first and only true love.

We didn't have to stand in the reception line if we chose not to. There was a roped-off area for the families to sit and rest. Granny stood the whole time. Greeting everyone was a way to occupy her mind. I don't know how she did it. The crowd kept swelling. They came but they wouldn't leave. They stood quietly. Some whispered while others quietly wept. They mingled through the crowd, looking for others they knew who needed comfort or who could provide comfort. Eventually, there was no room for any more people to enter. As people left, they let more in.

When the wake ended, we left for the hilltop. I never heard if everyone got in to see the boys or not. The city chartered buses to take the three families the short distance up to Randy's wheat field. We couldn't get the buses into the field because it was too wet. My mother and dad had to leave before the wake was over. Each bus with family members followed a flatbed truck that carried each coffin. They had side rails to prevent the pallbearers from falling off the truck. Unfortunately, and not according to plan, after each coffin was situated on its respective truck several other kids piled on until the trucks couldn't hold any more. Nobody stopped them. Only the pallbearers were supposed to ride in the back with the coffins. The kids wanted to take one last ride with their dead heroes. The procession moved slowly through town. On the hill, a number of vans were used to shuttle the folks who couldn't walk from the boundary road to the graves; it was easily the length of a football field. David, John and Guy were there when they dug the graves. They had their say as to how they were to be positioned. The boys' heads will face the south and they will be buried side by side.

The Requiem

Forget about the private burial. Everyone ignored that part. You couldn't keep them off the hill. People came and they kept coming. It was an anthill of hundreds of people. They all wanted to come as far as they could. Let them come, I thought. Mr. Simmons asked us if we should start the service. John O'Connor told Father Fitzgerald and Pastor Rice to wait and not start the committal service until everyone arrived. The crowd packed in around us. Were there hundreds or thousands? We stood there quietly for half an hour, waiting. In the pall of grief that gathered around us, I felt compassion and sympathy. I could feel it in the crowd that gathered. It was hard standing there that long looking at the three coffins. Then again, I wasn't in any hurry to get it over with. The police came and helped organize the crowd around us, and gathered everyone in as close as possible. Two news helicopters were above in the sky, but they kept at a distance during the service. There was a warm prairie breeze. The sun was getting low in the western sky when the service started.

It was brief. Pastor Rice read the Lord's Prayer and Father Fitzgerald gave a blessing. Pastor Rice threw a shovelful of dirt onto each grave and recited the committal prayer. Father Fitzgerald finished with the benediction. It was over in less than fifteen minutes.

Dozens of people, if not hundreds, brought shovels to help with the burial, which by prior arrangement was to be hand-shoveled. One by one each boy was lowered into the ground. On one end was Kyle, in the middle was Travis and on the east end was Brad. I wondered who made that determination. Why was Travis in the middle? Standing there looking at the coffins, I got it. It came clear. That's how they stood on the basketball court. The best plays were made with Kyle on the right side of Travis, and Brad lurking at the perimeter on his left side, ready for Travis to pass out to him for a three-point bucket.

When they started lowering Travis, Tanner lost it. He was too far away from us. I looked in horror as he fell completely apart. Like his dad, Tanner had bundled his grief inside him. The bundle burst. No one noticed. Everyone was transfixed on what Mr. Simmons' staff was doing. I saw it all. Tanner's contorted face, moistened with tears, struggled to contain the breathless sobs that began to erupt. Two of his cousins escorted him around on the other side of the dirt pile, out of view. They stayed there with him for a long time.

Soon, they reemerged with shovels. Then all we saw was shovels of prairie dirt falling into the holes. I could not separate one person who shoveled from another who didn't. Even the girls squeezed in between the men and boys. Everyone wanted to help. There were more helpers than shovels. I held tightly onto David. I knew he wanted to go and help. I didn't want him to. I needed him with me. Then, David's stepbrothers came with shovels. They all helped. It was okay. My sisters and family surrounded me.

It took an hour to bury them. They were done about 9 p.m. Some men had rigged up a tamping apparatus and periodically they would stop shoveling and tamp down the soil. When it was over, Rodger stood between the graves and the team huddled around him. Arm in arm, they stood there in silence in the gathering darkness. Soon athletes from opposing schools, so identified by the school jerseys that they wore, joined the huddle. I didn't know, but I wondered if all the Eastern Dakota Division schools were represented in that mass of humanity that stood there huddled in silence. The huddle grew larger and larger. We all stood and waited, and then when the huddle finally broke up, we walked back in the twilight to the buses.

Trevor Jensen

I felt the gentle sway of the bed, and then, suddenly, it jerked as the wheels sped over several switches where there were diverging tracks: click-clack, clickety-clack, clickety-click. Immediately, the speeding train shifted from jointed rail and continued its eastward journey through the night, gliding over continuously welded rail track. The soft muffled squeal of the wheels, as they ground tightly against the inside gauge of the track, was mainly what I heard as I tried to awaken and regain my bearings. At first, I thought I was in my own bed at home, but then, why was my bed swaying? I dreamt about my horse, Mr. Jed, and swore I heard him whinny in the night. I lay there wondering if I could move. My leg was stiff. If I bent it too much, the serous fluid from the wounds would ooze out from the bandages and soak through whatever I wore on top of it. The therapist taught me how to roll over to the edge of the bed without bending the injured leg. That maneuver enabled me to do a push-up off the bed. That process didn't work so well on this narrow train bunk. There was a knock on my door.

"It is three-thirty, Trevor. We are almost to Jamestown. We are ahead of schedule. You have about twenty minutes."

Babbs opened the door and made sure I was awake. She had a steaming hot cup of coffee, juice and a monster muffin. It is what every first-class passenger gets with the wakeup call, if they order it.

"Just get dressed and Jen will be here to get you off."

I thanked her and hustled. I almost hated to leave my first-class, single room. It was confining, non-threatening, cozy and quaint. I had everything I needed. If not, I could push a button and someone would bring it. I wished for an open ticket with no destination.

I didn't have to sleep with the crew, thanks to Rudy. I hoped he didn't have to bump a cash customer. I wondered what fib they told the passenger who would have been assigned to the room I had occupied for the past day and a half. Would they blame it on the computer? Would they put them in with the crew? Maybe they would sleep, like I have on occasion, on an upper bunk above one of the pastry chefs, who would snore and mutter all night because of all the greasy food they cook and eat. In the morning, the disgruntled passenger would demand a refund, but instead they would get a food voucher, a train video, and one hundred dollars toward their next train ride, provided they didn't travel during Christmas or summer or any other dates that the railroad predicted a capacity crowd of full-fare passengers.

I felt safe here on the train. I had no clue as to what I would do or say once I was there. I was anxious to meet the Olsens and then I wasn't particularly looking forward to it. I felt guilty about what had happened to their son. Will they ever know the part I had played in his death? Would I weaken and finally tell them that Travis died on my watch? Would I continue to feel guilt all of my life? I worried that my incompetence at the scene would be divulged during the court battles that dad said would happen. I had written out a personal message to Travis, but I wasn't sure I had the emotional stamina to read it. Maybe I could have somebody else read it for me. I was really terrified. During most of the trip here, I regretted coming.

Jen helped me off the train and wheeled me over to the lighted kiosk. I had a small carry-on bag on my lap. Jen hugged me and left. The train let out a short all-aboard whistle. There I was, stranded in Jamestown, North Dakota, in the middle of the night, with my arm in a sling, sitting in a wheelchair, holding a crutch and duffle bag on my lap. I had to really pee after drinking down a *cafe talla grande*. I locked the wheels on the chair and grabbed my crutch just as a man approached out of the darkness.

"Hello. Trevor. I'm David. Thanks for coming."

He bent down, put his arms around me and we hugged. He held on to me for a minute. It hurt so bad that I dug my knuckles into his shoulder blades. It was a long minute. *I wept.* This man should be hugging his son, not me. I kept sniffling as he pushed me in the wheelchair over to where I could hobble into his Suburban.

"I'm sorry, I'm kind of emotional," I said.

"Aren't we all?" he answered.

He opened the front door for me. I stood and steadied myself by grabbing onto the top of the door. I was trying to fish for a hankie that I didn't have. Man, did I have to pee. It was such a tremendous urge that I unzipped my fly, rested my arms on the door and began to empty my bladder. David put the wheelchair in the back, closed the rear door on the Suburban and walked around to the driver's side and looked at me. I stood there, still peeing. It was like I had dual bladders, and both were connected to an artesian well. I couldn't stop.

"You don't have bathrooms on the train?" he asked.

"They only work if you use them," I answered.

I couldn't see what he looked like in the darkness. We drove through the town, onto the interstate, and went about thirty-five miles east to an exit just beyond Cheneau Valley. We didn't talk much. He told me he was about at the end of his tether, after a week of it. After we drove on a country road for fifteen minutes, he turned into the farm. The first hints of daylight began to lighten the eastern sky. The house, except for a yard light, was completely dark. I passed the dog's sniff test as I hobbled through the back porch.

"This dog does a good job of sniffing. He could work for the feds," I said as I shielded my crotch with the crutch. The dog was invading my personal space.

"He's sniffing to see if you have been near Travis. This is Laser. He has been looking for Travis. He gives everybody the once over when they come."

David said the whole family was exhausted. They hoped to sleep late. The relatives were all coming for a late breakfast. Everyone was coming to meet me. He encouraged me to sleep the rest of the night, what was left of it. He walked me up to Travis' room, but would not step inside. He explained that he and Lynn hadn't been able to go in so far. He stood at the door and talked. There was a pungent odor of carnations. I hoped the smell wouldn't trigger my asthma, but I didn't mention it.

"A lady came and cleaned Travis' bathroom and changed the bed. We want everything left just as it was when Travis was last here on Saturday. Other than that, please make yourself at home. If you are not awake, I'll call you for breakfast. Have a good night. I appreciate all you did, and thanks again for coming back. I know the trip wasn't easy. I'm going downstairs to hit the sack for awhile."

David gently shut the door and left. I wasn't tired. I wasn't stressed. I couldn't believe I was here in the very same room of the man I hopelessly tried to save. I think seeing David and the deep hurt he carried affected me. I felt humiliated over crying right at the start. I didn't expect to do that. I get overwhelmed when anyone shows me compassion. They shouldn't.

As I glanced around the room, I noticed a pair of mud-caked jeans draped over a chair. There was a long-sleeve pullover and a pair of dirty white socks. There was mud on the carpet on the other side of the bed. The room was huge. I think it was larger than mine. There was a long desk across the opposite wall. Sitting on the desk was a laptop computer. Some pictures were hanging on the wall. I couldn't see them that well, but they were basketball pictures. There were three big trophies on the shelf. He must have been a reader like me. He had a large library. There was a shelf of videos and CD's. His bed was about forty acres long and twenty wide. I'd never seen a bed that long, but then again he was a tall dude.

It was 4:30 a.m.; dawn was breaking across the sky. I killed the lights and opened the window for some fresh air. The outside thermometer registered a chilly fifty degrees. The cold morning air blew in through the window. The stillness outside was penetrating. Suddenly, I could see something moving across the field, just behind the barn. It was a band of deer feeding.

I wondered what it might be like to be a farmer's kid. I saw several grain elevators, standing side by side. Behind were more metal cylindrical buildings. To the left was another house. I could see some corrals. There was a basketball court across the yard from my window. To the right was a huge metal building. Beside it was a big truck and trailer. There was some very complicated-looking machinery parked in front.

"My old man is a flipping big wheat producer!"

That's what I would tell anyone who asked who I was. I'd pound my chest as I told them the number of acres we farmed. Our yield per acre was always more than the neighbors. I never had to stretch the truth. I'd live in a great big house out in the vast prairie wilderness. There would be a big pond, right in front of my house, full of ducks. I'd have a barn full of fancy cars, trucks, tractors and machinery. My grain bins would be full of wheat. That is the same as cash. I wouldn't need a bank to hold my money. You only need trucks to take the wheat to the railroad. I'd fill up one hopper car after another and send my kids to the most expensive colleges and buy my wife a fur coat. Every year, I'd buy myself a new tractor. This Travis guy was a rich man's kid. Someday he could have inherited the whole spread. Me? I'll steal five million from my old man and disappear into the Dakota landscape. I'll emerge as the top producer of something, like wheat or whatever else they grow here. The state will build its own railroad just to haul out my crops. That's the only tune I'll dance to. I pulled my thoughts back in through the window and put them back in my brain and started facing reality as to who I really was and what I had to do. My old man is just a lawyer and he thinks I'm neck-deep in the smelly stuff. He's right. This whole speaking deal I got myself into today, it stinks.

I took out the handwritten notes I had prepared for today's

service. I started to read them. It really upset me. I dropped a big tear on it, causing a black smudge. Now I can't read it. The tear blotted out part of a sentence. I just can't figure out why I'm so upset over this dude dying. I'm afraid that, when I meet the rest of his family and see their grief, I'll be worse off than I was before coming here. I'm unsettled about what to say at the service. I guess I could say I'm sorry I messed up so bad, that your son Travis up and died. I'm sorry I didn't stand Travis on his head, keeping the blood in the head instead of the feet. I should have kept that Sanders EMT with me. Instead, I sent her away to take care of Aaron and Joey. They had Reyna. Travis and I had nobody. I'm sorry I didn't call for his mom and dad. If I'm ever in that kind of trouble, I hope the idiot who happens by will at least take my cell phone and call home. I bet David would have come. He would have loaded his son up and carried him off to the hospital. Travis would probably still be here with us. Thanks to me they have a dead son and the railroad can now pay out a kajillion million bucks in damages. I have to get my story straight. I should write out what the legal council approved me to say to the families and say no more. I can't tell them what really happened but then I guess I did and it is already in the paper so I'll just read the paper to them. There is nothing more to say.

I yawned. I had a light headache from smelling the white carnations. Do you suppose they would mind if I set them out in the hallway? David told me to move them if they were in my way. I set them out in the hall. I pulled off the comforter and the sheets smelled clean. I shed my clothes and crawled into bed. Suddenly I was exhausted.

David Olsen

As we all sat around stuffing ourselves on the buffet breakfast, I decided Trevor must still be in the sack. I went upstairs and rapped on his door. I called to him. There was not a stir. I picked up the carnations, dumped them out, and came back. I rapped on his door again. Nothing. I opened it and stood looking at him asleep in Travis' bed. He was sleeping in the same sprawled posture as Travis. The wind was blowing in the open window and the room was chilly. His head was covered. In that position he looked like Travis. He didn't quite reach as far down in the bed as Travis. It could have been Travis but it wasn't Travis. It would never be Travis. Travis would never, ever sleep in his own bed again. I spoke to Trevor. I touched him and he awoke a bit startled.

"Take your time Trevor, but breakfast is ready. It is nine-forty-five."

He grabbed his leg and tried to get up fast, but from the expression on his face I knew he was in some discomfort. He asked if there was anyone who could iron his new white shirt. I took it, still bound in the department-store cellophane wrappings, and went back downstairs. I gave it to Lynn's sister, Betty.

I heard the shower running and then in about ten minutes, down came Trevor. He didn't have his crutch and he didn't have the arm in a sling. He moved slowly down the stairs, holding onto the banister with both hands. He looked perplexed as, step-by-step, he negotiated the stairs. Everyone stopped talking and looked. For a few seconds he had holes stared through him. There he was, the man they were waiting to meet. They had a thousand questions, but no one spoke.

I needed to have time away from the others with Trevor. Tanner doesn't tell us accurately what Trevor tells him. Tanner gets confused and doesn't tell the same story twice. The cousins were getting impatient with Tanner's inconsistencies. They wanted to hear it first-hand from Trevor. They couldn't accept the fact that the truck hit the train. They think the opposite happened, even though the papers report differently. I think Trevor knew a lot more than he was telling Tanner and a whole bunch more than he told us last Sunday. I didn't like what I read in the newspapers. I didn't care to get my information from the press. Before Trevor talks to the media, he had better start talking to me first. I didn't care who he told, as long as I knew first.

The shirt was a no-wrinkle variety. Betty didn't have to iron it much. She brought it back on a hanger and hung it on the banister. She told Trevor what was on the menu and asked what he wanted. He said that he liked everything. She left to get him a plate of food. Everybody was gawking at him as he stood there.

"Everybody!" I announced. "Come and meet Trevor, but don't touch him. He is still recovering from some painful injuries suffered in the accident. Just yell hello to him."

There was a loud response from everyone as they crowded into the living room to yell the hellos. Just as if he didn't hear a word I had just said, Tanner made his way from the dinning nook in the kitchen, to the living room, stepped up to Trevor, and put out his hand. Tanner has never met a stranger.

"I'm the one that has been talking to you. I'm Tanner."

Trevor shook his hand but didn't let go of it. Trevor, while bracing his one leg into the banister to maintain his balance, pulled Tanner up one step to his level and gave him a hug. They stood there looking at each other a second or two. Tanner had a big smile on his face.

"Sit here with me while I eat," Trevor said as he sat on the stairs and straightened out his wounded leg.

From that point on, where you saw Trevor, you also saw Tanner. Tanner remained transfixed on Trevor the entire time Trevor was there. Tanner forgot about his cousins. Tanner wanted to be close to the man who rescued his brother and knew everything about the accident. Any information or knowledge that spilled out of Trevor, Tanner was there to swoop it up. Granny was there. She watched as Trevor walked down the stairway. She mentioned that he looked like an angel. Granny often gets spiritual presentiments about people. In Granny's mind, Trevor was that angel who removed Travis from the burning truck and handed him over to God, who was standing by. That is how she looked at it and that is how she regarded Trevor. Trevor was Granny's angel.

Karl Jensen

We landed in Minneapolis-St. Paul and quickly caught our flight to Fargo, landing there at 11 p.m. The next morning, room service knocked on our door at 7 a.m. I hoped the toast, oatmeal, and coffee would sustain me until I ate again, whenever that would be. I was nervous, agitated, and bewildered. The accident our son had been involved in was everywhere in the papers. I wanted to turn on the TV, but Susan was still asleep. I knew Paula and Amber would be out cold for another two hours. We had less than a hundred mile drive to Jamestown. I told the girls they were to be up by 10 a.m. and we were to be on the road to Jamestown at eleven on the dot. I knew it would take the girls at least an hour to primp and dress. I wrote Susan a note and went down to the front desk.

"Do you know, offhand, what hospital is used as your trauma center?"

"Probably Agassiz Healthcare North," the desk clerk said.

She gave me directions. The hospital was not far from our hotel. I knew both victims' names from the newspaper articles. I went into the hospital lobby and stopped at the reception desk. I asked about Aaron Richards.

"I have no information about him," the receptionist said.

"So he's not a patient here?" I asked.

"I have no information," she said again.

"I would like to see Joey Carlson or a family member," I said.

The receptionist acknowledged that he was a patient there, but would not give out his location in the facility. I told her who I was and why I was there. She made a phone call.

"Go to the critical-care waiting area and someone will page a family member." She smiled as she pointed me toward the elevators.

It seemed like someone was behind me, pushing me into this. Maybe it was Trevor. He doesn't even know I'm here. This is Trevor's deal. I should learn to stay out of his business, but he doesn't know what he is doing. He doesn't have a clue. He hasn't lived long enough for this. None of us have. He's in a whole heap of trouble.

Soon, they were paging Joey's mother, Lana. She happened to be in with Joey. She had spent the night there. She looked haggard, worried and distressed. She didn't look very huggable but I hugged her. She was glad to see me. I felt that sorry for her. My heart started to ache for these people. Lana had the look of death. I began to feel her pain.

"I know Trevor would want to be here, but I'm here in his place," I told her.

She punched in a code on the keypad and I followed her through the sliding doors when they opened. We walked three doors down, to a room by the nursing station. The curtains were pulled in the room, but the door was open and the lights were on full blast. Lana turned down a radio that was blaring out country-western music. It was Joey's favorite radio station, she said. The first thing I noticed was a bunch of get-well balloons tied to a piece of equipment by the bed. One wall was plastered from top to bottom with cards. There he was, a limp, lifeless body hooked up to life-support machinery. I couldn't tell at all what he would look like in real life. He was comatose, on a breathing machine. He was an average-sized kid. I couldn't guess his exact stature. His face was terribly swollen. His head was bandaged. There was an IV line attached to his neck, coming from three bags hanging off a pole. He was completely covered with flannel blankets. Tubes were coming out from under the blankets. His legs, she explained, were in traction splints until surgery could be performed. A large tube was connected to a bubbling device, which Lana said was coming from his chest in order to keep his lung inflated, and to drain air, blood and fluid from the pleural space. She said the collapsed lung was the most life-threatening injury that he suffered. It was the cause of the two cardiac arrests he suffered in the field. I took her hand as we stood.

"Is there a chance that he will recover from any of this?" I asked.

"I'm hopeful," she said. "The doctors aren't expecting permanent brain injury, but I don't know if he will ever play basketball again."

"Are you doing okay? Is there anything you need?"

I hardly knew what to offer or how to provide it if it was needed. She thanked me for my thought. Today, she said, she found it hard not being at the service. She was thinking about the families in addition to her own grief. I asked her about Aaron, and she said he was there and had been moved out of critical care. She told me the floor and room number. Aaron's lawyers and family do not want the hospital to release any information or acknowledge to a visitor that he is here. She said everyone knows where Aaron is.

She told me Joe Sr. would relieve her and her husband Bob would also be helping. She said Joey's dad couldn't take a full shift of standing vigil. She said her sister, who was also a hospital nurse, was helping her, but the sister was in Jamestown today to attend the service on their behalf.

"Joe goes to pieces after about four hours. It is hard for all of us to stand here by him. I don't want to leave Joey and then have them call me and tell me that he is gone. As long as I'm with him, I have this feeling that he will live. If I leave him and go to my room and sleep for a few hours, I worry he won't be here when I come back. I don't sleep, so I might as well be here with him. If anything happens, I want to be right here beside him."

"How is the care here?" I asked, hardly knowing why I even asked it.

"Wonderful," she said as she broke down crying.

She said the nurses and doctors were wonderful to her for the most part. She said the nurses talked sweetly to Joey while they worked with him, just as if he could hear every word that they said. They all handled him gently, she said. I told her to stay strong and that we would keep in touch. She told me to tell Trevor to come by as soon as he could. She wanted to meet him and thank him personally for his part in Joey's rescue. She said she wasn't buying what the papers were saying, about Joey's rescue being done too hastily before the firemen could implement the Jaws of Life.

"You tell Trevor, thanks to him Joey is still alive and I intend to keep him that way, as long as it takes. We're not giving up. I don't want to lose my Joey."

I approached Aaron's room just as a nurse came out. She was very bureaucratic.

"They are not receiving visitors and the family will not talk to anyone. You are not allowed to loiter here."

"My son, Trevor Jensen, assisted in his rescue. My son was injured in the accident and can't be here right now. My son wanted me to come by and wish him well. My son is very anxious about it. I would only be a minute. Can he talk?"

"I'm sorry, sir. There is a very limited visitor's list that the family has put together. Right now, they aren't allowing walk-in visitors unless you are on the visitation list."

I left for the gift shop, wrote on a card, took it back up, and handed it to someone at the nursing station, who said he would give it to Aaron's family.

I was quite perturbed when I arrived back at our room only to discover that no one had stirred. It was past 10 a.m. I woke everybody up and called room service. At 11 a.m., Amber was far from ready. She was taking excessive pride in her appearance and had completely filled the dressing table and mirror with herself and the contents of her vanity bag. Disgusted with her sister, who seemed to be competing for a Miss North Dakota pageant, Paula came into our room to apply her own makeup. I should have brought along a makeup artist for Amber; it would have been worth the price of the ticket. Susan went over to the girls' room to see if she could hurry things up. She preferred that to having me get on the phone and confronting Amber.

Trevor Jensen

I tried to convey some of my feelings to David as we sat on the edge of Travis' bed. It was the only place we could talk privately. I sensed that David was deeply upset by even entering Travis' bedroom. Either Tanner or Terri was at my side everywhere I went. They wanted to be close to me for some reason. Terri wanted me to hug her and put my arms around her. She wanted to be the center of my attention. It was awkward. One time she jumped up and sat on my lap, which started my leg scabs running again. Her mother is in a fog and doesn't see her doing this to me. She laughs and then in an instant she cries when someone shows her attention. Terri is a pretty little gal and the replica of her mom. If the kids saw my chest, they would understand my standoffishness. I unbuttoned my freshly pressed white shirt and exposed my black-and-blue skin. That got some looks!

As David sat next to me in Travis' room, he lamented over the situation of speaking at the service. He couldn't convince anyone from the family to speak for Travis. None of his cousins could do it. Terri and Tanner were too young. Everybody in the family was an emotional wreck, including David. He thought it would be a fiasco for any of them to try it. He said Travis wouldn't flinch to do it for him or anyone else in the family. He thought they were all a bunch of wimps.

He said Travis had always been an emotionally strong kid. It was part of his athleticism. David was wishing they hadn't agreed to what was sure to be a huge gathering in Jamestown. The media and publicity had completely overwhelmed the families. David told me he would be forever indebted to me for coming and agreeing to speak. He discussed the program scheduled at Jamestown. I wasn't a listed speaker.

I asked him to call Tanner and Terri upstairs so we could talk more about Travis. I told them I would do my best to speak for them. They wanted me to tell them again about how I first found Travis and the condition he was in at the time of the rescue. They wanted me to keep going over and over it. They were hanging on to bits and pieces of details. They wanted to stay connected to their brother. I told them they had to help me prepare for my part in the program. They told me a lot of things that he did and accomplished. I could sense how proud of him they were. I knew from that point on, that what I wrote on the way here was obsolete. It was completely inappropriate. I had to start over.

Then I asked David to do something that I knew would be very hard for them to do so soon after the burial.

"I want to go up to where Travis is buried. I need to sort out my thoughts from that perspective."

There were a few cars parked on the road below the gravesite. David said there was no way I could walk that far with my injured leg. David gunned the four-wheel drive pickup and we spun up to the top and around the barricades, going as close to the graves as possible. David wouldn't get out of the pickup. A man walked across to where we were parked. David didn't know him. He shook my hand and walked around to the driver's side and shook David's hand and then left. I stood there with a great big lump in my throat. Terri began to cry and I tried to comfort her. It kept me from breaking down. Standing there strengthened me. In the distance I could see the bridge over the valley. A train started moving slowly across it, but I couldn't look any longer in that direction. I braced myself against the pickup and stepped away from it. I could walk just fine without the crutch. I took another step toward the graves, and then another, and another until we were there. Tanner stood next to Travis' grave, looking down. He didn't budge. He could scarcely grasp his brother being there, under all that dirt. The dirt was humped up over the graves and covered with piles of flowers. Some people were there, but they stood back. Tanner knew them. He waved. It was respectful for everyone to stay back while we had some private moments. I thought maybe I would talk to Travis, but I felt no urge to speak.

"Is there anything you want to say to your brother?" I asked Tanner and Terri. They both shook their heads no. I put my arms around them and drew them up to me as close as I could without hurting my side. "Do you know why we don't speak to him?" I asked. "He is gone. He's not here. It wouldn't do any good. He is now in another world. I feel him far away now. Do you believe in the spirit world?" I asked. Tanner shrugged his shoulders. Terri continued to cry so I decided we'd better scoot. As we walked back to the truck a lady came up and hugged the kids and shook my hand. That was nice of her, I thought. The people here are very nice. They feel this, too. There was a family with three little girls. The girls had big bouquets of picked flowers from their backyard flowerbeds. One girl told David they would stop each Friday night on their way to the lake and put some fresh flowers on the graves.

Karl Jensen

When we arrived at the civic center there were already several hundred people standing in line to get inside. The parking lot was full of school buses. An usher told us that the people in line were waiting to see the picture displays that had been set up by the families. She suggested that we go in and secure a seat, as they were filling up. It looked like they would have to close the doors early once the civic center reached capacity. We followed that advice and were comfortably seated in a corner section, but with a good view of the podium. There was a hushed tone among the crowd. There was widespread visiting and talking, but no laughing. There were five sprays of flowers decorating the podium.

At 2 p.m. sharp the master of ceremonies, a Valley County Commissioner named Randolph Spencer, announced there would be a short delay as they waited for the governor of North Dakota to arrive. In fifteen minutes, there was an announcement for all to stand while the families and dignitaries were seated. The governor and first lady were the first to enter. Next was the family of Brad O'Connor, followed by the family of Travis Olsen and finally that of Kyle Hickles. The crowd was asked to remain standing for the color guard to present the flag. A band played the National Anthem. A minister gave the convocation. We were seated. A children's choir sang a medley of songs. Mr. Spencer introduced the governor, who spoke briefly, followed by the mayor of Cheneau Valley, followed by the high school principal, followed by Coach Rodger Epperson, who could hardly speak. After his message, the service became emotional.

Brad's older stepbrother spoke of their time growing up and told of the tricks they played on one another. Dana also spoke. It was hard but she managed, with her fiancé at her side. Jake, or Jakey as they called him, told of his friendship with Travis and how Travis inspired him to do well in school and to excel at football, which was Jake's only sport. As a result of his endeavors, Jakey was able to obtain a football scholarship to Cheneau Valley State. He thanked Travis for that. He said part of that scholarship belonged to Travis.

Mr. Spencer announced that they were honored to have Trevor

Jensen from Kirkland, Washington. Suddenly, Trevor appeared. He wore his black trousers, white shirt and black bowtie. That would be his most formal outfit. Had he worn a black coat, it would have been the same as a tuxedo. Jakey helped him up on the podium. Using the crutch, he slowly approached the microphone. I couldn't tell if he had any notes to speak from. Mr. Spencer asked him something, but I didn't hear what he said. When Trevor stood at the microphone, the crowd stood and applauded. It was a long applause. Trevor was completely shocked. He didn't anticipate that. Nobody did. The crowd did it spontaneously. I think he began to weep because when the applause ended he couldn't talk. He stood there looking at the crowd. My heart went into tachycardia. Susan and the girls started crying. I didn't know what was going to happen to my poor son. It seemed like he stood there the longest time. Then he rubbed his nose on his sleeve, brushed the tears from his face and delivered his message without once glancing down to any notes.

"I'm a stranger," he said, "but I can feel your love for Travis and some of it has spilled over to me. I'm feeling better, since being here with you all. North Dakota already has a part of my heart. Seeing your grief has helped me cope with mine. I was a friend of Travis for the last thirty minutes of his life. Thousands of you seated here knew him a thousand times better and a hundred times longer than that. I will remember him forever. I can't speak for him. I can't even speak about him, but I can keep the memory of my last moments with him. I listened while he talked of his family. He was brave. He was calm. I was very scared. He wasn't scared. I never heard him make one complaint about pain, or being uncomfortable, as I waited with him at the scene for help to arrive. He made it easy for us to help him. He thanked us for everything we did. I liked him. I wanted him to live. We risked our lives to give them all that chance. I don't know the why's and why nots about what happened. I'm sorry it happened. I can feel your pain. Being here will help me heal.

I hope I'll always be a trustworthy friend. Travis trusted me. He gave me his Rolex watch to keep until it was safe for him to have. He gave me his phone that opened the door for me to meet his family. He trusted me with his valuables. His goals were good. They are all worthy of achieving. Let's go out there using our full talents and achieve them for him. Let's all go out there and shoot ten for ten. I give my love and sympathy to you all."

He spoke fluently, confidently and with little emotion. Again the crowd applauded as he made his way back to his seat in front of the podium. His part was brief but it had a huge impact.

Sharon Hickles put the finishing touches on what would be the crescendo for the event. Without shedding a tear she spoke for her son Kyle as she clutched his teddy bear that was smothered in his cologne. Her poised demeanor forced a hushed silence through the teary-eyed crowd as she explained how Kyle, part athlete, part artist, was a complex kid. Along with his many talents, he had many flaws that only a mother could look past. He didn't fit anybody's mold. He was unique. They didn't agree on politics, on what clothes looked good and what clothes didn't. She constantly fought with him about his messy hair that he had allowed to grow just long enough to wear in a stubby ponytail. She told of the time she tricked him into letting her tie it up into a knot that he couldn't unloosen. He had to let it grow another couple of inches so he could cut the knot off. He never forgave her for that, but their relationship grew into something special in the last year Kyle lived with his mom in Cheneau Valley. The crowning event was the night of the state basketball championship against Bismarck Capitol, when Kyle did the behind-his-back layup and then jumped on Travis' shoulders. When the home crowd booed, Sharon said she jumped up and screamed. She wanted everyone to know she was Kyle's mom.

She hated the smelly cologne he wore, but Kyle insisted it

repelled the mosquitoes and attracted the love of his life, that being Shona.

"In Shona's eyes," she said, "he was beautifully flawed." She turned and looked into the crowd toward Shona. "Thank you Shona for loving Kyle and for loving me. I will always see Kyle through your eyes. The short romance you had with Kyle helped me see a beautiful side of him that I wouldn't have otherwise understood. Kyle no longer needed the teddy bear after he found Shona. He'd kill me if I told you this, but he slept with his teddy bear all though his teenage years. In spite of all his talent, wit and cockiness, he was very insecure. During his romance with Shona, the teddy bear sat on a shelf and was no longer kept on his bed."

Hugging the teddy bear, she ended by saying she hoped the fragrance, and the spirit Kyle left behind, would never fade. She sat down. The crowd stood and applauded. It was a most moving and poignant tribute.

A soloist beautifully sang "The Battle Hymn of the Republic" while a guitarist strummed out the melody. Next came the benediction and final announcements by Randolph Spencer. It was back to Cheneau Valley for the barbeque, where we would meet up with Trevor.

The Indictment

Trevor Jensen

What a relief it was to get that over with! I felt vindicated after speaking at the service in Jamestown. When we arrived at Cheneau River Park, there were tents, tables, food stands and lots of people. It was a party atmosphere. I stayed with Tanner and the cousins. Tanner said Travis loved to go to the park during the summer and cook hotdogs and play ball. It was the right thing, Tanner said, to come here and celebrate. It felt weird to me, so soon after the service. It was either this or back to the farm and cry. This was the better alternative. We sat down at a table in the shade reserved for the family. Our food was free, provided by a service club, and the menu was barbequed steak. Apparently, hot dogs were free for the public while they lasted, but you could, for a small charge, have a hamburger or upgrade the donation to include a steak with all the side dishes. My first steak was scrumptious, and the second was, too. I said no to the third. I couldn't finish the baked beans, potato salad, or the corn on the cob. I had to completely pass on the chocolate cake and ice cream.

I met several of Travis' buddies when they came by to say hello and give their commiseration to the cousins. They were all nice kids. They all wore the look of sadness and heartbreak, but the crying and weeping had ended. I knew this ordeal was not really over. It couldn't be. It didn't seem real: the hellos, hugs, the handshakes, the expressions of gratitude, and kind words. Suddenly, Jake, who was sitting directly across from me on the picnic bench, warned me that I was being approached. A girl came up from behind, put her hands over my eyes and rubbed my cheeks with hers.

"It has to be Amber," I said. "You smell like my sis. I can recognize that scent anywhere! Amber! It is you! What are doing here?"

I could not believe my eyes. Then came Paula. I wanted to cry but I laughed instead. I turned to the boys sitting at the table.

"These two ravenous females are my lovely sisters."

I still couldn't believe it. My dad was afraid to show himself, but mom came over right away.

"Would someone please throw a pail of cold water on my head so I can wake up and see whether or not this is real?"

I stood there looking at my mom and sisters in complete shock. Dad soon walked out of the shadows and we had a sweet family reunion.

"This is your trick, isn't it dad?" I asked.

It felt good. I'm sort of glad I didn't know they were in the crowd. I might have been more embarrassed if I had.

I had no more than recovered from that shock when Kyle's mother, Sharon, asked me to come with her and meet some people. If she explained who they were, I didn't hear her. She took me by the hand and I followed. I was walking pretty good and ignoring any discomfort I still had with my lacerated leg.

I connected right away with Sharon. We had a little chat before the service while we all waited before being seated. That was one reason for my emotional condition at the start. It wasn't a good time for me to go over all that about Kyle again.

"Everybody, this is Trevor. Trevor, this is Kyle's girlfriend Shona, her brother Ace, and their mom Sunny. They have to leave soon, and they wanted to meet you before they left."

Sharon completed the introduction and stood there with a smirk on her face. They all smiled at me like they knew something I didn't. I went to Shona first.

"I'm sorry about your loss. My condolences."

I stood there looking at her. She flipped a flock of red hair to one side, reached out and hugged me. It felt really good to be hugged. I wondered why it felt so good. I looked at Ace. I looked at Sunny. It was Sunny that I recognized.

"The ferret! I don't believe it! It's you!"

Sunny put her arms around me and we hugged. Shona started to cry. I turned around and hugged her some more. We walked off together. I started to talk to her. She wept quietly. We sat down on a bench and I held her partly in my arms as much as I could. They were still pretty sore.

"Did you ever get your coin purse back?" I asked.

She nodded yes. I told her how I had found it and desperately wanted to contact her to make sure she had it, but was forbidden to do so because of some floozy work rules. She handed me a gift bag. It had a card and small bottle of cologne. It was the same that Kyle always wore. I graciously accepted it. It was very aromatic. I remembered smelling it on Kyle. It was a nice gesture for her to give it to me. I didn't explain that because of my asthma I didn't wear scented colognes. She started to leave. Her mother had to go back to the restaurant in Jamestown and work. I didn't want Shona to leave. She looked so lonely and sad. I wanted to be with her awhile longer.

"Could you stay here with me? They are going to have some live music at nine o'clock."

She agreed to stay. My sisters, Shona and myself piled into dad's rental car and we went out to the accident scene. Travis' cousins followed us out in their car. When we arrived, a railroad representative was there to see that everyone stayed off the track. Apparently, there had been a steady stream of curiosity seekers who came to see the accident site. We parked, walked up the road to where it crossed the track, hiked up the hill, and down it to the exact spot where Aaron's truck had been. There wasn't a track or trace of debris. It was all removed and the surrounding area had been groomed. Except for a few faded bouquets of flowers, there was nothing left to indicate anything unusual had happened at that spot.

As we stood there I became like a robot, translated into a talking mime. I recited everything I remembered. Travis' cousins didn't know much of what really happened until I told them. I stood at the spot where Travis died. It felt like hallowed ground. I showed them exactly how he was positioned, where I sat when I talked to him before he died, and where I stood when they administered CPR. It all came back. It was like telling a story. I felt empowered and strong. I didn't know why I told them all that, but I did. We moved the flower wreaths over to the exact spot where Brad was and where Travis died. Amber cried, but the rest of us stayed strong. Jason, Travis' cousin, comforted Amber. I think he liked her. It set a somber mood. We quietly stayed a few more minutes. Jason and Amber stood together. In the end, it was Amber who comforted Jason. Everyone was broken up over it. For a moment I thought that it had been a mistake to come back there. It wasn't easy.

We arrived back at the park just as darkness settled in. The trip out to the scene took the wind out of my sails. Other than being with Shona, I didn't enjoy the evening after that. I don't think Ace liked me moving in on his sister so fast. When I first helped Shona on the train that night, before the fiasco with that lady's ferret, I knew I had to meet her. Wouldn't you know? Tonight I did. I can hardly wait to tell Dean and Reyna. I wish they were on tonight's train.

Kyle's dad came and told us goodbye. Shona said he would likely pair up with one of his women and get drunk, now that the funeral events for Kyle had ended. She didn't think too highly of him.

There was a continual march of people coming to say goodbye. I left Shona alone to say her goodbyes, found my folks, and spent the rest of the time with them. They planned to take me into Jamestown and wait for the train that was to arrive at 1:50 a.m. However, that all changed when Shona asked me to go out with her and some of her friends. We left the park when the band stopped playing, at 11 p.m., and headed for Jamestown. Shona was starved, so we stopped for pizza and I ended up at Shona's house and waited there until train time. I was sure wishing that I could take Shona with me on the train. I couldn't get enough of her. She was one beautiful girl. No wonder Kyle liked her.

It was 1:30 a.m. when Shona and I stood in the shadows at the side of the boarding platform, waiting for the train. I leaned over on my crutch and she patted my face gently and then we started kissing passionately. Fortunately, I had stopped using the sling. I heard the train whistle in the distance. It was just my luck. The very night you wished for a late train, it arrived early. I left her alone in the darkness and walked toward the train. I turned back and looked at her again. She stepped out into the light and waved. I could see she was crying. I wanted to go back to her, but I couldn't because there wasn't time. They stuck me in the crew quarters as a deadhead. All the dorm beds were full, so I had to sit up and wait until some of the day crew vacated their quarters. I tanked myself up with caffeine and curled up on the dinette bench. I dreamed of being with Shona. I soon conked out.

Lynn Olsen

I shook like a leaf when David answered the call from the State's Attorney's office in Cheneau Valley.

"They want us to talk to an agent from the Bureau of Criminal Investigation."

David's voice vibrated as it was transmitted over the shortwave radio from his truck, where he was doing some pre-harvest spot spraying.

"What do they want from us, David? I don't think I can do this right now," I pleaded, hoping to remove myself from the process.

"I don't think you have a choice, Lynn. It is this or they will subpoena us. The state is helping Valley County investigate the accident. If we don't talk, then it appears we are hiding something. We have nothing to hide."

I called Sara O'Connor. She said they had been asked to come in for an interview but John declined, saying they had no useful information to share. Anything like that would have been too upsetting for Dana, who is still there, trying to rethink her wedding and up at night having crying spells. John talked briefly on the phone to the agent, who left it open for them to come into the law enforcement headquarters any time they heard or thought of something that might be helpful in the investigation. Sara said that is what we should do.

David felt differently so we scheduled an appointment and went into town.

"I'm sorry about the loss of your son, Travis." The state's special agent from the Bureau of Criminal Investigation got right to the point. A highway trooper was also present. They recorded everything we said.

"When was the last time you saw your son?"

Agent Brent Ferguson looked directly at David as he asked the question. David didn't answer. He looked down and then up and then down again. They had hit a painful spot for David and I knew it. David couldn't talk about the last time he saw Travis. I blurted out an answer for him.

"David didn't actually see Travis either Friday or Saturday before the accident. He is devastated about going those two days without seeing or talking to Travis. David had an early breakfast meeting Saturday in Fargo and left before Travis was up."

The agent looked at me and began his questioning.

"Could you please, Mrs. Olsen, try your best to describe to me, in as much detail as possible, exactly what Travis did, who he was with, and please take us to the time you last saw him. I know this is difficult. I'm sorry about that."

I started crying. I immediately sacrifice any control or power over what I say when I break down. From that very point, I knew I was defenseless and further questioning would completely break me down. The agent said to take my time. I stopped crying long enough to explain that Aaron came by mid-morning and they went down to Kindersley in Aaron's new truck. They came back by late afternoon, washed the truck, and Aaron left for home. I said that just before I left to join David in Fargo, Travis left in the Mustang. He said he was going to a movie at the Buffalo Mall in Jamestown. That was the last I saw him. David sat silent. I sensed that the agent wanted David to talk when he looked at David and framed his next question.

"Mr. Olsen, did your son have easy access to alcohol?"

David shook his head no, but did not speak.

"Any possibility that the empty beer cans found at the scene of the accident came from your home, or any other place on your farm?"

Again David shook his head no.

"In the past, have you ever purchased alcohol for Travis to drink?"

After that question, David started talking. David told the agent about the code of conduct Travis had to live up to as an athlete. Travis didn't violate that code when he was in high school. He told the agent about Travis' five-year basketball scholarship to

NDSU. David said the Athletic Department there had a zero-tolerance policy for alcohol consumption by underage athletes. David said he never allowed any kids to drink on our property and he wouldn't approve of Travis drinking. David went on to say that he didn't agree with the rite-of-passage philosophy like some parents did when they allowed their kids to party in their presence when they became eighteen or otherwise. Next, the agent looked directly at me.

"Mrs. Olsen, was there any evidence that your son or Aaron had been drinking when they were together on Saturday?"

I choked. I didn't know what to say. I'm sure the agent knew I was keeping something from them. I tried to skirt around it.

"Did they take blood from Travis and test it for drugs and alcohol?" I asked, wanting the conversation to go in a different direction.

"Your son wasn't driving. I don't know the answer to that. I don't know if he was ever tested."

Obviously, the agent wasn't going to tell me anything about the investigation. He kept looking at me and didn't want to move on until I answered the previous question.

"Mrs. Olsen, was your son drinking on Saturday before he left for Jamestown?"

He wanted a yes or no. I couldn't say no. I didn't want to say yes. He knew I knew something.

"Is there some reason you can't answer that question?" The agent and state trooper looked right at me. They didn't say anything. I broke out in sobs. Poor David. He didn't know what I was holding back. I steadied myself by resting my hand on David's leg. I looked him in the face and confessed that I had noticed Aaron had been drinking, as he was stumbling around as he tried to wash his truck. I told them that Travis claimed they drank two beers each at Kindersley with their lunch, but I could smell the beer on Travis. I tried to apologize to David, but he made it easy for me. He told me to get a hold of myself and tell them everything I knew.

"In your analysis, Mrs. Olsen, did you think that Aaron was drunk?"

I nodded my head yes.

"How drunk?"

"I believe he was drunk, sir," I said.

"Do you know where or how they obtained the beer?"

"No," I said.

"Did you happen to ask him who gave it to him?"

"No," I said.

"Why didn't you ask him?"

"I don't know," I said.

I told them I assumed that Aaron brought the beer with him, because he has had beer in the past. I told them about Travis' birthday party last fall, when David wouldn't let Aaron, or anyone else for that matter, consume any beer during the barbeque. I told them that everyone around knew Aaron drank and likely he obtained the booze from his older stepbrothers, or from what they kept at home. I said that I had never heard of Aaron being drunk in public.

They thanked us for our time and said if we thought of anything else that might be helpful in the investigation of our son's death, to call them. They asked us to wait and talk to the State's Attorney. He came in shortly and asked us what type of justice we wanted. Considering the facts of the accident, with three fatalities and a fourth gravely injured, the State's Attorney thought there was prosecutable negligence involved. The strength of their case, he said, would depend on what evidence they uncovered in the investigation. He wanted to know how we felt about Aaron being brought to justice.

I let David answer that. David said he wanted to move past the tragedy and any so-called justice could not be a substitute for

Travis. He didn't want to see the town involved with any lengthy court proceedings that would only keep the wounds bleeding. He also didn't want to be fodder for a feeding frenzy in the media. David said he didn't want a pound of flesh from anybody. I wanted to discuss the crimes that they could charge Aaron with, and if convicted, what penalty each could carry. I really didn't know if I wanted Aaron prosecuted or not, so I just let it rest.

One morning I received a phone call from Susan Jensen, Trevor's mom. All I could do was cry while she talked. I didn't know this woman, but the way she talked to me, like an old friend, completely overwhelmed me. She spoke with a calming effect. She said Trevor was getting back on his feet, anxious to get back on the train. He was going to grief counseling, but she didn't think he was that enamored with it. Trevor and Shona talked every day. She said Trevor was infatuated with her. She wanted to know what I knew about her. I didn't know much, only what Travis said about her body parts being too small for him. She was no temptation for Travis. Then she asked if I knew that Shona was with Travis the last night of his life. Shona had told Trevor all about it. She would tell me sometime, if I wanted to hear it. I was afraid it would set me off on another crying spell. I didn't have enough strength to cry any more. She asked me if I had access to counseling. I told her I would look into it, and then Susan changed the subject. She told me Tanner called Trevor every day. They had become good friends, she said. I told her to call me often and she agreed to do that. We hung up.

Lana Delaney

"Look Ms. Woods, I don't have an oil derrick in my back yard. I do not make that kind of money working in the office for the Cheneau Valley School District. My husband is a salesman who sometimes only earns commissions when business is good. Right now, it isn't so good. It is my suggestion that you accept whatever my insurance pays and count yourself lucky. There is no way I am coming up with that kind of money in the near or distant future. I am not going to mortgage my house and I won't qualify for a huge jumbo loan, so you can continue to sit there at your seven-thousand-dollar cherrywood desk surrounded by fancy art on the walls and custom blinds on the windows."

"Mrs. Delaney. Please be reasonable here. You do understand that your health insurance policy, or the one the school district provides for you and Joey, pays eighty percent of what they view to be customary and usual. You have to pay twenty percent plus the difference between what they disallow and we bill. You haven't paid us anything. You also have a six-thousand-dollar annual deductible. We have taken excellent care of your son for the past two weeks. He has been assigned two of the most highly skilled and best-trained nurses in our surgical intensive-care unit each shift. Each of them provides quality care for him during their twelve-hour shifts. I won't begin to mention the many specialists and ancillary care professionals we have made available for him. We have cared for him twenty-four hours a day. Do you not understand that his prolonged need for this level of care strains our resources? We have, for the past two weeks, been required to hire more float nurses because our regular staff of nurses has been so consumed with his care."

"Ms. Woods, let me put it to you another way, if I may. My son Joey is eighteen. I'm not responsible for his medical bills. His stepfather isn't responsible for his medical bills. His dad Joe doesn't have a pot to pee in or a window to throw it out of. I'm your best bet here. I just told you, but you do not understand, that I'm not paying you over and above what the insurance will pay. If the insurance believes that a usual and customary charge for a twenty-five-minute helicopter ride from St. Catherine's to Agassiz North should be worth eight thousand opposed to the eleven thousand five hundred that you billed, I would say that you are overcharging by three thousand five hundred."

"Each of our charges are carefully assessed, based on the quality of service and the total cost of providing the services. The charges here at Agassiz Healthcare are not determined by reading off some nationally prepared chart of averages."

"So Ms. Woods, I'm holding a check sent me for eight thousand dollars from my carrier. A check you refused to accept, based on the fact it wasn't for full payment. Is that not correct?"

"Mrs. Delaney, Agassiz Healthcare cannot accept partial payment. If we accept their check, we have to sign off that the bill is paid in full. It's that simple. If Joey was on Medicare or State Medicaid, we could accept payment because we have to accept assignment for that much. You have refused to sign up for one of our convenient payment plans. Until you do that, I have no option other than to demand that you pay us the full amount."

"And how much, pray tell, is that going to be at this point?"

"The running total so far, Mrs. Delaney, is right at forty five thousand in unpaid charges."

"Great. Just great. I have had an enormous amount of living expenses since Joey's accident. I can easily use some of the insurance money for that, since you refused payment from the insurer."

"Mrs. Delaney, it would be fraudulent for you to keep the money intended for the hospital."

"But if you won't accept it, I certainly can use it. I'm not about to refuse a check made out to me for eight thousand dollars."

"Mrs. Delaney, our Life Flight Service is a very crucial part of our trauma center. Without it, we wouldn't be licensed to provide the level of service we do. If we don't collect sufficient patient revenues from our flights to cover our costs, then the service might not be flying tomorrow for the next accident victim. I'm sure you understand that."

"This is what I'll do, Ms. Woods. I'll resolve this once and for all. Tomorrow I plan to return to Cheneau Valley. I will de-enroll Joey from my policy. I would have to do that eventually if he doesn't enroll in college. Obviously he won't be going to college in September. Your office will enroll him in Medicaid and receive half of what my policy currently pays. Joey is unemployed. He is now disabled. Good luck getting your money."

I didn't slam the door in her face, but I felt like it when I left the business office. Roberta Woods! She is nothing but a money-grabbing, malicious, self-serving, individual. As if I didn't have enough to worry about, trying to keep my job going and being down here for Joey. Yeah! We'll probably get some money out of this mess, but when and how much and at what cost to me emotionally as I grapple with keeping sane and seeing that they keep my son alive. The hospital knows that, too. They know we'll get a big settlement, at some point. They're not going to take less if they think they can get more. They deal with this all the time. They can bill us up the ying-yang so that it puts pressure on my legal team to fight for a higher settlement. Whatever we eventually get for Joey, they will be right there with their grubby little hands out for part of it! This lady isn't playing that game with me. I'm not carrying this debt for the next five to ten years, or who knows how long it might take to get any money out of

Aaron Richards. They might be broke before I get paid. I heard the railroad is going after them to replace the signal and the train is suing them for damage to its passenger cars. What about the three he killed? Yeah right! Joey might be the last in line to get anything out of them.

If they are successful in bringing Joey out of his drug-induced coma today, I need to be in good form. I tried to explain that to dear Ms. Woods, but her office kept paging me and hounding me to come in. I was hoping they would accept my offer, but no such luck. I will follow up with my threat. I will take Joey off our policy. I can't expect Bob to work ten jobs to pay for the exorbitant debt Joey will incur as a result of his injuries. One job is all I can handle. I can't sign onto a payment plan with them when she is unwilling to reduce the totals. Every day he's here in ICU the total keeps growing. I can't work with that. I would forever be their indentured servant. Why should Bob and I work our butts off to pay up for patients they take in who are penniless?

Hallelujah! Joey is alive and we may soon know if he still has his mind intact. I turned my darn phone off before I went to the business office. The ICU had been paging me. I stood impatiently waiting for an elevator. I wish I had someone with me, just in case I don't get good news. They don't want to keep him down any longer, but when he wakes up the pain will be awful. They assure me they can manage his pain. He's been down ever since the accident. I've not yet seen him in pain or any other distress from this horrible event. I don't know if I can stand to see him suffer. It is round three with the ventilator. This is the third time they've tried to bring him back, but each time, he fought to breathe so they put him down again. So far, each time when they bring him back his neurology evaluation has been favorable.

It is true what Ms. Woods said about them having a stable crew of nurses with Joey. The nurses here have been exceptional and they stand next to him watching the computers, the monitors, and making sure nothing goes wrong. They are all dedicated and probably underpaid for the responsibility they have. I can't believe the fancy titles and board certifications the nurses carry to work here. The first night I was with Joey, one of the nurses, named Sandy, cried and told me she had a son Joey's age and she promised to take care of him just like she would her own son. I was a basket case. I begged her to keep him alive and not let him die. We both cried as she hugged me and then she said that they would all fight to keep him alive. If it hadn't been for Sandy, I'm not sure I'd still be standing straight after those first few hours Joey was in critical care. She let me stay with Joey twenty-four/seven those first few days. I even helped her with him. She let me do some simple things and apply some body lotion. She explained all the numbers that came up on the computers. When his heart rate went from seventy-four to sixty-four, I didn't panic. At first I got too hung up on the numbers. I tried to make too much sense out of every number I saw.

I had a big problem with one of the night-shift nurses. She told me I was in her way and asked me to leave. We had an immediate understanding. I told her I was not leaving Joey. Not for one minute! I intended to either sit or stand next to his ICU bed until I was sure that he wasn't going to die. Nothing more was said by her. The next thing I knew, a security officer came in the room and told me that if the nurse needed to uncover Joey, that I would have to leave. That was their policy. This nurse didn't like having me in the room looking over her shoulder as she worked. The next day, that same nurse, that officious little witch, came along with the doctors when they did their rounds. I was standing there by Joey and this woman had the gall to ask me again to leave while the doctors were examining Joey. I told her no. Then one of the doctors said, "She can stay!"

Phyllis, our social worker, came and took me to coffee. She

explained a few things to me. I had to give up control of Joey. I had to let go of Joey and put my trust in the nurses. Let the nurses do their job. It's all about trust. When a new nurse came on duty, I immediately stopped trusting and tried to take control. I had been there all the time so I thought I knew more than they did. I'm a control freak. When Sandy came on duty, I was at ease. I was relaxed enough to leave Joey and sleep a few hours. The social worker explained that each nurse is different in the way they perform their tasks. Just because one nurse suctions differently than the other doesn't mean she or he is doing it wrong. Every nurse working in critical care is highly trained to perform each task. She put me at ease. These people are trying to help me survive. I'm at the end of my rope.

My Bob is so weak in his knees; he nearly faints after being with Joey for longer than five minutes. I told Joey's dad he had better take some vitamins, grow up, and face reality. He is so devastated about everything that he sits home and rubs his worry stone. When Joey wakes up, I want someone with him around the clock. This horrible ordeal is just beginning, and I have no idea when or how it will end.

"Lana!" They called to me as I walked by the nurse's station. "He's awake. Go in and see him. We've been trying to reach you."

Three nurses were in his room, as was the neurosurgeon, who told me that he was pleased with how Joey had reacted to the verbal commands and pain stimuli. The swelling on the brain was well-controlled and the doctor wanted to bring him back to reduce the chances of serious infection. The problem in the next several hours would be weaning him off the ventilator. They said the ventilator was trying to adjust to Joey's breathing, which was faster than the twelve-breaths-per-minute rate of the machine.

"Breathe with the machine, Joey."

The nurses kept encouraging him not to struggle and fight

against the ventilator.

"It's like trying to breathe through a straw," the nurse explained. "It is difficult for the patients to handle."

His eyes were focused on me. He looked so natural with his eyes open, but he was stressed. The more he cooperates, the sooner he can be weaned off the ventilator.

"Joey! Joey!"

I caught myself before I cried. I put my cheek next to his. I kissed his forehead. I kissed him again and again. He was warm to the touch. He had a fever, I thought.

They told him not to try and talk, but instructed him to move his right hand, then his left hand. The nurses asked him to raise one finger for yes and two for no.

"Is this your mom?" He quickly raised his right index finger.

"Is her name Lana?" He acknowledged that, too. "Do you know your name?" He raised his finger. "Do you know where you are?" He raised two fingers. The nurse oriented him and explained where he was and that he had been in an accident. "Do you remember riding on a helicopter?" He didn't. "Do you remember what you were doing before the accident?" He didn't remember anything. One nurse explained to him that he had been asleep for two weeks. He didn't seem to react to that information.

"Joey, sweetheart, are you in pain? Do you hurt anywhere?"

I was so excited but tried not to appear anxious. I asked him too many questions and he couldn't answer them all. I had so many questions that I wanted to ask him. He looked like a little bishop with his white wrap-around bandage. The nurse had a mirror and showed him what I was talking about. He had no scars on his face or body, aside from the chest wounds that will heal in time. His legs are a different story. His right foot was mangled. He has a small bone break in the right leg and two bones broken in the left leg.

I immediately called his dad. For now, the staff suggested that only family visit. As soon as possible, we all needed to meet with the coordinator and review the treatment plan.

Phyllis will meet with Joey and go over all that happened. She will tell him that Travis, Brad and Kyle are dead. They told me that he has to be told when he asks. The nurses will not lie to him. They seem to be in such a hurry to tell him everything. Why? I don't know, but I decided to let the professionals handle it. I don't know how Joey will take it. I don't want to push too much on him. I can't face the boys being dead myself. It's too much. I don't want Joey to face it, either. Joey will be devastated, particularly when he learns about Travis. Joey has enough to handle right now. It might hinder his healing process. They want his dad and me there when he is told. I don't want Joe there. He will go to pieces. Joe can't talk about Travis, Brad or Kyle without falling completely apart. The social worker insists on Joe being there. She will brief us before we do it. She said that it was perfectly all right to fall apart. I just hope Joey doesn't ask right away. I can't handle too much at once.

Could it really be that our Joey is going to survive? Cardiac arrest due to trauma, particularly if it occurs at the scene of an accident, is almost always fatal and he had two the same night. The staff here says he is their miracle. There are so many people to thank for his life. I don't know who to call. I'm overwhelmed with joy. Joey's room doesn't have any windows. I wished I could open a window right now, stick my head outside, and thank the world for Joey's life. I think the first on my list has to be those two young men from the train who pulled him out of the burning truck. How lucky was it to also have a nurse at the scene able to restart his heart after it stopped? Then the Life Flight crew saved him again just before they left with Aaron. Again and again and again he got chance after chance after chance. Somehow, I have to find them all and tell them that Joey is still alive and awake. Sharon called me and told me that the young man who rescued Joey is talking to Shona every day. She has his phone number.

Shona told Sharon what he did in order to get Joey out of the truck. He risked his life for Joey. Had they not, Joey would have died. The only reason I don't call him is because I don't know what to say. All I could say would be to thank him and hang up. I was surprised to learn he was a ballet dancer.

Phyllis

This part of my job as a licensed clinical social worker is never easy. First I have to work at keeping this family intact and getting each of them to honor the other persons feelings above their own. Joey's dad, Joe Sr., is so laid-back, nongregarious, and inaccessible at times. He is grief-stricken over the deaths and what has happened to his son. I like Joey's stepdad, Bob, but he has no power over Lana. Neither of the men will talk when she is around. She completely takes over the conversation. I asked Lana to describe Joey's personality. She said he was introverted, just like his dad. Joe told me Joey was not introverted when among his peers, but he does not communicate well with his mother. So it was with this fractured family that I sat down and discussed with them the approach we would take with Joey, and how I thought we could best help him deal with the grief he would carry after we told him about the death of his three buddies.

Lana butted heads with me on every suggestion I made. I had to justify everything I said. Lana is the typical momma bear, wanting to protect her offspring from every tragedy in life. She thinks the timing is bad. She argues that Joey doesn't have his memory yet and wouldn't remember it, anyway. I try to explain that Joey is suffering from traumatic shock and a common cogitative reaction is temporary amnesia. Time is running out. The nurses will tell him. She can't isolate Joey from his friends who will be coming. He is eighteen. He can decide who he wants to see. The nurses will let them in. She can't stop them. We can't shield him from the media. We can't keep him in a bubble. My job is to prepare the family for Joey's reaction to the news. We have to help him work through it. One step at a time, I tried to transition them from denial to reality. I had to tell them he had already asked to see his friends and a nurse noted in the daily notes that he had asked for Travis, who is dead. That nurse is off for a few days, so I can't ask her specifically what she said to Joey. I hope she didn't tell him Travis was dead. Surprisingly, some of the nurses are not that familiar with the story; since Joey lives in Cheneau Valley, they don't know or remember exactly the names of who died and who didn't. I put a conspicuous note on the front of Joey's chart asking the nurses not to tell him anything until the family gets this sorted out.

Hearing about Travis, Brad and Kyle will hurt. Joey will suffer emotional pain, even if he doesn't react outwardly. It will change his life forever. It will be a turning point in Lana's relationship with him. It will change everything. We can't avoid it.

I entered Joey's room and introduced myself. He seemed to be having a good day.

"I'm Phyllis, the clinical social worker. I'm working with you and your family during your stay here. I popped in a couple times already just to see how you were doing. Do you remember?"

He shook his head but didn't answer audibly.

"That's okay, Joey. Don't worry about not remembering. I understand. You have been through a lot lately. Do you remember anything you were doing with your friends at the time of the accident?"

He shook his head again but didn't answer.

"Joey? Do you want to know what happened or do you want to wait awhile yet? It is up to you. We want to talk to you about what happened when you are ready."

"What do you mean? About what happened to me?" His expression and the way he answered confirmed that he was completely in the dark about everything. No one had told him about the three boys dying.

"I mean about what happened to you, to your friends or any other details of the accident that you would like to know or discuss with me or your parents."

"Well, sure," he said as he rubbed his nose and tried to turn in a more comfortable position. I suggested that I elevate his bed and reposition some of the pillows behind his back. They were all jammed up on his left side against the chest tube for when he coughed. It made it easier and less painful for him to cough. He wasn't coughing now and seemed better able to talk. I wanted him to be able to talk if he felt like it.

"Would you like for me to get your parents before we talk? Your dad, mom, and Bob are all here."

"Dad."

"I'll get your dad and we can talk. Is that what you want me to do?"

He nodded in assent to my question. At first, Lana was not happy that she was being excluded. However, she emitted a sigh from deep within that I processed as being a mixed bag of dismay, astonishment and relief. I reminded her that we needed to honor Joey's request and for her to stay strong because he would need her later. He didn't need her right now, when he got the bad news.

Joe stood by his bed on the opposite side from me. He was intensely nervous. This would be very difficult. I began the discussion.

"Joey, we have some very sad news to tell you. Would you like your dad to tell you, or would you like me to tell you?"

Joe started to weep. Joey focused on him so I gestured for Joe to begin. Joey took his dad's hand. He looked at his dad inquisitively and also had a bewildered expression. I don't think he had a clue about what was coming. Joe had huge tears running down his cheeks. He swallowed hard, then he came out with it in a sort of vague way. All he could say was that they died. They all died, he mumbled. At first, Joey looked puzzled. I didn't say anything. Joey didn't look at me. He stayed focused on his dad.

"What do you mean? Who died?" Joey asked.

"They all died except Aaron."

"Dad. Is Travis okay?"

"No son. Travis is dead. I'm so sorry son, but Travis, Brad and Kyle are dead. They died in the wreck."

Joey bit his lip. He looked at me and looked back at Joe.

"Why did Aaron live and not them? Why, dad?"

Joe was too broken to answer. He tried to gain control of his emotions but couldn't. Joe put his head down next to Joey's. I left them alone. They needed to grieve. We did it the right way and just in time.

[Police Headquarters, Jamestown, North Dakota]

Sunny

I never had a clue that I'd find myself with Shona sitting before a group of police officers at the center of an investigation as huge as this is. A Jamestown police sergeant began the discussion.

"Thank you both for coming in this morning to talk to us. I understand the accident victims are some of your close friends. I understand how difficult this has been for you. I'd like to just mention here, before we begin with the questioning, that my door is open. You can leave any time. We are not forcing you in any way to talk to us. We called you folks in today because we feel you may be somewhat knowledgeable about the events leading up to the tragic crash involving your friends on May thirtieth. Let me introduce Special Agent Brent Ferguson from the Bureau of Criminal Investigation."

The State's Special Agent was a fairly young, smooth-featured, preppy-looking fellow with a styled haircut. He looked more like a financial manager than a policeman. He spoke with a smooth, theatrical voice.

"When I spoke with you on the phone, you offered to provide me with a list of names. Do you have that list?"

I took out the list containing the names of the eight girls and handed it to Agent Ferguson. I had to drag Shona in there with me. She was too terrified to come alone. This has been like a never-ending nightmare for her. Thank goodness for Trevor. He encouraged Shona to cooperate with the authorities. She finally hooked up with somebody classy. That boy has class. She can't wait until he calls her, which is every day and sometimes twice a day.

At first she didn't want to rat on her friends by giving out their names. I'm the evil one who did it. I knew most of them, anyway, and when I included the names of two girls by mistake, Shona finally decided it was better to tell me all who were there than have someone's name on the list who wasn't. What they really want to know is who furnished the beer. Thank goodness, Shona didn't go drinking with them after the movie. She knew they had beer and intended to party. She just wasn't into that. Agent Ferguson took the list from me and looked it over carefully.

"Shona, is there any particular reason as to why you arranged for these girls to meet Aaron Richards, Travis, Brad or Kyle? Excuse me, I understand you were dating Kyle Hickles."

"I don't think Shona can really talk about that," I answered. "It is too painful for her. She feels responsible in part for arranging the evening that ended in the deaths of these boys. She is deeply grieved over it. She feels overwhelming guilt. She has not been herself since the accident."

"Let me do this. As I go down the list of names, would you kindly tell me whether or not each of these girls attended the movie with you?"

Shona nodded her head as he read each name. She shook her

head when asked if any names were missing. She confirmed that all the girls, as far as she knew, went with the boys afterward to the party. She also confirmed that she had not talked to any of them since. He was amazed when she said that none of these girls had been by to offer condolences. I confirmed that fact. I upset Shona when I said that the only reason Shona was involved at all was because Kyle pressed her to get some girls for the boys to party with. That's the truth. It was all Kyle's doing. He manipulated Shona into getting involved. These girls were Kyle's friends from when he attended school in Jamestown. Kyle knew these kids long before he met Shona. She contacted the girls on Kyle's suggestion. I told him Shona didn't hang out with these girls. Kyle should have done the arranging, not Shona.

"This girl, Layne Williams, was seen unloading several six-packs of beer from a car parked adjacent to Aaron Richards' truck when he was parked at the Buffalo Mall. Is that correct, Shona?"

Shona didn't answer Agent Ferguson. She glared at me. Shona had told me that originally. She said Layne had the beer. Shona thought it was Layne's brother who purchased the beer. Layne took it from her brother's car.

"Mother!" Shona mouthed it quietly as she stared at me.

"Shona!" I took immediate control of the situation. "We are putting all of our cards on the table. When we leave here this afternoon, everything we know will be told. That is the way I'm handling it. Period. It hurts me too much to carry this information around. I want to unload it."

So we left them all the information about who was involved. Shona disclosed that it was Bud Williams, Layne's older brother, who purchased the beer. On the way home, I remembered something. I forgot to mention that Shona said she saw Aaron pay Buddy for the beer. I'll just skip that part. Shona asked Agent Ferguson if she would have to appear in court. He told her that she might have to testify, but if it came to that she would be subpoenaed. Now Shona is upset with me for dragging her in there and creating the circumstances for her to testify against Kyle's friends.

[Agassiz Healthcare South, Rehabilitation Unit, Fargo, North Dakota (June 22nd)]

Special Agent Brent Ferguson

It's easy for law enforcement to gain access to a patient who is suspected of a crime. The security procedures set up for high-profile patients serve to isolate them from the media and other unwanted visitors. Security doesn't try to keep us out. We work through security to be as low-key as possible. We sometimes go in undercover without informing security. It just sometimes has to be that devious. The hospitals never hinder a criminal investigation. No matter where you are, if you break the law, you can't hide from us.

We came at a time when it was well-established that Aaron would be alone in his room and free to talk to us. We checked with the nurses to make sure that our visit this afternoon would not interfere with any aspect of his care. I was sure we'd only get one crack at him without getting entangled with his lawyers. We needed to get inside this guy's head and find out more details about what actually happened from his perspective. We need to determine guilt and intent. We asked hospital security to assist us by keeping everyone out of his room while we were in there. They obliged.

We won't be wearing a wire today. Nothing will be recorded. What he tells us today will be used against him if this case goes to trial, as I'm certain it will, and I'm the witness to what is said here this afternoon.

"Good afternoon, Aaron. We have to fill out some papers

regarding the accident. We can do that for you if you can answer a few short questions. We've been approved to visit you. This is for the state of North Dakota."

"I'm not supposed to talk to anyone without my folks or their lawyers present."

"I understand that. I have just a few questions. They are easy. I think you can do it without anyone's help."

"Okay. What questions?"

"Let me start with my name. I'm Brent and my partner here is Royce. How are you feeling?"

"Better now, I think, after the surgery."

"Do I have your full name spelled correctly for our records?"

"Yes, sir. Aaron Jason Richards."

"Do you have an alias or nickname that you go by?"

"My folks call me A.J. at home, but at school I always went by Aaron."

This appeared to be a very affable young man. He lay on his back against several pillows that supported his upper back and shoulders. He lay with both legs spread apart, slightly elevated. His position looked to be incredibly uncomfortable. He winced and pulled up on the support bar above his bed in an attempt to move to a more comfortable position. He had no tubes, no IV's or other equipment attached to him. He was watching TV. There was some type of game board on the bed stand. There was a cloth sheet attached to the sidewall with numerous cards. There was a huge red and white sock monkey attached to the bed rail. This was a two-bed ward but no patient was in the other bed. There were a couple of balloons floating above the bed rails. This man wasn't going anywhere. He was completely immobile. He had piercing blue eyes, a fair complexion, and shiny, perfectly aligned white teeth. His hair was very light-colored, but hardly noticeable as he sported a buzz-cut. He was tall, over six feet and of a slender build. He had husky-looking arms. There wasn't a scratch on his head or face. He looked robust and healthy except for the obvious leg injuries. My first impression is that no female juror will want to convict this young man of a Class B felony. The prosecution has their work cut out for them. I set that thought aside and began my questioning.

"How long have you been at Agassiz South?"

"Four days now. I think, anyway. I don't keep good track of time."

"What are they trying to accomplish here?"

"They want me to get my legs moving. Mainly, to get my whole body moving any way it can. I can't do much."

"How's that going?"

"It wears me out. I've been on my back too long. By the time they get me up and then try to work with me, I'm totally exhausted. But it's going better than it was."

"How's that?"

"Well, I've had two major surgeries since the accident. One is bad enough but two destroys you."

"What did they do the first time?"

"When I came into Agassiz North, they took me right into surgery. They thought I was bleeding and they found fluid in my belly. That is all I know."

"How did it all go that first night?"

"I don't know much about it. They had to take my spleen out. I was in a lot of pain and out of it for several days afterwards. They didn't have to give me blood."

"Is that a bad thing, to have your spleen removed?"

"They say you can live a long life without your spleen. They told me at the time why they had to do it but I don't remember now. It might have ruptured or something."

"Your legs?"

"Yeah, I got two broken legs. It's a total of three bones broken."

"That sounds painful."

"It was. Believe me."

"Are those breaks fixed now? Are they healing?"

"I hope so. They also did some leg surgery the night I came in and more surgery the next week. They didn't have the right doctor on duty the first night to do it all."

"That was unfortunate."

"It was."

"Overall the care and treatment is good here?"

"It's not exactly the Agassiz Hilton!"

"What do you mean?"

"Well you can fill a bedpan and sit on it for an hour before anybody comes. My food is cold half the time."

"The food? Is it pretty good?"

"Sometimes. It was actually better up at Agassiz North. I wasn't able to eat too much when I was a patient up there, but what I did eat seemed to be better than here."

"So, why doesn't somebody come when you need them?"

"I just don't think they have enough help. Mom says that all of us on this wing are bedridden and pretty much helpless. We can't do anything for ourselves. My mom has to give me a bath and empty my poop pan. I mean, it is ridiculous. The more she does, the more they let her do."

"Don't you complain?"

"It doesn't do any good. If you give them any crap they just boot you out. They tell you to go ahead and crap or piss in the bed and they will clean it up."

"Did that happen up at North?"

"No. The care I had at Agassiz North was really good. I was a lot sicker there, and I guess that is why they took such good care of me. This is rehab, you know. I guess that's why. You aren't supposed to be sick if you are here. At first, they said I wasn't medically ready for rehab and the doctor in charge of rehab was upset that I was even accepted here. He's got a real attitude about everything. He acts half the time like this is all my fault. I can't complain too much or they will kick me out and I'll have to go to a nursing home. I can't refuse to cooperate with them when they want me to do those stupid exercises that hurt me so much. My folks are too busy on our farm right now. They can't take care of me. When they threatened to expel me from the program, I decided to cooperate with them and not complain."

"But if it hurts too much you don't have to cooperate, do you?"

"It doesn't work that way. It's supposed to hurt or you're not doing it right. If you cancel out on too many therapy sessions, they'll give you the boot. They got more business than they got beds here. Mom looked into taking me down to Sioux Falls but that's just too far away from the farm."

"How long do you think you will be in here?"

"I don't know. As long as it takes, I guess. I have to go back to Agassiz North to have all the metal taken out at some point. I don't know when that will be. They tell me all this stuff, but it's too much, man. I don't remember it."

"We saw Joey Carlson yesterday."

"Oh sweet! How's he doing?"

"Pretty decent, considering. He's not out of the woods yet."

"Joey's a good guy. I like Joey. I hope he makes it. Have you heard if he has permanent injuries?"

"We haven't heard that he does. Do you have permanent injuries?"

"So far, they say, I should pull through this. I'm lucky."

"How do you figure you are so lucky? Just from my point of view, standing here looking at you, I see you as being very unlucky."

"When we were hit by that train, I could have been killed."

"Did you hit the train or did the train hit you?"

"Both!"

"Both? How is that possible? What really happened?"

"I tried to miss them. I veered off to my left, but they hit me and swung me around and pulled me up the tracks with them."

"Were you driving fast?"

"Not really."

"How fast?"

"I don't know how fast. I mean I was gunning it to get over the hump."

"Were you trying to outrun the train?"

"No man. I wasn't. I didn't see it until I was right on top of it."

"Why didn't you see it?"

"Somehow I got off on the wrong road. It was real muddy. The truck was throwing mud all over. I had to maintain our momentum or get stuck. It was a dirt road, man."

"So you had to drive fast?"

"We came to this, like incline and I started spinning out. I already had it in four-wheel drive, so I geared down and gunned it so we could get over the hump. I didn't see it as a railroad crossing."

"Didn't you know the tracks were there?"

"It was dark and the windshield was dirty. We couldn't see all that well."

"At what point did you see the train?"

"Like I said, when it was right on top of us."

"No one else in the truck warned you?"

"Someone screamed at some point. I don't know who it was. Joey didn't see it."

"Why didn't he see it?"

"He just didn't."

"Did you know what was over on the other side?"

"No, but I had to gun the truck to get up the steep incline and over the hump. I was following the road."

"If you couldn't see over the hump, were you planning to just go blindly over it?"

"No. That's just how I drive."

"Isn't that a bit reckless?"

"My truck can handle those kinds of roads. It's a good mud runner. I got power and good traction. If I slip off the road I can easily get back on again. We turned off the main road and cut east to take a shorter route once I realized where I was. That's the reason all this happened."

"But, Aaron, there are a lot of ponds around that country. We've had a lot of rain so far. They are all full to the brim. You could have driven into some deep water, either on the road or on the side of the road. You should have stayed on the main road."

"Looking back, I wish I'd done things differently."

"Back to the train, walk us through step-by-step, everything you remember that happened."

"I remember it all. Like I said, I steered away from the train. I missed the train completely. I reacted quickly. I turned in the opposite direction of the train, but it hit us and something caught on the truck, and it whipped us completely around."

"You continued to drive?"

"Yes. I did. I was trying to get free of it, but it pulled us forward. That train was moving. It was moving fast. It took us right along with it. We were wedged into it somehow. We were sort of dragged sideways until we hit something big."

"What point did you get hurt?"

"Oh man. Right away. When it turned the truck around and started pulling us forward, the impact did a number on my left leg. The pain was unbearable. The airbag inflated. I had to let go. I was in such agony; I couldn't do anything to regain control of my truck. I couldn't see, either. We were all being thrashed around, but I was pretty much pinned in my seat.

"Then what happened?"

"All hell broke loose. The train dragged us into something. All kinds of metal came through the windshield into the truck. I think that's when Joey bit the dust.

"Why do you think that?"

"He quit yelling then."

"The others? What did they do?"

"I don't know. I didn't hear much from them. There wasn't much they could do."

"That was it? It was over then?"

"Sometime, I think it was about then, the truck was thrown free of the train and it seemed like we turned over sideways. We went over and over and over again, and then end over end. I think I passed out and when I came to I smelled the fire burning underneath me. I started yelling for all I was worth. I didn't know where we were or if anyone could come and help us. The train kept on going so I didn't think it stopped."

"But someone did come."

"They sure did. It took awhile but suddenly there were two men there, but they couldn't get me out. Then a lady came and more people finally. One by one they took Kyle, Brad and Travis out. Then they got Joey out first before me because the lady told me he was worse off than I was. She told me who she was, but I don't really remember. She might have been on the train actually."

"But the two men put the fire out."

"Yes, they sure did. I am really grateful."

"Will you be able to play basketball again?"

"I'm not that concerned about basketball. I just want to be able to help dad on the farm and get on with my life."

"You were really good at basketball."

"I was good. I wasn't the best man on the team."

"Who was the best man on the team?"

"Aah! Well. That depends. Our game consisted of a lot of

different things. We had good shooters, rebounders, perimeter players, guarding. We had a good point guard. Man, I can't go there right now. It causes me too much pain. I can't deal with the grief part. They don't want me to. I have to heal first. Then I can deal with that later."

"What is it that you can't deal with? You have to face up to what happened. You have to deal with the deaths of your three friends."

"This lady comes to talk to me. She is some kind of psychologist or something. She's not a shrink, but they don't want me to get depressed. That won't help me heal, they said. In fact, they put me on some type of mood lifter. It's a light dose. They said it wouldn't hurt me or interfere with my pain medicine."

"So Aaron, you can lay here in bed all day watching TV, playing video games, and not think of your dead friends?"

"Of course I think of them. I try not to, but I can't stop thinking of them."

"Do you feel guilty? Is any of this your fault?"

"Of course I feel guilty. I was driving. I should have seen the train. I should have known where I was. I shouldn't have driven when I couldn't see. All of that lays heavy on me."

"Were you drunk when you hit the train?"

"I wasn't drunk. No! Not at all. I'll never admit to that. I didn't drink enough to be drunk. I couldn't have driven as far as I did on those muddy roads had I been drunk. That alone proves I wasn't drunk."

"Aaron, do you know the results of the blood-alcohol test they took from you the night of the accident?"

"I don't know about any results yet, but we were told the cops had blood drawn for that purpose. Do you guys know?"

"We don't have the quantitative results, but we know the qualitative results as far as being positive or negative."

"And? What were the results?"

"The yes-no answer is yes. We do know the results were positive."

"How much positive?"

"We don't know."

"What about Joey? Didn't they test him?"

"We don't know that either, but since he wasn't driving that information is unimportant."

"Joey was really plastered. That's really why he didn't see the train. Joey was helping me drive. He was looking out the window. I know he didn't see the train."

"There was a crossbuck just below the hump on the right, going up. Shouldn't you have seen that?"

"I never saw nothing like that. Besides, I wouldn't have done anything different if I didn't see the train."

"Didn't you see the headlight and ditch lights on the engine? They are pretty bright."

"Never saw nothing until I was right into it. Joey should have seen the railroad sign but he never said nothing."

"Nobody heard the train whistle, either?"

"Nope."

"Were you listening to loud music?"

"Nope. But the paper said one of the guys on the train said he didn't hear a whistle either at the time of the accident. Maybe the train didn't blow it. They don't always blow it at every crossing, at night especially."

"How much did you guys have to drink?"

"We all drank different amounts."

"How much?"

"I drank a few beers. I got a little buzzy-headed but that quickly wore off."

"How much can you drink and still drive?"

"I can drink a full sixpack and still drive just fine."

"And so is that how much you drank?"

"I might have drunk a little more."

"So, in essence, you feel that you could drink two liters of beer or more and drive safely?"

"Well yeah. It all depends on how much, how fast and over what period of time. I'm a big guy. I have a high tolerance for alcohol. It doesn't really affect me like it does some people. I had a huge meal before we partied. That always makes a big difference. I was really too full to drink much that night. I don't really like to drink that much when my stomach is full."

"How about the other boys. Were they drunk?"

"Man. They were drunk off their ass."

"Really!"

"They were."

"How did you get that much beer?"

"We get it."

"Where?"

"I'm not going to rat on my sources."

"Did you buy it?"

"Nope. All the store clerks know me. I can't buy beer. I'm always carded, anyways."

"Did you guys consume any other type of liquor?"

"Nope. We're beer drinkers."

"Aaron, we want to thank you for talking to us."

"You guys are with who now?"

"This is detective Royce Rodgers with the Fargo Police. I'm Brent Ferguson with the North Dakota Bureau of Criminal Investigation. Have a nice day, Aaron. I hope you heal quickly."

Karl Jensen

Trevor left on the train tonight. He was anxious to get back on the rails and didn't plan to enroll in college this fall. The employment physician cleared him for work. He missed his co-workers, and Wren especially. He wanted to work another year. So, if he starts college when he is twenty-one, I guess that is okay. There is not a thing I can say to convince him otherwise. He signed another contract with Intermountain Rail. He's been off work for six weeks. It has been wonderful to watch him heal physically and emotionally. He still carries a glint of despair in his eyes. It is very noticeable to both Susan and me. If he starts brooding over something, it shows up right away. When he gets his happy look back, I'll know for certain that the healing process is complete.

The grief counselor wants him to see a psychiatrist. She has stopped seeing him because, according to Trevor, he doesn't open up so she doesn't want to take any more of the railroad's money. She can't get through to him. He can be very impenetrable if he wants to be. That's honest of her, to admit failure. Trevor says he doesn't dislike her but he doesn't know what he is supposed to say. He is very passive during the sessions, so she doesn't know what he is thinking. She believes that he is still deeply disturbed over what happened and his involvement in it. Trevor has not agreed to see the shrink, and I can't force him to do anything he doesn't want to do. The company will pay for as many sessions as he needs.

There are many things out of Trevor's control that upset him. It's one thing after another. Valley County refused to release the 911 tapes to the media. The media threatened them about it. Since the case is under investigation I don't think they have to. I hope they don't release them any time soon. It will be a setback for Trevor if and when they do. A spokesperson for the county said the conversation between the people at the scene (Trevor) and the dispatcher was too upsetting to release to the public. I can't imagine the pain, fear and terror Trevor might emote through his voice during such a crisis. I certainly don't want to hear it. The media thinks it is because of a coverup. According to Trevor, he was pretty calm until Travis died. They don't want the families to hear that part of the conversation.

Rumors fly, gossip gets told, the media has hounded him relentlessly, and his friends call him with bits and pieces about the investigation, most of which prove to be untrue. The latest is that Dean has been subpoenaed to appear before a grand jury in Cheneau Valley later in July. Trevor has been called into the office here in Seattle repeatedly for interviews, and apparently he will have to testify in a formal hearing that the railroad is conducting. He fears that Reyna is in some trouble and rumors are that the railroad will be heavily fined by the Federal Railroad Administration for something they did or didn't do. Reyna tells Trevor to let the path of justice take whatever direction it needs to take and not to worry further about it. Trevor is an idealist, wanting to live in a perfect world where everything is in harmony with nature. I try to tell him that his perception of a perfect world just isn't the world we live in, and not to expect it or he will be very disappointed. He has been too sheltered to understand the many complexities of life.

Trevor wants to visit Aaron and Joey. Aaron's defense attorneys will not let Trevor visit Aaron because Trevor is a potential witness for the prosecution. He is also a witness for the railroad. Some attorneys in Fargo have already approached Trevor. They want to talk to him. We think they are working for Aaron. Trevor doesn't want to see any harm come to Aaron. I think they are going to try and build their defense on blaming the railroad. They are going to take Trevor and pluck him like a chicken. What a mess.

Trevor has talked to Joey's mom on several occasions. It looks like Joey's pulling through. She wants Trevor to come, but not until Joey can visit with him. She is going to let him know when the time comes. Apparently Joey lost his memory. He doesn't remember anything, so Lana doesn't think Joey would remember that Trevor was even there. She tells him when Trevor calls, but later in the day Joey doesn't remember who Trevor is or that he had called. Joey doesn't have a phone in his room so Trevor can't call him. The doctors are hopeful that Joey's memory will come back. When law enforcement came to talk to him, he couldn't remember anything.

The Indictment

The railroad is going to go after Aaron to recover the cost of replacing the signal that was destroyed by the truck as it was pulled down the track by the train. He'll have to pay for the HAZMAT crew that came to cordon off the diesel fuel that spilled into the inlet off Sanders Lake, since the fuel spilled from Aaron's truck. That area of the lake is a federal wetland. The *Mountain Daylight* is going after Aaron for repairing the five cars that had exterior damage. They estimate roughly a half million for the car repairs, track and signal work, plus cleanup. The civil lawsuits for wrongful death haven't started.

Everybody knows the boys were drinking, but no one knows for sure the results of the blood-alcohol tests. The results are back and the State's Attorney's office has told the defense, but nothing has been made public. I think that means the results are not good or the defense would announce it if it were in Aaron's favor. The results of the toxicological tests that were performed on the engineers have not been reported to the public by the railroad.

The railroad isn't revealing anything from its investigation. The event recorder is being analyzed in an attempt to see exactly how the engineer at the controls was handling the train at time of impact. Dean said the camera pack in the lead locomotive pretty much confirmed what the media had reported about the truck hitting the train. Apparently there was no image of the vehicle recorded on the camera. Dean also told Trevor that the train might have been speeding because they were trying to make up time. Before the accident, the train had just passed over an area where they had been replacing ties. There was equipment along the track. It seems, according to Dean, that the freight trains in the area had been given some type of bulletins about it and they were to restrict their speed. Either it didn't apply to the *Mountain Daylight* or they were never told about it or overlooked it entirely. Who knows? It could even be the dispatcher's fault if the *Mountain Daylight* was not informed. The engineer had just come back from vacation, so she wouldn't have known about the track work from previous trips. Trevor said she knew the territory and was considered to be one of the best engineers on the route.

Theoretically, had the *Mountain Daylight* been going slower Aaron would have made the crossing before the train arrived, thus avoiding the accident altogether. The real issue that troubles Trevor is the fact that if the engineer didn't blow the crossing, she could be decertified to operate any future trains. Dean said there was a whistle board a quarter mile east of the crossing but apparently since the location is so isolated some of the night trains didn't blow it. So now there is a huge investigation of the event recorders to see who blows it and who doesn't. The National Transportation Safety Board took the investigation away from the Federal Railroad Administration, but I guess the two federal agencies cooperate with each other to do as thorough an investigation as possible. Trevor says the National Transportation Safety Board stepped in, thinking that the relationship between the railroads and the Federal Railroad Administration was too cozy. It will be a year or more before anything is made public from their combined investigations.

The town of Cheneau Valley, according to the Olsens, is very polarized over Aaron's guilt and what should happen to him. That explains the State's Attorney's decision to go for a grand jury indictment. It's never a clear-cut issue.

So tonight it was with great trepidation that I said goodbye to my son at the boarding gate. He looked nice in his new uniform. When he went to say goodbye, he reached out and shook my hand, but I pulled him close to me and we engaged in a tender embrace.

"Take care," I said.

"I will, dad. I'll be okay. Don't worry."

"Will you see Shona when you stop at Jamestown?"

"We'll see." He smiled.

As he turned and walked through the gate, the tears started streaming down my cheeks. I didn't want him to go back on the train. It's a zoo there in North Dakota. I didn't want him back inside the cage.

Trevor Jensen

It was a muggy, hot day when we arrived into the Twin Cities. Seeing Shona, even for five minutes, made the trip worthwhile. I'm flying her out in August, when I'll take her to the employee awards banquet and ball. It's an annual event that Intermountain Rail holds to honor outstanding achievement among its employees. This year, Reyna, Dean and I have been nominated to receive awards for outstanding performance. On one hand we're regarded as heroes; on the other hand they secretly plot to make sure policies are in place that will prevent any of the service crew from detraining and assisting in a future crossing accident. The departing passengers at Jamestown had an eyeful when Shona and I embraced under the lighted kiosk. That was all I had time for. Shona will be there at 2 a.m. when I come back through on the trip west. This is a heck of a way to carry on a relationship, but this is turning out to be one heck of a relationship.

I went to sleep in St. Paul with the phone by my ear. David Olsen promised to phone as soon as they heard a verdict. He didn't call. We've been so busy tonight out of the Cities that I completely forgot about it until the news ricocheted throughout the lower deck of the train. All the crew heard it at once. I was stunned. I didn't want to believe it. Aaron was indicted on three counts of manslaughter. The State's Attorney issued a press release. They will ask that he serve the maximum of ten years. Aaron's blood-alcohol concentration was .06, just under the legal limit. There was no mention about Joey's test results. They arrested Bud Williams, who purchased the beer for his younger sister. He pleaded guilty to a misdemeanor charge. All I had were questions, so I immediately called dad for his opinion. I was screaming into the phone as I related the news.

"Dad! Is Aaron really going down?"

On the Roller Coaster

Lynn Olsen

I stopped at Greer's grocery to pick up a few things on my list. Just as I pulled up and parked, I saw Aaron's mom go into the store. I did not want to risk a chance meeting. I didn't want to face her. They didn't even send us a card after Travis died. Aaron's parents have remained in seclusion. Aaron was arrested yesterday while he was lying in his hospital bed. He was charged with felony manslaughter in the death of my son. I sat in the car thinking I could just skip it and go home. I took out the list again to see if there was anything I really had to have. I'm being really silly. Both of us have to coexist together in this town. I can't go around town trying to hide from people. Why should I? I've done nothing to them. I wondered, what would Travis do? That's even sillier. He would expect me to act as a mature adult, get the groceries I need, and go home. So that's what I did.

I caught a glimpse of her as she went around the frozen food aisle. I went down the canned goods aisle, expecting her to be in the checkout line already. As I paused, looking for what I came to get, there she was standing opposite me, trying to decide on a particular brand of something. She looked at me. I looked at her.

"Lynn! Oh Lynn!" She sighed as she came toward me.

I held out my arms and held on to her forearms. Thankfully, we were alone. No one saw us.

"I've been wanting to call you. I've wanted to come over. I don't know what to do. I've thought about you folks. I've cried for hours over Travis. He was a wonderful boy and basketball player. I hate myself for doing nothing. How are you folks doing?"

"Better, I think."

I couldn't really say anything to her. I stared into her face and sensed the pain she felt. She bore Aaron in her old age. I think she was at least forty when he was born. She was old enough to be Aaron's grandmother. She let her shoulder-length, gray hair hang. She tries to look younger than she really is. She's put on a huge amount of weight, and was out of breath just talking to me. She's a farmer's wife plus a farmer. She works in the field with the men. She's a hard worker. She didn't deserve this any more than we did.

"I'm sorry about Aaron. We don't wish him any harm. How is he doing?"

"Lynn, he cried for two hours when he heard about the grand jury complaints against him. Lynn, so many here in the town want him to do hard time for this. I don't think I can face the day they take him off to prison. You know Aaron. He's not a bad kid. He's never been in trouble. He doesn't even have a traffic citation. He made a terrible mistake. They will ruin him in prison, Lynn. He'll never recover. Under the law he could do ten years."

"We don't want him to go to prison. You tell him hello from me and you tell him when I get enough strength I'm coming down to see him. I can't do it just yet."

"Oh! Thank you. That is very kind of you."

"Do you have any idea when he is getting out of the hospital?"

"Not really. I think they'll send him home from rehab some-time in August. They have a treatment plan they want him to accomplish. He'll have to continue as an outpatient for some time and then be admitted back at Agassiz North for more surgery. This is all happening right in the middle of our harvest. We have so many legal hurdles to jump through. I don't know what will happen, Lynn. I really don't. Every day I get up and have to face this awful nightmare. My blood pressure has been way up and the doctor said if I don't get a handle on things I could have a stroke."

"So he's been arrested now, but when would he go to prison?"

"We don't know for sure yet. The judge has set an arraignment date for September tenth, when they estimate Aaron can be well enough to appear in court. In lieu of bond, he signed an agreement to appear in court on that date. The defense will push it out as far as they can, but the judge isn't going to be too lenient. The attorneys also want to wait until all of the railroad investigations are finished so they know best how to defend him. Otherwise they don't know for sure what they are dealing with."

"When will that be?"

"The NTSB said it could take them a year."

"Who sets the trial date? The judge?"

"Mainly the State's Attorney, who wants to move fast on it. We were told the trial could occur as early as six months after the arraignment. We know too many people around here. We don't know who the judge will be. A couple of the judges might have to recuse themselves."

"I'm sorry. I'm really sorry for you all."

"Lynn, you are worse off than we are. We have Aaron. You will never have Travis back in your life. I can't imagine how that must feel. As I try to work through my own pain, I think of you, Lynn. I really do. I think of you every day."

She began to cry. Some strangers came down the aisle, so we hugged and I left her standing by her basket weeping.

Shona

I went online, picked out the expensive light-green, silk chiffon halter dress and emailed my choice to Amber. I'm not accustomed to shopping at such classy stores. I'm to pick it up when I arrive there next week. Amber said they would charge it to their account and not to worry about it. I found a much cheaper cocktail dress at an online store. Mom and I found a real jazzy one here on sale. Mom said she would buy it for me, but I'll stick with what Trevor wants. He said to let his sisters help me with the banquet ensemble. I guess this affair will be too upscale for me to wear what I already own. I certainly don't want them to be ashamed of me. At least Trevor won't be worried about my appearance; otherwise he wouldn't be inviting me out there to be his date at the awards banquet ball. Trevor isn't that conscientious over fashion, anyway. He wears two colors: black and white, consisting of dark-colored trousers and some kind of light shirt. He'd look good in any color. Amber says Trevor is fashion's worst nightmare. Trevor sees fashion as purely black and white. Mostly, when I see him he is wearing the train's uniform. His sisters are the fashion plates. They spend a fortune on clothes.

My tickets and itinerary were sent by overnight mail. Trevor will be working on the westbound train I'm ticketed on and he also works on the train coming back. The train ticket was outrageously priced, but it includes four meals delivered to my seat. I don't know if Trevor or his dad paid for the ticket. Mother is more excited about me going on this trip than I am. She sees me as Cinderella, who just met my prince charming.

I love Trevor. Who wouldn't? I don't know him very well. It all happened too quickly. I was so numbed when Kyle was killed. I was vulnerable. I could fall for anybody. We live fifteen hundred miles apart. I don't know how to carry on a relationship with someone you only talk to on the phone. Like I keep asking myself, "Who is this person called Trevor?" I read about him in the newspaper. I talk to him on the phone. I read his emails and look at digital pictures he sends of himself. My boss at the dress shop believes no meaningful relationship can develop when one of the partners lives so far away. She told me to date only men who live in the same town I do. She thinks you have to keep an eye on them. Trevor has all the money in the world. Trevor can buy me anything I want. What money he doesn't have he can get from his dad.

I loved Kyle. Kyle couldn't buy me a hamburger. He could exist on whatever money his dad gave him or nothing. My brother Ace said he was a freeloader. Either way, it didn't matter. My heart still aches for Kyle. I can't talk about Kyle to anybody. Ace couldn't stand him and mother didn't care that much for him, either. They saw him as lazy and irresponsible. They are both too much into the work ethic. I'm not over it yet. I haven't let go. There is something I had from Kyle that I can't get from Trevor. I don't know what it is. It is more than the touchy, feely, handholding that occurs when your partner is close. I think it was more of a soul-mate consciousness. There was something about his personality that I loved. He was that "happy go lucky" guy and he took whatever life dealt him.

He was so much fun. He could make fun out of nothing. Kyle didn't need money to have fun. We'd find ourselves down at the shopping mall in Fargo. There we'd be, occupying space at the food court and not have a dime to buy anything. Kyle would sit there insisting he wasn't hungry. I'd be starving, get up and get myself a piece of pizza, and end up sharing it. Meanwhile, he is drawing portraits of people sitting at the tables around us. If it were somebody he really wanted to draw, he'd get into it; when they figured out he was fixated on them, they'd spook off somewhere else. He'd get so mad and then retaliate by making them into somebody really ugly. He would show me what he drew and we'd laugh our heads off. Maybe that's what it was! I never laughed so much as I did with Kyle. He kept a collection of those mall portraits. They were some of his best art, in my opinion.

He drew this lady one time. I think she might have been poverty-stricken or something, but she would sit there at the table watching people eat. If they threw part of it away, then she would go and dig the food out of the trash, bring back whatever she found to the table and eat it. She looked like a squirrel in the park, stealing table scraps. She was so precise. She ate so daintily. I could have killed him that day. We sat there for two hours while he drew her for a project in his art class. Just when I thought he was finished with her and ready to take me over to the movie, she fell asleep and he had to sit there and draw her sleeping. He wanted to sketch her every position. She laid her head down on the table. You could see the poor lady was exhausted. Then she eased down in the chair. Mind you, these weren't the most comfortable chairs for sleeping. She propped her feet up on the adjoining chair and locked her feet around the back of the chair. She laid both hands across her face, much like a bird would do when it tucked its head under one wing, and slept, unaware of the pandemonium caused from the overflow of hungry shoppers coming in to eat. Suddenly there was a scarcity of chairs. A big kid, looking in the opposite direction of the lady, reached around behind him and tugged on the empty chair she was hooked to. When it didn't give, he pulled on it. He pulled hard and pulled the poor lady right off her seat onto the floor. Kyle went right over and helped her up. Kyle was so upset at the boy for disturbing his subject. We never made it to the movie. That was Kyle. He was original.

I told Trevor I wouldn't meet him down at the Jamestown station platform this morning. I was too tired and I had to get my rest. I want to be able to relax and enjoy the trip. I'm pretty sure I heard the *Mountain Daylight* whistle at 4 a.m. when it went through to Chicago.

You'd think I'd be more excited. I leave for Seattle tonight, or tomorrow morning, however you see it. Trevor said he isn't going to let me sleep but I can't sleep during the daytime, when he does. I've never been west of Bismarck. I've never seen the mountains of Montana. I told him I don't function without sleep. Anyway, Trevor said they have a big crew on tonight and he is going to slack off and be with me. That's cool with me, but I have to sleep.

I'm not supposed to tell anyone I'm going. Well, I've already told everyone I know. Trevor is a celebrity and the media is after him for a story. The last time he went through Bismarck, they hounded him for his story. The media doesn't like the railroad, so they constantly find fault with it. Trevor is right in the middle of the controversy, with his statement he made to the press earlier about not hearing the whistle blow before the accident. Now they want him to comment about Aaron. He is being offered money to talk about what he knows. He's staying quiet. He flipped off a reporter who was taunting him at the station in St. Paul. There was a cameraman with him who caught Trevor's obscene gesture on film. They forwarded the picture to the railroad and Trevor was reprimanded.

Lynn Olsen

I took Susan Jensen's advice and told David I thought that I needed to see a grief counselor. David said to go ahead, but he wasn't interested. I heard about this group of behavioral-science practitioners in Fargo. They staff one of the clinics here in Cheneau Valley. I made an appointment and went. The lady was right on. She understood my feelings. She even said she had been following the story of Travis and the accident in the papers and had been deeply grieved over all that had happened. Before the next appointment, I asked David to come with me but he wouldn't. Men resist that sort of thing, I guess. She has helped me focus on elements of my grief that I can change. So we plan to anticipate future events that will trigger an episode of grief. She helped me identify these events and the circumstances surrounding them. We have to make plans for Travis' birthday coming up on September seventh. She wants Trevor to come on that day. She thinks it would be a good time for us to all come together and reward him for his friendship and heroism. She wants me to involve the other families. I hate to ask him to do that. She insists on it. His presence would help us cope. The kids love him. He's crazy about Shona. He wants to see her all the time. He might come again just for her.

Trevor came in July and helped us landscape the graves. He took time off and spent three days with us. It was hot the day we all worked on the hill. Trevor isn't afraid of hard work. David said he could tell Trevor knew how to work because of the way he handled the shovel. He knew how to use tools. Trevor said he has lots of experience shoveling out horse puckie from his barn.

A hundred people came and volunteered their help. We supplied the materials. We refused to use any of the memorial fund money, which was now over one hundred fifty thousand. They built a stairway up the bank, excavated the pathway, put down the weed barrier, and covered it with gravel. We boxed in the graves and rocked that area. In the days leading up to the project, the work crew had staked everything and mowed the weeds. We set up a large vinyl awning and served lunch and refreshments. The guys worked until dark. They went back on Sunday and finished the project. Some man, we don't even know who, is crafting three benches which will be installed next spring. The newspaper reporters followed Trevor around. He played into their hands and seemed to enjoy the attention. That kid loves to entertain. They took pictures of him. It's a big story. Everything went well. Then suddenly, about lunchtime, a beautiful wreath of fresh flowers appeared. It wasn't sent to any one of us in particular. I was serving refreshments when it came. I tried not to look at it. I was curious so some of us went over to see it, after the florist placed it in the center of Travis' grave. Just seeing it made me cry. The card attached indicated that Aaron had sent it.

Right now I'm torn up whenever I hear about any kid going to college. Jakey called and said he was starting early football practice and moving on campus. It really upset me. Travis won't be going for basketball practice. He won't be going to college. That tears me up. The counselor said to try and think about Terri being a sophomore and Tanner starting high school. She said to focus on what I have, not what I don't have. I don't have a college boy right now. I have two high school kids. That's what I have. I'm grateful for that, but I still look back to what I lost. The counselor wanted to know what plans Terri and Tanner had for college; what they planned to study and where they planned to go. When I told her I didn't know, she gave me an assignment. I was supposed to discuss this with them. She wanted me to come back and tell her. So I did.

I think she knows we were too much into what Travis was all about. I have to shift my attention to my other two kids. Travis is no more. I'm floundering in Travis' grave. I understood the message. I had to learn how to grieve, but not dig up the grave. Leave him in the grave and grieve. So when I asked Terri, she knew exactly. Terri wants to study elementary education at Cheneau Valley State, and her stepcousin Josie wants to study exercise science there. They plan to room together in the dorms. Tanner wants to attend NDSU in Fargo and study some aspect of agriculture. He wants to stay on the farm. He might specialize in crop production. That was easy. They have it together, these kids. Just knowing that Tanner wants to stay and farm with us has lightened my burden of grief. I had this right on my finger-tips and didn't know it.

David's stepbrothers don't want David on the combine. That leaves David with the grain truck and too much idle time. Tanner doesn't like to ride with him because there is nothing to do but sit. It's hard on David to be in the combine by himself. David and Tanner did it for a while but Tanner complained that David was too moody and upset. Travis' friend offered to come and run the combine, but he wrecked some equipment for some guy so David doesn't trust him. David won't let Tanner run the combine by himself yet. Travis was doing it when he was Tanner's age. We're finally getting all the wheat harvested, but it has been really difficult emotionally. Travis did most of the wheat harvest before he went back to school. Later, in September, David should be able to handle the soybeans. Travis was always in school during that time.

[Aboard the *Mountain Daylight* (Eastern Montana)]

Shona

I awoke with Trevor hovering over me. He was holding a hot drink of steamed milk with mint chocolate and whipped cream, the train's specialty for early morning. It was 7:30 a.m. and I had been asleep for more than five hours. He was off duty, showered and ready to spend time with me. The lady I sat next to had left during the night, so Trevor sat down and we shared the hot chocolate. He said the hot milk drink was perfect for his caffeine hangover. We were in Montana, along a big river. The landscape was big and dry, with high bluffs and huge hills everywhere.

"Who lives in this Godforsaken country?" I asked.

"The Indians until we drove them out!" He laughed.

Trevor took me downstairs, where he picked up my breakfast tray from the diner. I followed him at least half a mile through the bottom part of the train to a kitchen area occupied by the crew. Most of the night crew had already gone to bed. He pulled some scrambled eggs out of the cooler, slapped some bacon on top and heated it in the microwave.

I stayed with him there until we arrived at Billings, where he took me off to see the historical buildings there at the Depot Center. Billings is the mid-point service stop, where they resupply the train and refuel the locomotives. It takes them a half hour. After that, Trevor crawled into his bunk and I made my way back through the train to my seat and napped. We were in the mountains when I awoke. It was awesome country. I was glad Trevor was asleep so I could relax and look out the windows. I spent the day looking. We sat on a sweeping curve along the Missouri River, waiting for the other *Mountain Daylight*. Along the track, next to the river was an emerald springs flowing forth from underground and full of large fish. After we pulled through the tunnel on the Continental Divide, I saw a moose loping along the track. A short ways down, I saw some elk. I saw deer darting through the thickets. Instead of reading my novels, I studied the route guide in anticipation of the next river, town, or mountain peak.

Trevor called me at 5 p.m. to say he didn't have to work until Spokane. The extra crew was turning at Spokane and he would be busy after that. He's very entertaining in the way he tells about all the crazy things he did growing up. It was very romantic sitting listening to Trevor talk while the scenery whizzed by. I didn't have to say a thing.

The rail miles started adding up by Spokane. I didn't read my books, listen to music or watch satellite TV. After dinner I laid back in my chair, propped my feet up and dozed off, smiling and thinking of Trevor and his ferret. I didn't want to see another one.

I didn't see Trevor again until the next morning, in Seattle. He was tired, in need of a shave and some good deodorant. I was afraid Trevor was going to fall asleep as we sat in traffic, getting across the bridge into Bellevue. When he arrived home he went to bed immediately. I readied myself to go shopping with Paula and Amber. They had the day planned. All it takes is Paula, Amber, and a few charge cards at the most upscale stores in town for an "shabbily dressed" girl like me to have a blast.

[Aboard the *Mountain Daylight* (near Fargo, ND)]

Trevor Jensen

I've never seen such solid blackness at night as I sat looking out the upstairs lounge windows, recharging my fuel lines with caffeine. We're galloping across the Dakota prairie at record pace. We've had an early arrival at all stops. Tonight, the engineer slammed on the brakes just before the bright lights of Cheneau Valley emerged to my right, as we crawled over the bridge. I didn't look down on the fairytale town, nearly two hundred feet below us. My imagination tried to penetrate the black curtain hanging down from the sky to the north side of the train. I strained to see what was behind it. Through the darkness, the graves of Travis, Brad and Kyle were keenly engraved on my mind. I carry that image on my forehead, like you would a tattoo.

The night it all happened, I didn't touch Brad, but Kyle was still warm and Travis was very much alive. I don't have a spiritual background. I think that means I'm not a person of faith. We studied Solomon's ecclesiastical prose in the Bible during my advanced placement Literature and Writing class in high school. Solomon answered the question pertaining to the spirit of man's destiny when he wrote:

"The spirit of man that goeth upward, and the spirit of the beast that goeth downward to the earth..."

I don't understand what that means. So they go up, but where? If Solomon said it, it must be true. Are there two directions, up and down? So do the animals stay in the ground and we go up? Where is up? Is it light there? What do we see? Can we talk to each other? Are Travis, Brad and Kyle happy where they are? I was at least satisfied to believe that they weren't shivering in that cold blackness up on top of the bluff. That would be one cold place to spend the winter.

I stopped my macabre deliberations and tried to get back on track. No pun intended. I'm actually on a train, the track of which slopes downward. They say the prairies slope downward from Bismarck to Fargo. It all looks and feels pretty flat to me. I'm on an emotional roller coaster. When I get to Fargo in less than an hour it will be an all-downhill thrill ride. I'm leaving the train in Fargo. I need to sleep. I've been asked to spend most of the day visiting with Joey. He needs some emotional support. From me? I'm an "over the top" emotional guy. How does that go down?

This will be Shona's second week at NDSU and I'm taking her out for dinner tonight. It will be our last date. She knows it. She may cancel the dinner. She might have to study. I'm to spend the weekend at the Olsen's. The O'Connors are putting on a party for me at their place Sunday. Everyone is getting together there. Travis' birthday is Monday. I have agreed to talk to Aaron's lawyers. Dad says for me to tackle each event separately and not to mush them all together.

Oh, and if I get too overwhelmed I can call the crisis line and a psychiatrist on call will speak with me. How's that for service? I have the number right here in my wallet. I spent an hour with a shrink in Seattle. My counselor kept pushing and made the appointment for me. He was great. He dug right into me, and when I left the office I felt like a new man. Is that what they call psychotherapy? I'm rid of that sandbag of guilt. It all stemmed from being a rescuer and hero. When things don't turn out text-book fashion, we blame ourselves. Guilt smolders and burns inside of us, and if we don't get it under control we can have a blowup. I'm not crazy. I'm not depressed. I'm just me. That is exactly what the lead paramedic, Joanna, told me. I think the psychiatrist read from her book. I'm going to tell her that sometime. Man, I went way over the top with her. Hey! If I get myself boxed in somehow, I'll just call the crisis line and somebody will pull me out.

[Agassiz Healthcare North (10 a.m. that same morning)]

I slept three hours and caught a cab to the hospital. I stopped at the reception desk and announced my arrival. Phyllis, a social worker for the hospital, came to get me. I sat in her office and listened as she explained Joey's mental state. I was being told about Joey at the request of his family, who hoped my arranged visit would somehow be therapeutic. They are having difficulty managing his pain. He is unable to tolerate many of the commonly used pain medications and several others that they could use might have deleterious, long-term side effects. He does not talk. He won't cooperate with the therapists. He is giving up. He doesn't eat enough. It has been suggested that he receive more nutrition through an intravenous catheter, but he refuses to let them do that. She apologized for laying it on the line like that. In other words, he is just lying there wishing to die. If he doesn't cooperate, Lana might try for a court order on the grounds of his diminished mental capacity. She won't let him starve himself. They thought a visit from me might inspire him. Lana is pushing them to do more, but there is little they can do. Joey doesn't resonate that well with the psychiatrists and so far has refused antidepressants. They all agree on his diagnosis of depression. It's complicated, but not hopeless. He suffered severe chest injuries and that is still the source of most of the pain and will continue to be until it is all healed. He can eat anything and likes sweets. I told her I brought him candy. His legs are another issue but in time, Phyllis said, he'd walk again. After multiple surgeries on the legs, the bones are knitting. There is no evidence of a postoperative infection. Joey communicates with his dad, but not with Lana. He wouldn't respond during visits from his numerous friends, either. The caregivers are very understanding of his unresponsiveness, but at the same time they are all very concerned about his mental status. They had canceled some of his morning appointments so we could visit uninterrupted. He probably needs a reprieve from all the treatments he receives on a daily basis. I am to stay with him and force him to talk. His memory is back. They think he remembers more than he admits.

"What if he doesn't want me in there?" I asked. "What am I supposed to do?"

"In that case, of course, he can decide who he wants in his room and who he doesn't. If he orders you to leave, then there is nothing you can do but comply. We are hopeful for different results."

With that information, I picked up the two shopping bags of gifts and my shoulder bag and followed her to the door of Joey's room. There was a room divider in front of the door so he couldn't see us approach. She stood at the doorway and motioned for me to go in. I walked in with my three bags, set the shopping bags on the floor by his bed, placed my shoulder bag on a chair and spoke to him.

"Joey! Hi! I'm Trevor. Good to see you! You look great. I've been thinking about you. I've wanted to meet you for the longest time. I'm excited to finally meet you. I'm going to spend some time with you today. Are you feeling okay?"

I was running out of things to say. He studied me with his eyes. He said nothing. There was no acknowledgment of my presence. He had a round face with a cherubic look to him. He had dark hair with rosy cheeks. He was a good-looking fellow. The social worker said it was okay to touch him on his right side. She said to just take his hand and squeeze it as he does not engage in handshaking. So I clenched my fist to see if he would do a fist pound with me. He didn't engage me in that. I hooked my thumb around his thumb to see if he would pull back with me. He didn't. He looked puzzled. I smiled. He gave me a weird look. I gave up on doing more hand tricks. Maybe they don't do that here in the Midwest. The atmosphere was tense. I was really nervous. I didn't know what to do or what more, if anything, to say.

He cleared his throat. He looked like he was in some type of distress. I froze, watching him struggle to cough up some mucus. He reached for a tissue so I handed him two. He turned on his side and gagged on whatever he was trying to bring up. He motioned for me to hand him something. It was a yellow, shallow, kidney-shaped basin, which he spit into. He groaned as he tried to expectorate. I didn't want to look. I knew it hurt him to cough. I automatically placed my right hand over my ribs in sympathy. I could feel the pain.

"Dude! You are in some serious hurt here." He continued to cough. I caught the flash of the social worker as she whirled around and left the room. She was standing behind the screen, listening to my one-way conversation.

Immediately, a nurse came. She talked to him but he tried to ignore her. She helped position him so he could cough better. She elevated his bed, had him turn slightly and cough while she pushed the pillow into his left side. Next, she listened to his chest with her stethoscope. She told him there was still a lot of congestion. She told him to keep the bed at that level and not to lower it.

"Joey," she said. "Did you see respiratory therapy this morning?"

When he didn't answer right away, she looked at me and I shrugged my shoulders. I told her I had just got there. I didn't know. She left and came back, saying she had called for them to come and see him.

He stopped coughing and sat hunched over. His legs were

straddled. They were both in casts. His hospital gown was falling off his shoulders. So I stood up and started from square one again. He looked gaunt and thin.

"Dude. Do you want me to tie your gown for you before you lose it?"

"Okay," he answered.

Good. He can talk, I thought. I pulled his gown back over him and tied both the top and center together. He leaned back and thanked me.

"I brought you some things. I don't know if you will like them. I didn't know what to get you."

I put one shopping bag up on the bed and started showing him what I brought.

"For me?" he asked.

"It's for you."

"Why?"

"I don't know. I went shopping. I just wanted to bring you something, that's all."

"Oh," he said quietly.

"Look!" I said. "I brought candy. I heard you like chocolates. This lady makes the best candy on the West Coast. She has a store in Bellevue, close to where I live."

I took out three gift boxes of chocolate bars. They were wrapped in gold foil with a satin bow around each box.

"They look too fancy to eat," Joey said as he smiled. "Can I have some now?"

"Almonds, macadamia or coconut?" I asked.

"All three," he said.

I started to tear off the foil on each box.

"Save the bows," he said. "I'll give them to mom for my Christmas presents."

I laughed. I gave him an almond bar. I took a coconut and we ate them just as the respiratory therapist walked in. She was sort of unfriendly at first but she loosened up when I offered her a candy bar. She politely refused, but then she started to be a bit flirtatious with Joey. She smoothed back his hair, put her hands on his arm and asked him to take three deep breathes into a plastic apparatus she referred to as a spirometer. Evidently, she didn't like the results because she began to admonish him to improve.

"Joey! I remember you, honey, when you were on the vent in ICU. You don't remember me, do you? I worked hard to get you off that vent. We shouldn't have to be coming up here all the time to check on you to make sure that you do this. We're working hard here, not smart. You can't continue lying on your back here day after day without doing the deep breathing ten times an hour like you are supposed to. You are not doing your breathing exercises. Look! This is what you are doing and this is where you are supposed to be," she said as she pointed to the scale on the spirometer. "I know it hurts honey, but you are a young, healthy man. You have to do it. Your alveoli are going to collapse on us if you don't cooperate."

She made him breathe into the spirometer three more times. Then she told him he was looking really good and left.

He talked to me. I was relieved. I dug out the other items I brought him. I showed him the thermal T-shirt.

"All the winter fashions are in the Seattle area stores now. This is a North Dakota winter shirt, no?"

"If I wore this in North Dakota in the winter, I'd only wear it in bed!" Joey said as he examined it.

"Aw! Come on, Joey. You can wear this here in the winter. Feel it. It's warm."

"That prairie wind would blow right through this."

He was teasing me. He took it. I know he liked it. He sort of scoffed at the gift bag of skin-care products.

"What do I do with this stuff?"

"See?" I said as I set them out for him. "One is for your hands, one is a body lotion and a foot ointment."

"Huh!"

"Does your back ever itch? Have a pretty nurse rub some on your back tonight," I suggested.

"I never see any good-looking nurses. All my nurses are old."

"Not the one that was just here! She was okay."

"But she's not my nurse. My back itches all the time. I'll have mom try it out on my back sometime. My skin is dry but it's my feet that hurt. They itch, too." He stuck his finger in the container of ointment. "This would feel good, but my feet are encased in concrete. I can't reach them."

I gave him a shaving bag with exotic shave cream and shaver, and cordless hair trimmer. He liked that. I got him two print T's. I took out the video game console.

"Where's your computer?" I asked.

"Where? I got a messed-up computer at home, I think. Trevor, I forget what I have. I don't know. I lay here in a cloud most of the time."

"Isn't the hospital equipped with wireless?"

"I don't know."

"You have to have a computer, man. I got you this video stuff to play with while you are here in bed. If you had a computer nobody would steal it, would they?"

"Probably. Everything else disappears around here. I'm going to keep that candy in bed with me. Somebody will take that, too."

"That candy was good. I need a cup of coffee," I said.

"You do? Push that button and ask for one. They have coffee up front. They will bring it to you."

In a few minutes, a lady brought me a large cup of steaming hot coffee. She asked what we wanted for lunch. It was lunchtime and the staff was going to treat us. She asked Joey if he would eat some Johnny Dee's Pizza if they ordered it. They would deliver it to the room. Joey agreed and in about an hour we had eaten a large pizza between us and gulped down two Cokes. Joey said he had forgotten what pizza tasted like. I was so full I needed a nap. Joey was getting tired, too. I sat down in the recliner by his bed. It felt so good. I was soon asleep.

They woke us at 4 p.m. when the doctor came in to see Joey. I sat back and listened. The doctor explained that he was going to put Joey back on antibiotics if his chest didn't improve. He didn't want another bout of pneumonia. The doctor asked him to take deep breathes on the spirometer. It didn't look like the yellow piston moved very far up the scale. The doctor wasn't very pleased. The nurse unlocked his medicine drawer, gave him some pills, and left us alone.

I had to get back to the hotel, shower and prepare myself to face Shona. That was starting to give me a headache; it was so heavy on my mind. I forgot what time Shona said she was out of her last class. She is supposed to call me, but she hasn't yet. We haven't been talking that much since her trip out to see me in Kirkland. I asked Joey if he thought I should leave.

"No, dude. Don't leave. I want to talk to you some more."

I stood by the bed rails and we fist pounded. I told him to talk.

"What kind of work do you do?" he asked.

"I work on the train. I handle the passengers' personal effects, luggage, and stuff like that. I work nights between the Twin Cities and Seattle."

"Oh. What do you do when you're not on the train?"

"I'm a dancer. I love to dance. I studied ballet and Latin partner dancing."

"What?"

"Yeah. I dance. I love it."

"No. Dude. You don't look like a dancer."

"What does a dancer look like?"

"I don't know but not like you."

"Do you want me to do a trick?"

"Yes. Do one."

I put my right leg up on the bed rail and brought my right arm around it and did the splits right there in front of him, standing on one leg. I bent my body sideways and then backwards. He laughed. Next I bent one leg in and did a series of spins and about knocked over his bed stand. He was very impressed. I told him that sometime I would bring in my guitar and play him some music.

"When you go dancing, do you meet a lot of good chicks?"

"I do, Joey, if you count my two sisters that I often have with me."

"Do you have pictures of your sisters?"

"Yes. Here. That is Paula and this one is Amber."

"Whoa! They're quite the dames! They look too classy for me."

"They are good lookers, but they are very high maintenance. You don't want them, Joey."

"Do you think Amber would go on a date with me sometime?"

"Amber never met a boy she didn't like. I'm sure she would."

After we got through talking about my sisters, the conversation got onto a more serious note. Every now and then his face took on a very serious look. It was like he wanted to say something but couldn't come out with it. Suddenly he came out with it.

"When you came in this morning, I thought for a minute you were my friend Travis. You shocked me," he said.

"Travis Olsen?"

"Yes. That's him in the center picture, on the shelf above my sink."

"I don't look anything like Travis."

"No, but I thought you were him. I was thinking about him. Just when I was wishing I could see him again, you walked in. I miss him. We were friends."

"Those are nice photos of Brad and Kyle, too."

"How do you know their names?"

"Ah. I do. I just do. How did the glass get cracked on the pictures?" I asked.

"I couldn't take it anymore, so one day I was really down about everything. They left me sitting on a bedpan for the longest time. I threw the roll of toilet paper at the shelf and knocked the pictures all on the floor. The glass covers cracked."

"You don't want to look at them?"

"No. Take them and keep them."

"Well, why were they put there in the first place?"

"I don't know. They just appeared there one morning. Please take them down."

"Joey, I met Travis."

"How would you know Travis?"

"I took him out of the truck after the accident, Joey. He was alive. I talked to him."

"No. That's not true."

"What's not true? What I just told you is true." Joey gave a big sigh. He lay there with his mouth open. He was trying to find some words to put together. "Why don't you believe me, Joey? I was there that night. I know. I was with him when he died. I'm sorry Joey. Travis died that night. I spoke at his service in Jamestown in front of thousands of people. Joey! I was there. "

"How could you take him out when he had burned. He burned up."

"You didn't burn, dude. Nobody burned. Travis didn't burn. Where did you get that idea?"

"The news said they did. Mom said no, but I can't trust her. She tells me only what she wants me to hear. She's not straight up with me about anything. I can't trust anybody around here. They don't want me to grieve. I lay here all the time thinking how all my friends died in that stinking fire. It eats on me all of the time!"

"Dude, you misinterpreted what was reported. Maybe they meant only that the truck burned. The truck was on fire. But we put the fire down so none of you burned. When the fire crew arrived they completely squelched it."

"Honest?"

"Yes, Joey. Honest."

He looked like he was getting ready to cry. I got tense. I thought what I said was making him cry. He didn't cry. He told me about a paper bag he had in the locker across from his bed, where he stored some clothes. In the bag were several newspapers. He told of a hospital volunteer who visited him regularly. She buys him whatever he wants. One time he asked her to get all the news clippings of the accident together so he could read about it. She did. On top of the stack was a paper with a headline that read: "North Dakota's Mr. Basketball Dies In Fiery Train Crash." I started reading the story. I read it to him. There was nothing that said the victims burned. Joey still didn't believe me.

"No. They all burned. Don't lie to me. I know they did." He started to get very upset again.

"They didn't burn. Nobody did. Joey, listen to me. Please. Nobody burned. You aren't burned. Your legs aren't burned. Your face isn't burned. Your back isn't burned. Where are you burned, dude, on your butt? You were the second to last out of the truck!"

"You can't see my legs."

"I saw your legs when we cut your jeans off to stop the bleeding on your thigh. I saw it. You were stabbed in the leg with some metal that came through the windshield. Your legs weren't burned. Tanner said some of the kids took pictures of the guys in their coffins. All kinds of pictures must be floating around. Find out who took pictures and look at them. I bet Tanner has some. They weren't burned. The coffins were opened for everybody to see. I risked my neck to save you. I crawled inside the truck when it was still on fire and lifted you out of the truck. It wasn't easy. It was hot in there. I was scared for my own life as well as your life. I did the same for Travis.

"Tell me about Travis."

"Like what?"

"If he didn't burn then how did he die? Tell me, Trevor. What happened to him?"

"Well … he … he died at the scene. I was with him."

I didn't know how to tell him. I was getting really emotional. I didn't know what to say. I started to tear up. It was starting to cause me a lot of emotional pain again. I didn't prepare myself for this. Joey wasn't going to lay it aside.

"Did he suffer?"

"He was not in any pain. He died peacefully. He just went to sleep."

"Did you try to save him? What did you do when he died?"

"Everybody tried. They did what they could. He stopped breathing and they didn't get him going again."

"Why did he die? If he wasn't burned and was still alive …"

"Joey, he was bad, man. He was crunched. He was crumpled up like a piece of foil in the bottom of the back seat. He had a lot wrong with him. Brad was on top of him and Kyle was halfway out the back window. They weren't wearing seatbelts."

"Seat belts wouldn't have saved him. Back-seat passengers don't wear seat belts," Joey argued.

"The seat belt and airbag saved you, Joey. It saved your life, dude."

Joey got real redfaced. He was fighting back tears. I grabbed his arm and hung on to his hand and held it tight. We looked at each other for a few seconds. Tears were streaming down my face. We both got control of our emotions.

"Brad? What happened to him if he didn't burn?"

"Broken neck. Dean thought so. He took him out of the truck. I don't know for sure."

"Kyle?"

"Killed instantly. He suffered massive head injuries."

Joey whimpered, "They're all dead."

He turned his head into the pillow. I kept still for a minute or two. I goofed by telling him that it was maybe better that they died. It was wrong to say that. I slipped. I didn't mean it like that. It really offended him.

"How could you say that? It's never better to die," he said.

"Joey, maybe everyone's in a better place."

"No! I don't believe that. This is the better place for Travis, here, playing basketball for NDSU. He was a good guy. We were friends. We were best friends. We hung out a lot together."

"I'm pretty sure he was paralyzed, Joey."

"Paralyzed?"

"Yes. He couldn't move his arms. He had no feeling anywhere. I'm sure he was."

"Did a doctor say that?"

"Not that I heard. They did an autopsy up at Bismarck but nothing has been told to the Olsens. Joey! Listen to me, please. I've not told anybody that. The Olsens don't know that. Please don't tell anybody, but I'm sure Travis was paralyzed from the neck down. I know he was. I don't want Tanner or Terri to know that. It won't help them to know that. I shouldn't have told you that. I don't know that for sure. Maybe nobody knows."

He turned his head away again. He wouldn't look at me. We were both silent for a minute before Joey started talking again.

"If he was paralyzed, he'd never been able to play basketball again."

"But we don't have to worry about that, Joey," I answered.

"Did Travis know he was paralyzed before he died?" Joey asked.

"He knew something, because he asked me to take his watch off of him and keep it. He couldn't move his arms to do it."

"His graduation watch? He gave it to you? Do you have it?"

"He didn't want to lose it. David has it. He's wearing it."

"Did he know he was dying?"

"It was crazy. I don't know what he knew. He didn't indicate to me that he knew it. Everything was happening. My manager saved your life. Her name was Reyna. You quit breathing. Your heart stopped. She restarted your heart. She used a machine we carried off the train. Did you know that?"

"Mom told me a lot of it, but I don't remember from one day to the next sometimes."

"Reyna's coming to see you. I don't know when but she is coming. She lives in Minneapolis. She asks about you all the time."

"How did you know Travis was dead?"

"I left him for a few minutes to help Dean lift you out of the truck. We had to get you out and stop the bleeding. Reyna made that decision. She is the reason you are alive. I checked again on Travis and he was fine. I took his phone and called 911. Nobody else could get a signal to call out. He died shortly after that, before any help came."

"Did you not know he had died?"

"No. That possibility was the furthest from my mind. Believe me. Please. I didn't expect it. Nobody did. It just happened."

"Did Reyna help with Travis? Did she do anything for him?"

"Yes. She helped with his rescue and got him comfortable. I stayed with him until the fire and rescue crews arrived. They worked on him a long time but finally pronounced him dead. It's got to be painful, Joey, to lose your friends. No more losses, okay? I can't take it anymore. Losing Travis was bad, man. I cried my heart out over it. There's still a hole there. It still hurts. I can still hardly stand it to think of him dead. I have a lot of regrets about how it all turned out. You and Aaron have to pull through. You have to. It's worth it, Joey! Hang on to your life. You need to get well and get this past you."

"Aaron?"

"Yeah, Aaron."

"I hate him."

"Why? It was an accident, Joey."

"He drove us into that train."

"Joey, let's not go there. It's too soon for that. Deal with that later. Aaron's alive, you know."

"Yes I know. Have you seen him?"

"No. But I intend to see him sometime. We helped him, too. He was hurt bad. He's suffered a lot. He's in a lot of legal trouble now. I feel sorry for him."

"I hope they fry him."

"I don't want them to do that, Joey. I don't want to see the dude go down."

I thought it was better to change the subject. It was getting late. I had to leave. We both settled down. I told him goodbye. He wanted to know when I could come back. Just before I left he asked me to show him all the gifts I brought him. He thanked me for everything. He's good. He's going to make it. We bonded. It worked. He accepted me. I was relieved. They called me into the social worker's office. I spoke with Joey's stepdad and mom, who were waiting to meet me. They both hugged me tight; I left the hospital feeling wrung out, like a juiced orange. This visit was a heavy ride.

I took Shona to the old Great Northern for dinner. She expected that I would want to eat as far away from the tracks as possible. I saw this restaurant by the track, all lit up, each time I went through Fargo. It had old-fashioned class to it. I insisted on going there to eat my last meal with Shona, who is still the love of my life. The atmosphere was active and noisy. It was hard to talk. I was not very hungry after all the pizza Joey and I ate. I consumed half of my Philly cheese sandwich.

"How did the visit with Joey go? You look stressed, Trevor." Shona couldn't figure me out.

"It was tense for a minute or two when we were visiting. Have you ever gone up to see Joey?" I asked as she sat there eating.

"No. I haven't. I hear he's really spooky. I just haven't gone. They say he doesn't talk."

"I think you should go now. He talked to me. He has a lot to deal with right now. It's a lot of grief issues."

"I don't know him that well," Shona said.

So I changed the subject and tried to justify myself in not wanting to confine her to being faithful to me when I live so far away and since there are so many college hunks she could have just for the taking.

"Trevor. Stop it. You act like I don't have a brain. The whole evening you sat there telling me what to do. I have to do this. I have to do that. I have to see Joey. I have to date other men. You even suggested to me the type of man and what his personality should be. I'm a big girl now. I'm almost as old as you are. I'm in college. I can think. I'll survive. You never let me talk, or tell you what I think about all of your marvelous suggestions. You talk all the time. Do you ever stop talking and listen to someone else talk? Your motor mouth never runs out of gas. You only know what you know and never what anybody else knows. You still want control of my life, even from your vantage point in Seattle."

After she told me off, we finished dinner with dessert, and I asked her to take me to where I could get a laptop computer for Joey. I knew exactly what I wanted to get for him. When she dropped me off at the hotel, I begged her to let me call her and talk once in awhile. I wanted to be one of her best friends.

She said I could. That was sweet. She even let me hug her one more time. It felt just as good as the first time. She still likes me. Nobody hugs you like that if they don't.

I called the Olsens and told them that I needed most of another day with Joey. They came to the hospital in the afternoon. They had seen him before, but he didn't remember. I worked all morning on Joey's computer. We went right to it. That guy is a gamer. It all came back. I told him he must have had an addiction to video games in a former life. He thought that was possible. Lana said she would see that he got his cell phone back. Lana thought that since Joey is cognizant now of who is in his room, the gifts would not be stolen. I can email him and call him now. He visited well with the Olsens.

I poisoned the atmosphere when I brought up the issue of the truck fire. David and Lynn told Joey that none of the boys burned. I think Joey accepted what David and Lynn told him. I hate taking all the credit but I just let it ride. I'm still on a roller coaster.

Sunday was busy. I wanted to go over and see Aaron at his home, so I called his house. His mother Sally answered.

"Trevor, that is very nice of you to think of Aaron. I want you to come, but Aaron cannot talk to you. I can't allow it. The likelihood of you being a witness for the railroad or the prosecution is too great for us to risk a visit with you. Aaron talks and in the process he incriminates himself. Anything he said, they could ask you, under oath, to repeat it. What you say could be used against him."

"We don't have to talk about the accident," I told her.

"Aaron will talk about the accident. He will. That is all he thinks about. Aaron remembers you, the other man, and lady that were there on the scene. We are indebted to you. Trevor, I would like to hug you and tell you how thankful we are for what you did to put out that fire until they could get Aaron out of the truck. It saved Aaron's life. We know that. I can't see you now. When this is over, we'll get together."

"But I just want to see him and shake his hand. I want to tell him how glad I am he is okay. I brought him a gift. I don't know if I'm a witness or not. Dean is the one that actually saw what happened. I didn't see anything. Really."

"You are making this difficult."

"On Monday, I'm to meet with a Keith Markstein in Fargo. Do you know him?"

"Yes. He's on our defense team. I'll tell you what, Trevor; I'll get a hold of Keith and see what he says. You know the defense team doesn't want Aaron to answer the phone or anything. He's already in prison in his own house. It's awful, Trevor. I'll call you later."

I set that project aside and anticipated being together with everyone at the O'Connors farm. The dinner we had there was a banquet. Everyone showed me love. Each person was to bring a small, inexpensive gift for me. I was given one gift that was price-less. Sharon gave me Kyle's acrylic of the Dakota High Bridge. I couldn't believe it. I almost cried. I knew about it because Shona had told me how much she liked it. It turned out to be a happy event. Everybody knew it was Travis' birthday on Monday. He would have been my age, nineteen. They kept it happy. No crying. I entertained them with some funny stories from my childhood.

Dana cried when I played Brad's guitar. I sang as many songs as I could remember. I haven't been practicing like I should. He had an old Martin. After I tightened the strings, it played well. He had some music that I used. I enjoyed it and I think everyone else did, too. One song I could not sing was "Snoqualmie Pass." I was afraid it would evoke too much emotion.

Dana and Rod finally were married over the July fourth weekend. I liked Joey's mom, Lana. She has go power, that lady.

She could run the country, but I don't think Joey is going to let her run his life. He resents her power over him. His dad is nice, but so laid back. I liked Kyle's dad, Guy. They are all great. This party was a huge boost for my ego.

[Law office of Markstein, Williams & Collins]

I waited in the front office, nervous about the visit. I half wished I hadn't agreed to come. Dad said that since I was a neutral party it was okay to talk to them if I felt comfortable about it, realizing they might subpoena me to testify at some point down the road. The Olsens didn't want to crucify Aaron, so dad said as long as I was upfront with them he didn't see any harm in it. I followed Keith into the conference room and sat down at a round table. Four lawyers stared at me. Keith started the discussion.

"Thank you for coming to talk to us, Trevor. We really appreciate it. On your way out be sure and stop at the receptionist's desk for some gifts. What kind of food do you like to eat?

"I like anything. You mean here in Fargo?"

"Sure."

"Friday I ate at the old Great Northern. That's a neat place. I love food that is grilled and barbequed."

"How long are you here?"

"All week. I want to go to the court proceedings on Friday."

"You do? Why?"

"I want to see Aaron. I want to hear how it goes for him."

"It won't go well for him there. We'll work toward a better outcome at trial. We have an account at the Old Great. You can eat on our account there any time you want while you are in town. How's that?"

"Can I take guests?"

"Guests? Of course."

"Why do you want to see Aaron?"

"I want to see him. I've worried about him. I was the first at the scene. I tried to help him get out of the truck. It was horrifying."

"Are you on his side in this legal battle?"

"Yes. I don't want to see him suffer any more for just being in an accident. Sending him to prison won't help any of us heal."

"We heard you were hurt. Is that true?"

I told them everything that happened. I didn't mention how it all went down with Travis and they didn't ask. It didn't seem that they knew many details of the rescue. They were all nice, but I received a good grilling from all of them. What one didn't think to ask, the others did. Like dad said, they plucked until this poor little bird had no feathers left. They were following the story that appeared in the papers after my interview at home with the two reporters from Fargo. I was cautious about speaking on railroad issues. They wanted more from me on that. They thought I might know something. Dad said to never repeat hearsay. It's all right to tell what you know, but hearsay can wipe you out in court. I didn't like the way they pressed me so hard about hearing or not hearing the whistle. I said most of the time the engineers place their foot on the whistle and blow it unrelentingly. I hated that. It never stops blowing, especially when they are going maximum speed. I told them this engineer didn't do that. She didn't blow it all the time, just at crossings. That's all I said. But when they asked me if I could definitely say on the witness stand that no whistle was heard at the time of impact, I had to admit to them that I wasn't totally sure about it.

"Trevor, if you agree to be placed on our tentative witness list that we hand to the judge for the trial that's coming up in a few months, I can allow you to meet with Aaron. It would do him good to talk to you. You are a good man, Trevor. We appreciate what you are doing for the families. How does that sound?"

"Sure."

"You have to fill out some paperwork. We might have to do a background check on you. You have to be available to talk to us any time we need you before the trial. Can you agree to that?"

I agreed and left. The receptionist called the restaurant and had my name added to their account. I took the Olsens out to the Great Northern for lunch, compliments of Aaron's defense team. I called Sally Richards and set up a time to see Aaron.

As soon as I realized there was a small state university in Cheneau Valley, I put in a call to the chair of the Music Department and set up an appointment. Soon, I felt I was being hustled to come there and attend school. I took my guitar and sang "Snoqualmie Pass" for them. They liked it and I liked the campus. It was small, quaint and friendly. They have a small music program, but all the pieces were there that I needed in order to study undergraduate music. I met several instructors. A nice chick gave me a tour of the campus. The kids are friendly. I told the professors that I had signed a year's contract with the train and the earliest I could enroll would be a year from this fall. I was going to seriously think about it.

"Trevor, you can live here and go to college," Lynn said as she offered their home to me. "You can have Travis' bedroom. I'm sure it would be okay with Tanner. We just redecorated Terri's bedroom. She won't want Travis' bedroom."

My visit with Aaron was sad. I've never seen anyone so distraught. His whole life is in shambles. He is so fearful of the future. He told me how young men like him get beat up and abused in prison. He wouldn't be strong enough to fight. He is in anguish over what happened. He brought indescribable financial ruin on his family. The civil-court proceedings that will follow the trial will consume the remaining family assets. I almost feel more sorry for Aaron than I do the Olsens. Their grief will end someday. Aaron is much worse off than they are now. His trouble is just beginning. I just listened as he said he had no friends left. They had all abandoned him. They don't come to visit. They don't call. I told him I would be his friend. He said they tried to plea bargain right away, once the indictments were issued, but the State's Attorney wouldn't accept what they offered. Markstein wanted the charges reduced to negligent homicide and the sentence reduced to one year in county jail. If they did that, Aaron could work on the farm during the day and spend his nights in the jail. The sentence had to be a year or less if served in the Valley County Jail. Due to the seriousness of the charges, that can't happen. The State's offer is for Aaron to plead guilty to the three counts of manslaughter, and for that he would get his sentence reduced from ten years to five. The defense is trying to hammer out a better offer. If the state doesn't bend, then the defense wants to fight it. They think a jury will possibly find him not guilty. The defense said they will do everything they can to keep him out of prison.

The Judgment
[Valley County Court House (September tenth)]

Trevor Jensen

The weather turned ominous, mirroring the mood in front of the Valley County Courthouse as Aaron and his defense team entered. Aaron looked like a scared rabbit. His mom, dad, brothers, and other family members followed him inside. One brother pushed him in a wheelchair. Another brother carried a pair of crutches. I secretly caught his attention and gave him a thumbs-up. I wanted to go over and speak to him, but that would have blown my cover. The press didn't know I was in town. It was mainly the press that had come to watch. I wore a baseball hat, a pair of David's reading glasses, a hooded pullover and a pair of Travis' jeans and cowboy boots. David gave me the boots, but they were too narrow. My left foot is really wide. I could wear them for a short time but I wouldn't be able to keep them. They were beautiful boots. The top half of me was dressed like a Seattle hoodlum and the bottom half was dressed like a North Dakota cowboy. The press figured me to be a relative of Aaron. They made me remove the hat, which almost blew my cover, but I drew up the hooded part of the pullover and concealed as much of my head as I could. No one seemed to notice.

Aaron was read his rights and the judge waived the reading of the indictments as it was established that Aaron's counsel had explained the indictment to him and he understood the charges. He entered a plea of not guilty to each count. His voice was so weak and shaky that I could hardly distinguish what he said to the judge. A jury trial was requested. The prosecution was asked when they would be ready for trial, and the State's Attorney said they would be ready in six months. Aaron was ordered to stand trial for three counts of felony manslaughter.

The defense asked that the trial be postponed until all the railroad investigations were done, including the one by the National Transportation Safety Board. The defense team pointed out to the judge the mitigating factors in the accident that necessitated the National Transportation Safety Board taking over the investigation. The findings from those investigations might change the culpability factors. The judge asked the defense when they thought the investigations would be concluded. When the judge was told that it could take as long as a year, the judge rejected that argument, saying the National Transportation Safety Board would not influence the trial. He said the trial would proceed in accordance with the court's calendar and not the federal government's.

The proceeding took less than ten minutes. The trial was tentatively scheduled for March of next year.

After the proceeding I noticed several calls on my phone from Reyna. She wanted to know how it had gone. I told her. She asked if I could report to work tonight in Fargo. The train going west was very short-staffed on the day shift. She would be aboard and save a bed for me. I could sleep until just before Billings and work the following day. It was to be a permanent change of shift. My route was now clear through to Chicago. I knew what that meant. I had to load and unload the train in both Seattle and Chicago. I was stunned. She said I was getting a raise. I was on the train for longer hours and therefore I would make more money on each trip. Management did not want me off the train in North Dakota during the night. They wanted to isolate me from talking to the media that was following me across the state, popping up at each stop. Nobody at Intermountain Rail could figure out who was leaking my work schedule to the press. She doubted that the press would trail me across Montana, where I would be off the train during the daylight hours, as the story there was not as big. Intermountain Rail was getting dozens of inquiries from around the country from people who wanted access to me. The story was taking root everywhere. Reyna was so adamant about it; I didn't have the nerve to argue with her. Reyna said my sudden change of shift was a management decision beyond her control. I didn't want to leave my night crew. I'd have a new boss. Everything was changing.

It was a beautiful September in Montana until the third week, when the equinox storm brought snow. The locals said the storm, indicating a changing of the seasons from summer to autumn, happened right on schedule. The heaviest snow was in Bozeman. We pulled up through a blinding blizzard on the hill east of the Bozeman tunnel. We saw a jackknifed truck on the interstate. The wind, rain and heavy snow from the storm destroyed the brilliant fall colors that decorated the aspen groves situated at the base of the mountains, and also ended the blanket of orange, yellow, and red draped along the banks of the Yellowstone River.

When October came, we had clear, blue, cloudless skies for days and days. The passengers referred to it as "Indian Summer." It was the last warm weather we would have before winter. I loved waking up along the Yellowstone River going into Miles City. The ground was white with frost. There were whitetail deer along the river and pronghorn antelope in the grain fields. I could see numerous flocks of geese. One morning there was a huge flock of cranes flying south. The majestic bald eagle perched triumphantly in the cottonwoods along the river. The wildlife was easier to spot when the foliage was off the trees and bushes.

Actually, I love working the day shift. I get as tired as an old dog by the time we get to Chicago. The second day of work is draining. I can get more time off between trips, but I usually spin around and go back. I love making money. The more money, the more power I have over my life and the more independent decisions I can make. Many of the crews are short-staffed so I let them stick me wherever I'm needed.

One time I stepped off the train in Seattle and they shuttled me down to Boeing Field where I caught a private jet to Bozeman just in time to meet the train going east. I was the fill-in crew for a couple of sick kids who had to come off the train.

I talk to Aaron on a regular basis. They are moving Aaron's surgery up to early November. Just in case he lands himself in prison, he needs the extra time to heal. The lawyers said they wouldn't take very good care of him in prison. I told Aaron if wearing those casts on his legs kept him out of prison, not to let the doctors remove them. Aaron said it wouldn't matter. If the judge ordered him to prison, then he would go no matter what shape he was in. The prison would send out an ambulance and take him. He would end up in the prison infirmary.

The judge moved the trial out of Valley County. Aaron's defense team was not happy with that decision by the judge, who said he made the decision because of excessive media coverage. Bismarck agreed to take it, and they are trying to squeeze it in their court schedule. Aaron said the defense wants a jury that lived and worked in rural North Dakota, where there is more acceptance of driving under the influence. His lawyers have him convinced they are going to beat it. They are still working with the state on a plea deal. The state isn't budging on having Aaron do some hard time in the state prison. If he took the plea now, the judge could order him to prison. His health would deteriorate. He wouldn't get therapy or have the surgery he needed.

The lawyers don't want Aaron out in public. They want him to be silenced and closeted. They are afraid he will talk to the wrong person. His family is struggling to get the crops harvested so they have some money to pay all their medical bills and legal fees. Aaron said they had emptied their granaries to help pay the bills. There is nothing more to sell until the new crop is in. They grow a lot of corn. It comes in late.

The only contact I've made with Dean or Wren is by phone. Joey has to have two more surgeries, one on the left leg and one on the right foot. He also needs more therapy than the insurance will pay for. They are trying for some settlement money from Aaron's insurance but everybody drags their feet. Joey was offered two hundred and fifty grand but the lawyers didn't want him to accept it. They say he could get a couple million. Because of the severity of his injuries, they don't know how much he needs and if or when he can walk and work. He's out of the hospital now and is gaining some weight. He finally stopped throwing up after they took him off of all that medicine. The treatment plan includes an academic tutor, who they say he needs in order to get him mentally ready for college in a year. The insurance would not pay for the tutor and they said he reached his limit for the therapy. Lana had to hire a lawyer to help her deal with the insurance issues and manage Joey's medical bills. Joey said the tutor told him he was very bright. He might be able to start college next fall when I do. Joey wants to do it, so I think he'll make it. She convinced him that he would need to earn a living using his brain and not his brawn. The tutor charges a hundred an hour.

My sister Paula is in her last year of high school. She is going off to Cleveland to a fancy place to study elementary education and piano pedagogy. Amber is studying, shopping, or giggling on the cell phone with her girlfriends.

Shona said that since I broke up with her she couldn't get any dates. Everybody on campus still thought she was "Trevor's girl." She liked living at her mom's cousin's house and she invited me over any time I was in Fargo.

I'm still thinking about North Dakota. That is where my friends are now. Dad keeps quiet. He is stone silent when I mention North Dakota. I guess at this point he is just happy I'm getting off the train next summer. If I go to Cheneau Valley, I want to enroll in the music program and study voice and guitar. They want five years of my time to get through the two performance programs. It takes that long to complete all the recitals. I'm planning on going back there sometime to audition and let them see how good I am. I should be able to do it in four years. I might be able to get some credit for my previous experience. I'm at the professional level in guitar and, well, you can be the judge about my voice. I've had a lot of training. I'm not starting from scratch. I have to select a subject as a minor but what? They suggested I consider a minor in Spanish since I'm fluent in it already. They have affiliations with two universities in Mexico. They have a very good art program, too. Music is a huge major but I have to also fit a minor in with it. I have been emailing the department chair with one question after another. She emails me right back.

[The following March]

Karl Jensen

I paid an intern from my office to attend Aaron's trial in Bismarck. I want her to report back to me every day. Carlee arranged to get herself on the court's list of attendees. This is an interesting case even beyond the fact that my son, Trevor, may be a witness for the defense. The state is not using him in that capacity. Neither did the railroads in any of their hearings. They did, however, interview him privately several times. So far he has not had to appear anywhere. Now that they know what side of the legal fence he is on, the state isn't interested in him. I'm not sure what benefit he would be to them, anyway.

If there is going to be a plea bargain, it hasn't happened yet. Carlee is desperately trying to get information about it. She thought the defense didn't like the jury that much and that the defense may accept the state's terms for a plea bargain tomorrow before the trial got underway.

It seemed that the prosecution got the jury they wanted. The jury was mostly men who were born and raised in Bismarck and less likely to have been sympathetic to the drinking-and-driving culture that was more pervasive in farming communities where Aaron lived. A jury from Bismarck would be more apt to view Aaron as the culprit rather than the victim. None of the jurors worked for the railroad, abused alcohol, or had a spouse who did. It appeared to me, right at the start, that things weren't going that well for the defense. In my opinion, that judge did a number on the defense when he moved the trial out of Valley County. He knew it would be harder to get a conviction in Cheneau Valley.

The trial commenced March first, right on schedule. These North Dakotans didn't mess around. From what I could understand, the judge on the case was fairly inflexible but ran a good court. None of Travis' family is attending. They couldn't see that there would be anything accomplished, only more pain. They didn't want to face the press every day. Everyone knew, regardless of the verdict, that there wouldn't be justice. Justice was repaired lives and replaced losses. A life taken is an irretrievable loss.

The opening statements by the state were fairly compelling, I thought. All the statements they brought forth pointed to reck-lessness. The prosecution began by explaining the reason for the court proceedings. Carlee wore a wire and recorded most of it. She wasn't allowed to use a recording device. I told her not to risk getting caught with the wire but she slipped through security with it. She wanted to record the opening statements, which I considered to be one of the most crucial parts of the trial.

"Ladies and gentlemen, we are here today in court because Travis Olsen is dead. North Dakota's "Mr. Basketball" is dead. His career is over. We will never know the honor he might have brought to our state playing college basketball at North Dakota State University in Fargo. He obtained a five-year scholarship to play basketball for the Bisons. He planned to work on the family farm and use his college degree to grow and develop certified seed. We will never know what scientific advancements could have been made locally in the seed industry. He didn't intend to merely play basketball for five years. He was planning to under-take a double major. He also planned to study Animal Science. He graduated from high school at the top of his class. We can only predict that he would have been hugely successful. His life was sacrificed in a senseless, completely avoidable side collision with a speeding passenger train. The facts will show that Travis Olsen was a passenger in a vehicle that was being driven reck-lessly by an impaired driver.

"We are also here today because of the tragic death of Brad O'Connor. Brad was also a farmer. He planned to continue working with his dad. They were business partners. His death has brought irrevocable damage to the family business. He was an honor student, a basketball star, and a hero to his sister Dana. His life ended under the same awful circumstances that took the life of Travis Olsen.

"We are here because Kyle Hickles was also killed. He was an only son of his parents, Guy and Sharon Hickles, who mourn for him today. We'll never know the degree of success he might have achieved at Cheneau Valley State studying art. His paintings and drawings are the work of a genius. His artistic hands have been silenced. They will never again speak to us through his art. He also played basketball and was captain of his team. The Eastern Division named him Most Valuable Player. We can only imagine the degree of success he would have had playing basketball for Cheneau Valley State University, where he had earned a scholarship. As the facts will show, these three young men died at the hands of Aaron Richards, who is sitting here today in this courtroom.

Expert witnesses will explain, in great detail, how this crash occurred. You will learn, through their testimony, that the *Mountain Daylight* passenger train did not hit their truck. Aaron drove his truck into the train where it struck the second locomotive, flipped around and damaged five coaches. Ladies and gentlemen, that fact alone places all of the blame for this tragedy on Aaron. The facts as they are presented will absolve the railroad of any blame for the crash. Throughout the course of this trial, you will learn that road-grade crossing crashes are always the fault of the public who fail to yield to an oncoming train. Every grade crossing crash is preventable. The state's witnesses will provide statistics to show that such crashes are usually fatal. From this you would understand that statistically Aaron should be dead, as were three of his passengers. He beat the odds, because normally the majority of trains traveling these tracks are either one-hundred-thirteen-car coal trains or ninety-car grain trains that can weigh as much as twenty thousand tons. A train of that description, traveling sixty miles per hour, kills anybody they hit. But Aaron didn't hit a coal or grain train. The facts will show that he hit a smaller, lighter, passenger train carrying two hundred forty people. The evidence will show that he put himself, Travis Olsen, Brad O'Connor, Kyle Hickles, Joey Carlson, and the well-being of two hundred forty passengers in serious jeopardy of their safety and even their lives. The evidence will show that the crash was attributed to reckless disregard for conditions of the road subsequent to alcohol consumption. Expert witnesses will prove that the defendant, Aaron Richards, couldn't see because the windshield was plastered with mud. State's evidence will show how Aaron ran the truck off the road several times prior to hitting the train, and that he swerved back and forth down the road prior to the crash. At one location on the road, Aaron missed a curve and nearly rolled the truck. Experts will testify how they retraced Aaron's entire route before he hit the train. Tire tracks off the road were matched to the tires on his truck. From this evidence, it is clear that he had plenty of warning that the manner in which he was driving was reckless. The crash occurred, as the facts will show, because he chose to keep driving recklessly.

The state's expert will testify that Aaron was driving while impaired with a blood-alcohol concentration of .06 that impaired his judgment and reaction time. Ladies and gentlemen, do not be confused when you hear testimony about applying the *per se* theory in this trial. It is taken for granted, in a *per se* charge, that the driver was driving under the influence. The *per se* theory can be applied in all fifty states when a driver's blood-alcohol concentration is .08 or higher. In those cases, the state does not need to prove impairment. The *per se* theory has no relevance in this trial. Expert witnesses will explain that a blood-alcohol concentration of .02 in some cases causes impairment. You will learn that a blood-alcohol concentration of .05 causes impairment that interferes in performing a variety of psychomotor skills needed to safely operate a motor vehicle. We will show that in underage drivers, such as Aaron, impairment from having a blood-alcohol concentration of .06 is greater than it would be in a person of the same size and weight who is older. Aaron, from his own admission to investigators, admitted that prior to the crash he had consumed more than a six-pack of beer. Our witnesses will prove that there was impairment. The facts will show that reckless driving subsequent to alcohol consumption led to the deaths of Travis Olsen, Kyle Hickles and Brad O'Connor. The facts will show that this crash critically injured Aaron and his passenger, Joey Carlson. One passenger on the train was admitted to the hospital and one crewmember was treated at the scene. In addition, this crash caused enormous damage to the train, railroad and environment."

Carlee told how the defense began their opening statements by saying it was all an accident. In other words, it wasn't a crash but an act of God. There was no criminal negligence or recklessness. The so-called reckless driving was just a bunch of good kids out for some nighttime fun. They were mud running. They were using the truck to do what it was built to do. It was in four-wheel drive, as it should have been, going across country negotiating muddy terrain. It was not being driven where it was incapable of going. The fact that it was driven off road had nothing to do with impairment. Recreational mud running is a popular sport in that area. The more mud, the better.

"Ladies and gentlemen of the jury," the defense continued. "Are you aware that it is not against the law to drink and drive in North Dakota as long as you don't do both at the same time?"

The facts they would present would show that the drinking was before the accident. Aaron was not driving and drinking, according to testimony they would present. It is against the law to drive if impaired by drugs or alcohol. Aaron's blood alcohol of .06 was within the law. He was driving legally. The defense challenged the state's evidence, saying they didn't believe that the state could, beyond a reasonable doubt, prove there was impairment. The only logical way to establish impairment beyond a reasonable doubt would have been from a field-sobriety test administered by a peace officer. No sobriety test was given.

The defense went on to say that they would show how the crossing was of excessive profile, or "humped." That meant it was a crossing of restricted visibility. The crossbuck was not reflectorized in accordance with the newer Federal Railroad Administration standards. It would be harder to see at night. But Aaron did see the train. He didn't hit it directly. He compensated by swerving to the side. That maneuver saved his life, the life of Joey Carlson, and spared the two hundred forty passengers aboard the train possible harm in the event the train had derailed. In a split second, Aaron did all that anybody could do. If anyone was to blame, it was the railroad. The safest crossing is no crossing. The crossing is on the railroad's closure list. The railroad had been given money by the federal government to complete the work on several crossings across North Dakota but it had never closed this one. The railroad didn't reflectorize the two crossbucks, it didn't close the crossing, and neither did it correct the profile of the crossing that would have improved visibility. The railroad did nothing. The crossing was a sitting duck for disaster. Had the crossing been closed like it should have been, Aaron would have continued east, parallel to the track, where he would have found a better road leading to a safer crossing. This wasn't Aaron's fault; it was an accident waiting to happen.

Carlee thought the statements by the defense had an impact, but the arguments for recklessness were stronger as put forth by the state. She thought it was interesting how the state used the word "crash" but the defense used the word "accident" throughout their opening statements.

"If I had to gamble here, just based on the opening statements," Carlee said, "I'd bet on a conviction. The case that the state laid out in the opening statements was very convincing."

Throughout the trial, the state continued to present its case. They had numerous exhibits showing the route Aaron took before the accident. The pictures of the tire tracks, and how they were matched to the tires on his truck, were convincing. They showed where he missed a slight turn in the road, went down into the field, whipped the truck around, and drove back onto the road. They showed where he swerved back and forth from one side of the road to the other. They alleged that the erratic driving was due to impairment. It clearly didn't appear to be recreational mud running at 1:30 a.m., as the defense suggested in the opening statements. The jury was attentive. They seemed to be keenly interested in studying all the exhibits presented. Carlee thought the members of the jury were all well-educated and couldn't be easily swayed from the facts.

Carlee introduced herself to Markstein, telling them who she was, why she was there, and whom she represented. She convinced them she was not hostile to the defense. She made herself friendly, and one day the defense invited her to have lunch with them. They tried to find out if she knew anything more than what Trevor had told them regarding the railroad issues. Carlee could honestly tell them that she didn't know him, so she was no help.

It was interesting that the judge did not allow Joey's blood alcohol to be introduced, since the state didn't run it in their lab. They only ran Aaron's. Joey's test results were a part of his medical record. We heard a rumor that it was over 0.1. A level that high would have implied heavy drinking, but the judge wouldn't allow the state to present it. The judge, I think, felt that the number of beer cans that law enforcement found at the scene would of itself imply heavy drinking.

Poor Trevor. They dragged him off the eastbound *Mountain Daylight* in Bismarck at 2 a.m., chauffeured him to a hotel, and the defense took him to the courthouse at nine, later that same morning. The media recognized him immediately and tried to get a statement. They had a TV camera in the courtroom. He hadn't slept and was tired and nervous. He was afraid of what they were going to make him say. It was the same day that Dean testified about what he saw at the time of impact. He was a good witness for the state. He was believable. When the defense cross-examined him they asked if he had heard a whistle. He said that there was a whistle just before impact. Everything was either black or white with Dean. Then, he blew it when he went on to say that any time he was working on the trains, the engineers constantly blew the whistle. Of course the defense wouldn't let it pass. The defense wasn't interested in any of the other nights that Dean worked the territory.

"Was the whistle engaged on the morning of May thirtieth when it is alleged that Aaron's truck hit the train?"

Dean basically repeated what he just said, that the engineers always blew the whistle at every crossing. If they always did it, then he was basically assuming that they did it the night of the accident. Of course, the defense objected to that statement, which was based on speculation. The judge didn't allow the statement.

Trevor sat there all day and didn't testify. The defense decided not to put him on and have him contradict Dean. It would weaken their point about the whistle, if there was not absolute agreement between Dean and Trevor, given the fact that Dean was so credible about everything else he said. They knew Trevor was tired, scared, and nervous and would not perform as strong as Dean did on the witness stand. If Trevor disagreed with Dean, they feared that the prosecution would take that and run. Trevor wouldn't hold up under the pressure.

Later, Markstein said the whistle was moot until the facts emerged from the event recorder that the railroad had in their possession, and that it would be a few more months down the road before that information was made available to the public. Markstein said that when you subpoena the railroad, it gets really messy. They stonewall you, and you can never be sure you get what you are supposed to get. If they don't want you to know, they have a way of concealing it. He said they have been known to tamper with their own event recorders, and it is very easy to erase information that they don't want the public to know. He said it would be too costly to force them to turn it over before the National Transportation Safety Board is through with them. Only deep pockets can take on the railroad.

"One thing," he said, "is that they don't generally mess with the government."

Trevor never had his day in court. They flew him back here for a couple days off before he left again on the train. He made no statements to the media.

Joey took some of his settlement money and bought himself a used pickup. Having new wheels gave Joey more independence. He lost his car after the accident when he couldn't work and make the payments. When Joey had his last surgery, they did a complete reconstruction of the bones in his foot. He had to wear a special brace that severely limited his mobility. The brace might be permanent unless therapy could strengthen the ankle enough to support his weight. Trevor said Joey desperately needed a girlfriend. Trevor thought it would help him heal emotionally. When he couldn't do things and go places, his friends cut him off. Trevor told him to call up Shona and take her out to dinner or something. Joey drove down to Fargo three times a week for therapy at Agassiz South. Shona didn't have a boyfriend. Trevor pushed him to do it and Joey did. Joey took Shona out once, twice, and he is still dating her. On the first date, Shona asked Joey if Trevor had anything to do with him calling her. You can't fool Shona.

The case was handed to the jury on day ten. They deliberated a day and a half. It was a tense day and a half waiting for the verdict. On March the twelfth at 10 a.m. the verdict was read. It was unanimous. Carlee said the courtroom was packed. None of the victims' families were present. There was a huge presence by the media. She said the press kept asking her where Trevor was. Would she be the one telling him about the verdict? How could they reach Trevor for a statement? Carlee kept reaffirming that she had no contact whatsoever with Trevor.

By the end of the trial, Carlee didn't know which way it would go. She didn't know what to expect. It could go either direction, she felt. Still, she was flabbergasted when the verdict was read. The defense team stayed sitting in their seats. They didn't move. Aaron didn't express any emotion. Neither did his family. As the judge demanded, everybody left the courtroom quietly. Aaron's family would not talk to the media.

Trevor's westbound train was just arriving in Missoula, Montana, when I called him.

"Trevor! Dad here. They have the verdict."

"Shoot," he said.

"Guilty."

"No! No, dad. It can't be!"

"Trevor, it is. They threw the book at him. It is three counts of manslaughter to be served concurrently. They should have done a plea deal. What a mistake!"

"Did they take him to prison?"

"No. Not yet. The state wanted him sentenced in two weeks. I guess that was the schedule the judge was supposed to follow, but the defense bought more time. The judge agreed to a preliminary sentencing investigation and scheduled the sentencing ninety days out. It looks like he could go to prison in June."

"So, what do they do between now and June?"

"The defense will prepare their case in an attempt to convince the judge that Aaron should receive a light sentence. They will contact you, Trevor. You have to prepare yourself to get up there and explain to the judge why you don't want Aaron in prison. It might convince the judge to shave time off Aaron's sentence.

Bear in mind, there may be others that the state can find who would insist he go to prison. It's not over yet. I'm sure the state will push for the maximum of ten years."

"Dad, that is awful news."

"I know that wasn't what you wanted to hear, son. I'm sorry."

"I'll give Aaron a call tonight. We're pulling into Missoula, dad. I have to go."

On May the twenty sixth I received a call from Carlee. She was very excited. I actually thought for a few seconds she would tell me that her boyfriend had proposed. That was not the case. She wanted me to go to a web site where the National Transportation Safety Board posted the findings of their investigation into the accident. She had been diligently watching for that report. It was information that she thought, one way or another, would have an impact on the case. I carefully read the entire report. The government clearly blamed Aaron for the accident, as the probable cause was listed at the end of the report as failure to yield at a road-grade crossing. The accident was classified as alcohol-related. However, the most striking piece of information was what the event recorder established. The engineer didn't blow the crossing. At the speed she was operating the train, the whistle should have been blown at the whistle post placed one-quarter mile from the crossing. The engineer should have continued sounding the whistle until the lead locomotive passed through the crossing. Trevor was right. No whistle was sounded. The crossing was on the railroad's closure list. The railroad had fallen behind in completing several crossing projects, this being one of them. On further investigation, it was discovered that the crossing was not always recognized as active. Some employees thought it was a private crossing, as opposed to public, and that the railroad had no agreement with the owners to blow it. Other engineers simply ignored it. Daytime trains tended more often than not to whistle, whereas nighttime trains tended to ignore it. The crossing was remote and rarely used. The engineer handling the train only worked the territory at night operating the *Mountain Daylight.* She did not operate any daytime trains through the territory. She testified that she did not know it was a valid crossing. She also testified that the conductors working with her never told her otherwise. In addition, the train was speeding, pursuant to the condition of the track. That night, the *Mountain Daylight* failed to receive a Track Bulletin that specified a slower-than-timetable speed through the area of the track work east of the crossing. The engineer had just come off of her vacation time and had not operated trains through there during the tie-replacement project. Therefore, she wasn't aware of the necessity to operate at a lower speed. The track work was completed, but the equipment was still strung out along both sides of the track. The train's speed at the time of impact was sixty miles per hour, but it should have been forty if the engineer had carried the proper Track Bulletin. The engineer was in compliance with all the other operating rules. Had they known this, the defense could have argued that the accident wouldn't have happened if the train had been going slower, as Aaron would have made it over before the train arrived. Had the jury known that Aaron received no warning of an approaching train, they might not have convicted him of manslaughter.

The government did not fine the railroad. There were no plans to decertify the engineer for failure to blow the crossing or failing to operate the train at the lower track speed.

Carlee was sure this new information would have an impact on the conviction. I filed it away. I emailed the link to Trevor and asked him to read it. He remained upset about the possibility of Aaron going to prison. The railroad suspended the engineer but later reinstated her. The Brotherhood came to her aid, and they recommended against further disciplinary action because she did not carry the proper orders. Since the accident, the crossing has been officially closed.

Trevor thought the engineer could be prosecuted for manslaughter under state law, but a search done by my office revealed no such history of any prosecutions by the federal government or by any State Attorney General. Those rumors were flying around the train crew for quite awhile. There have been prosecutions in the aftermath of catastrophic loss and great bodily harm when the accident had been consequential due to drug abuse by an operating crewmember. In one such case, an operating crewmember under the influence caused an accident resulting in sixteen passenger fatalities. The toxicology tests on the *Mountain Daylight* operating crew were negative. I could assure Trevor that North Dakota's Attorney General would not be filing charges against the engineer for manslaughter. He finally calmed down about it and ignored the rumors. It was a serious violation to not blow the crossing in the event of an accident, because the engineer could be fined by the Federal Railroad Administration and subject to civil suit as well as criminal prosecution. Aaron could sue her and the railroad.

In real terms, what did this mean? Could the defense file an appeal? On May tenth, the defense team put forth a motion for a new trial based on fresh exculpatory evidence that they could not have anticipated, as it was discovered in the government's investigative reports made public after the trial. On May twentieth, the judge granted a new trial. The State's Attorney dismissed all charges against Aaron based on the belief that it was not in the interest of the state to expend further resources in prosecuting the case. Aaron went free. Public opinion changed from blaming Aaron for the accident to blaming the railroad. Under such circumstances, it would have been highly unlikely that the state could have obtained a conviction had they decided to retry the case. It was a lucky twist of fate for Aaron.

I was so relieved when Trevor finally left the train. He contracted a bout of summer flu in mid-July that ended up in a mild asthma attack. They took him off the train's roster for the remainder of the month and he officially resigned July thirty-first. He was excited and ready to enter college at Cheneau Valley State University, where he would study music and minor in Spanish. The guitar instructor specialized in classical music, an area Trevor had never explored. The forces pulling him to North Dakota were unstoppable. I worried about how his asthma would react during the brutally cold winters, or what allergies he might develop from the various crops they grow. My lips were sealed.

It wasn't a happy scene around the Jensen house that morning in late August when Trevor left for school. He let me buy him a new four-wheel drive sports van, a vehicle I felt comfortable sending him out into the world in. He was a huge fan of his sisters, and it was Paula who started it and her emotion carried over to Amber, who had been very jovial about his departure until that point. We all fell into tears, and Trevor was glad to be rid of us. When Trevor left, Susan and the girls went into the adjacent sitting room and continued the weeping. I shook my head in disgust and amazement and left for work.

As I drove into Seattle, I was pleased with how everything eventually ended. Paula leaves in two weeks for Cleveland. It's her first year away. Susan and I are stuck with Amber, the spoiled one of the three. I expended all my energy on Trevor and neglected my two girls. They are a credit to Susan. Amber will finish her senior year and then hopefully get admitted to the University of Washington, where she wants to study acting, dance and music.

Trevor decided to live in the dorm so he could experience the full benefits of campus life. He is a very social person, so I'm sure he'd want to spend his free time commiserating with his classmates. He declined the Olsens' invitation to live there and occupy Travis' room. When David took Terri and Tanner aside and offered Travis' room to either of them, they both said they wanted it kept for Trevor. When he needs some respite from dorm life, Trevor will spend weekends out at the farm. If I know my son, he'll be there for those kids. He'll be a good influence for them both. He'll be there in college when each of them graduates from high school. He can challenge David to a good chess game. Travis was the only one in the family who could, besides Granny. And there is no one in Cheneau Valley happier to have Trevor in town than Granny.

The End

Acknowledgments

First, I wish to thank Brandon Cesmat, my writing professor at Osher Lifelong Learning Institute, California State University San Marcos, who inspired me to write this novel. I thank my wife Vivian, who encouraged me to finish this book. Thanks to my nephew David, whose farm I've often visited during the wheat harvest. I am grateful to my nephew, Joel, for his advice in helping reconstruct the accident scene. He has dedicated his life to his patients, having worked as an ICU nurse, an ER nurse, and as a transport nurse both in the ambulance service and in medical helicopters. A huge thanks to Brad Cruff, State's Attorney, Barnes County, N.D., for walking me through the North Dakota legal system.

I also acknowledge the help of the following: Shawn Klimpel, Amtrak Conductor, St. Cloud, Minn.; Gary Blythe, Locomotive Engineer, Union Pacific Railroad; Gary Retterath, Fire Chief, Valley City, N.D.; Duane Ditier, Sanborn Fire, Sanborn, N.D.; Scott Miller, EMT-P, Valley City, N.D.; Kristi Favor, Clinical Nurse Specialist, Palomar Pomerado Health, Escondido, Calif.; Brian Weimer, Respiratory Therapist, Vista, Calif.; Kimberly Franklin, Director, Emergency Management, Barnes County, N.D.; Jason Kemp, Men's Basketball, North Dakota State University, Fargo, N.D.; Rich Winning, Guidance Counselor, Valley City High School, Valley City, N.D.; Curtis Hofmeister, Boys Varsity Basketball Coach, Mission Hills High School, San Marcos, Calif.; Dave Carlsrud, North Dakota High School Activities Assn, Valley City, N.D.; Randy Grueneich, Barnes County Extension Agent, Valley City, N.D.; Mike Lerud, Funeral Director, Valley City, N.D.; Dean Aakre, North Dakota 4H, Fargo, N.D.; Mark Peterson, Chief Deputy Sheriff, Barnes County,

Acknowledgements

N.D., Dr. Diana Skroch, Valley City State University, Valley City, N.D.; and Kent Peters, S.P.L., Catholic Theologian, San Diego, Calif.

I need to especially thank Joshua Coran, Seattle, Wash., for his critical review of the railroad content. Thanks to Luke and Tim Coulter for proofreading the first draft. Thanks to Peggy Lewis for her computer support and for proofreading the final draft. I am grateful to Mike Rasmussen, Oriska, N.D., for the excellent rendition of the Valley City Highline Bridge that he painted for the book cover. I remain indebted to several of you who provided information but requested anonymity.

Regarding my sources, I wish to make this disclaimer. The above-mentioned sources, including those not mentioned, provided information about their areas of expertise without knowing the contents of the book or how the information they provided would be used to construct the story.

Someday, Talgo double-deck hotel trains, designed for long-distance travel, may actually operate at speeds of 125 mph on a transcontinental route in America.

Every character in this story is fictitious. Any similarities to persons living or dead are strictly coincidental.

About the Author

Mr. Friedly had a long career as a Clinical Microbiologist working for the University of California, Irvine Medical Center. During his tenure there, he did technical writing and was a participant in several research projects. His work has been published in several scientific journals. He resides with his wife in North San Diego County.